A PLUME BOOK

THE MAJOR'S DAUGHTER

J. P. FRANCIS is a professor in New Hampshire.

THE MAJOR'S
Daughter

❧———————————————❧

J. P. Francis

A PLUME BOOK

PLUME

Published by the Penguin Group
Penguin Group (USA) LLC
375 Hudson Street
New York, New York 10014

USA | Canada | UK | Ireland | Australia | New Zealand | India | South Africa | China
A Penguin Random House Company

First published by Plume, a member of Penguin Group (USA) LLC, 2014

P REGISTERED TRADEMARK—MARCA REGISTRADA

ISBN 978-1-62953-146-5

Printed in the United States of America

Set in Albertina MT Std.
Designed by Leonard Telesca

For Jan Taigen

For winter's rains and ruins are over,
    And all the season of snows and sins,
The days dividing lover and lover,
    The light that loses, the night that wins;
And time remembered is grief forgotten.
And frosts are slain and flowers begotten,
And in green underwood and cover
    Blossom by blossom the spring begins.

                    —Algernon Charles Swinburne, 1837–1909

For if the end of loving is sorrow beyond bearing, is it not
better from the first to forswear love?

                    —Luke 23:29

Remember those in prison as if you were there with them.

                    —Hebrews 13:3

THE MAJOR'S
Daughter

In April 1944 one hundred and fifty captured soldiers from the German Afrika Korps arrived by train to a detention camp in Stark, New Hampshire. For two years they worked as loggers, bringing out pulp for the Brown Paper Company. In a world consumed by war, the German captives discovered an innocent haven, largely removed from the hostilities that raged across Europe and the Pacific. Working beside the New Hampshire loggers in the great northern forests, the German soldiers found commonality with their prison guards and lived through what one author on the subject called "examples of moral courage and decency holding out against crushing odds of baseness and depravity." Every act of kindness redeems the world anew, and in a tiny hamlet in the White Mountains of New Hampshire two enemies put down their arms and picked up saws and axes instead.

That was long ago. Camp Stark is a meadow now. The only reminder of the prison camp is a stone fireplace, tired and fragile, that keeps final vigil. Near the road, before one enters the meadow, the state of New Hampshire has placed a small plaque that outlines the history of these several acres. In all of its detail, the plaque does not mention Collie, a young girl whose war began as the Germans arrived. Nor does it mention August, her one love, who arrived in the White Mountains of New Hampshire on a train going north.

PART ONE

≈⊷ *Chapter One* ⊷≈

Collie Brennan woke to the sound of reveille as she had done nearly every morning of her young life. It was a joyful sound, she had always thought, and during her two years at Smith College she had missed it and often felt like a lay-a-bed in her morning languor. She could not confess such a thing to her father, but it was true nevertheless, and as she listened to reveille's final notes she opened her eyes and peered out the window that had begun to gather the light of a fine April morning. New Hampshire, she reminded herself. Camp Stark. Today, she knew, the German prisoners would arrive, and she imagined her father had been awake for hours, nervous and keyed up at the lack of materiel, the somewhat slapdash quality of the prison camp. Really, she should rise and get about the day, but the morning air, the bright mountains—what had they called the formation above the village? The Devil's Slide—rose like a granite frown on the western ridges and she let her eyes rest on it, contemplating its features. Beneath it was the lovely town, with a bright white church at its center, and a charming covered bridge that carried traffic into the small village proper—all of it cinched and held together by the Ammonoosuc River, a black band of water that arrived pure and sweet from the mountains. A postcard village, truly, and she had already sent a note to her dearest friend, Estelle, describing the features of the little hamlet. She had called it just that, a postcard village, and Estelle had written back with a tinge of envy that she remained trapped in Ashtabula, Ohio, a backwater town of no special beauty. She was in exile, she lamented, for the duration.

All of these thoughts spilled in with the fresh air, and Collie took them in a moment longer before pushing back the deep down coverlet. It felt cold outside the bed, even on such a glorious April morning, and she dashed lightly to the water closet down the hallway. She smelled breakfast cooking downstairs; Mrs. Hammond, she was certain, had breakfast well in hand, and Collie washed quickly, wondering if her father would return soon, and if he would bring anyone with him. Her father proved a magnet for men, which was another point, Collie remembered, that Estelle had made concerning their two different lives. With the men drafted and gone to war, Estelle lived among women; Collie, on the other hand, remained surrounded by men. It was an amusing observation.

Back in her room, Collie dressed quickly. She wore a narrow skirt with a jacket over a white blouse. The jacket had only two buttons, the maximum allowed during the war effort. She wore no nylons, naturally, because the war had taken them, so she made due with a pair of socks at the bottom of her bare legs. Afterward she spent a few minutes at the small vanity Mrs. Hammond had brought from somewhere in the house to her room. Mrs. Hammond said she was accustomed to male boarders, loggers and workingmen who populated the rooms above her, but she had found the vanity as if by magic. The mirror was clouded and insufficient, but if Collie bent close enough and carefully kept her shadow out of the glass, she could catch an impression of herself. Her soft, blond hair hung in loose curls down to her shoulders. Her mother had maintained she was an Irish colleen stepping through a backlit doorway, a description Collie always found accurate. The skin beneath the blond hair was darker than her hair would suggest, except where a moon-shaped scar ran along the right side of her chin. The scar was the legacy of a bicycle accident many years before, and she did not mind seeing it, though the sun brought out its lines and made it more visible in contrast to her tanned skin.

She gave herself one last look, pulled together her bed and tidied the room for a moment, then quickly descended the stairs to the large dining room. A crisp fire burned in the large hearth at the end of the room. Men had already collected there, some of them dressed for logging, others wore the uniforms of the U.S. Army. Collie said good morning, and the men answered, three of them beginning to rise at her appearance, but she made a quick motion of her hand to keep them in place. She crossed the room and pushed through the swinging doors that led to the kitchen, nearly bumping into the serving girl, Agnes, as she did so. Agnes held a large tray of cups on a wicker tray, and she looked uncomfortable with it, like a man jamming the butt of a violin under his chin. Collie held the door wide for her.

"Good morning, Agnes," Collie said. "A beautiful day, although I suppose it may cloud over."

"The Germans are coming," Agnes replied.

"Yes, I know. They have a pretty morning for it at least."

"Not that they deserve it," Agnes said as she slid past with the tray.

"Well, the sun falls on everyone."

Collie let the door swing shut behind Agnes, then passed farther into the kitchen, where she found Mrs. Hammond standing in front of the large cookstove, rashers of bacon and ham bubbling on a cast-iron skillet. Mrs. Hammond was a stout woman, with gray-black hair that flew away in wisps as the day progressed. She wore a starched white apron over her dress, and her hands went to it often to brush them clean of each cooking task. She had the back door propped open, but the cool morning air could not mitigate the swelter of the kitchen. When the heat became too much, she daubed her forehead with the hem of the apron, then returned to cooking with even greater energy. She reminded Collie of a steam engine when she stood in front of the stove, and Collie had learned in the three months they had been stationed here not to get in her way while food was in the equation.

"I'll just get the coffee," she said to Mrs. Hammond loud enough so the woman could hear her over the pops and sizzle of the cooking meat.

"Germans today," Mrs. Hammond said without properly turning to see her.

"Yes, it should be quite a day."

"Your father came by earlier in a vehicle. He said he'd return for breakfast."

"He's a busy man today."

"Almost ready here."

Collie wrapped a towel around her hand and carried the coffee out to the table. It was not her job to help, specifically, but she found it better to be busy. Besides, Mrs. Hammond was shorthanded; she had not bargained for the POW camp to descend on her small boardinghouse in the tiny village. No one in the town had bargained for such a thing, but it was happening all the same and Collie determined to do her part. She held the top of the pot as she went around the table, pouring coffee in a clockwise turn. Agnes finished unloading the cups at the other end of the table and hurried back to Mrs. Hammond for more instructions.

Collie had nearly emptied the pot when she heard a vehicle arrive outside, and a moment later her father entered the room. The collected men stood. It was prideful to relish the respect her father received, but she could not help it. He stood in the doorway for a moment, a white handkerchief pressed to his lips. The handkerchief signaled many things to Collie. It meant, mostly likely, that he had experienced a difficult morning. During the Great War he had suffered chlorine poisoning; his lungs had been glazed by the green, noxious gas, and now he carried the weight of the gas inside him, choking on it still, his health permanently undermined, his voice somewhat cracked and permanently pinched. He had turned fifty-two a week before, and though he was tall and slim and filled out his uniform admirably, quite handsomely, in fact, a sense of fragility clung to him in equal measure. The handkerchiefs he brought to his mouth occasionally muffled his speech; he had told her once that the Allied troops had been instructed to use cloths dampened by urine to protect themselves from the chlorine gas, and she could never see the handkerchiefs without thinking of that horror. She wondered how he could remain so equitable facing the prospect of German troops coming under his jurisdiction.

"Morning," her father said to the gathered men, dropping his hand holding the handkerchief to his side. "Will breakfast be long?"

"Shortly," Collie called to him, and he turned and smiled.

"Major . . . ," one of the men started, and Collie knew as she carried the coffeepot back to the kitchen that the man had buttonholed her father on the German subject. It was all anyone talked about, perhaps understandably, but she knew the topic occasionally wore her father out. He had traveled to Boston many times for briefings and was on the phone constantly with various political entities inside and outside of the military, but the truth remained that no one knew precisely how to operate a prisoner-of-war camp in what was a modified conservation camp. The facts were simple: pulp was necessary for the war effort, but most of the loggers had been drained away to the war or to the munitions factories farther south. Many of them went for better pay and safer work, and who could blame them? So the War Department had looked around at various conservation camps built during the Depression with government monies, and a few had been selected to become prisoner-of-war camps for the overburdened British. No one thought it was an ideal solution—and an avalanche of criticism followed the announcement that Camp Stark would be converted to prisoner-of-war footing—but now the theoretical was about to become the practical, and her father, for better or worse, was the lightning rod for every theory or opinion about the project.

Meanwhile, Agnes began carrying large serving trays of scrambled eggs and pancakes out to the table. Collie held out a second tray and received another pot of coffee, sausage and ham and scrapple, and a few pots of jam. Staples were often an issue, but today, at least, there was ample, and when Collie pushed back into the room she saw the men had already taken up their places, leaving the head of the table for her father.

". . . the Geneva Conventions says . . . ," spoke one man, a short, fiery little man named Johns who Collie did not particularly like. He was a saw sharpener, or something of the kind, and she found him too opinionated for the little he knew.

"Coddling them," another man cut off Johns, this time a soldier with a blank face and large, hairy wrists extending from his ill-fitting jacket. "These men have caused the world more trouble and pain by their actions, and when I think of them arriving in this town . . ."

"Hardly a town," someone joked, but Collie didn't see who spoke.

"Major Brennan," Johns asked, his hand taking a spoonful of eggs while he tried to make his voice heard over the murmur, "how do we know these men won't escape and kill us where we sleep?"

Gradually the table grew quiet. Collie watched her father gather himself. He appeared tired; she was certain he hadn't slept well these last weeks.

"A prisoner," her father said, his voice tightened as it sometimes did when emotion mixed with the effects of the chlorine gas, and Collie noticed the men tried to be quieter with their serving spoons and coffee stirs, "is entitled to fair treatment regardless of the forces that brought him to our door. They can be asked to work, and we must pay them in scrip if they agree. The officers may refuse and we may not put any of the men to work at labor deemed too dangerous. There's been some debate, as you know, to determine whether logging is too dangerous for captured belligerents, but Congress has given us authority to make them work. So now you know as much as I do about the proceedings, gentlemen, and I hope you'll let me sit with my daughter for a moment before the day becomes too hectic."

And that was all it took. The conversation turned to logging, the other great topic of the day. Collie finished with her tray, then quickly sat on a small chair pulled up at the corner of the table. She felt a moment's unease at sitting at a table full of men, and she would not have done so if her father hadn't been squarely in command. But he had held out her chair and kissed her cheek when she sat beside him, and she felt happy being near him.

"You're in for a full day, too," he said softly, buttering a corner of his pancake. "It's all hands on deck, I'm afraid."

"I'll be up right after breakfast."

"I hope we're ready. I suppose we'll find out soon enough."

"Everything will work out, Papa."

He raised his eyebrows in appraisal, his fork stalled halfway to his mouth. What choice did they have, anyway? she wondered. At times she felt they had all been swept out to sea. The editorials back and forth in the *Boston Post*, or the *Littleton Courier*, seemed like so much tedious bloviating. The war had entered every facet of their lives, and despite the editorialists' most cherished hopes, it would not rest until it found its own equilibrium.

Three short pops from the fireplace suddenly silenced the table. Faces looked quickly around, startled. A man nearest the fireplace stood and stepped on a few errant sparks, his handkerchief still in his shirt collar.

"Thought the Germans had arrived!" one man quipped.

And that brought laughter, though Collie thought, as she laughed with them, that the laughter had an underside of nervous fear. The enemy at last was to be made visible, and fear and curiosity divided most people's expectations, and not one of them, she felt, knew clearly what hopes they had in their hearts.

On the walk to Camp Stark from the village the sky clouded over and a few heavy drops of rain began to fall. It always astonished Collie how fast the weather could change in New Hampshire. Outside of Fort Dix, New Jersey, the place that Collie called home, the weather changed slowly and more predictably. In New Hampshire the winds coming across the Canadian plains made every weather system fiercer and more dramatic. It made it difficult to know how to dress in the morning; she found she relied on several layers of outerwear, peeling them or adding them as the day gained focus.

Collie might have hitched a ride from the many trucks going back and forth from the village to the camp proper, but she liked the walk and promised it to herself each morning. She had found a path, an angler's path, she supposed, that took her along the banks of the Ammonoosuc River. She had discovered a large oak about halfway to the camp, and beneath the oak a square slab of granite formed a perfect bench. It appeared almost as if someone had placed it there intentionally, but such a notion was not in keeping with the rough quality of life in a logging village. In any event, she had found it a place of contemplation, and she often stopped with whatever book she might be reading to spend a few minutes away from the noisy boarding-house or the clamor of camp construction. Whatever else the war might be, it was a loud affair, Collie thought. Life among men brought sounds she had forgotten in her time at Smith. Boots stamping, keys rattling against doors, the yawn of chairs as the men plopped into them, the greedy knock of their knives and forks against whatever plate passed near them—she had written to Estelle about these sounds, marveling that the men seemed not to notice their own cacophony. The only remedy for it, she declared, was the slab of granite next to the lovely river and a page or two of poetry to keep her level.

She felt guilty this morning, however, at the idea of stopping because of the arriving Germans. Her father needed her. Besides, the rain hurried her along. She heard the sounds of hammers before she saw the camp. The hammer blows echoed across the river and bounced off the Percy Mountains, the sharp break of the hammering rhythm cut and squeezed by the rush of water over rock. The camp had been built across from an old orchard, and Collie spotted the four guard towers slapped together quickly once the final decision had been made in Washington. Inside the fence, nine barracks stood in rows; they would be used to house the Germans. One hundred and fifty men, she knew, would make this their home. The refectory and latrines took up either side of the compound. It was not a perfect arrangement by any means, but, as her father said, the Germans were prisoners, not guests, and they would receive fair treatment, not a holiday.

This morning, however, the camp looked particularly dismal in the dull rain. The hammer blows came from a detail of men working to build a three-sided pole barn for the twitch horses. The horses would be required for logging, Collie knew, and she had helped process the procurement forms herself. Even now two large animals stood close to where the men worked, their heads down from the rain, their massive hindquarters slick with water.

Collie said good morning to the two guards at the central gate, then entered the small administration building on the right side. A potbelly stove gave off a solid wave of heat as she shucked out of her coat; she was grateful for the warmth because the walk had given her a chill.

Lieutenant Peters came out of her father's office carrying a stenographer's pad and a stack of invoices. Collie shared the outside office with him. He was a tall man, birdlike, with a diffident manner. He reminded Collie of a hen working sideways at a new spot of grass, his attention ready to dart elsewhere at a moment's notice. But he was devoted to her father, she knew, and he had been deluged with paperwork concerning the German POWs. He had done his best, but the army wanted everything in triplicate, so much so that it occasionally threatened to tie the office in knots. Lieutenant Peters managed it all with good humor, and Collie appreciated his forbearance.

"Morning, Collie," he said as he put his paperwork on his desk. "Today's the day."

"Are they on time?"

"From all reports. They've left Fort Devens. Hope you're ready with your German."

"Hardly," Collie said, blushing slightly at the thought that she, with her smattering of knowledge inspired primarily by her mother's love of German opera and lieder singing, would be counted on to communicate with the Germans. Surely, she thought not for the first time, the army could provide better interpreters, but she knew, also, that many had been commandeered for overseas work. It made her nervous to contemplate the potential embarrassment her rudimentary German might bring. Still, in a world of blind men, the one-eyed man is king, as her father said. She promised to do her best.

She settled into the morning's work. There was plenty to occupy her. She helped Lieutenant Peters with requisitions forms, answered the endlessly ringing telephone—the press, in particular, could not be satisfied and wanted more and more details about even the smallest details of the arrangements—and did her best to buffer her father from relentless questions. A barrage of men showed up to ask for clarifications: what planking to use for the boardwalks between the barracks and the latrines; what should be paid for hay; what food should be served the first night. The questions betrayed nervousness. Despite everything that had been said, the camp reminded Collie of a theater on opening night. The months of preparation suddenly ended; in a single moment the camp would go from being a proposal debated in a thousand forums to a tiny town populated by one hundred and fifty Germans. Everyone, Collie realized, felt keyed up and jumpy.

At noon her father came out of his office. It was time to go to the train station.

"Are you ready?" he asked her. "Lieutenant Peters, please keep an eye on things."

"Yes, sir."

"Off we go," her father said.

"Yes," she said simply, and gathered her coat.

The rain had lightened, but the sun still struggled to free itself from the clouds.

"I've been thinking of your mother this morning," her father said when they had climbed into the jeep that would whisk them to the village. "She would have enjoyed this day. She always liked a fuss. She loved parades and circuses, and she knew very well that I didn't. But she made me go just the same. She claimed it was good for me. It made my heart lighter, she said."

"I've been thinking of her, too. I'm worried that her German was much better than mine."

"Oh, I don't know if that's true. She never took a class. She learned it by ear, through music mostly. You received instruction at Smith, so I don't imagine you need to take a backseat to her ability. It's true she had a knack for languages, but you got that from her."

"You're about to see how little she passed along to me."

"You'll do fine. I have every confidence in you."

He smiled and patted her knee. He leaned to one side and drew his handkerchief from his hip pocket and pressed it to his lips. She heard his lungs rasp; he sat very still when that happened, as if to move might encourage his lungs to fail in their efforts to take in oxygen.

They arrived at the train station a moment later. A crowd of fifty or so waited in the rain, all of them peering east toward Berlin. It was a great irony, Collie knew, that the nearest town to Camp Stark was named Berlin. Everyone laughed at the odd coincidence. Meanwhile, two boys knelt near the rails, their ears pressed to the metal, their faces expressing equal measures of hope and excitement. Now and then they raised up to shake their heads at the crowd, then bent back down, listening to the rails for vibrations that passed through the earth.

⊰⊱ *Chapter Two* ⊰⊱

German prisoner-of-war Private August Wahrlich still felt the sea in his legs. That was not possible, of course, and yet it felt true. He imagined his legs contained water in sympathy with the sea, and that the rocking train reminded his body of its passage over the ocean to America. It was a nonsensical notion, but he was a young man given to poetic ideas and entertaining metaphors, and he deliberately gave his mind license to chase the thoughts it encountered for as long as it liked.

Some in the company called him dreamy or a rag catcher, he knew, but he did not mind. He understood the men's reactions came from his status as a former university student. One fellow soldier from Africa named Lingenheimer had called him Hamlet, after the equivocating prince of Denmark. The name had not entirely stuck, the reference being too obscure, but its residue remained, and his role as a translator of German to English calcified it. For better or worse, among the men he was known as a man of education, an impractical man, a man not as fully committed to German victory as his heartier compatriots. Whether his reputation was deserved or not no longer mattered. Men in wartime lived as semaphore messages, brief outlines that conveyed only the most cursory understanding of one another.

As his mind chased these thoughts, August kept his eyes outward, watching the passing scenery. Occasionally he caught his reflection in the dull glass window, and he would be surprised, again, to find it there. The steady swaying of the train made him see the reflection as though it were a puppet head rolling out beyond the tracks, and that thought, curious as it was, made him smile. He wondered, absently, if his mind had always been given to such odd flights of fancy, or whether the war had pushed him to give his imagination a wider leash. He could not say for certain, but he did not mind living inside his thoughts. Better, certainly, than the gruff exchanges of the men around him, the laughing brays of men confined too long in one place.

The more rational part of his mind took pleasure in the scenery. He had volunteered for service in New Hampshire; it had been advertised as a woodland, not unlike his homeland near Vienna, and he had been one of the first to sign up. Despite his compatriots' worries that they might be tricked into dire conditions, he had taken a chance. Some men, he knew, had been sent to potato farms in Houlton, Maine, while others preferred the dull monotony of prison life at Fort Devens. August had chosen the forest over the potato field, the scent of pine over the raw earth of farming. He had spent his boyhood in the forests, and now, gazing out the window, he saw the pines as old friends returned to him after months and months of fighting in the deserts of North Africa. It did his heart good to see them.

"We're coming into it," a man said behind him. "The train is starting to slow."

August let his thoughts continue to roam, while around him men became more animated. What were they coming into, after all? No one knew for certain; even the American guards did not know what to expect. Most of the guards would return to Massachusetts, to Fort Devens, on the return train. Though they talked about New Hampshire as a beautiful place, the guards let it be known that Camp Stark was rural and isolated. They had little interest in remaining, and they joked that the Germans better be prepared to speak French with the Quebecois. The idea of the Germans suddenly trapped in a small village appealed to their sense of humor, though August did not exactly understand why. It was one of many things that confused him about Americans.

Suddenly a large water tank came into view; it was a loading tank for trains, August imagined. Then he watched a band of boys running beside the train, some of them shooting imaginary guns at them. The sight of the boys made August look away. At the same moment one of the guards at the front of the car told the men to remain seated, because a few of them had begun to stand and move, preparing to disembark. The guard looked at August, and August stood, as he had done a thousand times in the last months, and repeated the command to his fellow soldiers in German.

"Stay seated!" August said in German.

"I'm sick of sitting," someone said at the back of the car.

"Tell them we're hungry," someone else said. "Tell them to feed us."

"Stay seated!" August repeated.

The train pulled into a tiny village. August was not sure why, but somehow his mind had tricked him to believe they might be met by celebration. Train arrivals often brought joy, but he glimpsed the serious faces on the civilians, the sharp attention of the military personnel, and knew he had been wildly mistaken. He had to remind himself that he was a prisoner of war, that this train brought only obligation, and that the village had been at war with his homeland.

"Wait while we see that everything is in order," the guard at the front of the car said. August stood and relayed the information to his fellow prisoners. They scarcely heard him. They were too busy looking out at the tiny village and ogling the women who had come to see their arrival.

A few new guards suddenly appeared on the train. They spoke quickly to the regular guards, then together they announced in loud voices that the men would dismount the train and form columns. No foolishness would be tolerated. They must leave by the front of the car and go directly into formation. August served as translator.

How peculiar it all was, August thought as he moved slowly behind the men in front of him toward the exit of the car. Life never ceased surprising one. It had not been so long ago when he had been on a different train heading for the transport boats to take him to Africa. How proud they had been, and so sure of their victory! Now the men in front of him looked like wraiths. Bright letters—PW— had been stitched onto their uniforms, front and back, so there could be no mistake about their status. Their eyes looked tired and beaten, and the color of their skin was ashen. Some of the men had worried that they were being sent to their deaths, and they glanced repeatedly out the windows, trying to assess the situation. For his part, August had stopped hoping for any specific outcome. It was better to be a kite and let the wind do what it wanted with you.

"The circus has come to town! See how they look at us!" someone from farther up in the car said.

"Silence," a guard said.

Someone cursed, and then, with one large, final step, August found himself on New Hampshire soil. He had a brief impression of faces, curious, anxious faces surrounding him. The citizens remained well back; a dozen or more guards stood with rifles at the ready, their chests puffed up like barnyard roosters. The same pack of boys he had seen earlier dodged in and out of the crowd, trying to get a better view. A few women regarded the Germans from the train platform, but August did not get a good look at them. Everything was commotion. As soon as the last prisoner had disembarked, the guards began forming them into tighter columns. They had not quite finished the formation when a man—an American, August guessed from his English—began yelling in a frenzied voice.

The guards stiffened. Someone, another American, went to the man and tried to quiet him. Gradually the man's words became clear: the Germans had killed his son, and he called them vile names and cursed them to hell. Around August his fellow prisoners whispered, asking what the man was saying. August could not distinguish all the words, but he whispered quickly the general sense. Someone in a low voice cursed back, calling the American father a shit-hound.

Then they marched. The guards flanked them all around while the prisoners marched past the length of the train. August felt the damp cold and tried to duck more deeply into his outer garment. His legs felt tired and filled with sand. At last, however, he smelled pine. The scent arrived on the quiet breeze, enhanced by the dampness, and August filled his lungs over and over again. It was the fragrance of his homeland, and he recalled his boyhood and let his mind roam to those early days, and he followed the man in front of him, his senses whisking him away, the rain falling in the river and making circles that drifted wider and wider until they returned once more to simple water.

The sight of the Germans marching peacefully toward Camp Stark filled Major Brennan with rancorous thoughts. Twice he touched his handkerchief to his lips, his breath coming in short, openmouthed pants, his eyes locked on the well-ordered columns. It was typical of the Germans to march well even in captivity. That aspect of the Germans he had always admired; as a lifelong military man he could not do otherwise. And yet hadn't the Allies given everything in the Great War to prevent exactly this? To keep Germans away from these shores? The sight of the German men marching in heavy cadence, their round, Teutonic faces straight forward despite their desire to see their surroundings, impressed him forcefully. He could not hate them, though he nevertheless despised them. They had robbed the air from his lungs, burned his pulmonary tract with gas, and yet, like some great, malignant wild creature, they did not intend it personally. A lion, after all, does not want to hurt you; it merely wants to consume you. That, Major Brennan felt, represented the German attitude.

Watching them, he also assessed their vitality and usefulness, despairing that the men would not be sufficient. *Blood from stones*, that was the common description given by his fellow camp commandants when asked about the usefulness of the Germans. He had read the reports: the Germans resented imprisonment, obviously, but they also betrayed a degree of haughtiness that was unusual in a captured people. It was as if, he had read, the Germans did not quite believe their country had been weakened. For many German prisoners the reports of German defeat remained a fabric of lies. Yes, they might be captured themselves, but the Fatherland, and certainly Hitler himself, fought on bravely and probably victoriously.

Major Brennan's job, however, was simple: *one cord per man per day.* The quota had been agreed upon by Sherman Heights, the president of the Brown Paper Company in Berlin, and by the regional commandant, General Lewis. Whether it was feasible was a different question altogether, and as Major Brennan rode behind the marching Germans with his daughter beside him, he had grave misgivings. They looked to be a skinny, ragtag outfit. Workingmen required calories, five thousand per day at least for the kind of work these men would undertake, but such nutritional theory felt laughable in the face of the emaciated men. Clearly they had suffered. It was evident in their postures, in the nervous eyes they cast about them. They were not loggers. They were German soldiers stripped of their pride, men left with only the vestiges of their wartime stature.

"What do you think of them?" Major Brennan asked his daughter, because he needed to be out of his own thoughts and because he trusted his daughter's powers of observation. "Do they look as you imagined them to look?"

"Less fierce," Collie answered. "They appear exhausted."

"They've had a rest at Fort Devens, but I agree. It will be a trick to get work out of them."

"When is Mr. Heights coming to see them?"

"Tomorrow. He was detained in Berlin."

"They need to be fed up a little. Look at that one there. He's as thin as a rail."

"I thought the same thing."

"Will you put them to work tomorrow?"

"They'll require a day to settle in. We need to find a few leaders among them. And we'll need to poll them to see if any of the men know the work. I doubt it, but it's worth checking. They'll learn the routine tomorrow."

"It will all work out, Papa."

Major Brennan nodded. At the same moment a vehicle—a converted Coca-Cola delivery truck carrying a few members of the press—pulled up behind them. The press members had been at the arrival; now they clearly wanted photographs of the men plodding toward the camp. Major Brennan watched them direct the military driver to bring them into position beside the column of marching Germans. The reporters hung out of the wide passenger door and snapped their pictures. The photographs, Major Brennan imagined, would jump onto the AP wire and be across the region before morning. It was not every day one hundred and fifty Germans arrived in a New Hampshire logging town.

As the first men began making the right turn into the camp proper, Major Brennan was pleased to see the sun push through the clouds. Perhaps it was an omen, he thought. Certainly it made the camp appear less dismal. He saw a number of the Germans turn to look at the Percy Mountains beyond the chain-link fences. A few elbowed the men next to them to look. Major Brennan wondered what they must think. He knew that Camp Stark resembled the German countryside in some regards at least. Perhaps the men felt relieved to be in a quiet haven, quit of the war. It was impossible to know. Perhaps, too, the men already searched for a path of escape. That was entirely possible.

His driver pulled the jeep over to the administration building, and

Major Brennan climbed out, turning to help his daughter descend. She looked lovely this afternoon, slightly misty from the rain and dampness. For an instant she reminded him of her mother, his wife, Mary Elizabeth. Before the illness, he amended. Before all of that.

"Form them up," he said to Sergeant Clydmore, a short, dense man who waited for orders. "Bring them to the front and I'll address them."

Sergeant Clydmore trotted off and began shouting orders, and the men herding the prisoners began forming them up. Major Brennan turned to his daughter.

"Are you ready to translate?"

"You put too much faith in me, Papa."

"I'll keep it short. The men will want to find their bunks."

"I'll do my best."

Major Brennan stepped onto the wide porch that fronted the commissary. He smelled the raw lumber; everything smelled of raw wood because it had been nailed together only in the past week or two. Many of the nail holes bled sap. He watched as the prisoners slowly formed ranks, their faces suspicious and tired at once. Many of them looked up at the four towers posted on the corners of the compound. That was only to be expected, Major Brennan thought. Slowly the men quieted. They were soldiers, after all, and they knew how to drill and when to listen.

"Welcome to Camp Stark," Major Brennan said, his voice somewhat cracked at the start from the dampness and the chlorine gas. "My name is Major John Brennan and I am the camp commandant. My daughter—standing next to me—will do her best to translate my remarks, but she is not a professional translator."

Major Brennan waited while Collie spoke a few phrases in German. Whether they accurately conveyed his meaning, he couldn't say. Her face had flushed. It surprised him, as it usually did, to hear a different language spill from her lips. She always had a facility with languages, but knowing that intellectually, and hearing it in practice, proved two different experiences.

"You have been brought here to help bring out pulpwood from the forests around us. It is good, healthy work, and you will be fed appropriately. You will work in teams of five and you will be guarded at all times. You will meet a quota each day."

He waited while Collie spoke. He saw the men watching her closely. Why wouldn't they? She was beautiful and they were men. When she finished she turned slightly to him and nodded.

"It is our intention to follow the rules set forth in the Geneva Conventions, and we promise to treat you fairly if you treat us fairly in return. You will have tomorrow free to adjust to your new circumstances and to form cutting teams."

Collie translated. Major Brennan tried to think of something inspirational to say, something to end their first contact together with authority, but that was not his personality.

"Get some rest," he concluded. And the men, after hearing Collie's final translation, turned and began filing into the barracks.

Collie had difficulty keeping her eyes off the windows that looked out onto the camp common. How quickly things had changed! Where before the area had been overrun with men building and carrying things, suddenly it had turned into a prisoner-of-war camp. She still found it remarkable that German soldiers, the Hun, had actually arrived. Certainly she had processed a mountain of paperwork to make the arrival possible, but to see the men lounging beside their barracks, smoking and talking, their eyes flashing to see what new thing might occur, filled her with strange emotions. She was glad, obviously, that they had been defeated, but a sense of something inhumane persisted about closing people in with wire fences cornered by guard towers. They deserved it, of course, there was no disputing that, but she could not regard them without seeing brothers and fathers, beaux and young boys. Remove the uniforms, the garish PW letters on their fronts and backs, and they might have passed for an equivalent batch of American GIs. The entire spectacle made her feel peculiar.

She did not, however, have much time for such speculation. The Germans' arrival had revealed the holes in their preparations. American soldiers streamed into the administration building, asking for decisions on this or that policy, requisitioning needed supplies, requesting clarification about a policing issue. The military questions she passed on to her father; the simple maintenance requests she tried to field with the cooperation of Lieutenant Peters. The entire day had been a mad scramble, and now in the late afternoon she felt tired and short-tempered, like a bear, she imagined, with bees swarming around it.

She put on the teakettle. Whenever she felt at odds with herself, she brewed a cup of tea. It was something her mother had taught her. No one, she had promised, could feel grumpy after a cup of tea or a long walk. Both remedies served her well. Tea, right now, in the darkening afternoon, seemed exactly the needed thing.

Perhaps it was the change in her position, but when she looked out at the common again, her hip against her desk, the teakettle sputtering and beginning to heat, her eyes fell on a handsome boy. At first, at least, he appeared to be a boy. He was tall and lithe, with a great thatch of blond hair, and he looked—what was she seeing?— somehow more groomed than the men around him. Perhaps it was only styling, or his trim physique, but his uniform did not hang and sag in the ghastly manner of the other men. The PW on his blouse appeared bright and solid, and when he turned to speak to one of his fellow prisoners she observed his splendid profile. Yes, he was very handsome, she realized, and he was not a boy after all but a young man about her age. Watching him, her mind drifted; she was conscious of watching him, while at the same time the world went on around her. She heard drops from the kettle sizzle and spatter against the hot stove, and she heard the distant drone of her father's voice on the telephone. Those noises registered on her senses, but she traveled down the line of her sight, taking in details that she wanted to recall later, seeing this young man apart from all the other men around him. She had often experienced this mild sense of being out of one's body when on the water in canoes, drifting with the summer breeze, looking down as her fingers dragged furrows in the still surface. It had always amused her to drift that way, half conscious and half given over to revelry, but she had never experienced it while looking at a young man. It was a faintly disturbing sensation.

The kettle brought her out of it, and as she fixed a cup of tea and knocked on the door to inquire if her father would like one, she tried to look out again and force her eyes to be clinical in their assessment. Yes, the young man was handsome, there was no mistaking that, but he was a German, too, and as she took the orders for her father and Lieutenant Peters, she mentally swept the young man into a pile with the other prisoners. She turned her attention to the pleasant job of fixing tea, and by the time she delivered two cups for the men, and one for herself, the German boy was gone anyway.

As she returned to work, the tea warming her, she imagined the letter she could write to Estelle. *This young man,* she thought, then erased that and began again . . . *This young German soldier.* Estelle would see right through her.

By sundown she had done as much as she could for one day. Her eyes hurt and her bottom felt sore from sitting. Her father planned to stay a little longer, and Lieutenant Peters was housed on the camp, so he would not return to the village. The weather had cleared and she decided to walk. Her father protested mildly, but he relented in the end.

"You put in a long day," he said as she left his office. "And there's another one in front of you tomorrow."

"Endless odds and ends."

"Are you sure you won't let me call a driver to take you back to the boardinghouse?"

"I need the walk and the fresh air, Papa. I'll be fine."

He kissed her cheek. She said good night to Lieutenant Peters and then made her way out of the front gate, a guard halfheartedly saluting as she passed. Then the gate closed behind her and she stood for a moment looking back inside. The river made a soft whispering sound. The moon, a half-horn moon, drifted in a troubled sky. The land smelled of spring and of the snow high up in the hills melting back to the soil.

❧ *Chapter Three* ❧

Henry Heights, twenty-five, walked slowly toward the mill, his attention sometimes diverted by workers passing by and greeting him with a good-morning. The workers called him Mr. Heights, a tribute to his place in the ruling family of Berlin, and he was aware of the inequity posed by his age and position. He was at liberty to address the workers by their first names and did so routinely on his leisurely stroll toward the mill office, and not for the first time he felt the injustice of the situation. He had been born to privilege, they had not, and that had made all the difference. His family owned the mill; his father ran it, as his father had before him, and so on back into the earliest memories of anyone living. Henry understood his place in the equation: he was to take over the mill, to run it efficiently and well, and then pass it on to his son in the appropriate season.

On this morning, the proposition of running the mill seemed nearly tolerable. It was a fine spring day and even the perpetual smell of pulp—an acrid, nearly sweet smell like certain tropical fruit left too long in a warm container car—could not diminish the sense of industry that surrounded him. Some of the pleasure he took in the easy morning air stemmed from his recent return from Bowdoin College in Maine, where he had graduated with a bachelor of arts degree in forestry. Absence did, in fact, make the heart grow fonder—even for his balky, rheumatic heart, the same one that had kept him out of the service, leaving him stateside like a child too weak to contest the great issues of the day. On this April morning, his first day returning to his long-anticipated career, he viewed the mill with fresh eyes. It was not a place of beauty, exactly, unless one took a utilitarian view that suggested function was beauty, but its pure energy impressed him. He mused for a moment imagining what his roommate and dearest friend, Wilbur Pace, would have said about the factory as church in the liturgy of American free enterprise and capitalism. Certainly the Brown Paper Company represented as much as any church to the people of Berlin, and in that sense he knew himself to be a young priest, charged with the community's spiritual and economic welfare.

He paused for a moment at the overlook to the Androscoggin River, where in bygone days men in spiked shoes rode logs through the churning spring runoff, assembling giant rafts of wood that choked the river and turned it brown. In 1938 the loggers had brought the detritus of the great New England hurricane, a gale that had done more damage in two days than loggers could enact with whipsaws in many decades, and the Department of the Interior had awarded enormous contracts to the processors. It was the high-water mark, at least in terms of industrial capacity, for the Berlin mills. Now the war was upon them, and the river drivers had given way to diesel trucks for delivery, the stink of engine exhaust mixing with the sweetness of the pulp. Henry felt the world changing, understood that it had, but he could not guess how it would come to rest.

He still stood transfixed by the river overlook when his brother, Amos, joined him. Amos was his older brother and was, by all measures, a rougher, hardier sort, a man's man who had lost two teeth on the left side of his jaw in a mysterious bar fight before he had turned twenty. He had not attended college; he had enlisted in the navy during the first months of the war, and his ship had gone down under him, torpedoed in the North Sea by a German submarine. Burning oil had scalded his waist and buttocks, and his left leg had been lacerated by exploding sheet metal. The bone in his left shin had been shattered, leaving him with a permanent limp that he could not hide. It was a wonder he had survived.

Now Amos clapped Henry on the shoulder and pretended to push his younger brother toward the water. It was not a serious threat; Henry could not have fallen over the stone retaining wall, yet it still made him stick out his arms like a cat falling. Amos laughed loudly and clapped him again.

"I was sent to get you," Amos said, his wide voice easily distinguished over the sound of the water and mill. "The military people are here to talk terms."

"Don't do that," Henry said, his voice surprising him by its edge. He had meant not to be drawn into this sort of thing with Amos, especially not on his first day.

"Do what?"

"Do that. That thing you do. That sneaking up and slapping me on the back, then pretending not to know what you have done. It's annoying. I don't do it to you."

"Well, feel free to do it whenever you like. It's a friendly gesture. Brother to brother and all that. What's got you all wound up? Is it so horrible to return to the fold? Rather be back at the old alma mater?"

"I didn't say that. It isn't about that. It's about you not sneaking up and slapping me on the back and pretending to push me into the water."

"Oh, for Lord's sake, you're a touchy one. Really, you are. Now come along. Father has them set up in the outer office for coffee. Major Brennan is here. He brought along his daughter, too, and she's quite an eyeful, I promise you. You'll be glad I fetched you."

What was the use of trying to reason with him? Henry thought as he followed his brother into the main rear entrance to the mill. They were as locked in their roles as Cain and Abel; it was merely a matter of time before one would murder the other. As soon as that thought crossed his mind, he amended it, however, and barred its insidious roots from digging into any possible soil. They would not kill each other, he promised himself, at least not literally, but in countless metaphorical ways he did not doubt they would vie for their father's approbation. For better or worse they always had, and sometimes Henry imagined them representing two halves of his father's brain: the rough, hardscrabble side harbored in Amos, and the more intellectual, refined side embodied in him. That was an over-simplification but true in its broad outline, and he wondered briefly if he could possibly discuss it with Amos, diffuse it by doing so, and thereby begin things on a better footing.

His thoughts lost their orderly parade through his head, however, when he stepped in the conference room and saw the major's daughter.

"Hello, boys," said his father, Sherman Heights, when they closed the door behind them. His father, heavy, with wide, bristling eyebrows, sat at the head of the table. He motioned to the others. "This is my second son, Henry. You've already met Amos. This is Major Brennan's daughter, Collie."

"How do you do?" Collie asked.

Her father nodded. She was in the middle of pouring him a cup of coffee.

Henry had difficulty taking his eyes off her as he made his way to one of the seats at the conference table. How had this happened? he wondered. So vividly did she seem out of place that it was as if a mythical creature had decided to pay them a visit. He had seen beautiful women before, many of them, in fact, at Bowdoin, but none matched the poise and ease with which she seemed to understand her own measure.

He sat across from her as she finished pouring her father's coffee. She motioned with her eyebrows to ask if they wanted her to pour them a cup. Amos shook his head, and Henry managed to say, "Thank you, but I've had mine this morning."

"You should know that Collie is the camp translator," Sherman Heights said, sipping his coffee. "At least this far into the campaign. You must be proud of your daughter, Major."

"Very proud," Major Brennan said, lifting a dull white handkerchief to his lips. His voice, Henry noticed, seemed sometimes to sink on the last few words, as if his lungs could not quite release them. "She's been doing more than her share in every way."

"Where did you learn Heiny talk?" Amos asked.

He slouched in his chair. He made Collie uncomfortable, Henry saw, and he deliberately used a slang word to deprecate her ability to speak German. Amos despised social conventions and did his best to disrupt them, but his hatred for Germans ran deeper even than that, Henry knew. Henry watched him with dull astonishment.

"My mother was fond of German opera and lieder music," Collie said, apparently ignoring his tone as she slid the coffeepot onto the silver tray at the center of the table. "We lived in Munich for a short time when I was quite young. My father convalesced there, and he also served as an adjunct during the peace discussions."

"That's very impressive," Sherman Heights said. "I may need to steal her from time to time, Major, if it comes to that. We depend on a fellow up in a logging camp here to translate when the need arises. A German fellow, but he's so long in this country that his language has dried up on him."

"I'll part with her reluctantly," Major Brennan said, "and only for the briefest periods."

"Of course, of course," Henry heard his father say. "Now, I should also mention that Henry has joined us permanently. He's going to be put in charge of shipping. It's his first full day, in fact."

Henry felt himself flush. He was aware of Collie, the major's daughter, glancing quickly at him. He had seen that look before: one of quick appraisal, then dismissal. What was a man if he could not join the service when his country needed him? He was young and outwardly robust, he knew, and he suspected that many people, hearing the news of his disqualification, attributed it to his family's prominence. It was emasculating. Any attempt to explain his circumstances only made the situation worse.

Fortunately, before they could delve further into the matter, they began discussing the details of their business arrangement: how many workers, how many hours, what terms, when the loads would be delivered, and so forth. Much of it had already been hammered out, but Henry nevertheless had difficulty keeping his mind on the discussion. Some of it was too new for him to comprehend, but he was also distracted by Major Brennan's daughter's presence. Collie, he reminded himself. What proved most distracting was trying not to look at her or to be distracted by her; he felt if he could simply give in and gaze at her as much as he liked, he might be satisfied with his study and turn his attention to the matter at hand. It was the surreptitiousness of his glances that complicated everything. When at one point the conversation paused and he realized he was expected to speak, he cleared his throat and simply nodded. That produced an awkward gap that his father hurried to fill with his own voice.

After the meeting, he joined his father and Amos in walking the Brennans out to their waiting jeep. Their driver held the door open.

"Good-bye," his father said, shaking hands with them both, "let us know if we can be of any assistance."

"Good-bye," Collie said to them all. "It was a pleasure to meet you."

Then with a slight grinding of gears, they departed.

"Lovely girl," Henry's father said. "She must have quite an impact up at the camp."

"It's a wonder the Germans don't rape her," Amos said. "Ugly bastards."

"Not every German . . . ," Henry started to say, then stopped. It was no use.

"Back to work," Henry heard his father say. But Henry's eyes remained on the jeep, the blond hair receding like a soft, yellow blossom.

It was a day for it, August thought as he watched the twitch horse heave against the traces in order to drag the raft of logs to the landing an eighth of a kilometer below. The flies swarmed fiercely and surrounded his ears with sound, but the sun shone brilliantly and the smell of pines drifted everywhere. It was the sort of day that his father might declare a *wandertag*, a day to wander in the Black Forest, backpacks and staves at the ready, afterward a visit to a *heuriger* for a meal of sausage and cheese and the bright happy singing of the accordion. It felt something of a dream that such an outing had ever been possible. But the weather at least was as fine as what they had known in Austria before the war. It was a spring morning and the birds had become crazed with its luscious warmth.

With Gerhard, one of the team members, driving the horse down to the landing, the men took a break. Two guards stood above them on the hillside, their rifles held lazily across their chests. Even the guards, August realized, could not resist such weather. At first both had stood guard resolutely, their faces locked in a neutral expression, their eyes alive to treachery. Gradually, however, the increasing warmth of the morning, the dull snore of the two-man saw working back and forth over the logs, had softened them. By midmorning they had devised a system where one of them would sit while the other remained alert. It had taken time, but the guards, August understood, had eventually realized that their captives would not flee into the woods at a moment's inattention. Escape *was* possible, certainly; that had become clear almost immediately. Too many men moving in all directions, combined with the horses, the odd Coca-Cola trucks filled with reporters, the newness of the daily routines, all held countless opportunities for flight. In the barracks the men had laughed at the security system. It was their duty to escape if they could, and some of the men already had plans to do so, but other men, men tired of the war and of hardship, had cautioned against it. It was one of the many threads of talk the men had engaged in freely, because the Americans, they soon understood, had no knowledge of German. The prisoners had tested the Americans many times over on the first few days, speaking a vile epithet to get a rise from them, but the Americans had been deaf to everything out of ignorance. The older German men, especially the hard core of Nazis who had already assumed command of the barracks, had ridiculed the Americans ceaselessly, calling them ignorant pigs.

But his cutting crew, at least, had no grudge against the Americans. August had already served as a translator to ask questions of the American guards: when did they think the war would end, and what did they miss the most from their wartime privations, and girls, what were American girls like? The questions had been light-hearted for the most part, and the Americans had slowly warmed to both the questions and the crew. Now isolated in the woods, at least two kilometers from camp, August felt at ease, though his hands had already blistered and his arms and shoulders ached from dragging the saw back and forth and limbing the trees with an ax. *Eine klafter pro kopf,* one cord per man per day. That was the camp's motto.

"All right, back to work," one of the guards, Private Mitchell, said when Gerhard returned with the horse. "We'll be here until nightfall at this rate."

Gerhard turned the horse in the clearing they had forged at the base of the small rise. Flies swarmed all over the poor animal, and the horse flicked his tail and lifted his hind leg to brush them away. The horse's name was Bob. Gerhard, the only farmer among them, had immediately taken charge of the animal. Gerhard was a solid, doleful character, who happened to be one of three Austrians among the prisoners. August felt a natural affection for him. He had known many men like him back in his home country—good, honest souls with square heads, men whose hands worked the soil and woodlands. Often Gerhard spoke longingly of the dogs he left behind, a breed he had fashioned himself by crossing wolfhounds and spaniels. He called them bread-dogs, kruh-hounds, and he outlined the animal's family tree as though they were human relatives.

"Ask them if we work on Easter, too," William said.

William was tall and skinny, with bad skin and a long nose above teeth too prominent for his narrow face.

August called the question up to the guards. The guards did not seem to know the answer. They discussed it for a moment before the second guard, Private Ouellette, responded that he didn't think so.

"Against the Geneva Conventions," Hans said, picking up the saw and extending the other end to Howard, the last member of their crew. Howard and Hans had similar builds, short and blocky, and they had both been meatcutters in civilian life. They went everywhere together, and talked about their trade before the war, and how, in time, the meat had grown rarer and coarser. Their discussion of meat seemed to be endlessly fascinating to them; they seemed determined to ride out the internment together.

"They must observe holidays. It's mandatory," Howard said.

"You put too much faith in the Geneva Conventions," Hans said. "They can bloody well do what they like with us."

"Not if they want their own boys looked after."

"There's a lot of ocean between here and there."

Listening, August wondered if anyone knew what the Geneva Conventions permitted or disallowed. Everyone talked about them as if they knew them to the last letter, but he doubted anyone in the barracks had ever read them. He certainly hadn't. Nevertheless, it was a magic wand that entered every conversation, used however it was needed for the moment. The Nazis in the camp laughed at the mention of the Geneva Conventions. They claimed such covenants were for weaklings.

August began limbing the next tree, a thick spruce with a sharply braided trunk. He used a broadax, chopping the smaller branches easily. Once he had the tree cleared of obstacles, Hans and Howard would saw it into five-meter lengths. Finally they would attach a chain to the trees and drag them down to the landing. From there a truck would eventually come and transport them to the mills in Berlin. But the truck would not come until they had a sufficient load, and so the day went round and round, not unpleasantly, but not easily, either. The work satisfied August, at least to some degree. It was straightforward and uncomplicated; it required none of the moral philosophizing that the war had carried with it day to day.

They worked until four o'clock. It was only their fourth day on the job, and August felt his legs tremble as he joined the crew for the walk back to camp. He felt hot and sweaty, and his hands stung horribly from blisters. In time, perhaps, they would grow accustomed to the work, but for the time being he marveled at the exhaustion that poured through his body. The guards, fortunately, behaved sensibly: they did not force the Germans to move faster than necessary.

In fact, the guards gave them permission to wash in Mill Stream, the small brook that ran down into the oddly named river at the base of the camp. When the guards first mentioned it, August watched the other men tighten. They worried about a trick, or some darker impulse that let the guards suggest a washup, but the guards' faces remained friendly and open.

"Go ahead, tell them they can wash here if they like. They worked hard today," Private Mitchell said, directing his comments to August.

"Does he mean it?" William asked.

"I think he does," August said. "If they meant to shoot us they could have done so already."

August stripped out of his shirt and shoes and dipped his face in the water. It felt wonderful. He stood on the bank and slipped out of his trousers, then stepped into the water and fell into a kidney-shaped pool that had been carved out of a stream bank. The others did the same, wading in and splashing, shouting and laughing now that they felt secure in taking a quick bath. August lay back and let his body float in the stream, and for a moment he remembered the heat of Africa, the burned bodies dangling like fuses from the Panzer tanks outlined against the wadis. It had all been hideous, not at all like the war they had been promised, and when the Anglo-American forces had surrounded them, the German company had surrendered on its knees like so many headstones. Yes, that was what he remembered as he lay in the water, feeling the coolness restore his body, the taste of soil and grasses mixed with the ripe scent of the stream. In the silence won by putting his ears beneath the water's surface, he saw the men splashing and laughing, watched the guards smiling, cigarettes in their hands, and a beam of light falling gently through the treetops. It called to mind a painting, something he had seen as a schoolboy, but now he failed to recall the name. It had been an impressionist, likely, a concentration of paint and light and bright colors, and as he let the water carry him to the heel of the small pool, he felt himself flying over the ocean, returning to his home, to his mother and father and his brother, Frederick. He did not know if they had survived, but in the stream light it seemed possible they may have lived, and he felt a moment's relief from his anguish and worry.

When he sat up, the men had turned, like so many weather vanes, to the sight of the commandant's daughter walking from the camp.

"There she goes," Hans said, and he did not have to identify further who he meant. She was the object of every eye in camp.

August sat up quickly to see her. She hurried past, obviously embarrassed to see men—German prisoners!—bathing in a stream. He watched her walk away, her form lovely and so different from the endless men who surrounded him. He smiled and looked at the other men and they all smiled as well. Even the guards could not pretend disinterest.

"*Sie ist hübsch,*" Howard said. *Very pretty.*

"What is her name anyway?" Gerhard asked, then revised himself in English. "Her name?"

He rested on his arms in the stream. He looked like a seal to August.

"Collie," Private Mitchell said. "Short for Colleen."

Mrs. Hammond served Easter dinner at two o'clock and it came off beautifully, with sufficient food for every taste. That was one benefit of having the prisoners, even Mrs. Hammond admitted: the War Department sent train cars of food into Percy Station. People grumbled that the German prisoners ate better than the American population, and that was partially true, Collie imagined. She had read the editorial, printed just the day before, concerning the scarcity of food across the country, the ceaseless rationing that touched every facet of their lives, while the Germans had food and gasoline made available to them. It seemed a grave injustice to the editorial writer, but Collie wondered if the author had seen the German prisoners up close. They had been through a great deal, obviously, and no one with an ounce of charity in his heart could begrudge them decent food. Besides, the men required the food for work.

Collie glanced out the window at the gloomy day. The weather was mixed and a cold front had lowered over the mountains to reclaim the last memories of winter. Collie sat with her father beside the sparkling fire. Her father, she saw, dozed off now and then, his head drifting rearward against the large chairback before he snapped forward and straightened it once more. He resisted sleep, she knew, because he wanted to visit the camp again before darkness. She had plans to go riding with the Chapman girls, though she was not certain if the weather would curtail the outing.

Meanwhile, she wrote a letter to Estelle, outlining in broad strokes what had occurred in the camp over the last several days. It was difficult to know where to draw a line in what she told her friend. She had already clipped out a number of the pertinent stories from the *Littleton Courier* and the *Berlin Reporter*; she had even drawn arrows on the photographs the paper published to show Estelle where the men went and how they lived. It felt like doing a report for school, and she realized, as she came to the last paragraphs of the letter, that she had perhaps taken greater delight in assembling the report than might have been entirely friendly. She had loved doing such work at Smith, and she was aware of allowing her friend to serve as a surrogate professor. Estelle, her faithful friend, would read every word of it and respond in kind. But Collie knew she did the report for her own benefit at least as much as she did to service their communication. She couldn't help it.

The phone rang somewhere in the house, and Collie heard Mrs. Hammond's voice speaking. A moment later Mrs. Hammond came in and said the Chapman girls would arrive by three. The weather, she said, promised to clear. Mrs. Hammond's voice stirred her father, who groggily climbed to his feet and put his back to the fire.

"Excellent meal," he told Mrs. Hammond before she departed. "Thank you for a lovely Easter dinner."

"It came out fairly well," Mrs. Hammond said, her face blushing a little at the compliment. "Tell me, though, Major, I've heard the Germans have a professional cook up at the camp."

"It's true. He was the head chef at a hotel in Munich. Apparently he's quite gifted. You have competition in your small valley here, Mrs. Hammond."

"I'm sure I'm not competition for a professional chef," Mrs.

Hammond said, obviously in a little turmoil at the news. "What hotel was that?"

"I don't know, but I'll ask and let you know. I guess he intends to plant a garden for the mess kitchen, which is a good idea in any case. He requisitioned a few packets of seeds."

"A garden is a good thing."

Mrs. Hammond left.

"That's quite a letter you have there," her father said, nodding at the papers surrounding her. "Is that for Estelle or the *New York Times*?"

"Estelle, Papa."

"Well, she'll be glad to have your news, I'm sure. This war can't last forever, you know. You can go back to Smith when it ends."

"Oh, I think that day has passed, Papa."

"Not necessarily. The Germans can't hold out too much longer, from what I hear. Their situation isn't good."

"We'll hope for a quick ending."

"So you are going riding with the Chapman girls? It was nice of them to invite you. You'll be riding the big draft horses, I'm afraid."

"Still, it will be fun."

"There have been cars all day up at the camp. People are using their gas rations to take a ride past the fence and stare at the Germans. It's like a zoo to them."

"The girls want to see the soldiers, too."

"So I've heard. We have a couple romances brewing. I've made it clear there will be no fraternization. That's the last thing we need."

"Life goes on one way or the other."

Her father's face suddenly turned solemn.

"Life should go on for you, too, Collie. I feel selfish that I have you up in this small village. You didn't enlist."

"We all have to do our part."

"That's true, but I worry that you should be leading a different kind of life. A life with parties and culture and—"

"And eligible men," Collie said, smiling at the theme he came to often when he turned serious.

"Yes, well, maybe. Why not? Your mother would be cross with me for bringing you up to a tiny hamlet like this one with nothing to do socially but go riding with the Chapman girls."

"You worry about it more than I do. I don't mind, Papa."

"I know you don't. You're not like that. That's one of your grand traits. You get along no matter what, but I shouldn't trade on your good will."

"We're lucky to be able to remain together as a family."

He looked at her softly, then nodded.

"I'm going to take this letter upstairs and get ready for the ride. Are you leaving? Going back to camp?"

"I suppose so. That fire felt awfully good."

"Well, you needed a little break from the camp. And Mrs. Hammond outdid herself. I think she may have a crush on you, Papa."

"Oh, good grief."

Their eyes met and they both began laughing. Mrs. Hammond was many wonderful things, certainly, but she wasn't a proper match for her father. Collie gathered the last of the clippings together, then kissed her father and carried the odds and ends up to her room. She washed quickly before climbing into a pair of old trousers and a heavy sweater. She peered out the window to check the weather. The Chapman girls had been correct: the sun had worked over the mountains and now bright sparks flashed on the Ammonoosuc River, and the afternoon shimmered like an animal lifting itself from the water and shaking itself dry.

They all appeared comical, Collie realized as she followed the Chapman girls up the Old Mill Trail. They rode three of the draft horses, one wider than the next, all of them massive and sleepy and annoyed at being rousted out on a vacation day. The saddles the girls had dug up from Lord-only-knew-where, looked absurd on the gigantic animals. Like a postage stamp on an elephant, Collie thought. They resembled a circus procession on its arrival into a new town.

Still, it was good fun. She liked the Chapman girls: Amy was her age, and her sister, Marie, was a lanky fifteen-year-old, all elbows and blushes. Marie, especially, amused Collie. She liked being with the girl, because Marie could not contain her curiosity about everything, and thoughts popped into her mouth before she had the adult sense to edit them. Her outbursts caused embarrassment or awkwardness at times, but nevertheless it was fun to be around her enthusiasm for life. She reminded Collie of a spatula leaping from one bowl to the next to stir the ingredients. She hardly cared what she baked as long as she was in motion.

Amy, in contrast, had a thin, nervous shell around her. At their first meeting, when Collie arrived from Smith, Collie learned that Amy had worn a chest-and-back brace as a young girl. The circumstances that required the brace had never been made clear, but it had left Amy with a rigid posture, as if she had been shaken out of a mold and left to stiffen in the open air. Her posture affected every aspect of her life, it seemed to Collie, and she wondered if Amy would ever loosen. Likely not. She was thoughtful, though, and intelligent: she had planned to become a schoolteacher before the war started. Now she helped around her family's farm and did occasional secretarial work for the Berlin Mill; she loved going to Berlin, and to the Rialto there. It was her favorite thing to do.

Collie rode Buster, a dark, gentle horse with a back as wide as a door. The muddy trail glistened in the late-afternoon sunshine; small rivulets of water flickered down the hillside like reflective veins of copper. Steering the horse was not required. It went where the Chapmans' horses went, climbing the grade with its heavy hooves sucking and releasing the damp earth. Amy took the lead on

Barrow; Marie rode Sylvester, a slightly mischievous horse that was a household wizard at getting out of enclosures and running loose.

"... says the Germans can hypnotize people simply by staring at them," Marie said, the last of a long litany of special powers apparently attributed to the prisoners by the local schoolchildren.

"Who says such a thing?" Amy asked, her body perpendicular to Barrow's large gray back.

"It's true!" Marie exclaimed in her eager voice. "Lenora walked past the camp the other day and a German soldier looked at her and she couldn't move! Her legs wouldn't work. Not *every* German has that power.... I'm not saying that. But some do. This one stared at Lenora until someone called him away. Lenora said she had to go home and lie down when it was over."

"That's ridiculous," Amy said. "Germans are people the same as we are. No one can mesmerize someone just by staring at them."

"They can, too! Collie, tell my sister the truth. She thinks I make up everything."

"No one has hypnotized me yet," Collie said. "But anything is possible, I suppose. They seem like normal men to me."

"Polly says they can dig through the dirt with their hands like moles or badgers!" Marie went on, turning back and forth to Collie, then Amy. "She says if you look closely, their fingers have curved nails."

"These rumors are absurd," Amy said. "You can't go into the store without hearing a half dozen crazy notions. It's embarrassing to hear such things. We're so provincial."

"We should go by the camp now," Marie said. "Please, can we? Everyone is going by today. The newspaper says people are coming over on a train from Berlin."

"I did hear," Amy said, turning all the way around to speak to them both, "that they took Mr. Chapin's rifle away. He threatened to go shoot the prisoners after what they had done to his son. But I guess his neighbors have agreed to watch him. His wife told the authorities about the rifle. They promised to give it back when the Germans are gone."

"I don't blame him for wanting to kill them," Marie said. "Daddy would kill anyone who touched a hair on our heads."

"People get killed in war," Collie said.

Then for a while they rode in silence. The sun hung on the tips of the mountains, still traveling in its springtime arc. When they reached Scooter Pond, a small impression at the base of a rocky outcropping, Amy climbed down. They always dismounted at Scooter Pond. Twice they had come across moose wading in the waters, but on this day the moose remained back in the woods. A kingfisher flicked along the shoreline, occasionally diving into the water to snap a dace from the shallows. Once they tied the horses to a line of shrubs, Marie climbed on a log that extended into the pond and began singing "Mairzy Doats." She had been singing it until she had driven everyone around her nearly mad, but now she pointed her toes as she balanced along the log, her arms out, singing the familiar phrases:

Mairzy doats and dozy doats and liddle lamzy divey
A kiddley divey too, wouldn't you?

She sang it three times through. She also used the lyrics from the bridge:

If the words sound queer and funny to your ear, a little bit jumbled
   and jivey,
Sing "Mares eat oats and does eat oats and little lambs eat ivy."

"I don't know why you like that ridiculous song so much," Amy said, taking a seat at the shoreward end of the log, "but you're driving me to distraction with it."

"Sing it with me. You'll like it," Marie said, breaking the song for a moment while she spun on the log to return to them. "Everyone likes it except you."

"Even the Germans sing it," Collie said, sitting on the opposite side from Amy. "They say it's popular in Europe, too."

"It's catchy, I'll give you that. But to hear it over and over . . ."

Marie began singing it again. Collie laughed at the pained expression on Amy's face. She couldn't help herself: she chimed in with Marie, and Marie, delighted, began singing louder. The sun felt good and warm and the camp felt far removed, Collie thought, and she sang right out, glad to follow Marie's nonsense. She grabbed Amy's hands and tried to get her to dance, but when she refused Collie hopped onto the log and danced with Marie. They did a silly minuet, pointing their toes and pretending to be grand ladies, all the while singing the delirious lyrics. It was infectious. Collie couldn't resist, and she led the next round, kicking higher now, laughing when Amy shook her head.

"Please, please, please, please, please, can we ride to the camp now? It's right on our way home," Marie asked when they came to a good stopping point.

"Will you promise never to sing that song again in my hearing range?" Amy asked.

"Never?" Marie squealed.

"For a week, then."

Marie jumped down off the log and ran to Sylvester. She turned and made a face, pretending that the words of the song tried to force their way up through her throat. She slapped her hand over her mouth, but her cheeks puffed wider, and she crossed her eyes to demonstrate the pain of not singing. Collie laughed. It felt good to be in the sun and good to laugh, and she linked her arm in Amy's and made her friend run with her to their horses.

*   *   *

August watched the traffic pass by: children laughing and pointing, cars creeping slowly past, civilians walking as if on an after-dinner constitutional, except that they had obviously come to gawk. It was difficult to avoid doing something to satisfy the American voyeurs. How odd the circumstances seemed to be, he thought. If the situations were reversed, and Americans were held prisoners in a camp, he could not imagine the German citizenry paying much attention. Prisoners, like sawdust to a carpenter, came from wars, plain and simple. To gaze at tanks and cannons on parade made sense to him, but to wander past Camp Stark and spend a day watching German men do nothing struck him as peculiar. He wished he could ask an American about it. He supposed it had something to do with the fact that Americans had little experience with war on their continent.

Boris—his barracks leader—had issued orders to do nothing about the audience. August had no intention of disobeying Boris, but it seemed like an opportunity lost. Wasn't it their sworn duty to attempt escape? If so, he thought, it made sense to speak with the citizens in order to find out as much as possible about the surrounding area. That only stood to reason. Boris had consulted with the Nazi leadership committee and had repeated the instructions to ignore the Americans staring at them through the fence. The Nazis were a group of older, brutal men, and August did not think seriously about defying them.

In any case, he was glad to have a day to recover. His hands hurt from the saw and ax, and his back ached from lifting and moving wood. He had eaten a good dinner—yes, Red, the Munich cook, was a talented chef—and now felt restless and bored in the growing shade. He considered walking to the canteen, where he might use his scrip to purchase cigarettes or beer, writing paper and soap, but he imagined the Nazi men would be stationed there. Better, he knew, to stay clear of them.

He had not moved from his station near the barracks when the

PA system crackled once and Mozart began to play over the speakers. For a moment, he could not believe what he heard. The radio sputtered several times, then seemed to fix on the appropriate station, and the music came through the system with quiet joy. He looked around him; everyone had suddenly slowed, their eyes meeting one another's with wonder. Such a thing hardly seemed possible, but as he listened more closely—what was the piece? He couldn't remember, but he recognized it as Mozart, his fellow countryman— he knew he hadn't been mistaken. Someone had gotten the notion to broadcast a concert, perhaps as an Easter present, and the music danced out into the muddy courtyard with incomparable beauty.

Several men wept at the sound. August stood, unable to determine a course of action for himself. What to do with the sudden happiness the music brought? He closed his eyes, positioning himself in the last strong sun rays of the day, and allowed his mind to travel back to Vienna, to the wonderful coffeehouses, the *kaffee mit schlag* steaming as the waiters carried them to the table, the snowy drift of a newspaper turning slowly, the steady pluck of the pendulum in the Black Forest wall clock, the scent of chestnuts cooking on an open brazier in late winter. The music carried everything with it, and it suddenly felt dangerous, as if it might puncture his heart in a way that would not mend. Nevertheless, he could not resist it.

When he opened his eyes he saw Collie, the major's daughter.

She stood on the other side of the fence with two young women beside her, three draft horses waiting like forgotten balloons on the leads behind them. Her beauty struck him; he had tried to see her every day, a glimpse of her as important to him as food or drink. All the men talked of her. She was like a lovely shooting star that came into view only briefly, always when least expected, and now, meeting her eyes, he raised his arms as if to dance with her and bowed. She smiled and looked down, but her younger friend, a slim, happy-looking girl, bowed back and held up her arms to mirror his own. He began slowly moving, pretending to dance, and the girl—how happy she looked, and how she blushed—followed his lead. They should have stopped, he thought, because it was a silly game, but he found he wanted to keep dancing, and she became bolder as the music continued, despite one of the other women saying a word that sounded like a name. Then the other woman—not Collie, but a third woman—reached out and put her palm on the young girl's arm to stop her, but the girl shook her off and continued dancing anyway. August felt tears build in his eyes, and he felt tremendously grateful for the girl who danced as his reflection. Other people along the fence line smiled, too, at their pantomime, and when the music built to a conclusion and then halted, they received a round of applause from the onlookers.

The girl blushed again and August bowed his thanks. The girl curtsied in reply, then scrambled onto her horse as lithe and as quick as a mink. For a moment longer he gazed at Collie, and he believed she gazed back, and when she moved to mount her horse, she could not keep her eyes from returning to his, the world around them gone while their stare continued, his heart following her.

❧ *Chapter Four* ❧

Time passed quickly. That was one thing Collie determined as the weather progressed and became warmer. The days seemed like a string of white beads, each one linked by news of the war, by more absurd songs pouring out of the radio, by mounds of paperwork and by the occasional shipment of new guards or the exchange of prisoners. Everything seemed transitory, impermanent, changeable. It struck her occasionally how adaptable humans could be. Three weeks before, the Germans had been a faceless enemy living somewhere distant and remote. Now, while they were still exotic, and remained the source of a thousand gapes from slack-jawed visitors, and continued to be the subject of hundreds of mostly ill-informed editorials, the fact of their existence had become widely accepted. "The prisoners at Stark," people said, as if mentioning a landmark or a geographical feature. They had become part of the community's mental landscape.

Except, of course, for Private August Wahrlich. Dressing on a fine May morning, Collie wondered if she would see him that day. He cluttered her thoughts, and when she saw him her heart grew heavy in her chest and she had difficulty breathing. It was a school-girl crush, she knew, something more fitting for Marie, who had not stopped talking about the day she had pretend-danced with the gallant German soldier. It had been the highlight of Marie's young life, Collie knew, and she enjoyed talking about it whenever she had a willing ear. As much as Collie pretended to be bored by the story, or disinterested, she relished hearing it again because she remembered the way she had exchanged a look with the young soldier. She remembered how handsome he had looked, his arms out, his eyes closing at times—she loved that detail—and how they had nodded slightly at each other. Yes, she remembered that, though at times she wondered if she had made that last part up. Had they really nodded? She couldn't say for certain, but she believed they had. They all agreed, especially Marie, that August Wahrlich was the most handsome German soldier by far. He was the most handsome soldier in the camp, Collie thought, challenged only briefly by a dark-haired young American guard who had been transferred to Houlton, Maine, after only a week of duty.

So she tried to see him, and that proved more difficult than she might have imagined. She could hardly lean out the window and gaze at the men like a lovesick heifer. Besides, the prisoners were gone most of the day, transported as far as Vermont to cut wood. She had her responsibilities as well, though they had changed slightly. Now, in addition to her responsibilities for translation, she concentrated primarily on the logging paperwork, attempting to keep track of what came in, what went out, who took it, at what cost, and so forth. The men proved to be unreliable accountants, and that made the bookkeeping more difficult. The Brown Paper Company wanted more pulp, always more pulp, but her father had remained a steadfast advocate for the fair treatment of the prisoners. He refused to be bullied. They met their quota, but he would not permit the Germans to be used as slaves as some factions desired.

After breakfast, she ignored Mrs. Hammond's admonition to wear a heavier coat, and she walked to the camp beside the Ammonoosuc. The trees on both sides of the river hung exactly on the edge of blossom. The leaves seemed to disappear if you looked at them directly, Collie thought, though they reappeared in slant gazes. The air smelled deliciously of pine and mud, and around the boardinghouse massive heads of lilacs painted the air.

She stopped at her stone bench halfway to the camp and pulled Estelle's latest letter from her pocket. She had deliberately avoided reading the letter earlier at breakfast for fear of spoiling it. Estelle had promised to see if she could arrange a visit; it felt too much to hope for. Collie opened the letter and immediately felt comforted by Estelle's lovely handwriting. She clutched the tissue paper to her chest when she spotted Estelle's promise to arrive in two weeks' time, early June at the latest. She smiled at the letter and teared slightly as she forced herself to slow and read it carefully. It had not been an easy thing to arrange, Estelle confided. She felt somewhat guilty, as if she were going off on a vacation while the rest of the world fought against the enemies of peace, but the war seemed to be tipping in favor of the Allies and it could not continue forever. Her mother had sensed Estelle's restlessness, and she had encouraged her to take a trip. Frankly Estelle had not been faring too well, she confessed, and her parents agreed a change of scenery might be the needed thing. So the plans, while still tentative, seemed promising. She couldn't wait to see her friend Collie, she wrote, and she wanted to experience everything Collie had written about: the funny horse rides, the grim German prisoners, and the bright forests of New Hampshire. She wanted most of all to take mountain walks and to have long conversations with her dear friend. She closed by extending her best wishes to Collie's father.

Collie read the letter twice before she folded it carefully and returned it to her pocket. Estelle! How she longed to see her friend! Collie felt an eager thrill in her stomach. Plans rushed it like a mad torrent: things to do, walks to take, small adventures to pursue. She would show Estelle everything, confide in her about every element of her life, and, in turn, hear all the many thoughts and emotions that had been stored in her friend's days. She patted the letter in her pocket and promised herself that she would read it again at lunch. Finally, reluctantly, she stood and began walking toward the camp in a quick march.

She had not gone far when she heard a siren begin to shriek. It built slowly, cranking until it filled every hollow space in the world.

She knew immediately what it meant: someone had escaped, or had gone unaccounted for, and the siren meant the camp had been locked down. It had gone off twice before, both instances terrifying, but each time it had proven a false alarm. Once, in fact, a young American guard had said he had seen a German Messerschmitt, or a Japanese Zero streaking at them in a deadly line. The boy had been relieved of duty a few days later, sent back to Rhode Island, where he made his home.

But this time the siren conveyed more seriousness. By the time Collie reached the camp, the guards ran about like hornets. The Germans had not been sent out for work; they lounged in apparent amusement, watching the Americans hurry to establish who was present. The siren died as Collie passed through the front gate, and she saw her father step out of the administration building, a cup of coffee in his hand.

A pair of strange thoughts assaulted her at that moment. The first was that her father did not look particularly alarmed at the possibility of an escape. He resembled a man going out to check on a delivery that had disturbed him at his breakfast. Her other thought was that her father had grown gray. It may have been the angle of the sun, or his placidity in the face of the turmoil caused by the siren, but he looked considerably older suddenly. She wondered how she had missed such a thing. She went to him quickly, as if she could somehow prevent his aging by staying near him. But he turned and smiled, then took a sip of coffee.

"Seems one of our birds has flown," he said. "It's a wonder it took them this long."

"Just one?"

"Apparently so. He slipped off into the woods from a cutting crew. That's the current theory. The two guards on his crew each say the other fouled up. It's hard to know what happened exactly. We'll sort it out eventually."

"What's protocol?"

"We'll put out a bulletin. Lieutenant Peters has already taken care of some of that, but there are still calls to make. It's doubtful the prisoner will get very far, but you never know. If he can get on a train and pass himself off as a Dutch soldier, or camouflage himself somehow, he might make it to Boston or New York. If he gets that far, he'll stand a good chance of permanent escape. If he tries to stay in the woods, he'll be out soon enough."

"You don't seem particularly worried."

"This is not a high-security camp. If a man is determined to get away, he probably can. The big thing is, people will panic when they hear about the escape. Once word gets out, the reporters will be calling."

"How can I help?"

"We're going to bring in his crew for questioning shortly. I will need you on hand to translate."

He smiled and bent down and kissed her. Yes, she thought as she looked at him more closely, his age had started to show.

She went inside and helped Lieutenant Peters make phone calls for a half hour. They notified all the proper authorities. She glanced out the window now and then and watched as the Germans remained in ranks according to their barracks. The headcount, distant and rhythmic, went on and on. Apparently they were having trouble determining the missing party, or perhaps, she thought, they had decided to keep the men outdoors while other guards searched the barracks. In any case, the Germans seemed somewhat smug at the guards' confusion. The vaunted German precision, Collie thought, would never have difficulty tallying a prison count.

When the count finished, her heart stopped to see August Wahrlich and his cutting crew being led across the parade ground to the administration building. It occurred so quickly that she did not have a moment to prepare herself. Guards flanked the Germans, herding them forward, and the Americans spoke gruffly to them. The missing man made more work for everyone.

Collie hoped she did not blush when the men halted on the small porch of the administration building. She leaned a little in her seat to see them. August stood a good head taller than the other men. Seeing him nearby for the first time, she realized she had underestimated his good looks. He was truly handsome, with a firm brow and fine eyes, a head of blond hair that lifted and inspected the breeze as it passed. His body looked trim from lumberjacking, and his stomach fell away from the cliff of his ribs into a valley that collected at his belt. He might have been a movie star, truly, and when he turned at something one of the guards said his profile rested in perfect symmetry. Studying him, she felt her blush deepen and she glanced quickly at Lieutenant Peters to make sure he wasn't watching. But he was still on the phone, repeating himself for the tenth time concerning the details of the escapee, and when she looked back to see August she nearly cried out when she discovered his eyes had again found hers.

She lowered her eyes instantly. A guard pushed through the door and asked if Major Brennan was ready for the crew. Did he want them one by one, or all in a group? Lieutenant Peters covered the phone with his hand and replied that the major would interview them one by one. Keep all the men here after they are debriefed, he added, in case the major decided to speak to them as a unit.

Collie felt grateful for the interruption the guard afforded her. He cut off the line of sight out to the porch, but when he peeled back outside she again found her eyes met by August. He smiled. She couldn't help herself from smiling in return. It could not be coincidence, she decided, that their eyes continued to meet. He deliberately found her gaze. No other explanation suited the facts.

Fortunately he was not the first to be summoned inside. A prisoner named Gerhard came in first. Her father called for her to translate and also brought in a stout, humorless guard who stood beside the prisoner. She entered the office and sat to her father's right. Gerhard remained standing. He was a square, blocky man, with unusually large forearms above heavy hands.

From a translating perspective, the questions were simple: who, what, where, when. The German answered straightforwardly. Collie listened to his responses carefully, trying to pick up on any discrepancies in his account. She reported the German's responses to her father faithfully. One by one the men came in, stood before her father, and reported the same story. They knew little; they had no idea where the man had gone. Each testified that the missing soldier had not confided in them. Her father treated them sternly and asked a rigorous series of questions to cross-check against previous answers, but it became apparent after the third man that they knew nothing of the escapee's whereabouts. Collie surmised the facts of the escape required little plotting. The man had drifted away on the walk back to the camp. That was the essence of it. He had gone precisely as the men reached the larger group of men returning for the day. He had mixed in, found his opportunity, then wandered away. It suggested nothing systemic. Nonetheless, it would have to be punished.

The last interviewee was August Wahrlich. He spoke English—he often served to translate English into German around the camp—and her father told her she could go back to the outer office. She passed close to the young German, measuring herself against him. She came to his shoulder.

She kept her head down and pretended to be busy at her desk, but her attention remained locked on the voices coming from her father's office. When Lieutenant Peters asked her a question, she answered it quickly, wanting silence so that she could hear August's voice through the walls. His English was only fair, she realized. It made her smile down at her paperwork to hear him say, *"Alles hangt vorl Kommandanton ab,"* then translate it into English, *Everything depends on the commandant.*

At last she heard him dismissed. The door opened and he stepped out.

"Good morning," he said in English.

Collie realized he greeted them both. The guard from her father's office stood beside him. Collie could not stop blushing. She kept her eyes on her paperwork, but gradually she grew aware that he remained in front of her desk. When she glanced up, he handed her a piece of paper.

"It is a translation of a poem," he said, the accents on his English phrasing somewhat blocky. "Ludwig Uhland. I remembered it from my school days. Do you like poetry?"

"Yes," she said. "I do."

"Your father said I could give this to you. I thought you might like it and perhaps help me with my translation to English."

He extended the paper farther. She took it and felt herself trembling.

"Thank you," she said. "I'm sure I will enjoy it."

"The translation was difficult and it is not very good, I'm afraid. I have the other German put there."

"The original?"

"Yes," he said.

Then the guard told August to step out. August smiled, and she smiled in return. She kept the poem folded and put it to one side, the paper nearly burning her skin when she touched it.

He did not like to do it, but Major Brennan issued the order to put the Germans on bread and water. It was a shotgun approach, one he doubted would be particularly effective, but he felt helpless in the face of the escape. The prisoners would not respect weakness, nor would they take the reduction in rations lightly. He was in a bind; they all were. Little had been gained by the interviews of the work party. A tall, thin German by the name of William Zimmerman had made good his escape. That was the long and short of it. From all accounts, he was an unlikely candidate for escape. He had always followed orders willingly, had labored with a good heart in the initial phases of the work, and had caused no trouble that anyone could point to. He had trusted no one with his plans, from what Major Brennan could determine, nor had he been part of any larger conspiracy. His approach had been clever. He had slipped away before evening roll call, just as the men returned from work, stepping behind a wagon or into the tree line beyond the camp, and from there he had until reveille to get away. Major Brennan did not imagine he would get far, but you never knew.

Meanwhile, he waited for the Brown Paper Company to get back to him. It was a ticklish predicament. By putting the men on bread and water, he undermined their ability to work, thereby reducing the available labor force for the extraction of pulp. Geneva Conventions had specific guidelines about nutrition and what was required in order to let a man labor. A diet of bread and water would make the men weak. It was a muddle, certainly, and he waited for the call from Sherman Heights, president of the Brown Paper Company, with a headache building along his scalp line.

"Collie?" he called into the next room. "Are you there?"

She came in a moment later.

"Could you bring me some aspirin and a glass of water, please?"

"Of course, Papa."

She disappeared and returned quickly. Coming through the door, he recognized her mother in her movements. He smiled softly to see it. He wondered if she knew how much she resembled her mother, his late wife, and wondered if she knew how beautiful she had become.

"Sit with me for a moment," he said, taking the pills and the water from her. "Thank you."

"Quite a day," Collie said, sitting in front of the desk.

"They'll be on bread and water for a time," he said, putting the pills on his tongue and then washing them down with water. "My hands are tied."

"Can they still work?"

He shook his head.

"I can't put them to that kind of work if they're not eating."

"How long will you keep them on it?"

He shrugged. He took another sip of water.

"You look like your mother sitting there. Do you know how much you resemble her? I'm not sure I've told you."

"I have some idea."

"You do, you know. It's in your movement as much as anything, and sometimes in your voice."

"Is it painful to see?"

"No, not at all, sweetheart. It's a delight. One of the few I can count on these days."

He looked out. The harsh light of midday had given way to the mountain shadows of early evening. He rubbed his temples. He watched her brighten.

"Well," she said, "if some good news will make you feel better, I should tell you that Estelle is coming for a visit. She confirmed it today in a letter. She'll arrive in a week or so. So now you'll have two young women to escort around the camp."

"Oh, I'm glad to hear that. She'll keep good company with you."

"I'll take her everywhere. I already have a dozen things planned out."

"Good. You need to consort with some people your own age. Maybe you could host a small reception to introduce her to people. Mrs. Hammond would let you use the parlor, I'm sure."

"I thought of that. But who would I invite?"

"Oh, the Chapman girls, and some of the guards. I don't know. Perhaps you'll invite your German beau."

He watched her blush. He smiled.

"He didn't pass along a secret plan for mutiny, did he? He's not asking you to spy, I hope. He said he had a poem for you."

"Papa! He gave me a poem and asked me to go over his translation of it."

"I see. Well, I probably shouldn't have permitted it. Be careful. The last thing we need is the story of the daughter of the camp's commandant becoming involved with a German prisoner. You understand that, don't you?"

"Don't be ridiculous, Papa."

"All right. But just the same, he's very handsome. Even as an old man, I can see that. But we're still at war with the Germans. These men were pointing rifles at us not long ago. Keep that in mind. Sometimes with the everyday routine of the camp, it's hard to remember, but keep it in mind."

"You don't have to remind me of that, Papa."

"Yes, but the heart wants what the heart wants. Help him with the poem if you like, but that will be the end of it, all right?"

"You're lecturing me like a schoolgirl."

"I don't mean to. Sorry, I'm annoyed with this bit of business about the escaped prisoner. The press will slaughter us over it. And I'll doubtless have to speak to the town fathers. It just makes for more work all the way around."

"I understand. Let me know if I can help."

Major Brennan stared at his daughter. It was rare to see her so uneasy about a young man. She blew air over her top lip and stood. Before she left the room, he sounded her out on something else.

"I'm expecting a call from the Brown Paper Company; they've invited us to a party and I didn't know what to tell them. Would you like to attend? I guess it's a small birthday celebration for the mother, Eleanor, I think it is. I can beg off without any problem, but I wanted to run it by you."

"When is it?"

"The day after tomorrow, I think. It's not particularly formal. No need for fancy dressing."

"We should go, shouldn't we? But I wouldn't mind dressing up, you know. It would do us both good."

"Probably," he said, and then the intercom buzzed. "That's the old man now. I'll tell him we'll attend, if it's okay with you. Give us a night out, anyway."

He watched his daughter leave the room. Then he pushed a button and listened as Sherman Heights's secretary informed the major that she had Mr. Heights and that she would pass him to the president immediately.

Henry Heights watched his brother, Amos, dance with a girl named Dolly, both of them drunk and vining around each other. Now and then Amos ran his hand up Dolly's side, trying to touch her breasts, and Dolly, in a gesture like a person pushing up on a wall, moved his hand away and put it back on her waist. She had performed that same act a dozen times during the dance. Amos was too intoxicated to care or take notice, Henry knew. Henry was drunk himself, and he had consumed only half of what Amos had consumed.

The girl next to him, Charlene, watched Amos and Dolly dance, too. She wore strong lilac perfume and drank a gin fizz. She smoked Camels and constantly dug in her handbag; that seemed to be her chief occupation. Henry could not quite remember her background: she worked in Mexico, Maine, or maybe it was Rumford, and she was up visiting Dolly for the weekend. She had leaned into him twice and put her hand on his thigh. Now, he supposed, she was inattentive because he had not responded. Amos responded instantly to women, staking out territory as if a date were a military campaign, but Henry simply felt uneasy in the haze of hands and drinks. He always had. Besides, he was tired and wanted to turn in, but he imagined Amos was set on having a big night and he doubted they would make it home much before dawn.

Amos and Dolly returned to the table when the jukebox flipped over onto a new record. Lester Young began singing "Stardust."

"You two not dancing?" Amos asked, his voice drunken and tight and watery. "What's wrong with my brother? Is he being a wet blanket, darling? He sometimes is, but he can't help himself. Is he being a wet blanket?"

Amos asked the question of Charlene, but she missed it for digging in her purse. Like a badger or groundhog, Henry thought drunkenly. Like an animal trying to dig into the earth.

"Let's have another round," Dolly said, wobbling a little on her feet. "We could use another round."

"Now you're talking," Amos said. "Now you're making perfect sense."

"We may have had enough," Henry said, though he knew it was futile to say it.

"Enough? Now come on, Henry, we have to have a little fun, don't we? This is our first night out in the old haunts in a long time. We're haunting the old haunts," he said again, evidently amused at his construction, then straightened and called to the bartender. "Ernie, another round, my good man. The same poison. The same concoctions. We'll keep trying till we get it right. Until we perfect them."

Amos sat and dragged Dolly onto his lap. Dolly was a Berlin girl, younger than any of them. She worked in the restaurant at the local bowling lanes. She had dark hair and a slim waist and she wore a bright black-and-white-checked skirt that made Henry think of checkers. She leaned back onto Amos's lap, yawning as she went. Some of her hair had come loose on the right side of her head and it dangled down. She fit Amos's lap like a viola. Now and then, despite her drowsiness, she shot a hand down to stop Amos from exploring too freely beneath the table.

"You're horrible," she said to Amos after one of his attempts and just before the next round arrived. "Did you know how horrible he is, Henry? Just the devil, your brother. Charlene, didn't I warn you? Didn't I say Amos is a devil?"

Charlene nodded. She looked up only when Ernie, the bartender and owner, appeared with the next set of drinks.

"This place is for the birds," Charlene said after Ernie withdrew. "Just for the birds. I thought we were going out someplace special."

"This is special," Amos said, nuzzling Dolly's neck. "This is where everyone goes. This is where the elite go to meet."

"Well, if this is the elite, I don't know where that puts me," Charlene said, taking her gin fizz off the cork-bottomed platter Ernie used to serve them. "Some big night out."

"This is the only place open this late," Amos said. "Stow that gab."

"Let's drive over and see the Krauts," Dolly said. "You said we could. I want to see them!"

"They'll be asleep now," Amos said, his hand beneath the table, making Dolly shift quickly on his lap. "They went nighty-night."

"I wouldn't mind getting out of this dump," Charlene said.

"You're a picky one," Amos said, turning a drunken eye on her. "Dolly, your friend is a picky one."

"They'll be waking up by the time we get there," Dolly said. "Can't we go? Can't we please, please go?"

She kissed Amos and wiggled a little deeper into his arms. Henry felt resigned to whatever happened. The last thing he wanted was to drive to Stark to see the German prisoner-of-war camp in the middle of the night, but he couldn't think of a way to get out of it without being again called a wet blanket.

"Your wish is my command," Amos said, chucking Dolly up onto her feet and grabbing his drink. "Let's go. You have to promise not to get fresh in the car, though."

Dolly laughed and slapped his arm lightly. Amos drained half of his drink. He took a big, breathy inhalation to steady himself. Henry stood and said he'd drive.

"The hell you will," Amos said. "I'm your big brother, so it's up to me to drive. You take a ride in the backseat with Charlene. Charlene, you promise to keep your hands to yourself in the dark?"

"Sure I do," Charlene said, coming alive a little at the prospect of a drive. "I love a car ride."

In no time Henry found himself standing beside the family Oldsmobile, its front wheels jammed up on the lawn beside Ernie's Tavern. Amos had wheedled a bottle of rye from Ernie. He grasped it as if choking its neck, the brown paper bag around it rolled back as a collar. Amos held the door open for Dolly and she slid inside. Henry did the same for Charlene and then climbed in beside her. She had apparently refreshed her lilac perfume, because she gave off a haze of fragrance, slightly tinged by the scent of gin.

"Now, this is an adventure," Amos said, pulling away from the curb. "You girls ready for a little adventure?"

"Of course we are," Dolly said, turning in her seat to glance at Charlene. "Aren't we ready for an adventure, Char?"

"My friend saw the German camp and she said one of the men had red eyes," Charlene said. "You wouldn't notice it right away, not in full sunlight, but right near evening his eyes caught the sun and she swore they were red. Like a wolf or something."

"A couple of them have tails," Dolly said. "I know that for certain. I have it on good account."

"What, were you in the showers with them?" Amos asked.

Dolly shrieked in mock offense. The car jerked across the road and Amos settled it back too rapidly and the tail fished out a little. Henry held the back of the seat in front of him. Charlene's perfume had begun to make him a little seasick. He rolled down the window beside him. Fog laced the roads and puffed as the car passed through it.

Henry dozed for a while. When he woke, Charlene had the rye

bottle in hand and shoved it against his shoulder. They had arrived at the camp. It wasn't much of a place, Henry saw. He took a drink and climbed out when the car stopped. Amos leaned hard on the horn.

"Wake up, you German shits!" Amos yelled in between honks. "Heil Hitler, you Heiny bastards!"

Dolly giggled. Charlene walked close to the fence and stared inside.

"It's too dark," she said. "I can't see anything."

"The guards are going to chase us off," Henry said. "We should go."

"I'll go when I'm good and ready," Amos said. "It's a free country."

He honked the horn in one long blast. It sounded terribly loud in the darkness, Henry thought. He walked off a few paces and peed against a maple, happy to be away from the horn noise. Amos joined him. Amos had trouble staying steady on his feet. Henry offered to drive back, but Amos shook his head.

"I got it," he said, zipping up.

He honked the horn some more. There was nothing to see, Henry reflected, except when the searchlight passed over the interior of the camp. He could make out guard towers posted on each side of a square, and he saw the fence topped by razor wire, but otherwise it was difficult to make out any details. It was too early, or too late, for the German soldiers to be about. They would still be in their barracks, asleep.

"Okay, let's go," Amos said, letting off the horn. "You girls satisfied?"

"We didn't see anything!" Charlene said. "I wanted to see something."

"At least you can say you've been here," Amos said. "Climb back in. I have to put my little brother to bed."

"I can put myself to bed," Henry said, bored with Amos's constant reference to his age.

"No, it's my job to look out for you, little brother."

Henry climbed into the backseat. Charlene climbed in, too. Amos grabbed Dolly and kissed her and rolled her a little on the hood of the car. Dolly fought him off and crawled into the car, laughing.

On the way back, near Eden Road, Amos pulled the car onto a dirt turnout and told the girls they had to take off their clothes to get a ride back.

"Stop it!" Dolly said, laughing. "You're so naughty!"

"I'm serious," Amos said in a voice that Henry didn't recognize as coming from his brother. "Get out and peel off. I want to see both of you. The whole package. Either that or you can stay right here and walk home."

A tightness entered the car. Henry couldn't read his brother's tone, though he imagined Amos was drunk enough to do anything, to mean anything. The girls didn't speak. Amos turned off the car. Light had begun to build in the east. It was a crazy situation.

"Amos . . . ," Henry started, but Amos opened his door and climbed out.

"Both of you naked," Amos said. "If you want a ride home, that is. That's the fare. You don't have to if you want to walk home."

"What a bastard," Charlene said. "I thought you were a bastard, but I didn't know you were this kind of bastard."

"I'm not doing that," Dolly said. "You stupid, damn gorilla."

"Okay, then both of you out," Amos said, his head propped in the driver's-side doorway. "Good luck getting back. Should be logging trucks along here pretty soon. Maybe you can hitch a ride with them. Now hop out. Henry and I are heading to Berlin."

Amos's head jerked sometimes in its drunkenness, Henry saw. It was an ugly thing to watch. The girls didn't move, except to glance nervously back and forth across the seatback, trying to read each other.

"You won't tell if we do it?" Dolly asked, weighing her words, Henry sensed. "You won't spread it around town?"

"You're not serious, are you, Dolly?" Charlene asked. "For this jack wolly?"

"You give us your word you will bring us right back?" Dolly asked. "If we do. You promise? Afterward? You promise?"

"Of course I do," Amos said.

His words slurred together so that it came out, "Course-sigh-dew."

Dolly slipped out the passenger side. Henry felt the booze and the lilac perfume linking together in his guts. He wasn't sure if Amos was being serious or not. It was low behavior, no matter what, but it still felt remotely like a prank. Amos told Charlene to get out, too.

"You're as bad as he is," Charlene hissed at Henry as she slid out on her side. "Letting this go on."

"Now right over here in the headlights," Amos said, pointing to a patch of grass in the center of the beams. "Just a little show, that's all. That's all you're doing. Just putting on a little theatrical performance. A little entertainment for the troops."

The women stood side by side. Neither made a motion to start. Amos reached into the car and grabbed the bottle of rye and took a swig. He stuck it through the window at Henry. Henry took the bottle and pretended to drink. He kept his tongue in the opening. That was easier than refusing his brother.

"You ready, ladies?" Amos asked.

He started clapping his hands slowly, wryly punctuating striptease music he made with his tongue and lips. A few June bugs rattled around in the headlights, creating a buzzing noise; twice, the bugs flashed off and bounced against the women and they flicked their hands at them to get them away.

"Okay, that's enough," Henry said through the window when Dolly started unbuttoning her blouse. "It was just a dare. Just a stupid dare."

"Like hell it was," Amos said, still clapping. "This is the cost of the ride home."

Henry climbed out of the car. He thought he might be sick.

"Come on," he said, and held out his hand to his brother. "Give me the keys and we'll head home. Drop the girls off and head home."

Amos made the striptease music louder. Dolly's hand paused on the buttons of her blouse. Charlene had reached behind her waist to undo the band of her skirt, but now she stopped. Henry reached for the keys in Amos's pocket, but his brother slapped his hands away. Amos kept his eyes fixed on the women. He clapped and smiled, egging them forward.

"They want an excuse to take off their clothes," Amos said, his mouth wet and borderless. "Don't you get it?"

"Let's call it a night," Henry said. "Let's head home."

Unsteady on her feet, Dolly took her clothes off. She did it quickly, automatically, her hands covering her breasts and her groin when she had dropped all the clothes into a mound beneath her feet. She kept her eyes down on the ground. Charlene didn't strip. Amos kept clapping slowly, then made a motion with his hand to have Dolly spin around. She did. Amos nodded. Henry looked despite himself. Dolly appeared white and pale in the early light. Still, he had never seen a woman completely naked before. Not like this, not right out in front of him.

"There," Dolly said, stepping into her skirt. "Satisfied?"

"I'm telling the police," Charlene said. "First thing when I get back, I'm telling them."

"The police won't do anything to them," Dolly said, snapping her bra closed. "Not in Berlin, they won't. It's their word against ours."

"Now, don't be sore," Amos said. "Because Dolly was so pretty, I'll let you ride home for free, Charlene. See? I can be generous."

Amos took a drink of rye. Then he walked the bottle over to Dolly. She slapped at him a bit when he held it out for her, but when she had her top back on she reached for the bottle and took a long drink. Amos put his arm around her until she kissed him. She laughed, too. She squealed as they climbed back in the Oldsmobile and said Amos was a devil.

Chapter Five

"We are used as *verheitz*," Boris hissed at lights-out. "Kindling wood for a larger fire burning beyond this camp. Bread and water!"

That had been the theme all evening. August listened from his bunk, tired of the virulence of the Nazi leaders. Camp life had made their extreme views more pungent than ever. They refused to believe the war had turned against the Fatherland. The reported appearance of Hitler at the funeral of Gauleiter Adolf Wagner had reassured them, despite the fact that the Führer had not spoken publicly. The mere fact of his ongoing life had heartened them, and they filled the camp with vows to continue fighting, to have faith, and all manner of other nonsense. Now William Zimmerman's somewhat absurd escape had proved a rallying cry. It had fanned the nationalistic flames and restored honor to men removed from combat months before. August wanted to point out that the German war effort now relied on schoolchildren to carry out the necessary labor, but he didn't dare raise his voice.

He turned restlessly on the bunk and tried to bury his hearing in the pillow at his head. Other voices replied to Boris's imprecations, their tones angry and layering on Boris's original statement. Yes, they were kindling wood. No, they would refuse to work if asked to subsist on bread and water. A general strike. On and on the voices went, hot and bitter, and August tried to send his hearing outside to the tree frogs calling in the spring air. Occasionally he heard the river passing over stones, the whisper it made as if carrying secrets from the mountaintops.

He also thought of Collie. He wondered if she had read the poem by now. He had copied it out as accurately as he could recall. He had memorized it many years before for a school exercise, but he could not be certain he had it right. It was a blessing, really, a poem by Ludwig Uhland called "Faith in Spring." He pictured her reading it, her golden hair catching the light as she turned to the lines. She spoke German! What kind of miraculous luck was that! She spoke German better than he spoke English, but between them they might make up a new language. It made him smile to think of it.

He fell asleep and did not wake until morning. That was a benefit of working outdoors logging; one slept like the dead. Boris, large and dark, his chest hair spilling over his undershirt, stood in the center of the barracks, stirring the pot once more. August ignored him as much as possible. He skirted around him and went outside, following the raised boardwalk to the latrines. He washed and used the toilet, and on his return ran into Hans the Butcher, a member of his work party, who informed him that William had been seized in Portland.

"He made it that far at least," Hans said, a towel draped over his neck. "A conductor asked a few too many questions and eventually William gave in. He's been sent back to Fort Devens. That's the report, though there are some here who won't believe it. Some think he was taken out and shot."

"Where did you hear it?"

Hans waved at the air to indicate it came from anywhere, everywhere, from the wind. Rumors.

"Will we work today, then?" August asked.

"If they give us breakfast, we will."

"I'd rather work than sit around all day."

"It's all the same to me," Hans said, and passed by to return to his barracks.

They served a full breakfast. August drank two large cups of coffee and ate a seeded roll with butter and a slice of sausage. He had been hungry since the dinner of bread and water. Rumors flashed around the refectory. Canteen privileges would be restored, he heard in one ear, and in the other heard the canteen would be closed indefinitely. William had been beaten horribly, one rumor maintained; in another rumor William had been captured not on a train, but in a high-priced cathouse with two women sharing his bed. In each new telling William gained the strength and cunning of a superman, and it was all August could do to stop reminding his fellow prisoners that William was a simple lad who had barely grown into his bones.

They assembled shortly after breakfast and Major Brennan addressed them.

William had been caught in Portland, Maine, the major said through his daughter, Collie. William had surrendered peacefully and was now being sent to Fort Devens, where the security would be greater. He said he understood it was their duty to try to escape, but given the rural quality of the camp, and the unlikelihood of their being able to return to Germany under current circumstances, he hoped they would reconsider their responsibility to their fellow prisoners.

Then he ordered them to work. It concluded that simply. August mustered with his work crew, now short one man for William's disappearance. As he passed through the front gate, he turned to the window where Collie worked. He saw her bent over a paper and he smiled at the sight of her. He willed her to look up, to catch his eyes, but she seemed intent on whatever she was doing, and he passed out to the twitch horses, a day in the woods before him.

The poem lived in her pocket as if it were a pet mouse. She was embarrassed to admit how carefully she had worked to translate the lines, each one desperate with meaning. She had already copied out her translation to Estelle, sending it with the morning post. In the letter to her friend she asked her opinion of the lines as if she meant the question merely as an academic exercise. She asked her, too, to bring a book of German verse. To bring anything, really, that might increase her understanding of the language. She passed it off as something required for camp life, but in reality she wanted the German verses to share with August.

That thought made her stomach flip and her blood push closer to her skin. How ridiculous she was! At certain moments she could take a step back and see herself clearly. She saw this absurd young woman poring over the scant German lines, ascribing meaning to each syllable, giving them the attention reserved for biblical passages. What had he said? It was merely a poem he remembered from his school days, so she should, she felt, attribute no special qualities to the poem, but she could not resist. The poem mixed with her memory of him standing before her desk, his broad shoulders nearly blocking out the light from outdoors, the sweet flow of his locks over his forehead and shoulders. She was worse than Marie in her romantic turn of mind.

At lunch, however, she carried a sandwich to the pole barn where the horses were kept. They were all out cutting now, so she sat in the sunlight on a cobbled bench someone had slapped together beside the horse stable. The air smelled of early summer, or late spring, and the scent of manure mixed in was not unpleasant. In the right breeze she sometimes caught the moist fragrance of the river, too, its water pressing southward toward the Pemigewasset and Merrimack. She ate slowly, taking pleasure in the silence. Noon felt sleepy and still, and it had come to be her favorite time of day. Red, the German cook, had prepared a sort of meat-loaf sandwich that was quite good. She ate it slowly and let the sun warm her, and tried, unsuccessfully, to resist pulling the poem out to read.

She wrapped up the second half of the sandwich in waxed paper, cleaned her hands on a small handkerchief, then edged the poem out of her pocket. Her copy lay within his. She read his German version first, then slowly read the English translation aloud.

> Now everything, everything must change.
> The world becomes more beautiful with each day;
> one doesn't know what may yet happen.

She loved its simplicity. She had wrestled with the word *change* in the first line, debating if it had meant *turn* instead. The difference was subtle but substantial. *Turn* changed the meaning into something more agricultural, she felt, while *change* spoke to the human condition. She preferred *turn* for its poeticism, but *change*, she concluded, was more accurate. It was something she would like to ask August himself if given the chance.

Naturally the poem meant more than that to her. What had he intended by giving it to her? That was the question her mind could not resolve. At the least he had meant it as an overture of friendship, not merely as an exercise in translation. It felt impossible to know what a man thought; add to that his German ancestry, and the task seemed insurmountable. She wondered, for instance, if he saw her as a woman apart from her role as daughter to her father, the camp commandant. Or was he, perhaps, of genuinely scholarly disposition, so that he saw the exchange of poetry as simple cross-cultural exchange? She wished Estelle would hurry, because she would like to put the question to her.

In the afternoon, while her father and Lieutenant Peters were out checking on two of the cutting teams, she transcribed a clean copy for Private August Wahrlich. She made a mistake the first time, blotting ink on the second line, and had to start over. It took her a half hour to make the copy to her satisfaction, then she stalled as she realized she might write a brief note of explanation to him concerning the translation. Her first attempt sounded too formal and condescending, as if she were doing him a great favor by tendering the translation. She scrapped it and began again, this time speaking directly from her heart. She kept it brief. She said—truthfully, she felt—that she had found the poem lovely and challenging at once. She raised the question of the word *change* versus *turn*, then concluded by saying she hoped soon to have a book of German verse that she might share with him. The last part, about the book and hoping to share it with him, made her nervous. Before she put the letter and translation into an envelope, she nearly crumpled the entire enterprise up and threw it in the waste can. But that wasn't honest; she yearned to pass along the note to him, and she finally sealed the envelope as quickly as she could and put it in the center drawer of her desk. It remained there beating—like Poe's "The Tell-Tale Heart," she thought—until the men began streaming back from the woods.

Luck worked in her favor. She heard a lot of yelling and laughing, and when she glanced out she saw the men—Germans and Americans together—ringed around something at their feet. Lieutenant Peters stuck his head into the administrative building and told her the cause of the excitement.

"They have a bear cub!" he said, obviously pleased with the discovery. "Come take a look."

"Where—"

"It was in a tree when they cut it down. No one saw it beforehand, and the mother bear must have been scared away. They've named it Bruno. Come and see."

On impulse she grabbed the letter and tucked it into her waistband. Then she followed Lieutenant Peters outside. The men formed a fence to keep the bear in the middle of their circle. She had a brief impression of something small and black scuttling around at their feet. The men pulled back when they noticed her, many of them holding out their hands as if, presto, they unveiled a great treasure.

One man, a German, rested on his knees before the tiny bear and provided a base when the bear needed reassuring. Collie felt her heart melt at the sight of the little orphan. Clearly it missed its mother, but it still toddled around, trying to make sense of what had occurred. The men treated it sweetly. The man on the ground, especially, seemed to feel some proprietorship over it. He guided it when it seemed shaky and twice lifted it up and held it like a baby. Whenever he let it run as it liked, it bawled for its mother and traced the interior of the circle.

August arrived with his cutting crew before long. Collie saw him, but he was quickly lost in the swarm of men who came to look. The bear served as a magnet; no one could ignore it. August, however, pushed his way to the front of the ranks. When the man in the center saw August he spoke to him rapidly in German. August smiled and translated, his eyes directly on Collie's.

"He asks if you want to hold it," he said, nodding toward the man in the center and the little bear.

"Yes, I would."

That seemed to please all the men in the circle. The man in the center lifted the bear carefully and handed it to Collie. Whatever discomfort she felt at being the only woman in a circle of men, disappeared the moment she held little Bruno. He was a darling! His fur felt fine and dense, and his black, inquisitive eyes did not leave hers. He weighed little, but what there was of him seemed vital and eager. He had four paws of good claws, and his pointed snout angled out in a brown muzzle. Around her she heard men exclaim in German. She wondered if they understood that she comprehended most of what they said. As if reading her mind, one man—the man who seemed the bear's owner—spoke to her directly in German.

"Do you like him? His name is Bruno."

"I like him very much," she answered in German. "I'm sorry he's an orphan."

"We'll take good care of him," the man said. "He can be our mascot."

"He'll get big rather quickly," said someone from the group of men.

"In Germany he would be used for the circus," said the man on his knees.

"Maybe you can teach him to ride a bicycle."

She did not intend it to be particularly funny, but the men gave a good, hearty laugh at the joke. She felt the laughter must stem from the idea of interacting with the commandant's daughter. At the same time it felt good to laugh with the men. She wondered what the editorial writers would say if they could see that Germans and Americans had so much in common after all. She passed little Bruno to Lieutenant Peters, though the bear struggled to stay with her.

"Were you able to translate the poem I gave you?" August asked in German.

He had crossed the circle and suddenly stood beside her. He smelled of pine and the heat of the day. She quickly drew the letter from her waistband and passed it to him.

"A few of the lines gave me difficulty," she said, "and I had difficulty with the meter. But I think I've managed."

"Thank you," he said.

"It was my pleasure. It's a lovely poem. I'd never heard of the poet before."

How strange and powerful it felt to be near him! She worried he would snap open the letter and read it in front of her. But fortunately the bear managed to struggle free from Lieutenant Peters at that moment and Lieutenant Peters hurriedly released him on the ground. The little bear ran to the man at the center of the ring for security, and the men laughed at seeing such a human behavior.

Gradually the men, tired and dirty from work, began to disband.

The man in the center picked up the bear and carried it like a baby toward the barracks. He made Bruno wave good-bye with his tiny paw. Collie waved back, then looked up once more at August. He smiled, and their eyes could not let go.

"Do you write your own poetry?" Collie asked, more for conversation than for anything else.

"Yes, a little."

"I look forward to reading your work someday."

"It's nothing important, honestly."

"I'm sure you underestimate yourself," Collie said.

"I am better at music. I have a few years of classical training."

"How wonderful. On the piano?"

"Yes. I am not so good, but I can manage. Do you play?"

"Only in the most rudimentary fashion. I've requisitioned a piano, because I thought it would be good for camp morale. But as for me, 'Chopsticks,'" she said the last word in English, because she had no idea what the word in German might be.

He made a puzzled face. She pantomimed two hands playing "Chopsticks" and he nodded immediately.

"Yes, of course. 'Chopsticks.'"

His mispronunciation of *chopsticks* endeared him to her. At the same moment, she realized the other men had disappeared, even Lieutenant Peters. Part of her wanted to say that speaking to a young man was perfectly respectable, but another part of her understood how obvious their attraction must appear. She felt nervous at the thought of it.

"A nice bear," he said, apparently finding it as difficult as she did to break away.

"Yes, a lovely little thing."

"Can you tell me," he asked, his face suddenly serious, "if the rumors are true that we will be sent to England after this? Still as prisoners?"

"I haven't heard such a thing."

"It's talked about in the barracks. We will work to make reparations to England for our bombing of London."

"I think it's too early to know what may happen."

"That would be very hard," he said, pushing his chin toward the barracks. "Hard on these men."

"Yes, I could imagine."

"Rumors are like mice. They live in the corners and feed on crumbs."

He smiled. It was a charming smile. For a moment she could do nothing but stay in his eyes. Finally she managed to excuse herself without panic. He thanked her again for the poem and promised to read it that night. She backed away and said good-bye. She wondered, as she climbed the steps to the administration building, if he felt even the smallest part of what she could not help but feel.

"If you ask me, the Germans should pay heavily, heavily indeed for their aggression," Sherman Heights said, his hand pushing away a large cigar from his mouth. "We can't let them up again. We should put our heel on their throats and not give them a breath. We went too easy on them after the First War."

"They think they have the right . . . ," another man began, but Major Brennan watched him get cut off by a reporter, a thin, serpentine man who wrote for one of the Boston papers.

"You said yourself, Major, that there has already been an escape. It's a bad precedent to have German prisoners on our soil. This war should be fought on European soil, not here," the reporter, a man named Whipple, or Whittle, Major Brennan couldn't remember, said from his position near the fireplace of the Heights' magnificent home. The reporter held a drink in his hand that threatened to slosh over the rim.

"We didn't have a choice in it," said Elman Thorne, one of the town fathers from Stark. He was a large, stolid man, with a farmer's neck and heavy shoulders. "Washington gave the orders and we followed. They play the music and we dance. . . ."

"Did the escaped German . . . did he make it very far? Are the reports accurate that he got stopped on his way to Boston?" the reporter asked.

Major Brennan could not accommodate them all. Everywhere he went these questions bombarded him, and he knew without doubt that no answer he gave would satisfy them. They spoke to hear their own thoughts; they spoke to top one another, to prove their insight into the war was greater than the next man's. It fatigued him. He had known as soon as Sherman Heights had invited him into his study, abandoning his daughter to the care of Heights's wife, Eleanor, that he had stepped into the lion's den. The men, huddling to smoke and drink in Sherman Heights's luxurious study, had fallen on him as soon as he had stepped through the door. Major Brennan understood he represented the faceless authorities, the government, the military, for men who felt removed from the war. Their questions betrayed a hunger for involvement, for understanding, that he was powerless to provide.

"The escaped German did not get far," Major Brennan said wearily. "Whatever you've heard to the contrary is mere rumor. He was not a—"

"The fact that he got out at all," Thorne, the town father, interrupted, "is a travesty. I'm all for a humane treatment of prisoners, I am, but in this case . . ."

"What I was going to say is that the prisoner was not what you would call an aggressive sort. He was a pretty timid boy, by all accounts. I think he was less on the warpath and more a simple case of homesickness."

"That may be," Whipple, or Whittle said, his drink going down too fast, Major Brennan saw, "but what about that next lad? Or the one after that? They're threats to the community and to the country at large."

Happily Eleanor Heights tapped on the door, then breezed in to tell her husband that he had run off with half of the party. She was a tall, handsome woman with a nose too large for her face. Yet the nose worked; it gave her a Roman dignity, a face not typical in Maine. Major Brennan watched Sherman Heights push out of his wingback chair, his cigar emitting a cloud above his head. He laughed and shrugged, giving in to his wife immediately.

"Cake is being served," Eleanor Heights announced. "You'll miss out if you don't come directly. And as it's a cake for me, I'm going to insist you men break this up immediately and come along."

Major Brennan followed his hosts out to the party proper. The last daylight washed the large living room in quiet grays. A maid had apparently delivered a three-tiered cake to the large dining room table, and she now busily lighted the candles that bristled from the top. The room lights had been lowered to add to the atmosphere.

"I'm fifty years old today," Eleanor Heights announced to the group around the table. "I know a woman is supposed to hide her age, but what's the use? I'm proud to be fifty. I have much to be grateful for, and I'm well aware of it. With luck, I may have another twenty years, perhaps even longer. . . ."

"Much longer," her husband said.

"Well, if you can stand it, I can stand it," Eleanor rejoined to her husband, and that brought a laugh. "Now once Mary here has finished with the candles, you all must sing to me and then I'll be done with my birthday. A half a century! That's a remarkable thing, and at the same time it's nothing at all."

Major Brennan liked Eleanor Heights's directness. He watched the cake lighting with genuine pleasure. Eleanor pantomimed turning away, then turning back and feigning surprise. Everyone laughed and then broke into a fractured version of "Happy Birthday." Major

Brennan suspected Eleanor had a theater background lurking somewhere in her past. He was going to say as much to his daughter—who stood almost directly across the table, her loveliness in the room a match for the candles—when a woman's voice spoke close to his ear.

"You must be the Major Brennan that everyone talks so much about," she said in a rich, husky voice. "I'm glad finally to see you with my own eyes. You're not such a horrible creature after all."

He made a quarter turn, as people do when they are supposed to be observing a ceremony yet want to talk unobtrusively, and saw a woman of about his age standing at his elbow. She had sharp gray eyes, a rather narrow nose, and hair the color of a corn broom that was held in place, at the back, by a large silver clip. She wore a simple lavender dress, slightly prim, beneath a boiled-wool vest.

"I'm glad to hear that," he said softly, his eyes meeting hers. "But I've already eaten three children today."

"Were they delicious?"

"Yes, as a matter of fact. Now, you have the advantage of me. Who are you?"

"I'm the town librarian and also the town widow. I'm the woman invited to round things out or to pull an oar on a social occasion. Lucinda Seaver. My husband was a lumberman about these parts."

Major Brennan nodded and said nothing while Eleanor Heights blew out the forest of candles. Everyone clapped.

"Please come to see me next time you're in Berlin," Lucinda said. "You're probably in need of a home-cooked meal. We could stand on ceremony and take three or four meetings before I extended the invitation, but I don't believe in that sort of thing. Besides, I want to come see Camp Stark and I hoped you would show me around. Your daughter has already volunteered you."

Major Brennan glanced quickly at his daughter, but she had her hand out to receive a piece of cake and he was reasonably certain she deliberately avoided his eye. He felt confused and flushed. It was one thing to answer questions from eager, ill-informed men about the camp, but it was another to contemplate sailing out on the vast sea that must be crossed between a man and a woman.

"I'd be a fool to decline," he said. "Thank you for the invitation."

"And bring your daughter, of course. She tells me she will have a friend visiting? From Ohio?"

"Yes, any day now."

"Well, you see? I will make a useful destination. Come to see me, don't forget."

She left to help with the ice cream afterward. Major Brennan stood in a slight daze, wondering what had just occurred. Before he could sort things out, one of the Heights' servants came to him and said he was wanted on the phone. Major Brennan followed the man into the kitchen and picked the phone off the wall. It was Lieutenant Peters.

"Something strange has occurred, I'm afraid," Lieutenant Peters said. "You probably should get back here."

"What is it?"

"Someone, or some group, has arranged the rocks up at the Devil's Slide into a swastika."

"The rock formation?" Major Brennan asked, to clarify. "The one above the village?"

"Yes, sir."

"How large?"

"Large, sir. It's quite visible."

"When did this happen?"

"It's hard to say. It was just a matter of when people began noticing it."

"All right. I'll be back directly. At first light, send a crew up to disperse the rocks. Downplay the whole incident as much as possible. It does no good to make a fuss over it."

"No, sir, I understand."

"Someone's sending a message of support, I suppose."

"That's how I read it, sir."

"There are plenty of Nazis in America."

"Yes, sir."

"We're just finishing up here. We'll be along."

"Sorry to interrupt, sir, but I figured you would want to know."

"Yes, of course."

Major Brennan hung the handset back on the wall. In the dining room, people clapped at something that had been said or done. Major Brennan brought his white handkerchief to his lips. If only he could draw a full breath, he thought. Things would be much easier if he could simply do that.

Henry Heights watched Collie Brennan slip into her jacket and thought that she would make a perfect wife for him. She was beautiful; that was beyond discussion. But she also possessed self-assurance, and a social ease, that was extremely attractive. She was smart and well informed, better informed, in fact, than many of the men who tried to show off with their knowledge of current events. Yes, he could marry her, he thought. She was exactly the kind of woman for him.

Nevertheless, he felt shy and awkward around her. He had taken a few jolts of whiskey from his brother's flask, but even that lubrication did not make it easy to approach her. Now, to his dismay, she was readying to depart. People surrounded her.

"Thank you again," she said to his mother, "it was so nice to be away from that dreary camp for an evening. I can't tell you."

"Well, you'll have to visit again. Next time bring your friend . . . was it Estelle?" his mother asked.

"Yes, Estelle."

"Please think of us as a port you can use whenever you need it. We have plenty of room."

"You're too kind."

Her hair dazzled. She wore a dark navy wool coat pulled close around her neck. Henry stepped forward and smiled, trying to act casual. He had wanted to speak to her alone throughout the evening, but the opportunity hadn't presented itself. Now he bowed slightly from the waist, and that, he understood, was absurdly out of place. His mother, however, apparently sensing the situation, moved away to bid farewell to the other guests. Collie glanced out the window, checking for their car.

"Do you like the cinema?" Henry asked. "I thought perhaps we could take in a movie. . . ."

"I love the cinema, but I'm afraid . . . ," she said, looking back.

"Your friend is visiting, that's right. Well, the more the merrier. Perhaps some day next week."

"That's very kind of you. I'll look forward to it."

"I'll call you then. I know where to reach you."

He meant it as a joke, but she hardly smiled. She looked out again for the car. He had overstepped, he thought. She had accepted—she *had* accepted, hadn't she?—merely because he had cornered her. It felt confusing. He didn't know if convention now meant for him to withdraw, or to stay and keep her company while she waited.

Fortunately her car arrived in time to save them both additional embarrassment. She smiled and pulled open the door.

"Thanks again," she said, stepping out. "It was a treat to get away."

"Thank you for coming."

His face felt flushed. He closed the door after her. When he looked back into the party he spotted his brother, Amos, shaking his head.

"So did she say yes?" Amos asked.

Amos had consumed more whiskey, Henry knew. Amos's face became lupine when he drank, heavy and slack, while his lips turned scarlet.

"Leave me alone and give me a drink," Henry said.

Amos passed him the thick flask he carried perpetually in his coat pocket. Henry poured a double shot in his punch glass.

"You'd be better off with Dolly and Charlene, but you won't listen to me," Amos said. "Your big brother knows a few things."

"You're all wet."

"That may be," Amos said, "but you'll come around to my way of thinking."

"Mom likes her."

"Of course, everyone likes her. She was made to reign in heaven."

"Is my brother being poetic?"

Amos shrugged. A group of departing guests cut off the conversation. Henry shook hands, helped with jackets, said good-byes. His thoughts remained on Collie, however. He pictured her stepping into her coat, her delicate throat covered by the topmost button. He didn't care what Amos said. She was the kind of woman he wanted, and he planned to do what he could to make her his own.

❧ *Chapter Six* ❧

August heard the beating in the middle of the night. He knew the tactic: the squad of Nazis pinned the blankets down around the victim, then beat him with their handheld boots. The boots bruised the sufferer less than fists or kicks might do. Boots never broke bones, and therefore the Americans could pretend not to notice. But the boots beat the skin and muscles mercilessly, and August had seen more than one recipient walk with difficulty after such an ordeal. The Nazi squad especially liked to ram a boot into the prone man's testicles. The pain was shattering, August knew, but the injury could not be traced to the guilty men.

The beating lasted forever, August felt. He closed his eyes and trembled, guilty that he lacked the courage to stand and fight. But then, of course, he would be next. That was the Nazi advantage. They thrived with stealth and secret communication, employing their aptitude for violence as a tool. If all of the other men organized and stood together, the Nazis would be powerless. But it required one man, maybe ten, to stand up and risk a harsh beating. August hated himself that he was too cowardly to do so.

He pushed his head deeper into the pillow. The beating went on with broad huffs, air ejecting out of the victim in violent, explosive puffs. From the sounds alone, August could not determine who received the beating. In all likelihood, it was Erich, a small, mouselike man, who had made the mistake of challenging a Nazi's contention that the war progressed properly for the German forces. They had entered a dispute over a radio report that Mussolini and Hitler had met at Klessheim Castle near Salzburg. The report was propaganda, according to the Nazis, because it called Mussolini "dispirited and unconvinced" of the Germans' ability to bring London to its knees. Erich, stupidly, had countered; he had not known he spoke to a Nazi, and so his name went on the list of "soldiers in need of discipline." That, at least, was as much as August could know for the moment. The beating might have been doled out to anyone, even to an innocent, simply to thicken camp discipline.

Finally it stopped. August heard the Nazi crew withdraw. The men stole out of the door and disappeared. When he was sure they were gone, August slipped quickly from his bed and went to find out who had been beaten. He had been correct: Erich, small and weak, lay bleeding in his bunk. His nose had been bloodied, his eye smashed with a boot. He seemed to have trouble breathing. August hardly had a chance to take an inventory of Erich's injuries when Gerhard arrived with a wet cloth. Carefully, they pulled the blankets back. Erich breathed in quickly from the pain of removing the blanket. It was like beating dough, August thought, the ribs and long muscles of the legs pummeled until they could not function properly.

"Don't move," Gerhard said quietly. "Rest."

"Dirty pigs," Erich hissed.

"Shhhhh," Gerhard whispered.

The other men in the barracks gathered around. They took one look at Erich and cursed. Many of them went back to bed. It was futile to stay and cluck, August knew. What could anyone do? Besides, some of the men might be Nazis themselves. They might simply pretend to sympathize, because the beating crews never came from one's own barracks. The Nazis were too shrewd for that. By raiding at night, they could administer their discipline, then leave behind spies to report the effects of their handiwork. Clever work, August conceded.

It took nearly an hour to staunch Erich's wounds and make him reasonably comfortable. By the time they finished, light had already begun to fill the eastern windows. August did not feel he could return to sleep. He invited Gerhard to go to breakfast. They would have to wait a half hour for food, he knew, but perhaps they could get coffee from the kitchen staff.

"We have to stop them," August said when they were clear of the barracks. "We're behaving like cowards."

"For all you know, I'm a Nazi," Gerhard said. "I may report you."

"If you are, then I despair about knowing anything."

"Their day will come."

"The Americans should step in. We could report them."

"And be beaten doubly for making trouble? It's not worth it. The war will be over before the year is out."

"You think so?" August asked, trying not to let his voice sound too hopeful.

"It's inevitable now. The Allies are too many against one. Italy is impotent. Trust me, the Nazis will have their sunset sooner than you think."

Gerhard's words caused mixed emotions in August. He did not want Germany to lose, of course, but he did not see any way left to win. Win what? he sometimes wondered. With difficulty he forced such thoughts from his head. He was hungry and in need of coffee. The morning, he felt, was sharp and clear. He looked up to see the stars still glittering in the pale sky.

Near the refectory, he nearly stumbled on Bruno. The bear had been tied to a stake beneath a large maple tree. The prisoners had built him a small house and had secured toys for him. He had a deflated ball near him, and an assortment of bear replicas made of sticks and cloth. The entire enterprise had become slightly tawdry. What had begun as an amusing diversion now struck August as an act bordering on cruelty. How ironic, he thought, that men imprisoned a creature while being imprisoned themselves. A groundswell of protest had begun to bubble beneath the surface, but for the time being, at any rate, the bear still served as a mascot. Even in its short time in captivity, however, the creature had grown beyond mere cuteness, so people did not willingly play with it. It could rake with its claws, and if its teeth sunk into a bystander's leg, it was no longer a puppy bite.

"Shall we let it go?" August asked Gerhard.

The bear was plainly visible in the dull light of the refectory porch. It chewed on a bone someone had given it, its paws curled around the white surface like a dog anchoring a leg bone for a better bite. August saw the cooks and kitchen staff passing by the lighted windows. He looked around carefully. No one was about.

"It may not leave," Gerhard said, "and besides, it can't get over the fence."

"It's a crime to keep it here."

"There are people who dote on him."

"They should have left it where they found it. The mother would have come back for it."

"People won't look kindly on your letting him go."

"Who will tell them?"

August looked directly at Gerhard. Gerhard returned his look for a moment, then shrugged.

"Go ahead," he said.

August worked quickly. Someone had downsized a belt to serve as a collar. August slipped it off and gave the bear a quick rub of affection. The bear didn't move at first, but gradually it stood and sensed its freedom from the collar. It made a deep, whining sound, then it moved back into the shadows and blended with the remaining darkness. August doubted it had the good sense to leave. It would likely circle around the camp, causing mischief wherever it went, then someone would return it to its post and collar. Nevertheless, it felt good to see the bear go free. He smiled at Gerhard. Gerhard patted him on the back.

"Let's see if we can get coffee," Gerhard said.

*   *   *

Collie had difficulty containing herself as she dressed for the day. Estelle was due to arrive later in the afternoon! Despite the quick telegram affirming her arrival dates, Collie could hardly believe her friend, her former classmate at Smith, would simply step off a train and find herself in Stark, New Hampshire. It felt as remarkable as time travel from a science fiction novel. She could hardly grant that a person might get on a train in Ashtabula, Ohio, spend a day or two traveling, and then, without any great fanfare, step onto a train platform hundreds of miles away. It struck Collie as profoundly normal, something so prosaic, at the same time so extraordinary, that it thrilled her to think of it.

It was all a whirl. Somehow the speed of news had increased. It seemed every day now brought news of a recent conquest over the German forces. Her father opined privately that the Germans could not hold out much longer. Eisenhower was said to be planning something formidable, something that could happen any day, and it would be a hammer blow that would send the Germans reeling. Collie fervently hoped so. She felt tired of the war, as tired as if she fought it herself, though she knew she needed to maintain a strong front for her father.

When she finished dressing, she made the bed carefully with fresh sheets. She had already tidied the room and cut flowers—irises and ox-eyed daisies—and placed them in a vase near the bed. She worried, briefly, that Estelle would find the accommodations rather humble, but then she scolded herself for thinking such a thing. It was unfair to expect Estelle to be judgmental about her housing. She knew very well what she was coming to see.

Downstairs, Collie helped Mrs. Hammond and the serving girl, Agnes, serve breakfast. The weather was fine, and the windows let in a cool morning breeze that seemed to wait for the heat of the sun to catch up to it. Mrs. Hammond had fewer boarders now. More men had gone south to the munitions factories. If not for the German prisoners, Collie knew from her father, the Brown Paper Company would be forced to cease production.

"There was a man by here this morning with a piano in his truck," Mrs. Hammond said, stirring porridge. "He was looking for you."

"Where did you send him?"

"Up to the camp. I figured someone would tell him where to unload it."

"What kind of piano was it?"

Mrs. Hammond looked up from her cooking. Clearly she had no idea.

"I requisitioned a spinet," Collie explained. "It's the most portable."

"Well, he had quite a list of things in the truck, but the piano had your name on it."

So that was the second great feature of the day. A visit from her friend, plus a piano! The idea of a piano called August to mind. She longed to see him play. He had not told her yet what he thought of her translation. They had not had an occasion to speak; it was complicated by his status as a prisoner. In quiet moments she imagined him reading the poem as carefully as she had, but that might have been a delusion on her part. It was possible, she imagined, that he read it once and then put it aside. She chided herself from making too much of the poem in the first place. She vowed to keep a better leash on her imagination.

Outside, the weather could not have been more perfect. She paused on the porch to look out at the river. It ran calmly by, its spring torrents gone to the sea by now. The deciduous trees had leafed out; everything shone green and promising. Before she could take a step toward camp, Marie suddenly appeared, dressed for school. She looked a proper schoolgirl, Collie thought, outfitted in a simple navy pinafore with a straw hat pinned to the back of her hair. The outfit made Marie appear younger, more a girl than a young woman. She clamored up the stairs and immediately began peppering Collie with questions about Estelle.

"Do you think she will be too tired tonight to have visitors?" Marie asked. "I won't stay long. I have to see her, though. I feel as if I already know her!"

This was a common theme by now and Collie tried to be tactful.

"She's come a long way. We'll have to see."

"You said she was very elegant," Marie said, as if confirming a mental picture she had adorned with her imaginings. "I wonder what she'll wear. Traveling clothes, I imagine. But what *are* traveling clothes?"

"She's very beautiful and very refined."

"And her father is a physician?"

"Yes, Marie, a physician. They live in a large Victorian house in Ashtabula, Ohio. Her mother is in charge of the local Society for the Prevention of Cruelty to Animals. They have a hundred pets about their house."

"I'd love to see that!" Marie said, leaning without a single bone in her body against the porch railing.

"A piano came today," Collie said, wanting to give the girl some satisfaction. "A spinet, I think. That's what I ordered, in any case, but with the war on one can never be sure. I didn't know if the order would ever be filled."

"Does Estelle play the piano?"

"Yes, she does."

"And you-know-who does, too," Marie whispered, looking around to see if anyone could overhear them.

Collie could not help smiling. Marie had a thousand stories in her head, all of them jumbled together and each one more romantic than the last. She had a horrible crush on August; the memory of their pretend-dance had not faded in time but had become even more important to her as the weather advanced. At the same time, Marie understood that she was too young for the German soldier, so she had entered into an unspoken spiritual contract with Collie, as though Collie might inherit his affections from her. It was, Collie suspected, a grand sacrifice in Marie's mind. Nevertheless, Collie didn't mind discussing August with Marie. She enjoyed speculating about him, and, besides, she could not resist Marie's infectious exuberance.

"We can discuss all of this later. Won't you be tardy for school?" Collie asked.

"Oh, it's all fiddle-faddle at this point. No one wants to be in school once the weather turns warm."

"I suppose that's true, but just the same. . . ."

"Yes. I'm going. What time will the train arrive?"

"You know very well. It arrives the same time every day."

"But today is different!" Marie laughed, hurrying off the porch. "Oh, I almost forgot. Amy said she had another horse for Estelle. We can all go for a ride together."

"Perfect. Thank you."

Then Marie dashed off. The young girl's enthusiasm made the walk to camp lighter and happier. Collie felt an immense sense of well-being. Part of it she attributed to the weather, but the rest, the larger portion, rested on Estelle and August, and the piano and just everything! Her mother had always called such a feeling a *pocket heart*, because one felt so filled up that one could hardly fit one's hand in her pocket for all the good treasures that rested there. It was an apt description, Collie thought, because today her pocket heart was indeed full, nearly to the point of spilling over.

It turned out that the piano found her. She had barely arrived at camp when she spotted it on the porch of the administration building. Lieutenant Peters smoked beside it, occasionally reaching over to plunk a key. He smiled when he saw her. The piano had been a will-o'-the-wisp between them, a requisition he had promised would never be filled.

"Here's your piano!" he said grandly when she came closer to inspect it. "I almost told them to put it in the refectory, but then I wasn't sure if that's where you wanted it. We can get some men to take it over whenever you like. It's still on wheels."

"I told you I could get a piano if I put my mind to it!"

He laughed and pretended to tip his hat.

"Is it in any kind of tune?" she asked.

"I don't know. I don't play myself. The cutting teams had left by the time this arrived, so you have first crack at it."

"Did Papa see it?"

"No, he hasn't been in, either. He went over to Berlin to confer with the Brown Paper Company people. But you must play, surely."

"Only a little."

"Give it a whirl."

She put down her handbag and then placed her fingers on the keys. It felt odd. It had been years, it seemed, since she had last attempted anything on a piano. She poked a few keys and found them sufficiently lively. The action on the spinet gave the sound a saloon tinniness. Still, it worked. She played "Chopsticks" for a moment, then ran up and down with chord progressions. Some of the keys seemed out of tune, but it was difficult to assess on an early-summer morning, playing standing up with a smirking Lieutenant Peters watching her.

She played a few more song beginnings that she remembered, though each score tumbled apart when her memory lost the notes. How fickle it felt. She had once practiced regularly and had attained a certain facility, but now the music felt blocked up behind the months at the camp. A touch of frustration seeped into her fingers and passed up to her head. She turned to Lieutenant Peters, prepared to explain, when she saw he was not looking at her at all. He swung down off the porch, his eyes on the barracks. He tossed his cigarette away and said, "Hold on, what's this?"

Collie followed his line of sight and finally spotted Bruno, the bear cub, pulling at an upended garbage can in the shadow of the most westerly barracks. The bear's chubby hindquarters counterbalanced its head; it had climbed three quarters of the way into the garbage can.

"That damn thing is becoming a nuisance," Lieutenant Peters said. "We should get one of the teams to take it out on their next cutting trip."

"It was probably a mistake to bring it in in the first place."

"The horses don't like it. They don't like its smell. It makes them nervous."

"Look how dark he is. You can hardly see him in the shadow."

The phone rang in the administration building. Lieutenant Peters ducked inside to get it. Collie watched the bear as she occasionally reached over to touch some of the keys. The bear dragged something out of the garbage can. Collie did not look too closely to find out what it was. Lieutenant Peters was correct. It was time for the bear to return to the woods.

She was still standing in the morning light with her attention divided between the bear and the piano, when Henry Heights pulled in with his vehicle. He climbed out quickly, then bent back inside to pull out a bouquet of flowers. He straightened his jacket as he walked toward the administration building. He was a handsome young man, Collie thought as she watched him. She wondered if she had looked at him carefully before. Yes, he was quite handsome and seemed to be a gentleman.

"I saw these and thought you might like them," he said, coming closer. "Just a collection of wildflowers, but my mother always preferred wildflowers to store-bought ones."

"For me?" Collie asked. "Well, thank you. You're kind to think of me."

The bear made a growling sound, and Henry turned to look at what caused the noise.

"Is that a bear?" he asked.

"Yes, it was the camp mascot, but it's overstayed its welcome, I'm afraid."

Henry studied the bear a little bit more, then turned back and held the flowers out. Collie took them. It was a charming bouquet.

"I was going past the camp, and I thought I might duck in to see you," Henry said.

"I'm glad you did," Collie said, because that's what one said out of politeness, and she wasn't entirely clear in her mind what she thought of Henry Heights. "We haven't made coffee yet, but it will be on shortly."

"Oh, thank you, but I should be on my way. I'm working with a surveying team not far from here. Mother asked me to remind you that she would love to see you again. I think she feels you are trapped here among a horde of men and require rescuing."

"Well, I don't know if I'd go so far as to say 'trapped,' but I take her point. Thank her for me, and tell her we'll come to visit soon. Estelle arrives today."

"Your friend?"

She nodded. Henry was better this morning, she conceded. He seemed more relaxed and, at the same time, more certain of what he wanted. He wore a tweed coat and was dressed for the outdoors. The change in his clothing suited him. Maybe, she reflected, his distance from his home, from his family, made him more his own man. In any case he seemed improved.

"Funny bear," Henry said, his attention returned to the animal.

"It makes me sad to see it."

"What will you do with it?"

"We'll get one of the teams to take it out, I suppose. It's for the best."

THE MAJOR'S DAUGHTER   97

"Did they ever get to the bottom of the swastika?"

"You heard about that?"

"Through my father, I suppose. Do you think it was an attempt to show local support?"

"I suppose so. Maybe the American bund. We tried to downplay it so as not to add fuel to the fire."

"That's probably the best idea. Well, I should be going. I hope you have a wonderful time with Estelle."

"Thank you, Henry. And thank you for the bouquet. That was very thoughtful."

He stopped with one foot in the door before climbing inside.

"I intend to marry you," he said, his eyes directly on hers. "I hope you understand."

She blushed brightly. It was such an uncanny thing to say that she felt it physically strike her. Nevertheless, it was flattering and confusing and absolutely absurd. Yet he appeared quite gallant and sure of himself now. She liked this version of Henry much more than the one she had met at the Brown Paper Company or even at the birthday party.

He nodded and slid behind the wheel of the car. She awarded him points for not lingering. What else could one say after such a statement? He honked at the gate and the guards, recognizing the vehicle and driver, opened the doors and let him go. The small black bear ran behind the car for a dozen yards, then veered off and disappeared into the woods.

❧ *Chapter Seven* ❧

Collie heard the train before it came into view. The sound arose as a deepening of air, then spread and gradually took purchase on the trees and stones on either side of the track. A pair of chickadees flittered to the nest they had built above the station door. Collie leaned a little toward the tracks in order to see the nest. Even with her improved vantage, she saw only sticks and grass and the busy heads of the birds. She wondered what the birds made of a train's arrival. It must seem like thunder to them, she imagined, and then she returned to looking down the track.

She felt nervous and excited and, to her surprise, somewhat shy. Estelle! It hardly seemed possible that her dear friend would step off the train any minute now. She felt as if she were at the beginning of a lovely meal, with the table set beautifully and the food sumptuous and plentiful. It was all ahead of her, the meal that had been so long in planning. She yearned to talk to Estelle, to unburden herself of every thought and fear, and, in turn, to take from Estelle whatever heavy loads she carried. Collie had already planned an itinerary, but that was merely the skeleton of the visit. The flesh of their visit, Collie knew without question, was their conversation, the communication of their kindred souls. It was nearly too much to hope for.

At last she glimpsed the train. It came up the river valley, the heavy engine pushing smoke into the blue sky. The railroad-crossing gate swung down across the road and the warning bell began a tattoo of rapid signals. The earth began to tremble, and Collie glanced quickly at the chickadees, but they had gone and she could not find the nest again in her excitement.

With a final whoosh the train came to a halt and a conductor swung down onto the station platform. He bent back and lowered a set of folding stairs.

"Percy Station," he called into the train.

A few soldiers disembarked. Collie looked quickly to see if she knew them, but their faces were not familiar. A small boy came down next, followed by his father, and the father glanced at a pocket watch before moving away from the stairs. Even that tiny delay made Collie mad with frustration! Where was she? A tiny web of panic began to fasten itself to her heart, and she walked a few paces toward the locomotive, wondering if Estelle had somehow missed a connection, or perhaps fell asleep. Anything might have happened, and she was on the verge of asking the conductor a few sharp questions when she saw a small shoe push away from the side plane of the train, and then a serge skirt followed, all of it belonging to her *amie de coeur*, Estelle!

"Estelle!" Collie called, tears suddenly hot in her eyes. "Here, here I am!"

In an instant, she had her friend in her arms, both of them exclaiming at the same time. A passenger behind Estelle—a broad woman with a masculine face—said *excuse me* in a weary, annoyed voice. Estelle began to laugh, and Collie did, too, and they moved away from the stairway, refusing to let go of each other but walking as if they had entered a three-legged race.

"I can't believe you're here at last!" Collie said when they finally broke apart. "I want to study you. You look marvelous. So beautiful, Estelle."

"And look at you! The camp translator!"

"Only by default, I promise. Where are your bags? I simply can't believe you are here, Estelle. Welcome to our little town. You won't be horribly bored by us, will you?"

"Not for a moment! I counted the days, believe me. Ashtabula is not Paris, you know."

"Well, even Paris isn't Paris these days, I suppose. Now let's get your bags. Do you have many? We can put them in the station here and send a car to pick them up later. Or if you don't have too many, we can carry them now."

"I have two, but they are spectacularly heavy. I'm afraid I'm going to have to depend on you for some outfits. I didn't want to bring too much. Father kept saying that a traveler with too many bags isn't a traveler at all. It's one of his many aphorisms. It turns out my father is filled with aphorisms when it comes to my life, but we won't go into that right now."

A porter inside the train began handing down bags. The conductor handled them expertly, lining them up for a half-moon of passengers waiting. Collie held Estelle's arm as they went to claim her luggage.

"That portmanteau is mine, I'm afraid," Estelle said, pointing toward a large trunk that would be impossible to carry any distance. "And that plain beige suitcase . . . yes, that one," Estelle confirmed with the conductor.

"Easily done," Collie said. "We'll send a man over in a truck. Two shakes of a lamb's tail. That way, we can walk and I can show you the river."

"I'd love that. I could stand to stretch my legs."

It was arranged. Moments later they began walking arm in arm toward the village. With her friend at last beside her, Collie felt she might pop like a bright balloon and go whizzing across the sky. At the same time it felt dislocating to see Estelle here in this tiny backwater of New Hampshire. Collie narrated their progress, telling her friend the name of the river, the various features in the hillsides, and finally guided her to her rock bench.

"This is where I read your letters," she told Estelle. "Somehow it feels more natural to read them outdoors. I have a little ritual when it comes to your letters, you know? I read them first here, but only quickly, just to assure myself that all is well and that nothing has happened to you. And then I take the letter with me to the office and I read it again. On the return journey I take it out once more and then I examine it like an ancient text. I've counted on your letters so much, Estelle. I'm not sure what I would do without them."

"I do much the same thing with yours. And I can see why you're drawn to this spot. How sweet it is. Should we stop for a moment? I'm taking this all in, and it's exactly as I pictured it. You look so lovely, Collie. So confident, somehow, and worldly in ways I can't begin to copy."

"That's nonsense, Estelle. I'm a daughter to my father, and that's the whole of it."

"Not at all. That's not how I see you at all. You have a position and responsibilities. I'm so envious of that. Here, sit beside me and let me see you in your proper setting. Yes, you match my imagination of this place. It comes surprisingly close, actually. Now tell me everything. I have so many questions, but my head is whirling. I'm grateful we have time for long conversations. I've yearned for them so much."

Collie sat on the rock beside her friend and turned her face up to the sun. Yes, she felt content. She had dreamed of this moment many times. She felt grateful for the fine weather; the camp and town could be depressing in the rain or inclement weather, and she wanted everything to be perfect for her friend. The day had co-operated. It glowed like a blue apple, bright and clean, nearly tart with its freshness.

"First, tell me about the train journey. Was it bearable?" Collie asked.

"It was long, I'll admit. I changed trains so often I lost count. But the countryside made it worthwhile. Everything was coming into springtime green. I've become a plant fancier, you know? I've written you a little about it, but gardening has filled many idle hours for me. Our home has a conservatory attached to the southern end and it gets good sunlight all the year round. My mother never much cared for it, and it was always a point of contention between my father and her. So I took it over and came across the most interesting Indian man who sells plants at a flower shop not far from our house. A true Sikh, with a turban and everything, living right in Ashtabula, if you can imagine. He's knowledgeable about plants and he has helped me select a good collection. I seem to have a green thumb, which is not something I ever cultivated. In any case, it's my one worry about being away. My mother will not care for the plants and my father is too busy and is mildly incompetent about them. . . . It's a muddle, although they both like the effect the plants have on the room."

"And so you watched the plants on the ride from Ohio?"

"Yes, I seem to respond to the natural world in that way. Plants, anyway. It's like bird-watching, I suspect. Once you begin noticing birds, you see them everywhere. Now I'm confronted by plants."

"I'm glad they kept you company. Were your parents very concerned about your trip?"

"Oh, I don't know. It's hard to sort them out. My mother kept asking why anyone would want to go visit a prisoner-of-war camp. It became a bit of a running joke to people who would ask about it. 'She's off to see the Germans,' Mother would say. Money is tighter than it was before the war, too. So a mixture of things went into the decision, but I've been a little depressed, as I wrote to you. I can't seem to get out of my own way some days."

Collie squeezed her friend's hand.

"Are you feeling better? Did the train trip help?"

"In fact, it did. Staying at home I began to feel like one of my potted plants sitting in the sun and remaining entirely immobile. Most of the men are gone and everything seems on hold. But it's not just the men. I don't mean to say that. Everything seems to be on hold and people keep saying, well, when the war is over. And I find myself thinking, well, we're alive now and who knows when the war will end? But now I've come east again and I am sitting beside my dear, dear friend. You really do look marvelous, Collie. You've changed, but all for the better."

"It's been interesting, I'll say that much. I made the right decision to leave Smith and be with my father. It was difficult at first. He was a little lost for a time when my mother died. With the war going on, getting any sort of extended leave was out of the question. Still, I'm not sure I would have been content to stay in a secluded enclave like Smith even without the force of my mother's death. It began to feel like make-believe, because the world had become so fractious and dangerous. I like it here. The work centers me."

"Well, it certainly is a pretty place. Are we far from your boardinghouse?"

"No, it's just a five-minute walk downstream."

"You would never guess there is a prisoner-of-war camp close by."

"You'll see the cutting teams from time to time, especially in the morning and evenings. The prisoners wear bright PWs on their blouses. You'll get into the routine soon enough."

"And when do I get to see the handsome August?"

Collie blushed. She leaned her forehead against her friend's shoulder. She shook her head and then lifted it again.

"You must think I've lost my mind," Collie said, her voice suddenly constricted. "In fact, there's another man I must tell you about. His name is Henry. His attention had been very confusing, but we can talk about that. I didn't much care for him at first, but then he showed up today and presented me with a bouquet. And he declared that he intended to marry me! And August . . . I have such strong feelings for him. You must think I've gone balmy."

"Not at all. I want to hear more about this Henry. As to August . . . do you know, I see my Indian friend sometimes and I think, well, he's a man and I'm a woman. My mother is frightened to death he will carry me off someplace and I can't help teasing her about it. But why shouldn't you admire a young German soldier. Is he very handsome?"

"Wonderfully handsome."

"You have feelings for him, don't you? True feelings?"

"Oh, it's hard to say. I don't know him at all, but we exchanged that poem . . . and now I'm not sure if he meant it as a language lesson, or if he has forgotten it altogether. I don't see him under normal circumstances. I mean, we don't see each other at church, or at meals, or anywhere else, really. I'm afraid I've given in to a schoolgirl crush."

"Stranger things have happened, certainly. I can't wait to see him. We're going to have so much fun. And you promise me we'll walk in the mountains? Ashtabula is so flat. . . . I'm not sure how I'd forgotten how flat it is. I feel as though I'm in the Alps here. Now, tell me, do you have the rest of the day free?"

"Yes, absolutely."

"Well, I wouldn't mind lying down for a short while. I didn't sleep particularly well on the train and I want to regain my energy. Tire me out, Collie. Get me out of my cobwebs."

"I promise I will. If I don't manage it, I have a young friend who will."

"This Marie you wrote about?"

"She's a hurricane."

"Good," Estelle said, standing. "I could use a little rough weather."

"She may be more than you bargain for. She can't wait to meet you. Amy will come by later, too. I thought we could have tea. Marie will not relent until she has a chance to be with you."

"It all sounds delightful. March me home. Keep me busy and out of my own head. I'm tired of my own thoughts, Collie. You don't know how tired."

Collie stood and linked her arm through her friend's. On their walk back to Mrs. Hammond's boardinghouse, Collie told her about the bear, Bruno, and about Henry's visit, and how the Nazi sympathizers had arranged the rocks into the shape of a swastika. . . . All and all a great rush of words that she could not contain and had no wish to.

"They are coming for you tonight," Gerhard said in a low voice, close by to a tree they were working up. "I overheard it in the latrine."

"Who is?" August asked, not forming the thought in his head. He had been lost in the steady thump of his ax.

"The Nazis," Gerhard whispered.

"For me?"

Gerhard nodded.

"I've done nothing to deserve a beating," August said.

"It doesn't matter, don't you see? It may be about releasing the bear or it may be about anything at all. They'll do what they like and reasons don't particularly matter. They may have caught wind of your poetry exchange with the major's daughter. Don't try to reason it out. It will just frustrate you."

"They'll get a surprise if they come for me," August said with a bravado he did not feel. "What do they care if I exchange a poem with a young woman? They're happy to look when she passes by, that's certain."

"Don't resist. It will only make it worse. They're eager to snatch on anything that can ensure discipline. Any transgression. It really doesn't matter what it is."

"Thank you for telling me."

"I'm sure I'm on the list as well."

August put down his ax. He had been busy limbing one side of a large pine while Gerhard worked the other side. Insects swarmed around them. They had both tied cloths over their necks to keep the insects from biting them on that tender flesh, but it scarcely made a difference. The guards called the insects no-see-ums, which had been a difficult translation, one that had no exact correlative in German. In the direct sun, the insects increased their attacks. Every breath, August thought, contained the scent of pine and the meaty puck of insects slamming into one's nostrils or mouth. The twitch horse had been flinging its tail at the insects all morning.

The news that he was on schedule for an attack shocked him. He had put on a good face for Gerhard, but the information sank like a dead weight through his body. He continued chopping with his ax—he had become quite expert by now, he knew, and his hands could work nearly without his mind's supervision—but his thoughts tangled with the image of the Nazis sneaking through the night toward his cot. He felt many things mixed with an overarching fear. He felt indignant and appalled that the men should carry the war into such a small corner of the world, but, primarily, he felt shame that he had never rallied his compatriots to stand up to the bullies. Now he would suffer from his lack of courage, and he could not say he didn't deserve it.

He tried to think of a plan, but his mind wouldn't settle. The no-see-ums buzzed around his ears and filled his nostrils until he coughed with the taste and rub of them in his membranes. He considered telling the two new guards who watched over them. Informing them, however, would merely delay the beating and intensify it when the time came. The guards could not be everywhere, and the Nazis demonstrated great patience. Sooner or later, they would come for him, and they would ambush him when he was alone, doubling the beating in recompense for his treachery.

He worked until lunchtime and then fell down in the shade when the guards gave them their food. Despite Gerhard's warning, he did not feel frightened precisely. He would endure what he had to endure; the war had taught him that much. The Nazis administered the beating as a means of maintaining discipline. They could be brutal beatings, true, but just as often the victims escaped with a solid pummeling, a reprimand handed down by a big brother to a smaller one. It was confusing. August knew, of course, who remained in sympathy with the Nazi movement, but he had difficulty believing their distance from the war would not eventually make them reasonable. How could men in a New Hampshire logging camp believe they retained any influence on the outcome of the war? It was madness.

He ate the stew put on his plate. The meat tasted of soap, and the broth was thin, but hunger was the best sauce, as the saying went. His new crew members ate with their faces close to their plates. Gerhard was the only one who remained from his original cutting team. The rest had been shuffled away; William had escaped and had been reassigned back to Fort Devens after his capture; Howard and Hans had been put in sick bay for several days before they, too, had been sent on a medical train back to Fort Devens. The new men had come from a different war, it seemed, and they stayed together as a pack within a pack. August found he had less and less in common with the latter waves of men.

"So what will you do?" Gerhard whispered.

"If they come for me? What can I do? They're angry because their cause is lost. I'm simply a convenient target."

"It's a beating nonetheless."

"True, but it hasn't happened yet. I could pretend to be sick and go to the infirmary, I suppose."

"You should."

"It would feel cowardly."

"Who cares, if it gets you out of a beating. You can come down with something this afternoon. There's no shame in it. Most people don't get a warning ahead of time."

"They'd really beat me because I released the bear cub?"

Gerhard made a dismissive buzz with his lips to indicate it didn't matter. August looked furtively at the new members of the crew. He did not trust them. He did not trust anyone except Gerhard.

"You should go to your friend and see what she can do for you," Gerhard said.

"She's hardly my friend."

"The commandant's daughter. She can set you right."

"I wouldn't presume."

"You're foolish then. She obviously has taken an interest. Only a fool would stand on pride at this point."

"I'll think of something."

"You better hurry. Lights-out will be here before you know it."

Then the guards hurried them back to work. Surprisingly, August found he worked with greater energy than before. He swung his ax with keenness and moved to get the work done. He would fight them, he decided. He was sick of the Nazis, of the whole damn war, and if it came as a small band of men to him in the night, well, then let it. He would fight back. He would not let them turn him into a coward. It was a tiny, absurd victory, but he knew, as he cut wood beside Gerhard, that he could not do otherwise. He had been a German soldier, a good one, and the scurrilous Nazis would find what it meant to stand for the Fatherland. He welcomed the chance to cross them. He would not back down.

"What they do is they take a man's jacket and cut it down to size. It works wizard! That's what they're doing in the city, because you can't get cloth with the war on, so they cut things into a more feminine shape and they can do wonders."

"Who can?" Collie asked Marie, and when she saw her young friend's face collapse in disappointment, she regretted holding the comments up to examination. "I bet we could find someone around here to do that. Who's the best tailor around?"

"Mrs. Jameson," Marie said without hesitation. "She makes everyone's dresses. There's a woman over in Berlin, Mrs. LaClerc, but she is for high fashion. Her work is very fancy. But for the everyday type of jacket I'm talking about, Mrs. Jameson could do it in a snap."

"Where will you get the men's jackets?"

"Oh, they're around. You can get them in the church bin. Naturally, the material will be coarser, but any salt is good when it's needed."

Marie stood and looked in the window of the boardinghouse, bending back and forth to see if Estelle had come downstairs. Collie smiled to see her impatience. Marie had come over directly after school, and she had been prattling on about any topic that came into her head. Estelle's nap had bled into the late afternoon. She must have been exhausted, Collie realized, traveling such a distance by train. She wondered, though, if she should tiptoe upstairs. If Estelle continued napping, she would have trouble getting to sleep at night and her rhythm would be thrown out of cadence. It seemed a shame to let such a lovely afternoon go by, but Collie remembered there would be plenty of days. Estelle had plans to stay at least a fortnight, perhaps longer, and so there was no rush.

As if Collie's thoughts were an incantation, Marie suddenly pressed her nose closer to the boardinghouse window, then turned with wide-eyed wonder.

"Here she is! She's awake! Oh, she's beautiful. She's just how I thought she'd look!"

"Oh, good," Collie said, "I'm glad she's awake. I worry she won't sleep tonight."

Marie tapped softly on the window. Collie stood and went to the door. Estelle walked toward her, her hair still mussed slightly from sleep, her face compressed from resting on the pillows.

"My goodness, I slept like the dead," Estelle said. "I'm so sorry. I didn't expect to sleep so long."

"I'm glad you did," Collie said, and opened the door to let her friend outside. "And we have a visitor who is eager to meet you. This is Marie, Estelle. She's been my good friend here."

Marie curtsied. It was so sweet, and so unexpected, that Collie couldn't help reaching over and hugging her. Then she turned Marie quietly to Estelle. Estelle took the girls' hands and held them.

"I'm going to ask Mrs. Hammond for some lemonade," Collie said. "Are you hungry, Estelle?"

"Not just yet, but I will be. I think I'm still adjusting."

"I'll be right back. You two sit on the glider. It's a lovely afternoon. Maybe we can walk up to the camp before dinner."

"Yes, I'd like that."

Collie went inside and found Mrs. Hammond cooking the evening meal. Agnes sat on a stool beside the large trestle table, her hands busy shelling peas. Collie glimpsed a bright red chicken standing on the back porch, its eye turned to peer inside. The scene looked to be a perfect little snapshot, and Collie regretted disturbing it by her request.

Mrs. Hammond pointed her to the lemonade, then went back to stirring something. Agnes lifted the bowl of peas and shook them to gauge their numbers. Collie poured out three glasses of lemonade and carried them outside to Estelle and Marie.

"Well, I'm afraid we've jumped right onto the topic of August, your young German soldier," Estelle said. "Marie confirms he's every bit as handsome as you've written."

"He's Marie's beau," Collie said, putting the lemonade down in front of them. "She had a dance with him."

"So she said. But she sensibly thinks he is too old for her, so she will surrender him to you. I think it's very generous on her part."

"He is very handsome," Marie chimed in. "He looks like Douglas

Fairbanks, only taller and with no mustache. He has very broad shoulders and a kind expression."

"Have you spoken with him at all?" Estelle asked, lifting the glass closest to her. "Since your last exchange, I mean."

Collie shook her head.

"He gave her a poem," Marie said, drinking a quarter of the glass in her excitement. "A man doesn't give a lady a poem just for his amusement, does he, Estelle?"

"I'm afraid I'm not much of an expert on romantic matters, but I suppose not. I've told Collie she needs to engineer an occasion to speak with him again."

"Do I need to remind both of you that he's a prisoner in my father's camp?"

"All the more reason to arrange something," Estelle said. "Don't you agree, Marie?"

Marie nodded. Collie understood that Marie would agree with anything Estelle said, so impressed was she with her new friend's elegance. Collie sat in a rocker beside the glider and drank some of the lemonade. It tasted bitter at first, then refreshingly sweet. A few swallows had already begun to slash at insects in the early-evening air. They flew close to the water's surface, their wing tips occasionally placing dimples into the current.

"I think communicating by poetry is the highest form of love," Marie said, her voice so transported by the thought that she hardly seemed to be speaking to the company arranged on the porch.

"You're nearly glowing, Marie," Collie said. "Estelle, tell Marie about your Indian friend, the one with the plants. That will distract her."

"An Indian man?" asked Marie, slowly coming out of her reverie.

"Well, yes. He owns a flower shop. His name is Mr. Kamal. He has become a good friend of mine. We drink tea sometimes and discuss plants and general things. The war, of course. He wears a turban because of his religious background. He does not believe in cutting his hair."

"Really? Oh my goodness," Marie said, obviously shocked and thrilled. "How wonderfully strange."

Major Brennan arrived before Estelle could continue. He had walked from camp, Collie saw. He looked tired but in good spirits. He moved quickly up the stairs and kissed Estelle's cheek in greeting. He took a step back to examine her, his handkerchief down at his side.

"You're entirely grown," he said, "and you're quite beautiful. It's strange, but I look at you, and now I see how Collie has reached womanhood as well. I suppose I hadn't seen it quite so clearly before. I keep thinking she is Marie's age, but now I see how badly mistaken I've been."

"Thank you, Major. And thank you for allowing my visit."

"Glad to have you. It's a funny way to spend the war, hiding out here in New Hampshire, but I imagine someone would have to do it so it might as well be me. Everyone pulls an oar."

"I told Collie that I envy her her position at the camp. I often feel of no use to anyone."

"I'm sure that isn't the case, but Collie has been a great help. It's true. Now, if you'll excuse me, I'm going to run in and wash before dinner. What does Mrs. Hammond have planned for us tonight?"

"Chicken and dumplings," Marie answered, though she had already said she had to go home.

"Wonderful. I'll just be a moment, then I want to hear about Ashtabula."

He went inside while Collie saw Marie place her glass on the coffee table near the glider and sigh. Clearly she was overdue at home. She left in small pieces, an elbow first, then a foot, each limb cast away as if she could not believe she had to depart. She made many promises to return whenever she could, then finally ran off, her books dangling from a strap in her right hand.

"She's delightful," Estelle said. "She's just as you described her. So sweet. I can't imagine we were ever like that."

"She said the same thing about you. That you were exactly as I described you."

Estelle stood and walked to the porch railing. She gazed out at the river. Collie watched her carefully. Did she regret coming all the way to New Hampshire? Did they all seem incredibly provincial? Collie had always felt slightly in Estelle's shadow, though it was a projection entirely of her own making. Estelle had never been anything but kind and open with her.

"I'm so relieved to be here," Estelle said, turning to look back at the porch and house. "You can't know how I counted on seeing you, Collie. I needed to get away. My parents . . ."

She lowered her voice. Collie studied her friend.

"What is it, Estelle?" she asked.

"You've already guessed at it. It's Mr. Kamal. I may be falling in love with him."

"And that's why your parents allowed you to make this trip?"

Estelle nodded. Then she shrugged.

"It's tangled up. It's not all one thing. My parents want the best for me, but they have misgivings about Mr. Kamal. They think I've seized on him because I am bored and restless. But he is such a kind, good man, and we have the most wonderful conversations. He's very knowledgeable and very well-read. He is a Sikh. I knew nothing about Sikhs until I met him, and I still know very little. I only know he's a gentle, kind man."

"I didn't know it had gone so far."

"It hasn't," Estelle said, and blushed. "I didn't write to you because my feelings had only been friendly toward Mr. Kamal. He was just an acquaintance, you see? But then our conversations lengthened and he began to tell me more about his background. He's had such an interesting life, Collie, I can't even begin to tell you. It's all very proper, so there's no trouble there. But my mother especially thinks it's better to nip things in the bud, and perhaps she's right. We are from very different worlds, Mr. Kamal and me. So you see why you have to hike my legs off my body? I need to be tired to the point of exhaustion."

"We can manage that. It will all be fresh air and exercise."

"Aren't we a pair?" Estelle said, and laughed. "You smitten by a young German soldier and me keeping company with a man in a turban. Did two sillier women ever live?"

"Not silly. Engaged with life, that's all. And that's not a crime."

"And you have a second suitor who we've hardly begun to dissect. What is he like?"

"At first I thought he was rather timid and awkward, but then he surprised me with the bouquet and he told me he was going to marry me. It was incongruent hearing it from him at first, but then, on second thought, it fit him perfectly well. He was joking, I think, or at least didn't intend to be taken seriously. But the words did pass his lips."

At that moment Mrs. Hammond began calling people to dinner. Agnes rang a small triangle that sent out a merry sound. Estelle smiled broadly at the noises and grabbed Marie's lemonade glass to carry inside. Collie held the door. She glanced once more at the river before following her friend. Yes, a walk later, she promised herself. It was not a day to retire early, not a day to hurry toward an end.

⊰ Chapter Eight ⊱

August lay in bed with a length of fire hose across his chest. The hose was the best he could do. He had searched the camp carefully, looking for weapons, but the Americans were thorough: they left no metal objects around, nothing that could be turned into a weapon. During the day, all axes and shovels and saws were strictly inventoried, each with a corresponding number. The Americans feared for themselves, of course, but the precautions, August knew, made them all safer. If the Nazis had access to weapons, they would use them. He had no doubt about that. And so he had scoured the camp and managed to find a heavy length of discarded fire hose. A feeble weapon, he knew, but he had chinked the bottom end into a handle so that he could whip it with potent force. At the least, it made a fine cracking sound when it landed, and he hoped it would serve to scare them away or make the attack too annoyingly difficult to carry off.

Meanwhile, he waited. His mind spun madly over various topics. For a moment he was back in his home near Vienna, and then he was in Italy, at a café, listening to two Italians argue about the war. Everything, it sometimes seemed, revolved around the war. Then for a long time he pictured his childhood dog, Chowder, who had been his constant companion. Dear Chowder, a dull gray mutt with crooked teeth. His father had named him, thinking it a joke, but the name had wounded August. He had wanted his dog to be noble and strong, a *shutzhund* if he could pull it off, but the name *Chowder* undermined all that. Nevertheless, he was a smart little animal, intelligent enough to go to the butcher's shop and beg at the back door for bones. He managed all that without getting run over by the trolleys, so, in the end, August did not have a noble dog but one that had a small reputation in any case, and people stood back when Chowder passed with a knucklebone in his mouth, laughing at the comical sight of such a small dog toting a huge meal. Even the butcher, Mr. Vankeuren, called it good advertising to feed the scrappy dog, so that, Chowder or not, the dog had found a way to earn a living. Yes, August remembered all that.

For a time, too, he thought of Collie, the commandant's daughter. He had seen her in the morning just in passing. Why was it, he wondered, that the sunlight seemed always to find her? Perhaps it was merely the presence of a woman among so many men, but everyone commented on it: beams of light seemed to find her more often than was explainable. She was uncommonly beautiful, but it was something about her step, too, that transformed her. She was light and obviously intelligent, and the men, he knew, yearned for her not as they yearned for the pinups of movie stars in provocative clothes but for the home she represented, the possibility of a fine wife and a happy laughter that could fill a house. That yearning— even more than a sexual yearning—struck deeper.

Those were a few of the thoughts that careened through his mind. Yet the primordial nut of his brain waited for the attacking Nazis. Let them come, he thought. That was one of the chief marvels of the war: he had learned he did not panic, but was, in fact, more deadly than he could have guessed. He had been good at war, he knew, and that knowledge did not trouble him nor did it embolden him. It remained in his consciousness like a simple tool, one that he could lift up and use when needed.

Twice, a thousand times, he heard them coming. Every creak of the barracks, every man turning on his cot to grumble and snore, every night sound shaped itself into the slither of the traitors coming to attack him. At those moments his skin prickled and his entire body seemed to vibrate and it took minutes for it to calm and re-settle. Then another sound triggered the reaction again and he gripped the fire hose tightly, ready to spring from the bed to take on the first attacker.

But the assault did not come. Not until very late and then August had drifted too close to sleep to protect himself properly. When they came at last—hands gripping him, a hiss in his ear—he managed to whip one of the men in the face with the hose. The man fell back and cursed. Then August broke free and made it onto his knees, flinging the hose back and forth until someone—it was dark, impossible to see—managed to tangle his own arm around the hose and anchor it under his body. That freed the other men and they fell on him, the shoes smacking him. Some of the men turned the shoes on their sides so the soles served as hammer blows, and August felt one such blow crack his nose, another peel back a portion of his ear. He raged against the arms holding him, but he did not speak. Another shoe landed on his face, ripping his lip, then he felt the boots pummeling his ribs and upper arms. They held him open so that he could not cross his arms to defend himself. Someone jabbed the toe of a boot repeatedly into his testicles, and August could do nothing but flinch crazily at the immense pain. Eventually someone close by said, "*Genug*," *enough*, but whether it was a bunkmate or one of the Nazis, August couldn't tell.

"Goddamn bastards," Gerhard said.

That was all August heard other than the scuttle of the attacking party hurrying out of the barracks. He did not try to inspect his pain; it was too much. He thought of Chowder, that ridiculous dog, and how one day he had returned with a bullet in his rump. The bullet had remained like a plug in the hairy flank of his friend, until his father had removed it with a pair of needle-nose pliers. After-ward the remaining hole had oozed blood, heavier and heavier, as if the bullet had been a lifesaving thing all along and they had failed to understand its role. Removing the bullet had been like removing the cap on an inflatable toy, and his dog, his Chowder, had collapsed in on himself, no longer the butcher's friend, no longer his noble companion.

Major Brennan did not know the name of the nervous corporal who woke him. The young man—how had they become so young, he wondered absently as he stood in his robe and pajamas and watched the man salute—handed him a telegram. The corporal's hands shook as he handed over the paper. Major Brennan took the telegram and told the corporal to wait.

Major Brennan had to read the telegram twice before he could speak.

"They've done it," he said to the corporal, his heart beating faster.

"Done what, sir?"

"They've landed in France. A second front. Eisenhower attacked Normandy. Five divisions went in, twelve thousand paratroopers, over a thousand warships."

The corporal held out his hand and Major Brennan shook it as though he had had something to do with it.

"The prisoners won't like it when they get wind of it," Major Brennan said. "A victory for us is a loss for them. That's why they've let us know."

"Yes, sir."

"It's called Operation Overlord. The invasion, I mean," Major Brennan said, still examining the telegram.

"They'll be on the run now," the corporal said.

"Let's hope so. What's your name, son?"

"Vincenzi."

"You've brought a car?"

"Yes, sir."

"Then hold on while I dress, if you will. I won't be a moment. I couldn't go back to sleep now if I wanted to."

When he finished dressing, he followed the corporal out of the boardinghouse and told the man to be quiet as he closed the door. He knew, almost without thinking about it, that he had just passed through a moment he would remember as long as he lived. History happened on a summer night in a boardinghouse in Stark, New Hampshire.

"We'll remember this night, won't we, Corporal Vincenzi?" he asked the young man as he climbed behind the wheel.

"Yes sir, I suppose so."

"Must have been a terribly bloody business."

"No doubt, sir."

"A beach landing."

"Yes, sir."

"Good old Ike."

"Yes, sir. He's got brass in him."

"Is it getting light beyond the river?"

"Yes, sir. Morning is already here."

It was no good, Estelle thought at the edge of morning dreams. She kept her eyes closed and listened to the river, hoping the perpetual hum of it might carry her back to sleep, but her thoughts betrayed her. She had determined to keep thoughts of Mr. Kamal out of her consciousness, but that was impossible. The trip had not erased him as she had hoped but had only made his hold on her heart more difficult to abide. The place in her heart needed to be cauterized, she told herself. Something sharp and wicked must end her association with Mr. Kamal, she knew, but she could not imagine what that could be. The trip had been her best opportunity to rid herself of her feelings; even her parents understood that. Yet here she was, listening to a New

Hampshire river whose name she could not pronounce or keep in her head, and thoughts of Mr. Kamal had only deepened.

She rose quietly from the bed and dressed. Soft sunlight barely illuminated objects in the room. Everything held a pale grayness, as if they had all been balanced on a pin and might as easily return to darkness as to morning. She carried her shoes in her hand and slipped out of the room without waking Collie. The risers creaked as she went downstairs. She found an old mackinaw hanging on a coat-tree beside the front door and slipped into it. Carefully making sure the door did not lock behind her, she crept onto the porch and sat on the same glider she had shared with Marie the day before. How long ago that already seemed! She pinched the rough wool of the jacket closer around her and waited for the sunlight to find her.

She nearly darted back inside when a car passed over the covered bridge and pulled up beside the house. Major Brennan stepped out of the back, his uniform jacket unbuttoned. For an instant Estelle worried she had caught him at some impropriety—an alley cat returning home—but he smiled when he saw her and asked if he might join her.

"You're awake early," he commented, falling into the rocker beside the glider. "Are you feeling all right?"

"I think my schedule is flippy. I woke right up as though I could run a race."

"Well, I've been awake myself. You'll be happy to hear we have invaded France. Normandy is the landing point. We've established a second front."

"Really? And what will that mean, Major? I'm sorry I'm not very knowledgeable about these matters."

"It's a tactic to divide the German forces. They can't be everywhere at once. If we establish a position in France, then we can close in on them from both sides. The Russians have the other side going."

"Does it mean the war is ending?"

"I think it's hopeful. I've just been on the telephone with people up and down the line and there is consensus that it marks a major shift in the war. Hitler cannot hold out much longer. The German people are suffering."

"How will you tell the prisoners?"

"I suppose straightforwardly. That's the best technique, wouldn't you say? No use babying them about it."

"I agree, Major."

"Still, it will be a tough pill to swallow. Some of them will be glad to hear it because it means the war might end sooner. But they'll worry about their families back home."

"Naturally."

Estelle watched him lean his head back against the chair and close his eyes. The sunlight had finally climbed onto the porch and had hardened into a bright white light. Estelle heard birds calling. She stretched her bare feet out into the light to warm them.

"Well," he said, his eyes still closed, "I should wash for the day and get ready to go back to the camp. Is Collie still asleep?"

"Yes."

"Are you hiking today?"

"I hope so."

"Oh, I almost forgot. Collie's young poet was injured quite badly last night. They brought him into the infirmary. He claimed he fell while visiting the latrine, but he's obviously been beaten. I looked in on him and it's not a pretty sight. His injuries are extensive."

"Who would do such a thing?"

"The trouble is, a dozen men would. Two dozen. The loyal Nazis have their own rules and they will only tighten them as victory becomes less likely."

"I'll tell Collie. Do you think we could visit him?"

"I wouldn't. I feel bad for him, but he's a German soldier after all.

It might not be the thing to do, visiting him. It might also put him at greater risk. It's difficult to read these things from their perspective."

He smiled and pushed himself up from his rocker. He walked to the edge of the porch and looked out at the river.

"Fine morning," he commented.

Collie felt sick with nerves as she made her way to the infirmary. She had picked her time judiciously; the cutting teams were out in the forests and the camp possessed a quiet emptiness that she had come to count on. She did not want to go against her father's wishes, but she could not imagine what it would be like for the young man, so far from home, beaten by his own compatriots. Everything felt jumbled together. Throughout the day, reports had drifted into the administration building concerning the massive casualties suffered by the landing forces in Europe. Her father said it best: the men had marched on their own blood. But now, as the afternoon grew taut and lazy with heat, she heard the radio report that Allied forces had been established concretely on the French mainland. The beach names made no sense to her—Omaha, Utah, Sword, Juno, Gold, and probably more. The names removed the assault from reality, somehow, as though someone had picked words from a hat and made everyone else play along. The fighting sounded horrible and the attack on August had been horrible and Collie felt sick with anxiety over both events.

"Take him some of the books I brought," Estelle had recommended. "It's a perfectly good excuse, and no one can hold it against you. Where else will he find German books? He's probably frightened."

"I may be the cause of the beatings. I could make it worse by going."

"You can't know that, Collie, and neither can your father," Estelle said. "I understand your father's concern, but one day the war will end. Today's invasion only proves the point. Even war must one day surrender to common decency."

"If I go, you will have to entertain Marie by yourself. You better prepare for an onslaught."

"I'm looking forward to it. Now go. You made me lug these books all the way from Ashtabula, so they should at last be delivered. I'll be fine here. I may even lie down and nap for an hour."

"I'm so ridiculously nervous about it."

"That's understandable, but don't dwell on it. Just put yourself on automatic."

"How do I look?"

"Perfect. You look lovely."

As Collie followed the path beside the river, her heart hammered in rapid beats. She carried three German novels—Gottfried Keller's *Green Henry*, Leo Perutz's *The Master of the Day of Judgment*, and Theodor Fontane's *Effi Briest*. She hoped a thousand things along the way. Obviously she hoped not to run into her father. For another, she hoped that August recognized her. She could not bear it, she felt, if she came to pay a visit and he failed to recognize her. That would mean everything had been in her head, and that was too humiliating to imagine.

She did not permit herself to look into the administration building but kept going instead to the small white house that served as a camp infirmary. It was a hopeful sign, she knew, that August had remained in the infirmary. More serious injuries went to Berlin, where a full hospital waited. As she went up the front stairs, she straightened her shoulders and drew on her determination. Nothing, she told herself, had to be one way or the other. She was paying a visit to a sick man, that was all. With that resolved, she pushed into the small vestibule where a receiving desk, staffed by a private acting as an orderly, took up the center area.

"May I help you?" the young private asked, rising to his feet.

"I came to bring books to the young German soldier. Augustus Wahrlich, I believe is his name."

"Yes, right through there, ma'am."

Could it really be that simple? Collie wondered as she nodded at the private and went in the direction he indicated. The infirmary, she saw, had been set up in what had once been a parlor. Someone had placed a vase full of wildflowers on the box stove in the fireplace. That caught her attention first. Then she saw a man—not August—lift his head at her approach. He lay in bed with a dark bandage on his forearm and hand. She had heard about him: he had ripped open his arm with a saw when it sprang out of its kerf and mauled his skin. The injury had been deep and worrisome, but now he appeared recovered and slightly bored. He nodded, not sure, it seemed, if her visit was meant for him.

In the next moment she saw August Wahrlich resting in the second bed. The sight of him wrenched her throat closed. His face had been beaten mercilessly; his nose had been broken, it seemed, and dried riverbeds of blood still marked where he had bled profusely. His eyelids, too, had been thickened to horrendous proportions. He looked like photos she had seen of boxers, their bodies bloated and swollen to protect whatever remained to be protected. A tube of some sort had been wedged into his mouth, probably to keep air passing into his throat. His right ear had been taped tight against his head, and his lovely hair, blond and full as wheat, held dark rings of dried blood mixed in with his softer locks. An enormous mound of something—she could not let her eyes examine it too closely out of modesty, but it was near his groin—pushed the blankets away from his legs and stomach.

Whatever fear or anxiety she had felt a moment before gave way to a rush of compassion. She walked carefully to his bedside and stood for a moment staring down at him. Then she could not help herself; she reached a hand to his soft hair and pushed it slowly off his forehead.

"August?" she asked. "Can you hear me?"

His eyes fluttered, but he did not wake.

"They gave him something to sleep," the man in the first bed said. "He should be out for a while."

"Are his injuries severe?"

The German man shrugged. What did *severe* mean in wartime? Collie wondered. It was a stupid question deserving no better answer.

"Who did this to him?" Collie asked.

The man—he was a dark-stubbled man with a rough face and thick shoulders—made a little pursing face with his lips. It was another naïve question, she realized.

"I brought him some books," she said. "Some novels. Would you mind making sure he finds them when he wakes?"

"His eyes will be too shut to read for a while."

"I guess that's true. But just the same. . . ."

"Set them by the bed on the table there. He'll get them soon enough. I'll make sure."

"Has he been conscious?"

"Oh, sure. He's young. He'll be all right once the swelling goes down."

The man nodded significantly at the mound near August's groin. She followed the man's direction. They had beaten his testicles, she realized. She had heard that before about other victims, but she had not imagined it in August's case. She felt a desire to strike back at something, at the brutality of such behavior. She wanted to tell this rough German that his side had lost today; that the Allied troops would bring France back to its ancestral governance, but that would be small and vindictive of her. Instead, she turned back and looked at August once more. Beneath the swollen lips and eyes, beneath the gunnels of dried blood beside his nose, she saw his handsome face. She reached a hand out again and ran his hair back away from his forehead.

"Will you tell him I visited when he wakes?" she asked the man in the first bed. "I'm the commandant's daughter."

"Yes, I know, ma'am."

"Our men landed in France today," she said, not to wound him but to let him know that the war might have an end.

"I've heard that," he said.

"This hideous war."

The man nodded when she glanced at him. And then she left.

❧ *Chapter Nine* ❧

They made a good company, Estelle thought as she watched Marie and Amy climb the trail ahead of her. She was third in line; Collie walked behind her. The day could not have been lovelier. The early-morning dew had burned off, and now in midmorning the trail offered secure footholds, and they climbed easily, pushing toward the top of Bald Mountain. On either side of the trail, fragrant pines waved their scent to them, the perfume growing stronger with the increasing strength of the sun. Red squirrels occasionally shot across the trail, and in the mountain thermals Estelle saw hawks gliding effortlessly, only the phalanges of their wings fingering the air as it held them aloft. For most of the morning—during the great heaping breakfast served by Agnes and Mrs. Hammond, and afterward in the noisy clatter about climbing equipment and supplies—she had fenced Mr. Kamal out of her thoughts. But now, climbing close to the tree line, she thought of how she could describe this moment to him, and how he, unlike any man she had ever known before, would understand the transcendence of the natural world. On this mountainside, surrounded by friends and spectacular scenery, she still could not keep him from intruding on her day.

"Not much farther. I can see the top!" Marie called.

"*How* much farther?" Collie called, seeking clarification.

"Not far at all."

"I've never been to the top of a mountain," Amy said, not for the first time.

"That's about to change," Estelle responded.

"Estelle climbed in the Alps!" Marie said, turning back to look and to confirm her statement, though it had been a theme through-out the morning.

"Yes, but never up to the peaks. We went from inn to inn, and it was marvelous. You'd arrive and be so hungry you didn't think you could fill yourself."

"I'm hungry now," Marie said.

"Hold off until we get to the top. Then we'll have a wonderful lunch," Collie said.

The trees faded behind them. A pine ground cover dotted with blueberries edged the trail. With each step the view cracked open to broaden its previous limits. The shoulders of the mountain became a simple fact. The mystery of the mountain had been vanquished, and now it lay exposed, a pile of granite possible to climb as it was possible to climb anything. Estelle told herself to remember that simple notion. One foot in front of the other brought one up a mountain, and that seemed extraordinary to her at the moment.

"Feel the wind!" Collie called from behind. "It could lift us up and take us away."

"We might want to lunch away from the peak," Amy said. "It will be cold."

"Let's get to the top, then we can decide," Estelle said, because she had more or less become the leader of the expedition.

"Oh, it's beautiful!" Marie said, and dashed up the last reach toward the summit.

Estelle turned and took in the 360-degree view when she reached the top. Her heart felt strong and happy. The wind ripped at them on the top, but she didn't care. This had indeed been what she needed. While the others pulled their jackets from their rucksacks and tucked their sweaters more closely around them, she opened herself to the wind. She wished for a moment that the wind could scrape her clean. She felt like the bow of a ship, plagued with barnacles, slowed in its passage through the water by the tenacious crustaceans. The wind scraped at her cares, and even Mr. Kamal, for the moment, fell silent. She made a small circle around the summit, gazing off into the wind and distance. The beauty stabbed her. She felt close to laughing, or to crying, and she would not have been surprised by either emotion.

"Look!" Collie said, her hand to her brow to block the sun. "Is that the camp?"

"I see the covered bridge," Amy said. "Follow the train line and you'll get your bearings."

"We should climb more mountains," Marie said, her face smiling and excited.

"I think we'll need to eat away from the wind," Collie said.

"If we get to the tree line again," Amy said, "we'll have some shelter. We passed a nice picnic spot not too far back."

Estelle understood they looked to her. She agreed. She made a last circuit of the summit. She held out her arms and let the wind push at them. She envied the hawks. She imagined letting the wind carry her up into the clouds, away from the world entirely, the land a patch of ridges and ribbons of water.

They descended after a few more minutes of gazing at the various landmarks. While the others commented about how good it felt to be out of the wind, Estelle regretted leaving the top of the mountain. Already, in the quieter realm of the forest, thoughts of Mr. Kamal returned. What was it, anyway? she wondered in frustration. What was it about this one particular man, foreign in so many ways, that drew her to him? To summon him, she merely had to shut her eyes and imagine the green shelves of his flower shop, the lacquered fountain table where they had shared tea so many times. She pictured his beautiful brown eyes, his inquisitive stare, his attention— yes, attention, that was much of it—as he nodded at something she had said. His radio played opera in the afternoons, and often their conversation stopped so they could listen to an aria, both of them staring down at their tea, clouds of cream floating in their cups, their desire for each other alive in every movement of their spoons. His company was addictive; she could not stay away. And yet she was not raised, educated at Smith, to throw herself away on a turbaned Indian flower-shop owner. That was not in her cards at all.

Her head still swam with thoughts as Amy finally called a halt at the spot she had mentioned. It was a small hollow in the pines with two large rocks positioned for seats. Estelle craved the wind again, but she forced herself to direct her concentration on the lunch. Marie dug ferociously through the picnic bag, calling out whatever item she came upon. Collie arranged them on the largest rock atop a red-and-white-checked linen. Estelle heard Marie call out cheese and bread, sausage and olives, lemonade and iced tea. Cookies, too, and some of the morning's leftover biscuits soaked in bacon grease and fried.

"I can't believe I'm hungry again after that enormous breakfast," Collie said.

"I'm famished," Amy said. "That was a rugged climb."

"We made it to the top. Wait until I tell father," Marie exclaimed. "He thought we would get discouraged and turn back, but of course, he hasn't met Estelle. I knew we would make it to the summit if we followed her. I told him so."

"He doesn't particularly think women should be hiking mountains," Amy said. "He's very old-fashioned in his thinking, I'm afraid. The war has made him even more wary than he had been before."

"Wary of what?" Estelle asked, leaning her legs against the rock and picking an olive out of its waxed paper wrapping.

"Oh, he thinks the world has turned upside and down, and I suppose he has a point. With women going to work in the factories, he thinks they've taken too much on themselves. He wonders how it will go back to normal."

"It won't," Estelle said, biting into the olive. "I don't think it can.

Women aren't going to be content to return to the kitchen and pretend the war never happened."

"We should pray for the soldiers before we eat," Marie said. "It's the least we can do."

She closed her eyes before anyone could say a thing and murmured a short prayer of thanks. Then she took a large chunk of bread and wrapped it around a thumb-size piece of cheese.

"Father says the landing in Normandy was incredibly costly," Marie said. "He says, think as we might, we can't conceive of how many died there. He listens to every radio report and he takes three newspapers."

"How are the Germans accepting it?" Amy asked Collie.

"They discount it, mostly, from what I understand. My father says it's posturing. Some of the men refuse to believe it at all. They claim we have made it up to fool them into despair."

"I don't understand how one small country believed it could defeat the entire world," Marie said, her cheek filled with bread. "I've never understood that."

"They are very powerful," Estelle said, "with great energy and a talent for organization."

"But the whole world?" Marie said.

Before they could go any further, a low hum suddenly came to them. Estelle cocked her head to listen and glanced at Collie. Collie held out her hand to still them, and then she nodded. By that time the origin of the low hum had become clear: it was the camp siren, calling the guards to report, letting them know someone had escaped. The sound filled the atmosphere and Estelle closed her eyes, wishing it to cease. But it kept going, like the war itself, and they had no more power over it than over the troops marching all over Europe and falling to battle.

*   *   *

Major Brennan felt the irony sharply: now that the war had taken a definitive turn toward termination with the landing on Normandy, the prisoners had been caught digging a tunnel. He felt many emotions at the discovery, chief among them betrayal. Yes, that alone was extraordinary. He performed a mental inventory and did not like what he found. He had treated them fairly, bending over backward at times to be humane, and they had rewarded him with this long conspiracy. It was his own naïveté that most disturbed him, however, and he made himself regard the facts squarely, coldly. The Germans labored as prisoners of war, and it was their duty, as soldiers loyal to the Reich, to attempt escape. He had persuaded himself, and by proxy the men under him, that the Germans could be pacified by decent treatment. Clearly that had been a miscalculation. He stood on the refectory porch now, staring at the prisoners, his anger difficult to control. He had assembled them more than two hours ago and had let them stand in the sun, contemplating their fate, while he had gathered as many facts about the tunnel as he could.

"As many of you know already," he began when he finally felt sufficient composure to speak, "we have discovered a tunnel leading from Barracks Seven toward the eastern boundary of the camp. The tunnel has been filled in and the prisoners from Barracks Seven have been shackled and sent to Fort Devens on the first available train. At Fort Devens they will be kept from the general prison population. We are in the process of gathering additional information about the tunnel, and any man found guilty of association will also be sent immediately to Fort Devens. We do not take this lightly, rest assured. Any man involved in any plan to escape will be dealt with severely. I hope that is clear."

Major Brennan waited for the full translation to finish. It was not Collie, unfortunately, with whom he felt his cadence worked, but with a newly arrived private who spoke German with his family. When it concluded, he nodded and continued.

"For the next few days, you will be put on bread and water. You will come off that diet when you have demonstrated by the strength of your labor that you understand your circumstances. The camp canteen will be closed until further notice. Those things that make life tolerable here are given at my discretion. I am under no obligation to provide you with any of those small luxuries you count on, so be advised. Your work in the next few days must persuade me that you warrant the canteen to be reintroduced."

Again he paused. He studied the German faces, many of them quite familiar by now. He had been glad that at least half of the soldiers from Barracks Seven had been avowed Nazis. He was relieved to be shut of them and their maniacal beliefs about the superiority of the German people.

He went on.

"Let me be clear: the war is coming to a close, and your side will lose. For those among you who believe this is a form of propaganda, that I am deliberately lying to you, let me sincerely urge you to look carefully at the facts. We are too many against you. Your nation cannot hold out much longer. Already it has been reported that you are sending boys to the Normandy front, because you no longer have men to fight. I take no pleasure from informing you of these facts. It is time for the war to end, I think you'll agree. The German people have suffered cruelly, and I am afraid they will suffer more as the war grinds to a conclusion."

Some of the prisoners nodded. Others looked down at the ground. Major Brennan didn't care. It was time they heard the likely outcome of the war. He had already received reports about the Allied attacks against Cherbourg. Six thousand German soldiers had surrendered on the Cherbourg Peninsula, more prisoners of war, more mouths and bellies.

"We have treated you fairly here. We hope to continue to do so. You must, at last, place your position in perspective. If you escape from here, where will you go? Is it your dream to jump aboard a boat and return to Germany? That Germany that you hold in your heart is gone. You are thousands of miles away from your home country. If you mistakenly believe you will find supporters among the American population, I hasten to warn you that you will find ten times as many Americans willing to put a bullet through your brain. If you do not understand that, you do not understand our country."

He stood for a moment longer, inspecting them. Then he turned and left. When Lieutenant Peters asked if the prisoners were to be dismissed, he told him no. Let them spend their day of leisure on their feet, he thought. Let them understand which way the rifles were pointed.

Still in her climbing outfit, Collie stepped into the infirmary, in her hand a small nosegay of wildflowers—purple grasses and wild violets. She felt happy and nervous, and her skin tingled where the sun had burned her. Her shoulders hurt from the straps of the rucksack, but the ache was a good one. It had been a glorious day; she had not had a better day in memory. When the others had ganged up on her, demanding that she visit the infirmary again, she had caved in without protest. She wanted to see August. She felt sure of that, and it made no sense to pretend she didn't.

The orderly at the front table stood when she entered. It was not the same young man from the earlier visit, but he behaved in the same manner, standing and pointing her to the parlor room. Collie took a deep breath and stepped into the room. The former patient with the cut hand and arm was not there. In his place a large, dark-browed man slept on his side, the round O of his mouth sucking air in audible gasps. Collie turned, wanting to ask about the man's condition, when her eyes crossed the room and met August's.

He smiled. Simply and beautifully. He smiled and she felt a smile spread on her face in return.

"You look better," she said, skirting around the first bed and coming to stand beside him. "How are you feeling?"

"Improved," he said in German. "Stronger."

"I'm sorry you were hurt at all."

He shrugged. He did not comment.

"I visited before," she said, "and brought you some books."

He nodded and reached under his blankets and brought up two of the volumes.

"You're very kind. They've kept me company when I could read them. My eyes have caused me some problems, but they are better now. Thank you for bringing them."

"I was happy to share them."

"My friend in the next bed, he is reading *Green Henry*. He is an interesting man. He looks rough indeed, but he is educated. I hope you don't mind."

"No, I'm glad you've enjoyed them. Please share them with anyone you care to."

"My English . . . I speak better than I can read," he said in English.

"How long will you stay here? Have they said?"

"For a few more days at least. The swelling has not gone down as it should."

He nodded in the general direction of his groin. Collie felt herself blush. But she had forgotten the nosegay of flowers and used that as a distraction.

"We went climbing today," she said, "and I saw these and thought of you."

"Spring flowers. Thank you. I have a cup there. Perhaps you would arrange them for me?"

Oddly, moving the things around on his bedside table and arranging the flowers felt more intimate than she could have anticipated. Her color was high, she knew. It felt a wifely thing to do, but she persevered and soon had the flowers arranged to her satisfaction. They brightened the room. She stood back. He surprised her by reaching for her hand and bringing it to his lips. He kissed the back of her hand, then moved her hand to his forehead and held it there.

From instinct, she nearly jerked her hand away. But he treated it with such gentleness that she soon calmed and let him press his forehead to it. She tightened her fingers slightly in his hand. She realized, watching him, that he was young and frightened and far from home. She did not mean that he was any less manly for showing such vulnerability. No, he was braver for doing so, and she could not help reaching her free hand out to push back his hair. He kissed the back of her hand again, and she saw that he wept.

"Are you all right?" she whispered.

"Your kindness . . . ," he said, and then shook his head.

"It's been a long, difficult war."

He nodded.

"It will be over soon. My father says that your people cannot resist much longer. He's confident this is the beginning of the final blow. I'm sorry for your country. Do you have family there?"

"In Austria. Yes. My mother and father and my brother, Frederich. I don't know if they are alive. I don't think they know where to look for me."

She nodded.

"I let the bear go," he said, and she squinted slightly, trying to understand.

"What bear?"

"The bear we found in the forest. I let him go so that he could return to his family. I could not stand that as prisoners we had made another creature a prisoner."

"Yes, I see."

"I'm sorry," he said, and gave her hand back.

She took an even breath. The man in the other bed made a gargling sound, then caught himself and returned to normal breathing. Outside she heard an announcement pass over the PA system. She could not decipher it.

"I should be going," she said. "I simply wanted to look in on you."

"We have not discussed the poem you gave me."

"Perhaps another time."

"Will you promise to visit me again?"

"Yes, of course. If you think I should. I don't want to make trouble for you."

"No, please come. I will feel better soon."

"I certainly hope so."

"Your father is a fair man."

"Thank you for saying that."

"Most of us understand him. A few do not, but you cannot worry about them."

"He does his best."

"Your mountains are not so different from our mountains in Austria. We have a beautiful country as well."

"I'm sure you do."

"Come again, please. You are the best medicine I could have."

"I will."

She touched his hand, and for a moment she let his eyes pour into his. She left quickly afterward, her heart violent in her chest.

"You've fallen in love," Estelle said from her place on the glider as she reached over and took her friend's hand. The night beyond the porch rested calm and quiet. Estelle heard tree frogs calling, their voices beaded by crickets rubbing their legs like violin bows. "It's the most natural thing in the world. You should not let it worry you. It should be cause for celebration."

"I hardly know him," Collie answered. "To talk of love . . . we sound like schoolgirls."

"We were schoolgirls only a short time ago, don't forget."

"He has a kind way about him," Collie said. "I've seen nothing not to admire."

"Love passes through the eye. Didn't we learn that in our poetry class?"

"Cupid's arrow. Ovid's *Romance of the Rose*. Yes, but this is everyday life."

"All the more reason for it to be exceptional and wonderful. The poets understood and so will you if you'd only let yourself."

"I'll admit I am attracted to him, but that's as far as I will go. The rest is just my imagination running wild."

"The heart knows its own course. That's another aphorism from my father. He says it whenever a poorly suited couple appears in our circle of friends. You've found someone who excites and interests you, and you would be a stunning couple side by side."

"Do you think so?"

Estelle nodded. And it was true. She could easily picture them together, their long slender bodies, their handsome curls. When she thought of them, then imagined herself as part of a couple with Mr. Kamal, the contrast overwhelmed her. No one would take her for Mr. Kamal's love. But Collie and her August, yes, they would command attention wherever they went.

"You would be a charming couple," Estelle said, returning her thoughts to her friend's predicament. "My only concern is his nationality. He will have to return to Austria when the war ends."

"Yes, of course."

"And if you did fall properly in love, you understand you might lose him? Europe will be in chaos. I don't know what his finances are, but he will have difficulty returning to the United States. Perhaps you could go to him, but where will he be? He doesn't know if his family is alive, does he?"

Collie shook her head.

"I'm not trying to throw water on the fire, but it helps to look all the way around things. I've become quite expert at it, you know. Mr. Kamal is my professor."

"Have you fallen in love with him, Estelle? Truly?"

Estelle took a long breath and weighed the question. She could not be certain she knew the answer. Yes or no—both answers came too quickly and too easily. She could simply dismiss him as inappropriate, but what about his tender personality, his warm brown eyes? Why did she so love speaking to him? Was it possible to fall in love purely with a man's voice and eyes and gentleness? She wondered if that could be true. The books never talked about that sort of love. The books concerned Collie's type of love with her handsome German beau. So what answer could she possibly give her friend to such a simple question?

"I don't know. In the books they talk about love taking us whether we want it to or not. Do you believe that can happen, Collie?"

"Yes, absolutely."

"That love is a force that exists outside of us, so to speak? That we have no control over who we love?"

"I wouldn't go as far as to say we have no control, but love is the equal of hate and envy and spite. I don't believe we can resist it completely. It has its own agency."

"I don't want to love Mr. Kamal, but I'm afraid I do. Isn't that horrid? To be afraid of love? He is a good man. I don't doubt that for a moment. Even my mother can see that, and she has only met him a handful of times. But he is from a different world, a profoundly different world from my small circle in Ohio. Do you know I've heard people call him a nigger? Ignorant, vile men, but still that's the word they use. They don't care that he is from a distinguished family in India or that his lineage goes back much further than their own. There are people who refuse to enter his store despite his way with flowers and arrangements. He is by far the best florist in our community, but the prejudice runs so deep that many of my mother's friends refuse to patronize him."

"And so to love him is to cross a great barrier."

"Yes, I'm afraid so. And I am a coward. I detest that weakness in me. I would take a knife and cut it out of me if I could."

"Has Mr. Kamal shared his feelings with you?"

"No. He is afraid to, I suspect. But his feeling is in every look we share, every topic we discuss. He gives me books, copies out poems. He has a vast library. He has thought of opening a bookstore beside his flower shop. . . . There is an adjoining storefront available. The book customers and flower customers would blend back and forth to the benefit of both. He has talked to me a great deal about it as though he is waiting for my commitment to the idea."

"As a wife?"

Estelle felt herself blush. She couldn't help it. Tears washed the corners of her eyes.

"Yes, I suppose, although it's never overtly stated. He, too, must cross a great barrier, you see? For all I know, his family would not be pleased to find him joining his fate with an American girl. It's a pickle, as my father would also say. How funny life is, isn't it?"

"I wish I could give you some sort of wise counsel."

"You are. Merely letting me talk about it is a great help. And today, the hiking . . . that was splendid, Collie. I'll remember this day a long time. Marie and Amy are sweet and very good company."

"I think so, too."

Estelle dropped her friend's hand so that she could wipe the small tears away from her eyes. She snorted a little with laughter at their absurd circumstances.

"We are a pair," she said. "Who could have guessed where our hearts would lead us?"

"The war has upended everything. You said so yourself."

"Of course. Now is it time for us to sleep? It's so lovely sitting out on a night like this, but I am tired. The hike wore me out."

"Yes, it's time."

"I'll fall asleep as soon as I hit the pillow."

"And not dream of Mr. Kamal?"

"Tonight I have reduced him to a small, inconvenient ache. I intend to sleep like a dragon."

"Thanks to Marie."

"Yes, Marie. She's quite brave about letting you have August, you know. It's a great gesture on her part."

"I don't have August."

"Yes," Estelle said, "in fact, you do."

◈ *Chapter Ten* ◈

At midday the barracks stood empty. August limped slowly down the row between the bunks, his body exhausted from the short walk. He carried Collie's novels in his hand, a canteen of water, a bottle of aspirin. His testicles ached; they had ached for days, the hurt receding like a tide slowly pulling back. The rest of his body sent up messages of distress as well. His ribs hurt at each breath, and his ear, where it had been ripped by a Nazi blow, felt as though it had been attached by the slightest thread, so that any movement might shake it free and leave it resting on the ground.

As he approached his cot, he spotted the fire hose beneath the mattress. It rested like a large snake, green and pocked with fiber, its dull life confined to hiding in the shadows. Gerhard, he knew, had placed it there. Gerhard had twice visited and had twice filled him in on the barracks news. Many of the Nazis had been sent away as a result of the tunnel episode. Major Brennan had not bothered with questions after the discovery of the tunnel, or with second-guessing, but had come down firmly and quickly to rid the camp of the worst elements. Things had improved, Gerhard said, and August tried hard to believe him.

He had broken into a sweat and trembled visibly by the time he reached his cot. He placed Collie's novels carefully at the foot of the bed—he could not bend over to put them on the floor—then collapsed in pieces onto the thin mattress. He felt nauseated and mildly disoriented. His tongue felt fat and swollen in his mouth, and his body jerked several times to release the muscular tension created by exercise. He closed his eyes and fell asleep instantly, the sound of distant pigeons fluttering in the barracks' eves bringing him peace.

He slept for hours and woke only when the men returned. Gerhard, tan and smelling of wood chips, came immediately to his side and asked how he felt. August sat up and put his back against the iron headrail.

"Better," he said, "stronger than yesterday."

"You look tired. I thought they would keep you longer."

"They need the beds. It's just a matter of time now before I am better."

"Well, it's good to see you back. And you'll be happy with the changes."

Gerhard looked around him before he leaned close and whispered, "The shit-hounds are gone," referring to the Nazis. "They got caught one too many times, and the few who are left are impotent without the numbers behind them. They're cowards and bullies."

"If they come for me again, they will have to kill me."

"They won't be back. Even they see how things are going. The war is dropping away. Germany is in retreat."

"Is it really?"

Gerhard nodded.

"The longer it goes on, the weaker we will grow," Gerhard said. "No country can make war forever. Hitler is a confused, weak man now."

"There's still venom in him."

Gerhard shrugged. A few other men came by to say hello, to ask after August's progress, and August told them straightforwardly how things stood. Everyone eventually went outside to smoke before dinner, and August, with difficulty, joined them. His body felt slightly better. He found a seat on an oil drum and positioned himself in the sunlight. He had not been there more than a minute when he heard someone call his name. As he turned, the sun made it difficult to see, so he had to stand and lean to one side and then he saw the little girl he had pretended to dance with so many weeks before.

"Hello. I remember you," he called. "What are you doing here?"

"I'm going to a musical program at the school. I saw you there. I hope you're feeling better."

"Yes, much better, thank you. Remember me to Collie, please."

"Yes, I will, of course."

She stood for a moment on the other side of the fence, apparently unsure what else to say. Then, to amuse her, he bowed gracefully from the waist. She curtsied in return, and with a great show of laughter blew a kiss to him and ran off. August smiled and went back to sit on the oil drum. Better than yesterday, he told himself, though not as good as he would feel tomorrow.

Seen dispassionately from the outside, Estelle mused, Henry and Amos were precisely the correct men, and they had taken them to the correct restaurant, and this was a perfectly correct evening. At one point in her life, she knew, she would have reveled in a night like this one. The restaurant, a club restaurant where the Heights apparently had a limitless credit arrangement, was small and intimate. It overlooked a golf links, and the furnishings, thick and heavy, with brocaded curtains hanging stolidly from massive curtain rods, struck exactly the right note. The waiters seemed to be old friends, and they called Amos and Henry *Mr. Heights*, each one addressed solemnly, with due reverence. The entire evening felt a little like a performance, but it was a friendly, somewhat lavish performance, and Estelle felt certain that it had turned many girls' heads to imagine themselves part of the Heights' fortune and sumptuous lives.

Amos, however, required watching. He frequently slipped his flask out of his coat pocket and applied a thin stream of whiskey to his glass. It was not that he couldn't drink—he ordered horses' necks for them all—but that he couldn't drink enough in front of the waiters to satisfy himself. His mischievousness, from what Estelle could discern, bordered on something darker, something he had either to encourage or stamp down in his spirit. He was a puzzle and a hazard, and Estelle felt nervous in his company.

Henry, on the other hand, struck Estelle as softer and more an obvious heir to the family's wealth and position. He spoke respectfully to the waiters who moved demurely around the room, and he did not attempt to register his authority in any low manner. He was handsome, too, although she imagined his looks would not fare well in old age. He might go to fat, or to a deskbound heaviness that would not be attractive. It was difficult to say.

A greater revelation was Collie: how light and gay she could be when called upon to play her part. That was a new aspect of her character, or at least a recently enhanced element. She looked beautiful in the room; the bright crystal, the red-rimmed plates, seemed to pick up her color and improve it. She fit perfectly in this room, in this life, actually, and Estelle felt certain Henry saw it. In fact, the only person who did not see it plainly was Collie herself, and that added to her charm.

"I'm tired of the Germans," Amos said after the waiter had delivered their entrees. "I'm tired of thinking about them. They're a nuisance. I don't mind fighting them, really, but I simply want them to go away."

"Go away how?" Henry asked.

"Oh, I don't know. Puff, disappear," Amos said, his drink making his tongue lazy, Estelle heard. "I heard about those swastikas appearing above the camp, you know? There are people here in sympathy with them. . . ."

"You're off your head now," Henry said, turning his attention away from his brother. "Let's not talk about the war or about the Germans. I want to hear about your experiences at Smith. That's where you two met?"

"Yes," Collie said, picking up her knife and fork, "as freshmen. We became friends almost at once."

"It was at once," Estelle agreed. "Then we had several courses together. Remember Professor Stevens?"

"Professor Stevens," Collie lowered her voice when she pronounced the last part of his name. "He had a deep, bass voice that sounded like thunder. He taught classical literature, and he took himself very seriously."

"But he was a good teacher for all of that," Estelle said.

"You always thought so. I wasn't quite as taken by him."

"I don't know why a woman needs college anyway," Amos said, his fork running furrows through a pad of mashed potatoes. "My mother never went to college. Neither did my father, for that matter."

"Amos resents the fact that I attended college," Henry said, "and so he has to run it down as soon as the topic comes up. Don't take it personally."

"I was too busy fighting in the war," Amos said. "College is a luxury not all of us can afford."

"It certainly is," Estelle said, tasting a piece of her cod fillet. "I won't argue that at all. But that's not to say there isn't a benefit to it."

Their primary waiter, a short, dour man with a head of sparse gray hair, came to inquire about their meal. Henry thanked him and said it was excellent. The waiter backed away.

"I believe in forests," Amos said, slipping his flask out and tilting it into his glass. He glanced around to see if anyone would join him. When no one took him up on his offer, he slipped the flask back in his pocket. "I believe in pulp. In land. I never cared for school. Hated it, in fact. What's the good of a bunch of musty old books?"

"You only prove your ignorance by asking that," Henry said, then deliberately turned away from his brother. "Anyway, I'm glad you had a good experience. You left after two years?"

"Yes," Collie said. "Mother was ill, and the war was everywhere. . . ."

"It was difficult to rationalize staying in college when the war—" Estelle said, but Amos cut her off.

"It wasn't hard for my brother," he said.

Now, Estelle saw, Amos truly was drunk. His head moved in jerky, twitchy increments, like a windup dog feeling the inevitable pull of its spring. How unfortunate, Estelle reflected. Amos might have been an attractive man if not for the loose, primitive aspect of his personality. She watched his last comment sink in with his brother, Henry. Apparently Henry had heard it before, because he simply continued eating, effectively ignoring the remark.

"We'll drive you back to camp," Amos said when they had completed their meal and took coffee on the outside patio overlooking the eighteenth green. "It's a beautiful night for it."

"It's a lovely night," Collie agreed, "but we don't mean to trouble you. We can take the train. It drops us at our door."

"Don't be absurd," Amos said. "What kind of escorts would we be if we let you take a train? Is that the type you take us for?"

Estelle felt a tingle of apprehension. Amos looked to be in no shape to drive, and besides, she didn't trust him to be a gentleman. She tried to catch Collie's eye, but in the dimness it was difficult. Amos signed the bill and stood shortly afterward. He led them to the Oldsmobile that was parked beside the pro shop. He held the door open for her and Estelle climbed inside. Collie slipped in behind her. The two men sat on the left side, Amos at the wheel.

They had not left the country club grounds before Amos reached across and put his hand on her knee. Estelle moved it away, but it returned immediately, this time with more force. She moved her knee from under his hand, and he did nothing for a moment. He kept his eyes straight ahead, his hands returned to the steering wheel. Then, after taking a right turn, he reached over and tried to work his hand up under her skirt.

"Stop it, please," Estelle said.

Amos looked over and grinned.

"Stop what?" he said.

"You know very well what," Estelle said. "Stop it."

"Amos . . . ," Henry said.

"Just being a little playful," Amos said, driving with his palm on the wheel, his free hand lurking like a patient spider on the seat between them. "We're allowed to be a little playful, you know. This isn't supposed to be a funeral."

He slipped his hand under her skirt and ran it up to her knee. Estelle slapped at his arm, but it was impossible to avoid him. He kept the accelerator pressed down, so she had that worry, too. She felt Collie reach over the seatback and try to restrain Amos's arm, but it was no use.

"Two on one," Amos said, "that isn't fair. Of course if that's how you like it . . ."

"Cut it out, Amos," Henry said. "I apologize for my brother."

"And I apologize for *my* brother," Amos said, and lifted his hand and raked it across Estelle's breasts. He laughed when she squirmed away. "Try to be a little friendly."

"Pull over and let us out," Collie said, her voice commanding. "Do it now."

"Like fuck I will," Amos said. "A pair of college twats."

Collie slapped him. Estelle cringed against the side door. Amos swung his hand back and fought off Collie. Henry suddenly jerked forward, grabbed the keys from the ignition and turned the car off. The engine made a tight whining sound. For a moment the car simply glided on the flat, dirt road. Estelle was conscious of the trees floating by, the headlights gone.

Then Amos reached under his seat and pulled out a revolver.

"Get out," he said when the car stopped.

He waved the gun at them all. He nearly tripped as he climbed out himself. He pulled his flask from his pocket and drank from it.

"Give me back the keys," he said to Henry when he lowered the flask.

Estelle felt cold suddenly and dead in her stomach. Collie moved closer and linked her arm with Estelle's. Estelle wondered if they could somehow run away, hide in the forest, do anything to save themselves. Henry was their only hope, and he did not seem a match for Amos.

"I'll run them back to Stark," Henry said. "You start walking toward Berlin. I'll pick you up on the return trip."

"Fuck you, too," Amos said.

"You're drunk," Henry said.

Amos fired the revolver in the air. The sound shocked Estelle. Its echo seemed to fill the woods on either side of them.

"Take off your clothes," Amos said. "Take them off now."

Henry hit his brother. Not with his fist, Estelle saw, but with something like a tire iron. It was a quick, deadly strike, and Amos went down without a struggle. He made a gurgling sound as he lay on the ground. Henry walked over and removed the revolver from his brother's hand.

"I'm sorry," he said, but whether he meant his apology for their ears or as a statement to his brother, Estelle couldn't say. "Terribly sorry."

"Take us back," Collie said. "Leave him here."

"I'll put him in the backseat and you two can ride up with me. He won't be any more trouble, I promise."

"No, leave him here," Collie said a second time.

Estelle watched Henry regard her friend, then he nodded. He put the revolver under the driver's seat and pulled Amos off the road. He left him in the weeds. Amos made no additional noise; Henry, Estelle noted, did not check to see if he had killed his brother. He acted, almost, as though Amos was beyond killing. It was extremely peculiar.

"Climb in," he said. "Let's go before he wakes up."

They both climbed in front. Collie sat next to Henry. Estelle maintained her place by the passenger door. Not until the car had moved away from the spot where Amos remained did Estelle allow herself to breathe freely.

"What did you hit him with?" Estelle asked after they had driven for a time. "He went down like he was shot."

"It was a shillelagh. My father collects walking sticks. He must have left it in the car."

"Thank goodness for that," Estelle said.

"He's not really like that," Henry said. "Not really. It's the drink."

"Then he did a good imitation," Collie said. "Because he certainly seemed authentic."

"He was better before the war."

"Yes," Collie said, "weren't we all?"

Chapter Eleven

Collie heard the piano across the prison yard. It came in fits and
starts, and it had played for some time at the edge of her consciousness before she tuned into it and recognized its presence. The
camp felt empty and hollow; the men had gone off to cut wood, and
her father and Lieutenant Peters had left to attend a policy seminar
in Boston for the day. Estelle had gone to Berlin with Amy and Marie
after school had let out. They had plans to see a movie. Collie knew
Estelle had deliberately given her some time alone to catch up on
work. Estelle was faultlessly considerate that way.

The music distracted her. She had worked briskly through past
inventories and a mound of requisition sheets, and had made a
dozen calls to suppliers to dicker about prices or check on delivery
dates. A typical day's work. And now, in the quiet afternoon, she felt
hazy and sleepy, and the piano, when it ran in full passages as if
someone remembered what the keys might do, made her moody
and happy at the same time. When the music disappeared, as it did
frequently, she found she missed it. When it returned, she put down
her desk work and listened. She understood enough about the piano
to recognize fluency in the pianist. She allowed the music to push
her to her feet so that she could make a cup of tea. She went to the
window and listened as the kettle boiled. When she had her tea, she
walked toward the refectory, where the piano waited.

It was August, of course. She had known that obliquely; she had
not permitted her mind to wander there. He sat in front of the
spinet, his elbows at right angles to his body, his hair long and blond
in the afternoon light. Cooking smells came from the kitchen where

Red, she knew, worked to prepare the evening meal. She realized as she entered that August had been placed on the cooking detail. He wore a white apron over his prison uniform and had obviously taken a break at the piano while the meal preparation got on without him for the time being.

"It is you," she said in German, stepping into the refectory. "I heard you practicing. Are you playing it by memory?"

He turned. His handsomeness arrested her.

"Yes," he said, smiling and standing. "Bach."

"I'm glad to find you up and around. Marie was the last to see you."

"So that's her name. I'd forgotten, or perhaps I never knew. Yes, we had another moment together. She has a wonderful spirit."

"Yes, she's delightful, but please don't let me stop you. Sit. I only looked in because the music made me curious."

"I think I'm finished for now. I've lost my way in the piece. And I am wanted in the kitchen."

"How do you feel? You look stronger."

"I'm a cook, as you see," he said, and spread his arms to indicate his apron. "A potato peeler. I'll be put back on a cutting crew soon, but the infirmary doctor wants me to wait a few more days."

"I'm sure that's for the best."

He remained standing. She sipped her tea. The room possessed an afternoon feeling. Sunlight passed through the windows and climbed over the tables. It reminded Collie of summer camp, or a shore house she once visited on the sands of Asbury Park, New Jersey, where the afternoon proved a time to be still and quiet while the day swirled on toward evening and rest. She took more of her tea to have something to do.

Then for a moment everything stopped except their eyes. She could barely swallow her mouthful of tea. Everything she had wondered about him, everything she had felt, suddenly existed between them. She could no longer deny any of it; she knew he understood, and he did not move but let his eyes rest on hers. The war meant nothing for the instant, and the clamor of pots and pans, the whine of a screen door, the scent of a cigarette and a match light, served only to underline their attraction to each other. She did not move and neither did he, but she felt as if she were a plant and she bent toward him as toward the sun.

"Is it too much to hope for?" he asked.

She shook her head. He stared a moment longer, then nodded as if he confirmed something in his mind, and then he spoke a line from the poem they had shared.

"The world becomes more beautiful with each day," he said.

"One doesn't know what may yet happen," she answered.

"Now everything, everything must change."

He nodded. She felt her cheeks burning. She sensed his eyes on hers and her heart could not catch itself. This was the man she wanted, she realized. It was no use to pretend otherwise. Before either of them spoke again, a voice began calling for August. The voice sounded weary and impatient. August smiled and held out his apron to prove his powerlessness. She smiled in return and nodded to let him go. With a sigh he pushed into the kitchen, his voice calling to Red that he had returned from break. She left the way she had come but stopped for a time in the sun to finish her tea.

Estelle recognized the handwriting as soon as Mrs. Hammond handed her the letter. She forced herself to take the letter casually, thanking Mrs. Hammond and commenting about the fine afternoon. Yes, she said to Mrs. Hammond, the motion picture had been wonderful. In fact, Marie had insisted they stay for the second picture, *Here Come the Waves*, starring Bing Crosby. It was better than the first, *Henry Aldrich, Boy Scout*, so all in all the afternoon had been a success. Estelle marveled at her coolness in conversation with Mrs. Hammond, while all the while her hand burned with the letter. She yearned to tear open the letter and run upstairs, but she forced herself to slide it into the pocket of her skirt and converse amicably with Mrs. Hammond. Mrs. Hammond promised evening tea and sandwiches if she, Estelle, had enough room left over from eating all the popcorn and candy that went with the movies.

She climbed the stairs and found Collie had left a note to join her at the sitting rock. She said she had important news. Estelle paused, wondering if she should take a few moments to read Mr. Kamal's letter. She pulled it out of her skirt pocket and felt its thickness. Yes, he had written a long letter. She decided she did not want to rush through it. She did not want to squander his voice or his thoughts. She grabbed a jacket instead and hurried out to meet Collie.

The late afternoon had turned to early evening. A kingfisher hunted at the edge of the river, lacing its way from tree to tree as if it meant to keep company with her. It felt good to be outdoors. The river sent up an embracing chill that seemed to spring free from the heat of the day. Crickets scattered as she walked. The mountains caught the angle of the falling sunlight and turned bronze; the phenomenon reminded her of the alpenglow she had encountered in the Alps. Legend held that the mountains drew the light inside and stored it for the following morning. Light ran like sugar into the peaks.

She found Collie perched on her meditation rock, watching the river. Estelle deliberately scuffed her foot to warn of her approach. Collie looked up and smiled. Estelle felt a moment of great tenderness toward her friend. When she reached her, she leaned down and hugged her. To her surprise, Collie hugged her in return with great force.

"Is it possible to love someone so easily?" Collie asked. "Am I simply being foolish?"

"What happened today?" Estelle asked, taking a place beside her friend. "Did you see August?"

"Yes, he was playing the piano in the refectory. I knew it must be him. We shared a moment together. . . ."

"Did you kiss him?" Estelle asked, and grabbed her friend's forearm.

"No, I'm not that brave. But we recited poetry to each other. And our eyes . . . I could barely breathe, Estelle. I know I can be silly about these things. I have a romantic bent, I suppose . . . at least I've always felt that I am a bit too easily excited by poetry and music. . . ."

"I'm sure he felt the same."

"I think he did," Collie said, astonished as she said it. "I'm fairly certain of it."

"I'm sure he did. It's as good as a declaration."

"I'm the only woman he sees, really. He might be susceptible in his condition."

"You don't give yourself enough credit, Collie. You're beautiful and intelligent and would do any man credit. Is he working in the kitchen now?"

"Until he's completely mended," Collie said. "He looks better than he did, but he's still recovering. Estelle, he's a prisoner! What hope do we have? He can't leave the grounds without a guard. And we can hardly approach each other with several hundred men watching us. I would never want to put my father in an awkward position. Really, I think it's a crazy idea."

"The heart wants its way. You know that."

Estelle drew out Mr. Kamal's letter. She handed it to Collie.

"He wrote?" Collie asked, examining the letter.

"I haven't read it yet. I can't bring myself to open it."

"Would you like me to open it?"

"No, please. I need to sit alone and read it. If I had half a brain, I'd throw it in the river and forget about it."

"Here," Collie said, and jumped to the edge of the river and held the letter over it.

Estelle jumped after her, and Collie began to laugh. Estelle took the letter back and returned it to her skirt pocket.

"How absurd we are!" Collie said.

"Let's go back. Mrs. Hammond has promised me a sandwich. And I have to tell you all about the movies we saw. Marie insists."

"Did you have a good day?"

"I had a lovely day."

Estelle hooked her arm through her friend's as they began to walk. The kingfisher had departed and the alpenglow had changed to a dull, wan light. Evening rested on the peaks like a bird waiting to come to the feeder.

"If the war would end," Collie said, "we might have a chance. But until it does, it's hopeless."

"Yes, a great deal will change when the war ends. The world will be different. Not entirely, of course, but it will be changed. Can you ask your father what will happen to the prisoners at the end of the war?"

"I doubt he knows for certain. They will have to be repatriated eventually. August heard a rumor that the men will be sent to England. They will be put to work as prisoners again."

"Germany will be destroyed."

"Still, they will have to go back. Opinion would not stand to let them stay here."

"So you have fallen in love with a man who will be taken from you?"

"Yes, that's why it's ridiculous to let my heart go in that direction."

Estelle squeezed her friend's arm with her elbow.

"It's funny, you know," she said, "if I had made this trip a year ago I would have told you to take hold of your heart and protect it. But now, after meeting Mr. Kamal, I know it's not as easy as it sounds.

It's far more complicated, isn't it? At the same time, it's far easier. Simpler. What else should we do but follow our hearts?"

"Will you follow yours, Estelle?"

"I'm not sure it's a choice any longer. I'm afraid I'm lost."

"And society will never approve."

"No, not really. We can pretend people will be generous in spirit and accept these differences, but not in Ashtabula, Ohio, I'm afraid."

"Could you return to India with him?"

"He would never ask. Besides, he likes America. He is growing rich here, at least by his former standards. His business is quite successful. His family in India counts on his resources."

"My mother used to say that time is the oil of life. She said that patience is the greatest tool. Most things resolve themselves if you leave them alone."

"I wish I could believe that."

"The war will end someday, Estelle, and then people may look at Mr. Kamal differently. Not everyone, of course, but the people who count in your life. What feels impossible now may seem prosaic later on. You never know."

"I don't have your confidence, Collie. Prejudice is a sharp, angry thing. Intolerance. Mr. Kamal tells stories that would wrench your heart. In the final analysis, your chances with August are greater than mine with Mr. Kamal. And I am not entirely sure of my own heart as you are sure of yours. It is my own grain of prejudice, you see, that poisons me. I don't like that about myself. But it's there. . . . I see him as different, but he is just a man like any other man."

"And your parents would object. . . ."

"I would be ostracized from everything I know. It's true, believe me. No one would mean to do it, not in their conscious minds, but they would think twice about inviting me to a party, or a wedding, or any social occasion if it meant also inviting Mr. Kamal. Then in time they would persuade themselves it was out of kindness toward me . . . because they would not want to make me feel awkward. You know how these things go, Collie. Little by little I would be on my own island with only Mr. Kamal for company. And if we had children . . ."

"I get your point. But I will always be your friend, Estelle. I promise that."

"Yes, I know you would. I've always known that about you. Now here we are, and if you don't mind I am going to go up to the room and read Mr. Kamal's letter. You know, I think it's time I stopped calling him Mr. Kamal, don't you? He has invited me to use his first name, and I do sometimes, but with others . . . it's easier to use Mr. Kamal."

"What is his first name?"

"His full name is Neem Karoli Kamal. His mother calls him Neem."

"That's beautiful."

"It reminds me of rainfall. I don't know why, but it does. A soft rain on a spring morning."

"Go read your letter. I'll tell Mrs. Hammond you are hungry. Now, go. I'll build a moat around you."

Estelle hugged her friend again. Then she ran up the porch stairs and went straight to their room, her hand against the letter to keep it from sliding out by accident.

The moon rose above the Devil's Slide. August sat on the porch of the refectory and watched it climb above the last brow of pines. A summer moon. He fanned the apron to bring air under his clothes. The kitchen had been mercilessly hot all afternoon and evening, and one of the men, Simon, had become light-headed and had to be sent to his barracks to rest. The cutting crews talked of swimming in the many woodland creeks when they came back for mealtime, but that was not permitted for the cooking detail. August had worked straight through, first peeling potatoes, then carrying service ware to the tables, and finally washing an avalanche of dishes. His hands felt scarred and raw, and the front of his apron pushed its sodden weight against him. A funny thing, he thought, to spend the war washing dishes in a military prison somewhere in the United States. Nevertheless, he felt grateful for the work and to be alive to see the moon climb into the sky. He hoped his brother and his parents watched the same moon. He prayed they still lived and that they had not given up hope.

He started to rise to his feet when Red came out for a cigarette, but Red grabbed him by the shoulder and kept him where he sat. Red pulled an upside-down bucket close to August and handed him a beer. The beer sweated with glistening rivers of ice; the label had slipped away from the brown bottle.

"Lousy beer," Red said, his fingers reaching into his pockets for a cigarette. "But lousy beer is better than no beer. Skoal."

August tilted the tip of the bottle toward Red, then took a deep drink.

The beer tasted watery.

"Not as good as ours," August said.

"Not close. Pig piss. What I wouldn't give for a few Bavarian lagers."

"It's a pretty moon just the same."

"Yes, very pretty."

Red lighted his cigarette. In the flash of the match, August saw his profile. He appeared older in the dim light, as if the man beside him was a faded copy of the chef who ruled the kitchen.

"I'm not sure how many of these I would have to drink to feel drunk," Red said, alternating between sips and puffs from his cigarette. "They are weak. Hopelessly weak."

"They have different tastes, I suppose."

"Yes, but there are plenty of Germans in this country. You would think they could teach the Americans how to brew a proper beer."

"We only know this one place."

"True," Red said, apparently giving up on his condemnation of American beer. He blew a white funnel of smoke into the air. A few June bugs rattled the light over the back door. For a time neither of them spoke, and August concentrated on the coolness finally touching his skin.

"How is your Fräulein?" Red asked. "Have you seen her?"

"Earlier today. At break time."

"She came to see you?"

"She heard the piano."

"Ah! Music is the cheese for your little trap!"

"It's not a trap."

Red laughed, then took a large drink of beer. He rolled the empty bottle into a corner, then went inside and brought out two more beers. August finished his and rolled it after Red's. The bottles clinked. Red lighted another cigarette as he sat.

"Women . . . ," he said, then lost his thought or his tongue.

"What about them?"

"What else do we have but women? That's the great misery of war. What sane man puts himself in a barracks full of men miles away from available women? We must like it, because we continue to do it. War turns us into bachelors whether we like it or not. It makes no sense."

"Did you ever marry, Red?"

"I did, but she didn't!" he answered, and then gave a loud, hearty laugh. August guessed he had employed that remark many times.

"My Fräulein is the commandant's daughter."

"So? Everyone is someone's daughter or son. You can't let that get in the way."

"I can't approach her."

"But you already have, don't you see? The heart always finds a path. It's like water . . . it keeps seeking its own level. You two will not be able to stay away from each other. Trust me."

"They'll send us back afterward."

Red shrugged.

"Who knows what will happen?" he said. "We all may be dead tomorrow. Hasn't the war taught you that much at least? Enjoy each other. If it doesn't work, *pffft*. It's not the end of the world. But if you don't take her seriously, you may regret it. Do what you can and see where it takes you."

"Thank you."

"Nothing to thank me for. It's nature, that's all. All the wars in the world won't prevent men and women from finding each other. You watch. Your Fräulein will find a way. She has more freedom than you. And the war is ending. You can feel it, can't you?"

"It's not finished yet."

"No, not for a time yet, but the end is inevitable. Hitler should have stopped a long time ago and sued for peace. He should have taken his gains when he had them."

"That's not his personality."

"No, of course not. He's the great Napoléon of our age. He had bad counsel around him. That proved to be his Achilles' heel. They made him believe he was invincible, that the German people would sacrifice anything for him. But there is a limit to what people can endure. His counselors should have warned him."

"What waits for you at home, Red?"

"More kitchens," he said, flicking his final cigarette away. He drank off his beer. "For me, the world is a kitchen. For you, maybe it is that Fräulein's sweet arms. Now come on, let's finish. I'm tired and I want to go to bed."

❧ PART TWO ❧

⇥ *Chapter Twelve* ⇤

Estelle waved for as long as she could still see the station. Twice she watched Marie jump into the air, her lovely young face covered with tears. Then Estelle saw Amy gather her little sister into her arms. The poor child, Estelle thought. Marie had been inconsolable at the thought of them all separating. She had asked repeatedly why Estelle needed to return to Ashtabula, and it did no good to remind her that Estelle had always meant to visit, not change addresses permanently. To every reason put forward—time, money, missing her parents, her home life—Marie had countered with a cry from her heart. She wanted Estelle to stay, that was all. Estelle had never felt more admired by anyone in her life.

So she waved and she watched her three friends wave in return. The train moved up a slight grade and then turned gradually around a bend. Pine trees blocked her view of Percy Station at last. Her friends disappeared. She fell back into her seat and felt a wild mixture of emotions clawing in her chest.

She was going home. Back to her house in Ashtabula. Back to her parents. And, of course, back to Mr. Kamal.

Nothing had changed, she realized. Even now she carried his letter in her purse. How many times had she read it? Rocking slowly in the train, the pines clustered and rich in either direction, she drew out the letter and read its opening again. Besides giving the news of Ashtabula, the gossip among the merchants, a few mentions of the society page, it contained, buried in several lines, expressions of his feelings. She had showed those passages to Collie and Collie had concurred; they had been placed carefully in the letter to convey his feeling for her. He could not simply declare himself, and so he had hinted, and made references to earlier conversations, all of it expressing to her his deeper, truer feelings. He waited for her; he looked forward to resuming their afternoon teas; he had new plants to show her; he had thought of a concert they might attend. All innocent, all friendly, and all an invitation to step closer.

She had not replied. She had tried several times, coached in several attempts by Collie, but words failed. She did not want to encourage him; she did not want to encourage herself. The letter remained like a burning ember wherever she carried it. She did not dare expose it to common air for fear it would explode into fire.

With an act of will, she pulled down the window of her train car and dangled the letter out the window. She let the sheets go one at a time. She did not care what other passengers might think. The pages flung themselves rearward along the train, swirling back like memory or loss. She watched them go and told herself it was for the best.

Marie insisted on dancing. She had lingered at Mrs. Hammond's boardinghouse all afternoon after Estelle's departure, depressed and unhappy, and to buck up her spirits Collie had agreed to a single wish if Marie would simply smile. Amy had cautioned against it, but Marie had jumped on the offer and moved immediately to the radio in Collie's room and turned up the volume.

"It's too hot for that nonsense," Amy said. "People don't need to hear us tromping around up here like a herd of elephants."

"You promised!" Marie insisted.

"I didn't promise," Amy replied. "I hate to say it, Collie, but this is your ticket to punch. She'll dance your legs off."

"What else do we have to do today?" Marie asked. "We can't just sit around for the rest of our lives."

"You're the one who was moping all afternoon," Amy said.

THE MAJOR'S DAUGHTER   167

"I'll dance," Collie said, "but not forever . . . do you promise, Marie?"

Marie nodded and turned the music up louder. The windows stood wide open, but barely a touch of wind found them. It felt like rain coming. They had already watched the clouds forming, spotting shapes and animals in the thunderheads, but the rain refused to fall. Collie used a folded newspaper for a fan. The humidity clung to her and made her feel as though she wore a second skin.

"I'll be the boy," Marie said, standing in front of Collie with her arms open.

"It's too hot," Amy said, and fell back on the bed.

"You're a funny-looking boy," Collie said as she stepped into Marie's arms, "but I'll dance with you anyway."

Marie counted them off, then pushed Collie away and made her spin. Collie burst out laughing and stopped.

"What dance are we doing?" Collie asked.

"You have to follow, that's all."

"But shouldn't we have some idea of what we're trying to do?"

"You wouldn't ask that of a man, would you? That would be terribly rude. Now come on, you promised."

It felt ridiculous at first, but gradually Collie found the fun in it. She allowed herself to be pushed away, spun, then nearly strangled in a complicated hand exchange that Marie had learned somewhere. Amy laughed and clapped from the bed. On the second dance, they both kicked off their shoes as a dark, gusty wind began pushing against the house.

A crack of lightning suddenly sprang across the Devil's Slide and Amy let out a little whoop. Marie used the lightning as an excuse to dance faster. She began holding her finger up and wagging it, saying *hidey-hidey ho* over and over again, when suddenly she jerked Collie's arm hard and pulled her to the window.

"Look!" she said.

"What?" Collie asked.

Amy jumped up from the bed and crowded to the window with them.

It took only a moment for Collie to see August running through the rain with his shirt off and his trousers in his hand. The men wore their khaki undershorts, but nothing else. Obviously his cutting team had been at the river for a swim when the rain hit. The American guards trotted behind them, fully clothed, their rifles held loosely in their arms. The men laughed and shouted; Marie pulled the girls down lower in the window so they could watch without being observed. Collie thought she had never seen men so free and wild. This is what they are like, she realized, when there are no women around. It felt as though they watched a herd of deer, or a flock of birds, and Collie felt enormous attraction.

August carried a bouquet of wildflowers in his right hand. For an instant he disappeared under the eave of the roof, and Collie heard his heavy tread on the porch stairs. An instant later he had returned to running with his mates. They greeted his brief departure with hoots and laughter. One man ran close to him and ruffled his hair. The American guards laughed, too, and then their voices mixed and became jumbled with the squish of muddy steps and the clink of a canteen. At last they passed down the road far enough so that they could not look back and catch them watching from the window.

"Men are always laughing at a joke I don't understand," Amy said, sitting on the bed again. "I comprehend English well enough, but it's as if they speak a different language."

"I'm going to run to the porch and get the bouquet," Collie said.

She hurried down the stairs. The porch door stood open except for a screen, and Collie watched as water poured off the roof. It made a curtain, a prismatic sheen of dark light. She saw August's bare wet footprints on the porch boards; the footprints shimmered in contrast to the wood when a stroke of lightning touched the mountainside. She found the bouquet on the glider. He could not leave a note, naturally, but he had tied the bottom of the bouquet with strands of grass, so that it did not fall apart when she lifted it to her nose. Wild black-eyed Susans, tansy, Queen Anne's lace, a stalk of cornflower. She didn't know all their names. Flowers from her suitor, she told herself. She carried the flowers quickly upstairs, where Marie examined them for hidden meaning. She made Collie pluck off the petals of the black-eyed Susans and repeat the ageless questions *Love me? Love me not?* while the rain fell in hurried gusts and the smell of the summer became locked in her memory.

"My father would kill me if he knew an Austrian soldier had delivered flowers to me," Collie said. "I can't encourage him. I should speak to him and tell him to stop."

"Are you insane?" Marie asked, her voice riddled with disbelief. "It's the most romantic thing I've ever seen. He thought of you and he didn't mind showing all those other men that he wanted to bring you flowers! He's perfect!"

"He's German," Amy said.

"Austrian," Collie corrected, although she knew that wasn't the point.

"It's a dangerous game you're playing," Amy said, turning down the music. "What does my father always say? A falling knife has no handle. Be careful, Collie. You may reach for something and it might cut your hand."

"Oh, you're as old as a dinosaur already!" Marie said. "I swear, what kind of old wet blanket are you?"

Amy smiled, but the corners of her mouth remained tight. Collie met her eyes and nodded.

"Thank you for agreeing to see me again," Henry Heights said a week later from his seat in Mrs. Hammond's parlor, his hat in his hand. "I can't begin to apologize sufficiently for my brother and for our behavior the other night. It was unforgivable. My brother suffers from dipsomania. He cannot control himself when alcohol is present."

"I understand. You've made that point."

"He's promised to get treatment. This last incident brought that plainly to light. His condition worsened after his return from the war. This is all a family matter, and I'm sure it's tiresome to you, but he is not the man he was the other night. He's changed from the war."

Collie nodded, her gaze carefully assessing him. She granted that he had made a heartfelt apology. He had sent flowers twice, both times with accompanying notes asking to see her. He had also sent a note to Estelle, begging her forgiveness, but it had arrived too late. She had forwarded it to Ohio, and then Estelle had reported on the content. Collie still did not know what to make of the evening with Amos. It had been sordid and terrifying, certainly, but it had not been Henry's fault. She believed he was as appalled by his brother's behavior as he claimed to be.

He twirled his hat lightly in his hand. Collie heard Mrs. Hammond clank something in the kitchen, cleaning up after dinner. It was half past seven and dinner was over. Agnes occasionally passed through the room with a tray in her hand to set the breakfast table. Henry Heights fit his apology into the gaps when they were alone.

"I appreciate your good intention, Mr. Heights . . . ," she said, but he cut her off.

"Henry, please."

"All right, Henry then. I do appreciate your intention. I won't say all is forgotten, because I won't soon forget that evening, but I accept your apology. I can't speak for Estelle, but I don't suppose it matters. She won't be back here again. We could have brought legal action against your brother."

"Yes, I know."

"If my father had known what jeopardy you placed us in, he would have taken serious action."

"You didn't tell him?"

Collie shook her head. She still wasn't sure they had been correct to not inform her father or any authority. It seemed better at the time to put the entire evening out of their minds. Estelle refused to speak of it afterward.

"Give me another chance," he said, then stopped when Agnes swung through with a tray of silverware.

"A chance?"

"I have a feeling that we could get along very well," he said. "We could not have gotten off to a more horrible beginning, I grant you, but please don't hold that against me forever. The Woodcutters' Ball is in a month's time, and I was hoping you would accompany me. It's a gala evening . . . well, at least it was before the war. Now we've had to cut back, but it's the social event of the season in Berlin."

"I don't think so, Henry."

"Tell me, are you saying no because you have no interest in me, or because of my brother's abhorrent behavior?"

He appeared so vulnerable as he asked that she couldn't help but feel pity for him. And what did she really feel? It was true that her heart felt on loan to August, but he was a prisoner of war, a German, and it was unrealistic to place her hopes on such a thin string. Henry, on the other hand, came from a prominent family in New Hampshire. He was an American, college educated, attractive, and he seemed sincere in his repentance.

Before she could answer, Mrs. Hammond appeared. She said hello to Henry but took no time to hear his reply. She carried a sewing bag over one shoulder and a quilt against her chest. Collie knew Mrs. Hammond was headed out for a night of quilting and gossip at Mrs. Cutrer's. It was her regular Tuesday night, her one break in her demanding week.

"Almost forgot," Mrs. Hammond said at the door, "our little Marie is ill. Her mother called over this afternoon from their neighbor's house. They don't have a phone, you know."

"Is it serious?"

"Apparently it is. They thought it was the simple influenza, but it's taken a turn. It's hard to know how these things will go."

"But she'll get well?" Collie said, sitting up.

"I expect so, but the girl wanted to see you. She thinks the world of you, you know?"

"She's a dear. Henry, you'll have to excuse me. She'll think I've abandoned her."

"Give her my best, and tell her mother I'll do anything I can to help," Mrs. Hammond said.

"Thank you, Mrs. Hammond."

"We're all in God's hands," she said, and then walked off, the quilt like the soft prow of a ship.

"I'm sorry, but I have to go to her," Collie said. "May I think about your invitation? I'd like to sleep on it."

"Certainly," he said, rising. "And I hope your friend has a speedy recovery. Do you need a ride?"

"No, she lives close by, thank you."

He nodded and turned to go. She gave him credit for not dragging things out.

"Thank you for the flowers," she said as he opened the door.

"I'd always bring you flowers," he said, then he left.

Estelle dressed carefully, slipping into a peach-colored gown that suited her, she knew. It was not a new gown, but her mother had it cleaned and ready; Estelle slid it over her head, adjusted it past her hips and breasts, then turned and watched the fall of it as she moved. Yes, it worked. It had always worked, that was the point, and she understood her mother took pleasure in seeing her daughter "come to her senses." That had been Estelle's resolve, formed as the train left Stark and confirmed as she traveled closer to home: she was done resisting. She comprehended what her parents wanted from her, *of her*, and she endeavored to give it to them. She had not seen Mr. Kamal except briefly, and then only out of politeness. She had stopped by casually, ducking in to buy an arrangement of irises for her friend, Ginny Babcock, and she had braved it through with Mr. Kamal despite his pleading eyes. Her coldness had wounded him; it had wounded her as well, and on returning from the shop she had gone directly to bed, claiming a headache. She had cried until her eyes had become pale, sandy deserts. She had lost her taste for everything, and now the world seemed dull and flat and empty. She moved through her days, but she felt herself an imitation of what her true self might have been previously. In giving up Mr. Kamal, she had forfeited herself.

Nevertheless, she must put a brave face on things, she thought, turning again to see the dress in the mirror. Of course the meeting had been strained; he had wanted more from her, a greater indication of her interest, but she had retreated to a cold, lofty place in her consciousness, and she had treated him with an attitude bordering on condescension. He was a merchant, that was all. He had expressed his hope that she would visit again soon, and that he was eager to hear more about her experiences in New Hampshire. She smiled and accepted the bouquet of flowers. She promised nothing.

And now she had a date to a country-club dance with George Samuels. George, dear George, was not unlike the peach dress she modeled for herself in the mirror. He was tried-and-true. He came from the right stock, from the right schools, was determinedly heading in the right direction. Nobody found anything exotic about George, which, she confessed to herself, was a relief. It made her parents happy to see her dressing for a dinner dance with George Samuels, and it was not a deficit of character for parents to want the best for their daughter. Even his name, in its blandness, seemed a relief to her mother; several times Estelle had caught her mother emphasizing the correctness of his name when she mentioned her daughter's plans to friends on the phone. George and Estelle. George Samuels, of course, the boy left out of the war due to some form of hernia.

Estelle sat at the vanity in her room and applied the last of her makeup. She spritzed a tiny cloud of Chanel from her atomizer and ducked her head through it. The lighting proved flattering; she looked, she admitted, like a young woman going out with a man to a country-club dinner dance. Her mother's pair of small diamond studs glittered in her ears, and a triple string of cultured pearls dangled at her throat. If she could not feel the part, then she would have to act the part until feeling came. That was her plan.

Her mother entered as Estelle put a wrap around her shoulders. Mrs. Emhoff was a tall, graceful woman in her late forties, with a blond bubble of hair that had recently tilted toward gray, and a pale complexion that burned easily in the sun. She wore dramatic red lipstick that occasionally left a pink sheen on her teeth.

"Oh, you did go with the peach," her mother said, although why she should be surprised Estelle could not imagine. They had discussed it a thousand times.

"It's what we talked about, wasn't it, Mother?"

"Yes, of course. You look so lovely in it. And George just pulled in. Your father is answering the door."

"I'll be down in a moment."

"Let him wait a little," her mother said. "Men hate to wait, and that's why it's good for them."

"I wasn't aware we were playing a game."

"Always, dear, always. Now, yes, the pearls are just right. Spin and let me see you."

Estelle did as her mother requested. When she finished she watched her mother's happiness spread like something spilled and expanding on a kitchen floor. Her mother wore a dark gray at-home dress, and it was possible, Estelle thought, that she had selected it to provide contrast to her daughter's pastel outfit. It tired her to think such a thing, and she took her mother's hands in sympathy. It seemed unfair that she, Estelle, had such power over her mother's happiness.

"It's just George," she said, "and just the old country club."

"George is making his way, make no mistake. You look lovely, dear. You'll meet the Elvinsons at the dance? You'll make quite a smart set."

"A dream come true," Estelle could not prevent herself from saying.

"What is it that you're looking for, dear?" her mother asked, bending to flounce the hem of her daughter's dress a little. "Why this fatigued-with-the-world demeanor? It's very tiring and not particularly attractive. You're a lucky girl to be going out to a dance while a war . . ."

"I know, Mother. I'm sorry. I promise to behave."

"George is a perfectly nice young man, with a good future in front of him. You grew up with him, Estelle. His parents are friends."

"You're right, Mom. I'm sorry."

"Now go down and save the poor young man from your father. He'll probably be in a full sweat by now."

Estelle hugged her mother. She didn't mean to be cross and difficult. If anything, she should be grateful to her mother, she knew, but her mind felt like a scramble of warring emotions. She had been cruel to Mr. Kamal! Yes, cruel. And now she wanted to be cruel to her mother, and to George, the ox of a man who wanted nothing more than to be her escort for an evening, and maybe for life. Estelle knew herself to be a difficult daughter, and as she went down the stairs she scolded herself that she would be better, would improve, and that George, her bovine boyfriend, would be the first step in her self-reclamation.

She found them in the living room drinking highballs. They had not bothered to sit but stood next to the portable bar, their glasses like bronze candles in their hands. George wore a dinner jacket over a white shirt with a crisp black bow beneath his chin. He had put on weight since college and his face looked fleshy and supple, a camel's neck and face, with eyelids that fell over his eyes and achieved a sleepy, bemused expression. He seemed always to be tilting his head backward, as if his vision needed the flat expanse of his cheeks to see things properly.

"There she is," her father said. "Would you like to join us, dear?"

"A short one, please. Hello, George."

"You look smashing," George said.

George borrowed English phrases and made them part of his vernacular; she had forgotten that about him until her recent re-acquaintance with him. His immersion into business had only made it worse. She imagined he thought it made him more refined, or continental, or merely different.

"Thank you, George. You look very handsome."

"Is your mother coming down?" her father asked, shaking out a highball.

"Right here!" her mother said, whisking into the room. "Hello, George. You're a picture!"

"Thank you, Mrs. Emhoff."

"Who's playing tonight?" her father asked.

"The Jefferson City Two Tones," George said, his voice a tad watery. "They've got a smashing brass section."

"Do they?" her father said. "I've never heard of them."

"Yes you have, dear," her mother said. "You've even danced to them, but you don't remember. They have that Puerto Rican trumpet player who everyone admires."

"You can't beat Puerto Ricans on horns," George said. "You know the band, don't you, Estelle?"

"Yes, sure. Didn't they play last New Year's?"

"No, that was the Walker Brothers," said George.

He passed along a highball to Estelle's mother, then raised his glass.

"Here's how," he said.

"It's so nice to see you again, George," her mother said. "And doing so well."

"It's a dog-eat-dog world, but it turns out I'm a bit of a dog myself."

That brought a laugh. Estelle smiled and drank. She decided she would need several drinks to make it through the night. She looked at the faces surrounding her. This was the path she was meant to take. Her mother stood between the two men on one side of the circle, directly across from where Estelle stood. Boy-girl, boy-girl, like a game on a children's playground. For an instant she tried to imagine Mr. Kamal standing here. He would not drink, for one thing, and he would wear his turban and pass his doleful eyes over everything. Like a crow trooping among doves. Wasn't that what Shakespeare said? She drained her glass and passed it to her father.

"Knock me again, please," she said.

"Steady on, old girl," George said, smiling.

⇥ *Chapter Thirteen* ⇤

In the center of his barracks August stood on the outside of the circle of men, listening to the stories told by the newcomers. They were all hungry for news of the war, news from *their* side, not the versions given by the American press, and now, almost by magic, two newcomers had arrived from Normandy. They were young men, nearly identical, with red cheeks and golden hair, both with dented chins as if screws had been inserted into their jawlines to secure something deeper in their skulls. Their arrival had caused a stir; even the American guards had been interested in their reports, because they brought firsthand knowledge of the fighting. They had been captured near Coutances in France. It was a hellish battle, on that everyone agreed, but here were two young German soldiers, fresh from the Fatherland, their fates bringing them to this tiny camp thousands of miles away. So miraculous was their arrival that some of the men had believed them to be infiltrators. If they were, August decided, then they possessed theatrical skills beyond anyone's comprehension.

"We killed over a thousand Americans and Allies, and they gained a mere two hundred meters of ground. They paid with blood, believe me," the youngest of the pair said. "Our tanks are better than theirs."

"They outnumber us, though, isn't that true?" a voice from the ring of men asked.

"Yes," the older of the pair said. "Like ants on a wedding cake."

"The British Second Army tried to forge into the Cotentin Peninsula, but we pushed them back," the younger said. "You would be proud of our forces. They are fighting like demons."

"We never hear that from our guards," Liam said.

He was a short, blunt man who had moved onto August's cutting team the week before.

"What of Germany itself?" August asked. "What news do you have of our countrymen?"

"They are Germans. They stand united," the older boy said.

"Yes, but are there supplies and food?" Gerhard, August's friend, asked.

"Not as much as is needed . . . and medicine is in short supply. Very short supply. But we soldier on. You will not hear protests."

August studied the speaker. He could not determine if the young soldier, the one who had finished speaking, told the truth. Or, rather, he could not say if the young soldier merely repeated things he had been told or heard.

He met Gerhard's eye and motioned with his chin that he intended to step outside. Gerhard nodded and went with him.

"What do you make of those two?" Gerhard asked when they had moved a safe distance from the barracks. Gerhard lighted a cigarette. Night had come at last, and a soft rain fell and made tiny explosions on the camp's metal roofs. It smelled wonderful and fresh and August thought of his parents' kitchen garden for an instant, the earthy scent of newly turned soil and manure.

"They believe what they're saying, but they don't know any more than we do," August said.

"That's how I took it. But I believe them about the fighting. Even the Americans say it's bloody."

"We're lucky to be out of it, really," Gerhard said, blowing smoke into the air. "We're not supposed to say that, of course."

"I wonder if my brother is in the middle of it," August said. "He was too young when I left, but he's at least as old as those two."

"They're babies."

"We were babies once."

"I don't think Germany can hold out forever, and Hitler is too prideful to strike a peace agreement. He'll lead us off a cliff, I'm certain."

"The time to sue for peace may already be gone. The Allies will want revenge. It's only human nature."

Gerhard shrugged. At that moment August spied a familiar shape coming through the guarded gate. Collie ran past the guards and jangled a key, obviously coming to open something in the administration building. August put his hand on his friend's shoulder and turned him slightly. Gerhard strained to see, then nodded. August left him and went to see what had brought Collie to the camp so late in the evening.

A guard stepped forward and challenged him.

"What do you want?" the guard asked.

Then the guard, a middle-aged man named Howard, recognized August, because he lowered his rifle.

"It's you," the guard said. "I still can't let you approach the gate."

"I wanted to speak to the commandant's daughter."

"Who doesn't?" Howard asked with a quiet leer. "She's in to use the phone."

"Is something wrong?"

"Well, if it is, she didn't tell me."

"We've talked sometimes," August tried to explain.

"Yes, and I'm Kaiser Wilhelm. Go back to your barracks. I don't want to put you on report."

August started to turn, but Collie reappeared on the porch. August could not see her well, but she seemed in distress. Her usual calm had been eradicated, and she paced on the small porch, obviously impatient for something.

"Collie?" he called. "It's August Wahrlich."

She came to the edge of the porch and peered into the darkness.

"Let him pass," she said quietly to the guard. "I know him."

"It's against regulation, miss. At this time of night . . ."

"He may be of help to me. Now, please, do as I say. I won't keep him more than a minute."

The guard moved off to resume his usual position near the center gate. August stepped quickly to the small porch where Collie waited.

"What is it?" he asked. "You look upset."

To his astonishment, she walked into his arms. He heard the loud wracks of sobs passing through her body. He wondered for a moment if something had happened to her father. At the same moment, the sensation of having a woman in his arms, even with such sadness attached to it, felt overwhelming. It had been years since he had experienced such comfort. He couldn't help it; he kissed her hair and tightened his arms around her. In time her crying slowed and she pushed away, bringing a handkerchief out of her pocket to dab at her eyes.

"I'm not usually like this," she said, "but Marie . . . the young girl. You know her, don't you? We talked about her."

"Yes, the one I danced with?"

Collie nodded.

"What is it? Is she all right?"

"She's very ill and they're not sure she will make it through the night. The family doesn't have a phone, so I came here to use the office phone, but now the doctor is out delivering a baby. He is supposed to call and I'm to wait here, but I feel as though I'm about to explode. She's raving. Her fever is horrible."

"I'm sorry."

"The doctor is at least an hour away, and that's if he could leave this moment. The delivery could go into the small hours. It's a first birth, his wife said, and those are typically the slowest."

"We have a medic who could look at her," August said. "His name is Schmidt. Wilhelm Schmidt, and he's a good man."

"I've seen the name, but I didn't know he had a medical background."

"He was a doctor, or a medical student in Hungary. I don't know which. But he takes care of the men here. I could fetch him and ask if he would go see the little girl."

"Yes, please, would you do that? It can't hurt. I'm afraid she's going to die and we won't be able to do anything for her."

"I'll be back in a moment. Stay here and I'll bring him."

August hurried off. He hoped he had not promised too much. He found Schmidt in the middle of a chess match against another Hungarian. They sat on opposite bunks, cigarettes burning, a cloud of smoke obscuring the checkerboard propped on an empty bucket between them. The game appeared advanced; only a few pieces remained on the board.

"It sounds like the Spanish flu," Schmidt said when August finished describing the situation. "If it is, she'll be lucky to survive it. I've seen many cases."

"Will you come and look at her?"

"The doctor may not like such interference."

"I think it's critical."

August watched Schmidt weigh the information. He was a good, kind man, August knew, but he suffered in camp life. He was older, for one thing, and the work exhausted him. Apparently he felt some apprehension; if the girl died, August realized, then the fault might be laid at Schmidt's feet, and who knew where that might lead? But eventually Schmidt stood and ran a hand through his bushy gray hair. He stubbed out his cigarette in an old B&M bean can. He knelt with difficulty to retrieve a suitcase from under his bunk. He handed it to August.

"Where is the girl?" Schmidt asked.

"In a house nearby."

"Will they let us off grounds?"

"They must."

Schmidt stopped in the latrine for a moment, and when he emerged he had obviously washed his face and run a wet comb through his hair. He looked better, more groomed, and his demeanor had become crisper. August spotted the glimmer of what the man must have looked like before the war, before Africa and the dirt and heat. It heartened him to see it.

August led him to Collie and introduced him.

"Do you think you can help?" Collie asked.

"I can look. I make no promises," Schmidt said in German.

"She's very ill."

"We need to break the fever or she won't survive. I've seen this illness before."

August stood beside Schmidt as Collie went to speak with the guard. He heard Howard's reluctance; it was against protocol. August could not imagine what it required on Collie's part to persuade an American guard to permit two Germans to wander off from the prison at night. He heard her speaking emphatically, her voice slightly raised. She mentioned her father, who was apparently unavailable at the moment. That much he overheard.

In the end, August listened as they summoned a second guard, a young man named Jules, to accompany them to the girl's house. The young guard appeared nervous as a kite string. He stood with his hands roaming over his rifle as if he expected the Germans to make a break for the woods at any moment.

It rained a little as they walked to the white house at the base of the orchard. August realized he had not been off the camp at night in months, and then only to return from a job that had taken them far away. He looked up at the stars; rain obscured them, but the moon, a half-horn, rolled slowly through the passing clouds. When the wind blew, the trees rocked and sent down showers of water from their boughs. The ground underfoot felt sodden and slippery with summer grass.

"You can keep watch on the porch," Collie told the young guard. "I'll call out if they make an escape attempt."

Schmidt laughed. The young guard, August saw, seemed troubled but lacked the confidence to suggest anything else.

August followed Collie inside. A young woman met them. It looked to be an older sister to the little one he knew as a frequent passerby. The house, August realized, had become abnormally quiet.

"It's not good," the woman whispered.

"This is Amy," Collie said, to introduce the young woman. "Marie's sister. Marie is the sick girl."

Schmidt bowed slightly from the hips. August did the same.

"This man, Herr Schmidt, he is a medical man. A medic."

"Where is the doctor?"

"Dr. Shepherd is delivering a baby. I spoke to his wife. He will be here as soon as he can make it, but in the meantime I thought it wouldn't hurt to let Herr Schmidt take a look. He's familiar with Marie's condition."

August watched Amy study the old medic. Here, exactly here, the entire war resided, August understood. All the deaths, the combat, the blood pouring into the rivers of Europe, were represented by the look of mistrust that sugared the appraisal of the young women gazing at a German doctor. What hope did any of them have for peace if they could not even trust one another in this providential moment? He watched as Collie squeezed Amy's hand and nodded. It was meant as reassurance. Amy took a breath and whispered that her mother was upstairs and that her father had gone out, unable to stand the agony of watching the illness advance. They suspected he had gone for the priest, but they didn't know for certain.

Amy led them upstairs. The temperature in the house seemed to rise the higher they went. It was a poor house, August thought, but clean. He had always wondered what the inside of an American home looked like, and now he knew. They were constructed of wood, unlike the homes in Austria, and they felt insubstantial as a result.

Marie's mother met them at the door to the sickroom. She looked vexed that Collie had not brought Dr. Shepherd.

"Where is he?" the mother asked, referring to the doctor.

"He's over near Littleton, delivering a baby," Collie said. "I'm sorry, but this kind man has agreed to take a look."

"He's a German!" the woman said violently.

"Yes, Mama," Amy said, "but he is a medical man."

"I won't let a German touch my daughter. I don't care what it brings."

"You're tired, Mama, and not thinking carefully," Amy said. "Dr. Shepherd will not get here until midmorning at the earliest. That's our guess. This man . . . Herr Schmidt . . . he has kindly offered to do what he can."

"I don't want Germans in my house," the mother said. "Get them out. Get them out now. I never agreed to this."

"It's for Marie," Collie said. "Think about Marie. Whatever can help her . . ."

Then Schmidt, to everyone's surprise, slowly reached into his vest pocket. Carefully, so as not to ruin it, he held out a photograph toward Amy's mother. August glimpsed it briefly; it was a portrait of a young girl.

"My daughter," he said in broken English, holding the picture so that the woman might examine it. "She died in the first weeks of the war . . . in bombardment. . . . Death has no friends."

August watched the mother deliberate. Eventually she nodded and stepped away to let them enter the room.

"Be done before my husband returns," she said, "or there will be hell to pay."

Estelle waited for George to come around and open her car door. The Duck Pond Country Club looked festive in the evening air. Through the windshield, she watched couples moving toward the front door, their calls and greetings merry and filled with promise. When George popped open her door, music met her. It came as a bright, happy sound, drifting out over the eighteenth hole of the golf course and filling everything with rhythm. She recognized the song as something by the Andrews Sisters, though she could not remember its precise name. She wished for a moment to have the intrepid Marie by her side, because Marie knew every song that tumbled out of the radio. How Marie would love the sparkle of the country club, the white pillars, the trimmed hedges, the glint of automobiles coming to discharge their passengers! Estelle made a mental note to write her and tell her all the details. Marie had already written twice, and Estelle, in her painful self-occupation, had been too blasé to answer back. She promised to change that tomorrow.

George held out his hand.

"The place is hopping!" he said, smiling. "Soldiers are coming back, and the young folks are taking over."

"It sure looks lively."

He tried to steal a kiss. Just like that. He leaned in, trapping her between the door and his arm, and he kissed her. It was all she could do not to pull away, so she stood rigidly and let him rub his lips against hers. Then he smiled.

"You look like you're taking medicine you don't like," he said.

"I hadn't expected to be kissed."

"Loosen up, Estelle. Tonight's about fun."

"Yes, of course," she said, and when he ducked in for a second kiss she forced herself to meet his lips squarely. His hand brushed discreetly over her hip and up toward her left breast. She broke off the kiss and pushed him gently away.

He held out his arm for her to take, and she did, glad to have fresh air after the staleness of the automobile. George, Eternal George. As children they had danced together at this club; they had escaped the summer heat in the pool, and, yes, she had kissed him plenty of times before. Several times as teenagers they had petted while lying in sand traps, or on the hills leading up to greens. He was within his rights to expect a kiss or two, but she wished she felt more in return. He was George, Eternal George, a solid, dependable wheelbarrow of a man. He squeezed her arm several times with his elbow as they approached the front door, like a rider, she thought, spurring on a horse to greater speed.

But the club did look wonderful, she admitted. The dance committee had brightened the entranceway with flowers and decorative pennants. Someone had dreamed up a nautical theme—there was always a theme, however dreadful—and Estelle imagined they were supposed to be coming aboard as they entered. How strange, she thought, that they should be playing at going to sea while their countrymen pushed onto foreign soils and risked drowning in the seas that carried them. But that was a gloomy thought, not appropriate for the evening, and she turned to let George slip off her wrap and hand it to the check girl. As usual the dining room had been turned into a dance floor, and she looked down the lobby and past the men's grill to see dancers twirling past, the light and music stirring them into an eager broth.

"This place is jumping and jiving," George said, scanning the room, obviously happy to be out on a Saturday night.

"It looks very jolly," Estelle agreed. "Babs Walker was in charge of the dance committee, wasn't she?"

"You should get on one of those committees," George said, taking her hand and walking her toward the dance floor. "The best social sets . . ."

"I was away," she interrupted, choosing not to hear him about social sets or making the right connections. A flash of Mr. Kamal— what he would make of such a dance, how he would appear stepping through the door, nodding to acquaintances—came to her, and she forced it away as too absurd to entertain.

"Drink or dance?" George asked when they finally made it to the dining room where the couples whirled past.

"I think a drink, please."

"Now you're talking. See that Puerto Rican fellow on the horn? He can wail."

Estelle nodded. George bent close and winked. She had no idea what that meant, but she did not want to rain on his happiness. He grabbed her hand and led her around the dancers, finally pushing through the French doors that opened onto the patio overlooking the eighteenth green. The nautical theme had been extended even here, and the bar—with Apples, the old colored bartender, standing behind a papier-mâché boat wheel—had been transformed into a pirates' deck. Apples wore a French admiral's hat; beneath the hat his face, as usual, remained set in a stoic frown. Estelle wondered how she had never noticed as keenly before the casual mockery they made of Apples, a man who had served them all for many years. She knew Mr. Kamal would resent it—he saw all men as equal and did not care a moment for skin color—but to George, Apples was merely part of the decorations.

"Two sidecars, my good Apples," George said. "I like that hat, Apples."

"Thank you, sir."

"You look like you're out of *Mutiny on the Bounty*."

"Yes, sir."

"You should take that hat off if you don't like it," Estelle could not keep herself from saying. "If it gets in the way of your work."

"Miss Walker asked me to wear it," Apples said, his hands busy with brandy and lemon and orange liqueur.

"He looks like Napoléon," George said.

Before the drinks came, and before George could say anything else, an avalanche of partygoers came off the golf course. They had obviously been enjoying cocktails at someone's house and had walked across the course; the women carried their shoes, and the men played piggyback with one another, wrestling and shouting, yelling *giddyup* as if they had mounted horses. Estelle recognized almost everyone at a glance; it was the familiar crowd, running perhaps on more alcohol than usual, but the old gang poured up off the eighteenth fairway and came into the bright patio area.

"Whale ho!" Robert Tailor, a ginger-headed man known to them all as Polly, shouted at the sight of the bar, perhaps, though Estelle couldn't say. "Libations all around!"

"Apples, you look positively regal!" Missy Kent exclaimed, her quick little feet nibbling like mice as they came onto the patio stones. "Hello, Georgie Porgie! And there's Estelle. I didn't know you were back, or I would have insisted you come to the trough for drinks this evening."

"Doesn't Apples look like Napoléon?" George asked the crowd. "Doesn't he really?"

George took charge of their drinks and passed one to Estelle. He raised his glass in a mock toast.

"At Dirty Dick's and Salty Dans, we drank our whiskey straight, and some went upstairs with sweet Marleen, and some, alas . . ."

"With Kate!" the others shouted in a merry explosion.

"Is that that little Puerto Rican I hear playing?" someone asked.

Estelle could not see who asked; she took a drink and smiled.

"Like Gabriel blowing his horn!" Polly said, his voice on the edge of hilarity. "A dark Gabriel, you understand. Not the shining blond-hair version."

"Apples, we're parched!" Missy Kent said, sliding into her heels. "You could strike a match on the back of my throat."

"Who's got a cigarette? I need a cigarette," Kenny Lindsey said.

He had just let his rider slide off his back, and he came onto the patio, straightening his jacket and running his hands over his hair. He was tall and lanky and played tennis at the Duck Pond, where he had twice won the club championship. He was a lean lefty whose serve, people said, was illegal in seventeen states.

Estelle stepped back from the bar. She didn't believe for a second that Missy hadn't known about her return; it had been a deliberate snub, but one, Estelle granted, that she probably deserved. George, in fact, would normally be included in any of the group's shenanigans, but by asking Estelle to the dance he had made himself an outcast at least for the night. Estelle understood all that. In a sense, she should be grateful to him, but she didn't feel that way.

"To our men in arms!" Polly said when he at last had his drink. He raised his glass and the others followed.

"Vive la France!" Missy Kent said.

"It won't be long now until they have Hitler on the run," Polly said, his voice carrying over the fading embers of a song ending. "The Kraut bastard."

"Polly!" Martha Guthberson said, her voice hiding a laugh.

She was as tall and lanky in her own way as Kenny Lindsey was in his, and people linked them together whether they liked it or not. Estelle always mused that they were as suited as livestock for each other, sure to make terrific babies who'd grow up to play basketball and could reach anything on a high shelf. Martha wore a long string of pearls, an accent reminiscent of flappers, and it didn't quite work for the type of evening they had in store for them.

George dripped his hand around Estelle's waist. She smiled at the sensation, though she imagined it was a tight, steady smile, like a person wading into cold water. He slid his hand down in a quick movement and cupped her rear end for a moment before whisking it back up to her waist. No one saw his grab and he kept his eyes straight ahead. She took a drink. She decided that she needed several drinks.

Then the dance floor emptied. The French doors swung open and the dancers hurried out, their faces flushed, while the band members slowly descended from their stand. A second bartender, a colored man Estelle did not recognize, came to help Apples behind the bar. The man wore a white sailor's cap, and he was young and appeared slightly frightened. Apples spoke to him in a low voice, Estelle saw, but she could not pick up the words.

"Get me another drink, would you, George?" she asked, shaking the ice in her glass. "Keep them coming."

"I say," he said.

"Don't say anything," she said. "Just find me a drink."

⊷ *Chapter Fourteen* ↞

Moonlight ran across the snow. On another night, for another purpose, Collie would have found the vision of the snow beneath the green pines a perfect wonder. The snow rested like a white sleeve on the side of the hill, its frigid center causing the air around it to feel damp and heavy. August had known its location from his work with the cutting teams, and she had hiked beside him, along with the young guard, Jules, each of them carrying an empty rucksack. Now she knelt beside the snow and held the top of her rucksack open, while August employed a short, military shovel to fill the interior with snow. Jules already stood with his pack filled; August's pack waited, its sides bulging. Snow for Marie, Collie thought. Snow to fight a fever.

"Nearly finished?" Jules asked impatiently.

Jules, Collie knew, felt uncomfortable without his rifle. Hiking into the mountains with a German and a woman had been a difficult proposition for him. Collie glanced at him. He was a slow, cautious boy, she observed, with a wild creature's mistrust of things threatening him.

"Ya," August said, then asked softly in German, "will this be too heavy?"

Collie shook her head. August poured two more shovelfuls into the interior, then held the pack steady while she cinched the top. He told her to turn around, then lifted the rucksack onto her back. The cold passed through her body and took hold of her ribs. She felt her lungs contract and she had to open her mouth to breathe. It was heavy, too; the weight pushed down on her shoulders and made her knees weak.

"Let's go," Jules said, then addressed August. "You go first."

"We're coming," Collie answered.

August swung his pack onto his back and started down.

It *was* beautiful, she admitted. She had never hiked at night, and the trail—a twist of soil among rocks—ran like a pale stream down the side of Bald Mountain. She followed Jules. She understood he wanted to be near August in case August made an escape attempt; Jules walked with his hand perched on his sidearm. It was foolishness, but she had promised to abide by Jules's rules; that was the only way he had agreed to accompany them to the snowfield. Regardless, he could not insulate them from the beauty that surrounded them. Clouds threw curtains across the moon and the light fell like smoke or river fog across the mountain's shoulders. The cold pack dripped down her back and legs.

Her mind spun as she walked. She pictured Marie in her thin white shift, her poor, exhausted face twisted in anguish. She pictured Marie's mother, grim and accepting, as she watched Herr Schmidt take the child's pulse against the stopwatch Amy found for him.

"How is the weight, Collie?" August called back to her.

"It's heavy, but I'm all right."

"How about for you, Jules?" August called, kidding him, Collie knew. "Not too much?"

"No. Keep walking."

It was not far. A half mile at most, Collie calculated. The snowfield hung this far into the summer due to its position on the northern slope, not from altitude alone. Pines provided shade. Those thoughts and observations worked into the rest of Collie's troubled imaginings. She felt she had no filter for her inner workings, could not fasten to one specific thing. She concentrated instead on the weight of the backpack and its cold pressure against her spine. The town and camp came into view as a haze of lights, and she walked toward it, bending forward like a miner carrying a hod of coal to the surface.

Herr Schmidt met them on the back porch. He dotted out his cigarette when he saw them. He did not appear confident. When he spoke, he whispered.

"*Gut*," he said. "It's critical now."

"How is she?" Collie asked.

"Floating," he said in German. "We must bring her back to earth. Come with me and we will put her in the bathtub. Her sister is ready to help."

Collie shrugged out of the backpack and left it on the porch. August said he would mind it. Collie looked at him in passing. He nodded and touched her hand.

She followed Herr Schmidt upstairs. Amy sat on one side of the bed, her mother on the other. Collie bent close and kissed Marie. Marie's skin felt warm and dry as sand. She looked tiny in her bed. Her lips sometimes moved as if she tasted something the rest of them could not detect.

"We're here," she whispered to Marie. "We're going to make you well, but first you must endure a little cold."

"We will put her in the tub and pack her with snow," Herr Schmidt said, turning to Marie's mother. "With your permission."

"I don't know . . . ," the older woman said, her voice shaky with indecision. "We should wait until her father returns. These are the kinds of things he decides."

"Her fever . . . is too hot," Herr Schmidt said in his broken English. "Her brain . . ."

He looked to Collie, then explained it quickly in German. If the fever was not brought down, the protein in the brain would bubble and dry. She risked being brain-damaged if the fever could not be controlled. He was not certain the snow would work, but he was certain doing nothing would bring about her eventual death. Collie translated his words to Marie's mother.

"It's time to try something, Mother," Amy said. "She won't last this way. She's being burned from the inside."

"How do we know he's telling the truth?" her mother asked. "He's a German."

"What could he gain by lying? He's not a monster, Mother, he's just a man trying to help us."

"We need to wait for your father."

With those words, Amy's mother stood and smoothed the sheet over Marie. Collie felt paralyzed and could barely manage to look at Amy. Herr Schmidt turned and stepped into the hallway. Collie smoothed back Marie's hair. The poor lamb, she thought. How could such vitality, such joy and merriment, turn so quickly to such a fragile state? It seemed impossible. Collie wanted to argue for the ice, but she did not know for certain that Herr Schmidt was correct. If they insisted on the ice, and Marie failed anyway, it would be a catastrophe. Marie, Collie knew, possessed unbounded energy and a great, seething love for life, and she imagined the young girl would resist and fight until she recovered if anyone could. She wished, for a moment, that her father would arrive, although matters of sickness and medical procedures rested outside his purview.

She had not had time to advance in her thinking before she heard a gruff voice speak from the hallway. Collie knew instantly that Marie's father had returned. She turned from the bed and stepped into the hallway only to discover Marie's father holding a kitchen knife leveled at Herr Schmidt. Father McIver, a young priest from Littleton, stood at Mr. Chapman's shoulder, his eyes darting back and forth from the knife to Herr Schmidt.

"You filthy slime," Mr. Chapman said to Herr Schmidt, "what are you doing in my house?"

"Easy," the priest said. "Let's all slow down."

Herr Schmidt did not look afraid, Collie noted. That was a remarkable thing. He stood with his shoulder brushing one side of the hallway, his body slack and relaxed as if he had confronted many men in his life and this was merely one more. The priest, on the other hand, appeared panicked and uncommitted to any course of action. Collie felt empty and weak, but she did not duck back into the bedroom. Her main thought was for Marie, and now these men had come and suddenly nothing felt clear. The knife reminded her of a snake, its body undulating in Mr. Chapman's hand.

"I am here to help your daughter if I can," Herr Schmidt said in German.

"He's here to help Marie," Collie translated from habit. "Dr. Shepherd is unavailable."

"I want Dr. Shepherd," Mr. Chapman said. "I don't want this Kraut bastard."

"I asked him to help us," Collie said, "for Marie's sake."

"I'll stick this knife up his ass and twist it until I have his liver. Tell him that in your Kraut talk."

"He'll leave if you want him to leave," Collie said. "He hasn't given her any treatment. He simply gave advice and took her pulse."

"He's escaped from camp and it's my duty to kill him. Your own father would tell you as much."

"He's trying to help!" Collie said sharply, then beseeched the priest. "Tell him, Father. If we don't bring down her fever, she won't survive. We have snow from the mountains to pack around her if you'll only give your permission."

Mr. Chapman waved the knife. No, it was not a snake after all, Collie realized, but an eager cat's tail whisking across the floor in anticipation of a rodent's dash for safety. As she thought it, Mr. Chapman stepped forward and the priest put a hand on his shoulder. Mr. Chapman brushed the hand away and advanced.

Before he took a second step Mrs. Chapman and Amy appeared, Marie's frail body balanced between them. Collie moved aside. How small Marie looked, Collie realized. How sweet and gentle and kind. The two women shuffled slowly, moving their feet in unison so as not to disturb Marie more than necessary. Collie watched Marie's tiny hand drifting like a flower in the air below her. For a dreadful moment, she believed her friend had died.

"Kill him or let us tend to her," Mrs. Chapman said to her husband, her voice strained with desperation, "but don't stand about and make a nuisance of yourself, Harold. We're going to put her in the tub and then pack her with ice and then we'll pray to God to have mercy on her sweet spirit. If you have a better idea, then speak it now, because I will not stand here and watch my child die while you fight a man you've never met before."

"Father, come with us," Amy added.

And they carried Marie down the hallway, past Mr. Chapman and the priest, and turned in quarter steps to bring their patient into the bathroom, her pale skin red with heat and trying.

Estelle felt her head spinning and she clung to George for balance. She was aware he might mistake the tension of her arms for interest; he had twice groped her, leading her to dark places off the patio where he could wrestle away something necessary for him, something juvenile and naughty, his breath like insistent pops in her ear. She understood she should be firmer with him. He was like a young dog in that respect, mindful only when he was brought up short. The liquor had made her soft and supple, she comprehended, but that knowledge was, in its turn, also dull and hazy. She let him paw at her and kiss her neck, and she responded only enough to encourage him not to think her a complete prude. He knew she had limits. That had been established long ago, and when she took his hand and led him back to the dance floor he went without protest, his face flushed with liquor and excitement, his demeanor grateful for such a visit.

Now she danced. The music had taken on a late-night plaintive quality that she found irresistible. The French doors remained open and cool air from the golf course swept in and made the dining room tolerable. The Puerto Rican horn player was marvelous, just as George said, and he seemed to anticipate the cool winds that passed through the club, a dark-skinned Pan calling them all to a midsummer frolic. Around her men and women danced in tilted pairs, their bodies leaning together, their faces conspiring over some plan, or emotion, between them. George, for his part, held her tight and released her only when a song ended, or when another couple floated into view and he felt the need to smile and acknowledge them.

Then suddenly Babs Walker announced that the dance was finished, she didn't want the police to close them down, drive safely, Godspeed, a last round of applause for the dance committee, thanks to the great band, everyone pitched in, thanks, thanks, and she received a large bouquet from her date, Alan Bremen. Everyone applauded, and everyone booed when the band broke into "Auld Lang Syne." Estelle began to cry. She didn't know why. Or, rather, she knew a thousand reasons why. The music struck her as incredibly touching. Good-bye to everything, she thought. That's what the music made her feel. Good-bye to all the brave boys dying in Europe, and good-bye to Mr. Kamal, and good-bye to gracefulness and summer nights, and even poor doltish Georgie, Georgie Porgie, who held her in his arms and danced her nobly around the floor. It was the liquor's fault, she knew. That's what had made her emotional, and when the band finally ceased, closing with a gentle, quiet completion, she accepted her wrap and followed George out to the car.

"That was lovely," she said to George inside their car after they had shouted their good-byes to a dozen similarly departing couples. She meant what she said. There had been some talk of going out to the Wayward for last call, but the idea had never gathered momentum, and she was glad now to be heading home, the windows down, the soft summer night inviting them to not retire, to never retire.

"I told you that skinny Puerto Rican can play," George said, backing up and fiddling his way out of the lot. "It's in their blood."

"I hope the air marshals don't flag us down for using our headlights."

"They're all buddies. You never mind. Now scoot over here and pretend that you know me."

He held his arm up, and after a moment's hesitation, she slid under it. He drove expertly; she gave him that much. He let his hand drop lazily down to touch the side of her breast. She didn't resist, though the gesture tired her. She would have almost preferred, she thought, a full-on assault rather than these unmanly raids. Amos, in his vileness, was nearly preferable. She opened her mouth to tell him as much, when he surprised her by starting to talk about their future.

"We make a swell couple, Estelle," he said, his driving hand playing patty-cake with the steering wheel as he negotiated the turns and twists back toward her house, "and everyone knows it except you. I'm not scolding you, I promise. I'm asking you to step back and take a look at the long run. Will you do that? I'm doing okay in business, if I do say so myself. You can ask around and confirm that. I know I should be over fighting the Hun, but my hernia, well, you know that whole story. Some of us have to stay behind anyway. Look at Kenny Lindsey! He's a demon tennis player . . . don't I know it . . . but he's got a little trick knee that says no way, no how he's going to fight the Krauts. That's just the way it is. Anyway, I'm getting turned around about all this . . . what I want to say is we could both do a whole lot worse than ending up together. You know that. We kind of fit together, we have a crowd to run with. Wasn't tonight fun? I thought it was fun, and we can have plenty of nights like these. These are our kinds of people. We fit here, Estelle, at least I think we do, and I bet your parents would back me up on it. So what I'm asking is maybe you think about it a little, and stop being so sure there's a better life waiting for you someplace else. Maybe there is, I don't know, but this isn't a bad life, is it?"

He looked over at her. The booze had made him talky, but she couldn't deny the dull wisdom of his words.

"I'm sorry, George. Sorry if I've been distant. . . ."

"There was some talk about you taking an interest in that Negro fellow who runs the flower shop. I told people that couldn't be true, but there were rumors."

"He's not a Negro, George. He's an Indian."

"If it walks like a duck and talks like a duck . . ."

"There is a difference, George, not that it particularly matters."

"Well, anyway, I'm betting you don't want your name associated with him in that way. Not if you're smart and want a future at the club and in our set. You know what I'm saying. Birds of a feather fly together."

"He's a very nice man. Very well-read."

He leaned a little away, his face cut into a look of appraisal.

"Say," he said, "you were sweet on him, weren't you?"

"Not sweet on him, George. I just told you. He's a nice man, and he's well educated. I enjoyed talking with him. That's not a crime."

George let out a long whistle. He lost the line of his driving and had to hurry the wheel back in place.

"I'll be a monkey's uncle," he said when he stopped whistling.

"You're making more of it than it was, George. I'd prefer we drop it."

"Consider it dropped."

"Let's go to the lake," she said on impulse.

"Now?"

"Why not?"

"I thought you were tired."

"I am tired, but this night . . ."

"Pretty damn night," he agreed.

So they went to Lake Mindowaska, a brown, liver-shaped body of water not far from the club. It was a popular place in the summer; the town sponsored a waterslide in a roped-off area, and the local Kiwanis had put up grills and picnic tables, and the Boy Scouts had built a fire-pit where people from the Audubon Society, or the Fish and Game Department, sometimes gave talks on wildlife. Officially, the swim area was closed at sunset. It was popular for neckers and kids with nowhere else to go, but at this hour, Estelle saw, they had the place to themselves.

As soon as George turned off the headlights, Estelle pushed out the car and ran down to the water. She left her heels at the sandy edge; wading in, hoisting her skirt to her knees, she called to George to join her. But he lighted a cigarette instead and stood watching her, his face illuminated by the red glow of his rhythmic puffing. She felt slightly drunk, and a little crazy, and she wanted to take big bites of the summer night. That was impossible, she knew, but she felt it anyway, and when she came out and saw George flick his cigarette away, she knew what he had in mind.

He led her to one of the picnic tables and he pushed her down, his hands fumbling under her skirt. She pushed his hands away, but she had invited this, she knew. How strange she felt. For a moment George seemed to be everywhere at once, at her mouth with his lips, then his hands on her breasts, then down below, down where she could not let him go but did anyway. She lay back and gazed up at the moon, at a quarter moon, and she knew this was a sort of bargain she had struck. She was not sure with whom, or why precisely, but she let him do what he wanted for a time, just a short while, then she sat up and said it was all right.

"Jeepers," he said, backing away, his balance thrown off by drunkenness and the unexpected. "What a night this turned out to be."

"Do you love me, George?"

"I do," he said. "I really do, Estelle."

"I hope you do."

"You don't think I'd . . . be like this if I wasn't serious."

"I'm not sure what you would do, George. I've never been very good at figuring all this out."

"It means we're kind of steady, doesn't it?" he asked.

"I suppose so."

"That makes me real glad. Real glad. I think we're swell together."

"I don't want to think about anything anymore, George. Will you keep me from thinking about things?"

"You've got it, sister," he said. "You got whatever you like."

"Wouldn't that be lovely? To have whatever one wants."

"You can have it, baby. I'll bring you the whole world and set it up on a snack table."

"If you say so, George."

"I do."

Then he kissed her some more. This was it, then, she realized. This is how people went forward and made plans and ended up married. She thought of her parents, and thought of Collie and August, thought of a half dozen married couples. They all began like this, she thought. In some ways, she realized as she pushed up from the table and straightened her clothes, it was no different from picking out an outfit. One went over the selections, considered the events ahead, determined what one strived for, then made a choice. Maybe her dates with these different men were simply outfits to hold up against oneself in front of the dressing room mirror, to model the gown and see where it struck the knee, how it flowed against one's legs. It was simple, really, entirely obvious, and she wondered how such knowledge had escaped her. Maybe, she thought, women always knew this but never passed along the secret to the newer candidates.

George lighted another cigarette and sat on the picnic table and blew smoke up at the sky. She went to retrieve her shoes, the sand now cold and gritty under her feet.

"I'm tired now, George," she said when she came back to join him.

"I'll take you home, honey."

"How do you know if I'm the right person for you?"

He looked at her and shrugged. He dotted out his cigarette on the picnic bench, then flicked the butt toward the water.

"You just are," he said.

"But how do you know? Aren't there a thousand women out there who might be the right one for you?"

"You talk crazy sometimes, Estelle."

"You haven't answered the question."

She felt the alcohol in her blood now more than before, she realized. The cold had done it, and his hands had done it. Something bitter and empty worked around in her stomach, but she couldn't name it.

"There's always someone else, if you want to frame it that way," he said. "I mean, people die and then the surviving spouse gets remarried, so, yes, sure, you're right. But I don't look at the world that way, Estelle."

"How do you look at it?"

"Straight ahead."

"And I'm a good match in most ways?"

"Sure you are," he said.

"I wish I knew how to be more like you, George."

"Stick around. It rubs off, I promise."

Then he took her back to the car. He held the door open and she climbed inside. He tuned in the radio as they drove back to her house. The secret, she realized, was not to wish. Wishing was the cause of too much heartache. George was right. Straight ahead was the way to go about things. She saw that. He reached over and held her hand for some of the way home as they traveled the streets beneath the great trees. She held one hand out the window and let the wind lift it and settle it down as it liked. When they came to her house, she let George come around and open her door.

"Good night, George," she said on the front porch when he walked her to the door.

"Good night, baby. You're terrific."

He kissed her. She waited, curious, to see if she would kiss him back. But no impulse pushed her further into their embrace, so she smiled when they broke apart and dodged through the door like an actress, she reflected, tiptoeing offstage.

Dr. Shepherd arrived close to dawn. Marie still hung on by a thread; she had come out of her ice bath flaming and hot. Herr Schmidt did not say as much, but it was clear he held out little hope. He and August had been escorted back to the barracks by Jules, the young guard. Now Collie worked in the kitchen beside Amy to make coffee and cut slices of bread. Father McIver administered last rites, then came to the kitchen and sat in a chair, his face drawn. He accepted a cup of coffee when Amy offered it; Collie carried it to the table and put it in front of him. It was good, she felt, to have something to do.

"Are you hungry, Father?" Amy asked. "We are toasting some bread and we have cheese, I think. . . ."

"The coffee is plenty," he said. "Thank you."

"Where did Papa go?" she asked the priest.

"He went out. It's difficult for him to be upstairs. He feels helpless."

"We all feel helpless," Collie added.

"Yes, in times like these . . ."

"I'll bring a tray up to your mother and Dr. Shepherd," Collie said. "You take a rest, Amy."

"Thank you. I will."

Collie prepared a tray. She doubted they would eat, but at least they could have coffee. She went up the back stairs, walking as softly as possible. She overheard Dr. Shepherd saying something about fevers breaking at sunrise and sunset. Collie could not tell from his tone if he said such a thing merely to provide hope for Mrs. Chapman, or whether he truly believed it.

"Some coffee?" she asked when she came in the room. "And Amy sent up some toast, if you're hungry."

"Thank you, dear," Mrs. Chapman said.

Dr. Shepherd held his hand to Marie's forehead. He had placed a thermometer in her mouth, but the instrument had fallen to the side. It was not much use, Collie realized. It would report the obvious.

She arranged the tray on a small table in the corner of the room, then added cream and sugar by request. She handed the cups to Mrs. Chapman and the doctor. The cups rattled on their saucers, and it was not until she heard the sound that Collie noticed her hands shook. Mrs. Chapman took a brief sip, then put the cup on the bedside table. She stood and went out, as if the sip of coffee reminded her she had a body still. Collie took her place beside the bed, the doctor across from her.

She had hardly taken a look at him on his arrival. Now she saw he was a gray-haired, handsome man, a little stout, with a heavy beard this early in the morning. He had not been home, she realized. His hands moved well when he lifted the coffee cup; they were steady and certain, and she felt a spark of confidence in seeing them. A dark scar lined his right eye socket. His brow obscured it, but it was there nonetheless, and she wondered how he had come by it. As a result of her own bicycle scar, she always had an interest in others' injuries, because, she felt, they suggested a narrative about the person. One lived into one's scar somehow, and she had become an expert of sorts, though naturally now was not the time to talk of it.

"How is she?" she whispered instead.

"Very weak."

"Was the ice . . . ?"

"Yes, it was fine. I'm not sure it made much difference in the end."

"*Is* this the end?" she asked, her heart suddenly fluttering.

He gazed at her and pursed his lips. It was not an answer.

"She is such a sweet soul," Collie said. "Such a light."

"I delivered her," he said, sipping the coffee. "She came into the world very easily."

"I'm sure she would."

"She's strong . . . but . . ."

Collie leaned forward and took Marie's hand.

"With the war going on, you don't think about regular, everyday people becoming ill."

"They do all the time, I'm afraid," he said.

"I don't know how you stand it."

"Sometimes your work bears fruit. This evening I delivered a little boy to a woman who had wanted a child for a long time. She had a difficult delivery, but both came through. It's all a balance."

"Everything is a war, isn't it?"

"No, not everything. Sometimes it's a very graceful ballet. It's not one thing or another. You'll see as you go along. There's as much beauty as suffering. At least I've always found it so."

"She doesn't deserve to be this ill."

"Does anyone?"

"The old might. She hasn't had her days."

"Who can tell?" he asked, and sipped his coffee and put it on the floor beside him.

He took the thermometer out and examined it. He squinted to see, and it was at that moment that Collie realized the sun had slipped above the mountains. The first edge burned like a searchlight, and she saw it spread and flow over the hillsides, over the river and the covered bridge. It was a tender, quiet beauty. The light came and rested on a glass pitcher beside the bed, and it fell in a prism of color on the thin sheet over Marie.

"It's lower," Dr. Shepherd said, shaking out the thermometer. "Just a little lower."

"That's a good sign, isn't it?"

"Where there's life, there's hope."

Collie squeezed Marie's hand gently. Light continued to spill into the room. Collie moved Marie's hand so that the light found it and warmed it. *The sweet young lamb*, she thought. *This happy, happy creature. This happy creature despite this gloomy house. This happy creature who was the only sun this household knew. Wake up*, Collie thought and sent that thought to Marie. *Come back*. A rooster crowed as she formed the thought and a hammer began working somewhere. The world had started again, Collie realized, as it always would, as it would with or without Marie, as it would without any of them, and she closed her eyes at the terror of such notions, and opened them again to capture the beauty once more.

"Will you sit with her a moment?" the doctor asked, sliding his cup and saucer from the floor onto the side table beside the bed. "I'll be right back."

"Yes, of course."

He left. The floorboards marked his parting and the sound of the boards squeaking followed him down the hallway. He went downstairs. Collie stood from the chair where she had been seated and squeezed onto a small space beside Marie's heated body. She pushed the girl's hair back. Her forehead was moist with sweat. Collie dampened a cloth and brushed the girl's skin carefully.

"You mustn't do this," she whispered to Marie as she worked. "You mustn't leave us all. It's not time yet. Stay with us. Don't go, Marie. Please don't."

And yet she knew the time had come. She wanted to call out, to bring back the doctor and Marie's mother, perhaps Amy, but it was too late. She watched her young friend's chest fill over and over rapidly, as if searching for air it could not find. Choking, Marie sat up partially, her eyes suddenly opened, her right arm lifting slightly as if being handed something. Collie could see that Marie understood what had happened, what was about to happen. Collie clasped her in her arms and held her. The heat of the poor girl's body was intolerable. Nevertheless she put her lips to Marie's ear and whispered, "Mares eat oats, and does eat oats, and little lambs eat ivy." She sang it three times, holding Marie closer and closer, her lips touching Marie's skin. It was morning now, Collie thought, watching light take over the room. It was a new day.

Then for an instant Marie's body turned rigid. It sprang straight and nearly leapt from the bed, and Collie felt her friend's spirit pass away. It entered the light of the morning sun, and Collie held her softly and whispered that someday she would be married in the covered bridge, that the whole town would attend, and that she, Marie, would be the most beautiful bride ever. She would glow in a white gown, and Collie promised a swan boat, a beautiful boat that would glide to the shore and take Marie and her husband away. The band would play, and it would be summer, and people would throw flowers into the water at sunset. They would all glide down the river, and Marie would turn and wave. *Good-bye, good-bye, good-bye,* she would call. *I love you all. I am leaving now.* The town would call back and their voices would blend and echo up into the hills where this sweet child was born, and night would steal softly on all of them and the river would turn to glass and carry the reflection of the sky like a great ribbon tied properly around the world.

⊰ *Chapter Fifteen* ⊱

"I'm sorry to bring it up at this time, with Marie's funeral just concluded. . . ."

"I understand, Papa."

"Do you?" he asked, his voice sharp. "I don't think you do. To take two German prisoners off the prison grounds in the darkness, and one of them, this young man . . ."

Collie nodded. She felt her skin turning hot. She felt horrible that she had put her father in such an untenable situation. She sat on the edge of her seat in her father's small office, her eyes still raw from crying at Marie's funeral the day before. She could not look up to meet his gaze. Of course it had been ill-advised to bring the German prisoners with her to help with Marie. She had known the risk at the time, but she had gone through with it anyway. She would have done anything to help Marie, but it had failed, in any case. Now her father had been lampooned in the *Littleton Courier* as a commander who ran an open prison for the inmates. The editorial page had posted a cartoon of him standing next to a turnstile, a stack of free tickets fanned out in his hand, a grotesque German soldier passing through on his way to a carnival. It didn't matter that the German prisoners—August and Herr Schmidt—had worked to preserve the life of an American citizen. To let German soldiers out at night, under dubious supervision, was all anyone needed to stir the pot.

"Under the circumstances, I understand. I do," her father said. "You've been an invaluable help here. But there are rules governing these matters. . . ."

Collie nodded. She had no energy to fight.

"I won't make that mistake again, Father," she said.

"You should not take it on yourself to plead for special privileges. That's an abuse of your position here. I'm sorry, but it is. It blurs too many lines."

"Yes, Father."

She heard him sigh. He stood and came around the desk and sat beside her. She had started to cry. She couldn't tell if the tears were for Marie or for herself or for the stupidity of the war and the restrictions it placed on them all. It didn't matter, she reflected. She felt tired and thin-skinned, unhappy with everything. When her father reached over and took her hand, she let him hold it for only a moment before drawing it back to her lap. She kept her face down.

"I'm sorry," he said. "I know this hasn't been easy for you."

She nodded. Tears came more rapidly into her eyes.

"Marie was a darling girl and she was your friend," he said. "I understand. And of course the newspaper men and critics . . . they don't care about context. They want a headline or an excuse to drag us through the mud. I know you meant no harm."

She nodded again.

"You have feelings for this young man. I understand that. You may not think that I understand, but I do. I was young once, too. From all accounts, he seems like a fine soldier. He's well educated, and I see that he's handsome. But under these circumstances . . . surely you see how impossible it is. I don't want you to get your feelings hurt, or to place yourself in a compromising position. I'm sorry, I'm probably ham-handed at these fatherly sermons, but you understand me, Collie. You know what I'm saying, don't you?"

"I understand you," she said, looking up.

He handed her a handkerchief. He always had fresh handkerchiefs about because of his pulmonary condition. They smelled of the pine box where he kept them. She wiped her eyes and tried to compose herself. The world felt fragile and empty at the moment.

"Is that all?" she asked.

"Next time I'll be more stern. But there won't be a next time, will there?"

She shook her head. He patted her shoulder.

"What about the Heights boy's invitation?" he asked. "The Woodcutters' Ball? Wouldn't a night away from this camp be a good thing for both of us? Mrs. Heights, Eleanor, offered to put you up rather than your making the trip home late at night."

"I don't feel much like dancing these days, Papa."

"Naturally it's difficult. But just to gain a little perspective," he said, "just to shake out the cobwebs. We're too cooped up in this camp. The prisoners have made prisoners of us."

"It doesn't feel respectful of Marie."

"Oh, now come on. Did anyone ever live who wanted so much to dance as Marie? She would insist on it, as you know very well. It really is supposed to be quite a night. It marks the end of summer. The ballroom where it's held is reportedly sumptuous for Berlin. I've been there to lunch in the grill and it's nicely appointed. Please say you'll consider it."

She nodded.

"The Heights boy, Henry, he has his cap set for you, you know."

"That's not true."

"Apparently it is," her father said, rising and returning to the other side of the desk, his voice lighter now. "He's made it quite clear. I've heard it from different quarters."

"That's ridiculous."

She saw her father shrug. Then he sat behind his desk again. He pulled a stack of papers closer to the lamplight. She knew he had said as much as he would likely volunteer.

She went back to her desk, glad to see that Lieutenant Peters had gone out. She felt nervous and upset. She tried to bring order to the papers on her desk, but her attention kept wandering away. She thought of Marie a good deal; she remembered her friend's warm body, the terrible heat of her life baking away. The funeral, held just the day before, had been a dismal, horrible affair. It had rained and turned everything to soup, and the priest, Father McIver, had gone on too long in his eulogy. His words had seemed like an overwrought apology, as though he could ask forgiveness for the Lord's plan to take a girl who brought such joy to those around her. Afterward, the Chapmans had invited people to return to their home, where they laid out a paltry board, everything hurried and inadequate, the entire ordeal lacking the grace and pleasure that Marie had sought to find and bring into her life. It had been depressing, and Collie felt unable to shake free of the funeral's dark tones.

At noon she went to sit with the twitch horses, but they were all out. She hoped, too, to meet August, but he did not show up as he occasionally did. She was just as glad; she did not know what she could say to him. It was clear her father did not want her to see him anymore, to encourage him in any fashion. That was a sensible plan, certainly, and she decided, given the complexity of her situation, that she should accept Henry Heights's invitation to the Woodcutters' Ball. Her father had a point; it would give her perspective. She would be able to see Henry with the benefit of a new light. You could not always give in to your heart, no matter how strong the impulse to do so might be. That was part of growing up.

She found Amy waiting when she returned to her office. Amy sat on the edge of her chair, her posture betraying her unease at being in the camp. She smiled when Collie sat at the desk beside her. Amy's skin looked pale and her eyes were red. Collie reached over and took her friend's hand.

"I bought you these," Amy said, sliding a packet of papers toward her. "They wouldn't mean anything to anyone else. They're just a girl's secret thoughts, but so many of them are pointed toward you and Estelle that I felt you should see them. She writes about you with great tenderness."

"I'll treasure them," Collie said, taking the bundle and holding it gently in her hands.

"I still can't believe she's gone," Amy said. "You know, she always shined the brightest. Don't pretend otherwise, please. You would think an older sister would be jealous, but I found her just as amusing, just as extraordinary as everyone else who met her."

"She *was* extraordinary, it's true. She brought light to the world."

"Yes, that's it, isn't it? I hadn't thought of it just that way. But she found such joy in things that it was impossible to remain in her company and not feel joy one's self. Peculiar, really. Anyway, I thought you might like those pensées, I suppose you would call them. She was as good in her private reflections as she was in life. I've stayed up these last nights reading her diaries, and they are the most remarkable pages. She never complains and she never finds fault. I felt both encouraged by what I read and also diminished by my own shortcomings. I would give anything to have her here for one last long conversation."

"Yes, I'm sure you would."

Amy smiled. She put her face down and teared up. When she raised her face again, she pushed onto her feet.

"You must have better things to do than listen to me," Amy said. "I'll leave you."

"I do have some work, but I haven't been able to bring my mind to it. You must promise me that you won't compare yourself to Marie, or to think of yourself as lessened by her in any way. You played a wonderful part in her life. She loved you most of all."

"Oh, I was such an old maiden aunt, honestly," she said, blinking away tears. "I look back and I hate what I see. I'll do better, though. That's what I've promised myself. I will steal a little of Marie's joy and keep it for myself. That's the treasure she gave me."

Collie stood and took Amy in her arms. Amy took a deep breath, then turned and went out the door. Collie went to the window and watched her make her way out the guarded front entry. Above her the sky looked to be building clouds.

Henry waited patiently for Collie to finish in the ladies' room. He had darted off to check their jackets, then had returned and taken up a position near the lush red banquet set against the center pillar of the Holland Arms Hotel foyer. From where he stood, he could see the social buzz of the ballroom as well as the arriving guests; he recognized nearly everyone who passed through the doors, but he tried not to be distracted. He wanted to be attentive to Collie. She was fragile, exceedingly so, after the death of the young girl in Stark. He had learned about the death only a day later, and he had sent a wreath to the funeral, hoping the flowers struck the correct note, and was relieved when Collie assured him they had. There were precious few flowers, she said, and so the wreath had been that much more welcome. She said Marie, the young girl, would have appreciated them.

It had been a tricky business to re-invite her to the Woodcutters' Ball. On one hand, he did not want to press her. On the other, he wished to be clear about his intentions. The flowers, fortunately, had paved the way for a follow-up call. She had agreed to go in stages, giving in to his gentle persistence. She had hedged, at first, over her period of mourning, but the funeral came and went so quickly that she had had three weeks to get her feelings under control. He called her often, trying to involve her in the amusing details of the ball's preparation—his mother played a great role in the celebration as an organizer, so he was privy to all the obstacles—but he could not determine if Collie took a genuine interest or only listened out of politeness. Nevertheless, something in her attitude toward him had changed. He did not want to let himself become too hopeful, but she did not erect such a wall between them as before. The child's death had softened her.

She came out a moment later. She wore a crimson ball gown, delicately teetering off her shoulders, with a white string of pearls adorning her neck. Her hair, above all, dazzled him most. It was pushed up in a sort of chignon, and it provided to the back of her neck, and her profile, the most alluring angles. She was stunning; he had already seen the looks and expressions of interest as she dropped her coat into his hands. He felt lucky to be her escort, as if he had been given the genie's lamp but could not quite trust his good fortune.

"It's a madhouse in the ladies' room, I'm afraid," she said as she rejoined him. "I hope I didn't take too long."

"Not at all."

"You could make a fortune selling pins and tucks of fabric in there," she said, her eyes passing quickly over the room. "Everyone has ripped something, and they are all in dire need of a stitch. It would be comical if it wasn't all so desperate."

"But you escaped unscathed?"

"Yes, as a matter of fact, I did."

He held his arm out for her and she linked her arm through his. It was a proud moment. He escorted her to the short reception line where his mother and the other committee members greeted the partygoers. Music filled the room behind them. A quick glance told Henry that the decoration committee had met its usual high standard. The ballroom had been transformed into a bright confection of balloons and paper streamers. The back doors opened onto the river and he felt a brisk breeze coming through, keeping the heat from building. The breeze moved the balloons and streamers, giving the night a sense of motion and restlessness that he found appealing. Fall had entered the air at night.

He listened as Collie greeted everyone, introduced herself when appropriate, or stood and allowed him to introduce her. She was a marvel of social ease and confidence. He noted how the organizing committee of the Woodcutters' Ball regarded her. She was a bright white bird in a room full of dun sparrows.

"Now the music has started . . . ," his mother said at the end of the reception line, her eyes scanning the crowd to make sure everything had begun correctly. "Make yourself at home. Enjoy . . . Henry, see that she dances and meets everyone. Oh, you know what to do. You both do. And keep an eye out for Amos, will you? He's not very good at these sorts of evenings."

"Yes, Mother."

"We put you at the young people's table, but of course that's just for a sense of order. I don't mean young people's table as though you are children . . . just as young people who are out for fun. You can roam anywhere you like. Make sure you show Collie the outside deck. . . . Well, you can't miss it, of course. Now, go ahead. I'm making too much of things as usual. Your father is around here somewhere, probably with a cigar and a drink he doesn't need. . . ."

"I'm in good hands, I'm sure," Collie said, then took Henry's arm and walked beside him toward the dance floor.

"Would you like to dance first, or perhaps some refreshment . . . ?" Henry asked.

"A drink, please."

"You look absolutely showstopping. I hope you know that."

"Showstopping, is it? That's a new one."

"I shouldn't be so complimentary," he said. "You're probably too accustomed to it. You should be tortured a bit more."

"No one ever said I was showstopping, I assure you."

"Here we go," he said as they arrived at the bar. "How does a highball sound? Two whiskey and sodas, please. Tall glasses."

The bartender, a short, eager fellow named Tad, Henry knew, said, "Yes, sir, Mr. Heights," and began shuffling glasses and ice together. Henry signed the bill when it came to him. He took the two drinks from the bartender's hands and passed one to Collie.

"To the woodcutters," Collie said.

"Yes, to the woodcutters."

"In the past, you know," he said, clinking her glass and sipping, "the Woodcutters' Ball was a sort of lumberjack competition. A bunch of jacks would meet out in the woods with a barrel of questionable liquor and they would have a ball. People still tell stories about the earliest ones. They actually danced as they do right here."

"Sounds quaintly primitive."

"Oh, it was, I suppose. Lots of fighting, of course, and dares and foolhardy challenges. The Frenchmen were the worst, according to legend. One fellow had a moose he could ride and he would spend the early part of the night drinking on moose-back. Someone shot the moose later in the season for stew meat. It caused a terrific riff."

"You like the romance of it, don't you?" she asked.

He took more of the highball and nodded. He wanted to say more, to have her interest firmly fixed on him, but soon a party of young people swooped down on them. He knew them all; they were Berliners, local children from local families. He introduced Collie around the half circle they formed against the bar. There was Jack Pillton and Annie Scott, Bill Biels and Sarah Clement, and Edward Gates and Betsy Rice. The girls all wore gowns, but none fit them as well as Collie's gown fit her. The boys spoke with the high, nervous tone in their voices that sometimes fell on men around attractive women. Henry knew Collie had been the subject of much speculation already that evening.

"Did you find a pin?" Collie asked Betsy Rice. "You looked to be in a panic."

"This strap broke," Betsy said, pointing to her left dress strap, and Henry remarked how easily Collie entered their world. "My kingdom for a safety pin."

"It was a madhouse in there, wasn't it?" Sarah Clement said, her voice slightly drunk already. "They should set up more mirrors if they intend to have this kind of crowd. Henry, take a note for your momsy. Tell her the young set demands more mirrors."

"Demand," Bill Biels said, "make sure you frame it as a demand."

"Who needs another drink?" Edward Gates asked, his voice lush with liquor. "Oh, Gunga Din, you're a better man than I am, Gunga Din. See here. Eight of your best highballs, young Tad. Though I've beaten you and flayed you . . . does flayed mean to remove one's skin? Is a simple whipping a flaying as well?"

"I don't think whippings are ever simple," Sarah said. "Not simple at all. But a flaying is the taking off of skin. I'm fairly certain about that."

"How dreadful," Betsy said. "Who started us on this topic? It must have been Bill. Bill's been odd all evening."

"Cut her off!" Jack said, then he made a moan like a steam whistle. It went on too long, Henry thought, but there was no stopping it. Afterward, Jack said, "Throw the girl a life preserver."

The drinks arrived. Henry caught Collie's eye. She smiled. She was a good sport, he realized. She had entered into the fun, and he admired her comfort in diving into a new situation. Some women might have stood back, or remained superior, but not her. He suspected the others found her a good egg, too.

She took the second highball and hoisted it when the others toasted.

"To the jack with the biggest balls," Bill Biels said.

"To the biggest balls," the others repeated.

It was an old profane toast, one that could be said with impunity on this single night. Even his mother would raise a glass to it, Henry knew.

He watched as Collie blushed but drank. She smiled when she

lowered her glass. She was exactly, exactly the kind of woman he wanted in his life.

It felt wrong to be merry, but Collie couldn't help herself. The drinks had fueled some of it, she knew, but the rest, the majority portion of it, had to do with Henry and the lively atmosphere of the Woodcutters' Ball. If she were honest with herself, she realized, she would have admitted that she had expected to have a horrid time. The ball followed too closely on Marie's death; and she was with Henry, not August, and that, too, should have mitigated against much merriment. It felt like a small betrayal. But all of that counted in, it was a lively evening. Part of it, she suspected, was the season. The night had turned crisp and bright, and someone had the good sense to jam the door open so that they could pass freely out onto the wide verandah overlooking the river. Stiff breezes came in throughout the early part of the evening, seeming to stir them as leaves might mix in the corner of a building. The party convened as much outdoors as inside.

The crowd also—this was a revelation—had a sense of humor about itself. Yes, they were dressed in finery, and yes, the band played demure numbers, but behind it all rested the legacy of the true Woodcutters' Ball. It was meant to be an outdoor festival, the demarcation of summer's ending, and something riotous and good-humored remained in the fabric of the event. Even the toast, slightly scurrilous, worked to make everyone less stuffy. Although she had never been to it, the evening reminded her of stories about Mardi Gras, some crazed evening where the sole intent was to let loose and to bury any worries about the future. That's how it felt, anyway.

And Henry . . . yes, he had been a perfect gentleman and escort. He was fun and well suited to his social environment. It was obvious, she mused as she stood on the verandah waiting for him to arrive with what she had made him swear was the final drink of the evening, that he was well liked by his friends and family. What she had taken in him previously as a sign of timidity and a failing of confidence was really, she sensed now, a basic shyness mixed with the desire to cede to others the center stage. His talent, in fact, relied on his standing back and surrendering the social battles to others. It was easy to picture him as he would be in later life: diffident, patient, perhaps wise in an unusual way. In short, he had a sense of himself, a very proportionate one, and she had reassessed him throughout the evening, clarifying her image of him against the backdrop of the ball.

How strange life could be, she thought. She turned and looked out at the river. It reflected the moonlight and seemed to be in a rush to arrive somewhere. Now and then she heard logs knocking together. They had been corralled in what Henry called a boom pier. Or an alligator pier, she wasn't quite sure. It was fun to hear them talk about wood and logs as if they discussed the habits of acquaintances. Underneath it all, she imagined, there was significant land and wealth, although they never made much of it. She liked that about Henry and about his family and friends. They wore their riches lightly.

"Here we are," Henry said, reappearing with two more drinks in his hands. "I hope I wasn't too long. Poor Tad is overrun and the two spare bartenders they've signed on aren't up to the challenge, I'm afraid."

"No, you're just in time. I was beginning to think you'd gone off."

"I wouldn't abandon you to this pack of wolves," he said, raising his glass and nodding over it. "They may look safe, but they're loggers when all is said and done."

"They've been nothing but polite."

"Oh, it's early still, I promise. We haven't had the ritual fistfight out in the parking lot. That's part of the festivities, but it requires the proper alcohol levels. It's a delicate balance."

Collie looked at him closely.

"I wanted to thank you for inviting me, Henry," she said. "I've had a lovely evening. I was hesitant, as you know . . . with Marie, and all of that. But I'm glad now that I came. I'm glad I got to know you away from the usual run of things."

"Well, I had no choice but to try to make up for our first date."

"Yes, that was a spectacular something, certainly. But even without that in the balance, I've had a wonderful night. I needed to get away more than I realized. Camp life can be wearing."

"I would imagine so."

"So thank you. I appreciate your patience with me."

"I'm fond of you, Collie. I intend to marry you. I told you that."

She studied him. He'd had a few drinks, unquestionably, but she did not think his statement came from that. He seemed to mean what he was saying. It was the second time he promised to marry her, and she looked at him curiously, trying to gauge him.

"You should be careful," she said, "because someday someone will believe you."

"I'm hoping you will believe me."

"I think you've had too many drinks, Henry."

"I'm on the level about this, Collie. I picked you out as soon as I saw you. I've always thought you were the right woman for me and everything since then has confirmed it. I can't be plainer about it. I'll ask you to marry me someday. Not right now, because I know you aren't prepared to answer. But I will ask, and then we'll see. I think we would have a good life together. I think you think so, too."

She turned and looked out at the river, her mind racing. He had no right to speak this way so soon in their friendship, and yet he didn't seem to do it for shock value or to appear daring and fascinating. He struck her as sincere, which was extraordinary. He was either hopelessly naïve, or wonderfully candid.

"Don't worry," he said, "I won't mention it again. Not for a time, anyway. I'm a patient man. You don't know that about me yet, but I am. And I usually get what I set out to get."

"Am I something to get?"

"I don't mean it like that. You know I don't."

"Yes, I do know that."

"Unless you hate me, Collie, I hope you'll let me see you often. I won't press, I promise. I want to see where we might go together. Will you give me permission to do that much at least?"

Her mind flashed quickly to August. It flickered to Estelle, and to Marie, and to poor Amy sitting in her office, downcast and heart-broken.

"You can ask, and I can answer," she said, because she did not know what else to say at the moment.

"That's a small victory, then," he said, raising his glass. "Now I hope you'll dance with me, and we'll check to see what fistfights are brewing."

"Yes, let's," she said, and led him back toward the ballroom.

But there were no fistfights. Henry took her glass and set it beside his on their table. The table had long since been abandoned; the night was exploding outward, each table like the site of a detonation. People either danced or stood outside, taking the air. Some, she was certain, had already left. She had seen her father depart an hour ago.

She danced with Henry. He was not a particularly good dancer, but neither was she, she knew. Still, he was game and he led her around the floor to the tune of "Smoke on the Water" by Russ Morgan.

She did not feel the electricity she felt when she was in August's presence. She could not delude herself about that. She couldn't say what it was about August, but he thrilled her, touched her in a way that Henry, despite his good nature, could not replicate. It struck her as perverse that the feelings between men and women worked in such a way. How much easier it would have been, she reflected, if she had felt passionate about Henry. She could have a comfortable life with him. It was absurd to hold out for August; August might be sent away at any moment, and what, in the end, had they meant to each other so far? A few haphazard meetings, that was all. She had visited him in the infirmary, and she had seen him running through the rain to leave a bouquet for her, but how did that calculate against the solid warmth of Henry's companionship? She wished, even while in Henry's arms, that she might discuss everything with Estelle. Estelle would bring light to the subject. She always did.

The song ended and they went back to their table. Amos had found them, she saw. He had been drinking, too, by the looks of him. He sat slouched in his chair, his tie loosened, his thick frame thrown on the chair like an old set of clothing. He raised his glass at their approach.

"The Mayor and Mrs. of Lumbertown," he said, toasting them. "You make a dashing couple, you know? Everyone says so. You've made the evening sparkle."

"Where have you been?" Henry asked.

Amos waved to indicate the universe.

"How do you like our provincial festivities, Miss Brennan? Are they up to your standards?"

"It's a lovely evening."

"But a bit rude and boorish, wouldn't you say? A bit déclassé, isn't it? To someone who has been to the Continent, who speaks German . . . why, we're a bunch of hillbillies when you come down to it."

"Amos, don't start," Henry said. "Can't you for once just have a pleasant evening?"

"Oh, I'm having quite a pleasant evening, I promise. The sight of you two has been a highlight. Your hair and gown . . . well, they're a triumph, Miss Brennan. But never mind that. I've come to get you both. Our old friend, Fox, has entered a significant wager that I thought you might like to witness. It's really quite marvelous. He plans to shoot an apple off his dog's head. It's about to happen and I thought you should see. They have the dog, but they're in search of an apple. Funny, you would think it might be harder the other way around ... to find the apple but not the dog ... but Fox has had his dog for a decade or longer. You know him, Henry. The old retriever that's always with him."

"How did this come about?" Henry asked.

Amos raised his glass to indicate alcohol and shrugged. Then he stood.

"Just out here," he said. "Out in the lot."

"It sounds like simple cruelty to me," Collie said.

"Does it? Well, Fox stands to gain a good deal if he can manage it. You see, the thing is he loves the dog. Everyone knows it. So Parker McMahon set the wager at twenty acres of prime land, which is more than fair, I daresay. They always devil each other. But Fox is a good shot, so it's an even contest anyway you look at it."

"I think we'll pass," Henry said.

Amos pursed his lips and left. He touched the backs of the chairs as he went, using them to steady himself.

"Not a fistfight after all," Henry said, picking up his drink again. "Something straight out of *William Tell* instead."

"Can they be serious?"

"I'm afraid they are."

"I want to stop it. It's horrible."

"Too late, Collie. There must be a little blood sacrifice to these evenings. That's always been the way. This is a new wrinkle, I'll grant you, but the theme is an old one."

Collie put down her drink and moved to go outside. She intended to stop it, but by the time she reached the parking lot the entire crowd had beat her to it. Looking around, she saw the garish expressions of those watching the event. A few men had turned on their headlights to form a court of illumination. In the center of the ring sat a black dog with an apple on its head. The dog was aged and slightly stout. It sat the way an old dog that is no longer supple in its hips must sit; one bandy leg stuck out from under his rump. He looked like a small old man, his gray muzzle pale white in the harsh light.

They had cleared the area behind the dog. Fox—she did not know the man, but he was evidently the owner—stood in front of the dog with a pistol raised. He was a large man with reddish hair and a bright pink complexion. He breathed with difficulty, his mouth sucking in air like a fish of some sort. He sighted down the barrel, then lowered the gun again. He pulled off his jacket and threw it aside. He stood in his shirtsleeves, obviously agitated and unhappy, but powerless to swim free of the current that had trapped him.

"You said twelve strides," the man, Fox, said, his eyes casting back and forth between the dog and his position. "This is fifteen at least."

"Shoot the apple!" someone yelled, and the crowd laughed.

"You can move in a foot," a man nearby said.

Parker McMahon evidently, Collie surmised. The whole scene struck her as a primitive mass. She could not take her eyes off the poor animal. It sat in the headlamp light oblivious to what was about to occur. She had never seen anything sadder. Now and then the dog's tail thumped the ground as if, even amid this insanity, it sought to be a friend to its owner. The apple rested on its head, held by an elastic of some sort. The dog appeared to be wearing the equivalent of a child's party hat.

"Stop this!" she shouted. "This is barbaric!"

People shushed her. They wanted to hear the interplay between Fox and Parker McMahon. Henry called out, too, but she noted he did not sound insistent. He implored Fox to think about what he was doing, but Fox—what kind of man was named Fox? she wondered—was obviously too far in his cups to think clearly.

Fox stepped a stride closer to his dog. He raised his gun again. The crowd became silent. And then Collie heard the most horrible sound.

Fox called the dog's name. "Buster," he said, getting the dog to turn to him, and then he fired.

The dog flew sideways. It made no sound. Neither did the crowd. Collie looked away, shivering. Then she heard Fox stepping across the gravel, and she heard a second shot, this one truer than the first, and then a third one put punctuation to everything. No one moved, and the sound of the river, forgotten and then suddenly remembered, covered this small tragedy.

❧ *Chapter Sixteen* ❧

In a single instant Collie knew everything: she knew that she loved August. It came at the most inconvenient moment. She stood on the porch of the administration building watching three cutting teams loading for a prolonged stay in Vermont. August's team was going, too. She knew that; she had supervised the paperwork, so that much was not a surprise. But what did catch her unawares was the slant of afternoon light, the warm autumnal sun, the patting of dry leaves on the oak that stood next to the building. She did not want to love him. She had avoided him for the past few weeks. She had avoided him after Marie's funeral, finding his presence unbearable in her desire to walk into his arms and be comforted by him. She had set her clock by him. She had departed the dining room when he entered, entered when he departed. Yes, it was childish and obvious to anyone who cared to watch, but she stuck to the plan, containing her exposure to him as if he were radioactive or contagious. She hoped that absence would rid her of his place in her heart, and until this moment, this precise instant, she had persuaded herself that it had worked. She had even enjoyed several dates with Henry, going once to Portland to the theater, attending the movies with him, going to a family Sunday dinner. She had kissed Henry twice, forcing herself to accept his advances, writing to Estelle afterward that it was for the best after all. No, she explained, their kisses had not been passionate, but passion could grow, she hoped, if planted in the soil of respectability and mutual respect.

Then she saw August and she felt herself thrown back into her former feelings. He did not see her at first. He wore his prison clothes, and she noted at once that he had lost weight. He looked thin and reedy, as if the work among the trees had turned him into a vine. He also slouched, coming to a stop beside his friend Gerhard, and she saw his hair lift in the autumn breeze, his eyes at first on the bus, then slowly, inevitably, they came to rest on hers.

She tried to look away. Honestly, she tried. She imagined some excuse to go back inside, but it was her responsibility to mark off the passengers, to write down the equipment and further provisions. Lieutenant Peters stood among the men, counting them, talking and laughing, occasionally turning to her when he required some nuance translated. Perhaps he had forgotten about August until the moment he appeared. But when he did, sauntering up from his barracks, his duffel bag casually perched on his shoulder, she understood that the others watched their interaction, watched them as you would watch two horses released in a meadow of high grass.

August did not speak. He stood with his hip out, his leg cocked at an attractive angle, his casualness intensely appealing. His posture suggested he had accepted her indifference, her constant absence, her deliberate effort to stay away. Perhaps he even approved of it, she reflected, and comprehended its necessity. Watching him, her eyes on his, she wanted to rip out her heart and throw it away. It would only bring pain, she thought. It would only bring upset and turmoil, place her father in an untenable position. No, she was better off with Henry, with anyone else, really, even with the bashful guards who sometimes tried to capture her attention for a moment when she walked to the refectory or accepted a ride to an appointment. Why did she react as she did to this one young man? It was maddening and cruel.

"All right, boys, let's load up the bus," Lieutenant Peters called when he had made the final tally. "Do you have everyone, Collie?"

"Yes, twenty, right?"

"Twenty it is."

"I have them all."

"I'll count them as they board anyway," he said. "Double-check."

"Okay."

Before they started climbing aboard, August stepped close to the porch and reached in his breast pocket. He pulled out a chain of clover flowers intricately woven with grass blades into three bands that resembled strands of pearls. Collie examined them, her hands shaking as she tried to hold the clipboard steady.

"In my country," he said in German, "when two lovers part, they give each other such a chain. Each day you remove one link. When the flowers are all gone, then your promised one will return. It's a custom in our land, and people set great store by it."

"But I have nothing for you," she said.

He smiled. She loved his smile.

"To know you will remove a clover and think of me is my present. If you keep it under your pillow, we will see each other in our dreams. That's what my mother always said."

"Did you make it yourself?" she asked, accepting it.

He nodded.

She placed the clipboard on the arm of a chair and held the clover necklace out to inspect it. The rest of the men had continued to board, but she knew they watched. Lieutenant Peters watched, too, although he pretended to be busy with the list of riders.

From her position above him, she bent down to kiss his cheek. It was wrong to do it; it was wrong to accept the flowers in the first place. Here she was making a spectacle of herself in a public square. But she could not hold back. She intended to kiss his cheek in a friendly manner, to make light of the flower necklace, but as she moved closer she felt a force pull her toward his lips. It was useless to resist. She felt herself falling into him, his eyes on hers, his breath suddenly mixed with her own. At the last instant she did not kiss his lips but managed to move an inch toward his cheek, but that left the edge of her mouth pressed to his. She felt the world still and become quiet, and even the men, who she imagined would hoot and make lewd comments about such a kiss, said nothing at all.

"Every day, one flower," he whispered.

She nodded. Her lips touched his and then broke away.

❧ PART THREE ❧

PART THREE

❧ *Chapter Seventeen* ❧

It was to be a house wedding. The news caught Collie by surprise. Estelle's letters had grown infrequent over the fall, and somewhat veiled, and so her request to have Collie act as a bridesmaid, to attend a wedding held in Estelle's house, perplexed her initially. Naturally the news also brought joy for her friend, and she had used the office phone to reply, leaving a hasty message with Mrs. Emhoff that of course she would attend, that she would follow up by a letter, that it was magnificent news and she was flattered to be asked to be a bridesmaid. Georgie Porgie had won the day after all, and Collie's letter to Estelle had seemed to open a gate between them, so that notes flew back and forth as before, the missives dotted with news about dresses and colors and cakes. It was a whirl, Estelle wrote. Once decided, they saw no reason to wait, so the engagement was brief and the wedding, as the enclosed invitation suggested, was planned for the first week of December. Christmas and the wedding, Estelle added in her letter, had somehow formed their own union, so that it was difficult to separate the two. They had early snow, thank goodness, and the yard and trees were white. Her papa had decided to hire two sledges for visiting guests, an old touch but a whimsical one, and Estelle stated that she felt she had decided to get married in Dickens's time, not her own. It was all rather comical and gay, and she asked Collie to arrive three days before so that she might help her keep a level head. Of course there was also the dress to fit, and hair. . . . It was all a lovely confusion.

And now she was on a train traveling to Ashtabula, of all places, on a wintery day at the start of December 1944. Collie looked out the window, her face tired and happy. The train slowed; they came into a station, not Ashtabula, and she watched the conductor swing off the train and call something to the waiting passengers. A quiet snow fell, and it looked beautiful in the afternoon light. The open doors allowed frigid air to pass through the car. Collie enjoyed the sensation of the cold resting just outside, while they remained in warmth, hurtling through the day toward the wedding.

When the train got under way again, she decided to go to the dining car for hot chocolate. She had perhaps an hour and a half to Ashtabula.

Snow fell harder outside as she found a seat on the north side of the dining car. For a moment Collie felt she traveled through a snow globe, a make-believe world. The porter came and took her order. He also left a bowl of hard-boiled eggs and a saltshaker. Collie didn't feel she could face eating an egg, and she turned her attention to the countryside, her eyes roaming.

She thought of Marie. She thought of her every day, her sweet, gentle presence like music heard at a distance. She did not allow herself to remember the funeral, the ponderous, heavy ceremony that had demonstrated no understanding of the girl. Instead, she recalled the day that Marie had danced on the log at the halfway point of their ride, her joy at singing that ridiculous song. *Mares eat oats, and does eat oats, and little lambs eat ivy.* She had danced and twirled on the log beside Scooter Pond, and everything about her, every molecule, had called out for joy and happiness, for adventure and promise. Collie missed her friend, that sparkling girl who met the world each day with hope.

In time, after the porter brought her hot chocolate and she had sipped the rich foam from the top and spooned out the dollop of whipped cream, she let her mind wander to August. He was out in the snow somewhere, likely Vermont, cutting large pines and dragging them through the frigid woods. She had already removed today's flower, but she pulled out the remaining strand of clover buds and spread them on the table in front of her. They were fragile; they had dried and started to crumble apart, but she treated them like valuable jewels. Each day, a flower. He had been gone for close to three months, working in a camp that had twice been relocated for greater access to timber. She followed his journey on paper, but she had not shared a word with him in all that time. She wondered, frankly, if his feelings for her had been driven out of him by the harshness of the winter work. She wouldn't blame him if they had. But for her he was still fresh, remarkably fresh, in her mind. She no longer resisted thoughts of him. It was futile to do so. And when she accompanied Henry to the various events and occasions he found for them, she could not be unencumbered. They had gone to the movies; they had gone bowling and on a picnic. But she did not love him. Her heart did not rise up for him as it did for August, for the young German's ethereal beauty; she had no control over it in the end.

The porter passed by and asked if she wanted more hot chocolate. She shook her head. When she looked out at the countryside again, they seemed to be passing through the outlying region of a town. Maybe Ashtabula, she thought. She drank the last of her hot chocolate. Her lips touching the chocolate made her think of August, the kiss they had shared. Their bodies, so long deprived, had met in perfect wonder. What had started as an innocent gesture— had it ever been innocent? she wondered now with her head against the train window—had begun to glow and smolder between them. She could not feel that for Henry; she had never felt it for any other human.

She needed Estelle, she decided. She needed her help to sort things out. It was Estelle's wedding time, of course, but Collie hoped for a moment, an hour, when they might lay out the last months since Marie's death like a game of patience. Estelle would help her turn over the correct card, make the proper play. Collie felt too tired to think on her own, too confused by her heart to know how to go forward.

Estelle watched the door to the flower shop from the opposite side of the street. She pretended interest in the shoe-shop window directly in front of her, Towne's Shoes, but in reality she used the reflection in the window to keep vigil. Her head felt jammed with impossible thoughts and emotions, and she chided herself for being here, being across the street from Mr. Kamal's shop, when she had a thousand chores to distract her.

What did she want? What possible good could come of seeing him? She might have asked what good was morning, or evening supper, or a well-made bed. She could not resist, or pretend to ignore the ache in her stomach, and she glanced repeatedly in the window of Towne's Shoes only to catch the square reflection of Mr. Kamal's storefront.

Collie was scheduled to arrive in slightly more than an hour. It was unfair, she realized, to spend her time here, absurdly looking in the shoe window reflection like a lovesick schoolgirl. But there it was. She saw two women, both carrying hand muffs, step out of the flower shop, their heads bent conspiratorially toward each other. For no reason whatsoever, she despised them. They were free to visit Mr. Kamal whenever they liked, while she, by her own manipulations, had made the flower shop off-limits. She was affianced, all but a wife, and she did not imagine George, or even her mother, would look kindly on fanning these old embers to life.

She pulled a small pad and pencil from her purse. She had become a great list maker with the preparations for the wedding, and she scanned the items now, hoping for one sufficiently pressing to pull her away. But she had deliberately cleared off time for Collie, and she had this forty minutes or so to spend. . . . She tucked the moleskin pad away and threw the pencil in after it.

She took one last glance in Towne's window, then simply turned and walked toward Mr. Kamal's store. As simple as that. Why make it more complicated? she asked herself. He was a friend; true, there had been feelings, but she was engaged now, and George was a fact of life, and surely she could visit Mr. Kamal without danger. In fact, she told herself, as she stopped to let a cab pass, then stepped sideways when a man pushing a wheelbarrow of ashes hurried across the street near her, it was precisely the thing to do. The wedding plans had inoculated her, she was certain, and seeing Mr. Kamal now, observing him for what he was rather than what she imagined him to be, might serve to relegate him to the past. She owed it to herself and to George, not to mention the entire wedding party coalescing around her, to set matters to rest.

She did not hesitate at the door. She pushed through, triggering a familiar bell, and Mr. Kamal, his eyes squinting slightly at the brightness of the front room as he came out from the back of the store, raised his hand to protect his eyes. The gesture made him appear old. A shopkeeper after all, she realized. She could not imagine George making such a gesture. She smiled at the newly won knowledge.

"Ah," he said, smiling. "You have returned at last."

"Good afternoon, Mr. Kamal. It's been too long."

"Yes, for me, certainly. How wonderful you look. Positively radiant. As a bride is entitled."

She stopped in front of the counter. His words had surprising force. A bride! How had he known? It pleased her that he knew she was to be married, that he had followed her life even when she had not included him in her affairs. Doubtless he had read the papers; he had told her long ago that reading the engagement announcements was part of his business. He often picked up jobs that way, sending a discreet card with a handwritten note that offered to be of whatever assistance he could provide to the marrying couple. Yes, she was sure, he had followed her engagement announcement.

"How can I help you today?" he asked. "Would you care for some tea? I was just putting the kettle on when you came through the door."

"Thank you, no," she said, "I have a visitor arriving on the five o'clock train."

"Ah."

"I was just passing by . . . so many errands, as I'm sure you can imagine."

"A marriage is a great undertaking. I understand."

"And I thought to myself, I have not seen Mr. Kamal in such a long time. I had a moment to look in, and so I did."

"I'm glad you thought of me."

Oh, what was she doing? Her feet felt rooted to the ground; they had sprung thick taproots, like a beech, knuckling into the ground, tearing up the soil as it grew. What a colossal mistake! She thought, suddenly, that she had always mistaken his intentions. Yes, that was clear! Maybe he had merely been polite, seeking her business, and she had interpreted things entirely wrong. She wondered, too, how conversation had always flown so easily between them. Now it felt stilted and awkward, and it was everything she could do not to turn and flee, despite the rooted feeling in her extremities.

"So George Samuels is the lucky fellow. Is that not correct? My heartfelt congratulations."

"Thank you. It happened rather quickly."

"So I gathered," he said, his eyes, for a moment, betraying feelings about her abandonment. "I didn't know you were fond of him."

"We go back a long way."

"Yes, of course."

"I think of him as the Eternal George. He's always been around."

"Ah, yes, I see. That is the same as in our country. People can be promised to each other at an early age."

"I was never promised exactly. . . . It just seemed a natural fit."

He smiled. For an instant, Estelle saw the hurt she had inflicted on him. He, naturally, was not a perfect fit. That was clear; it always had been clear, she saw now. She allowed her eyes to pass into his. Yes, the feeling was still there, summoned at once when their eyes touched one another. He was handsome. She had perhaps been aware of it before, but now, with his brown eyes locked on her, his white turban starched and fresh atop his head, his hands spread on the flower counter, she saw he was a fine figure, a flesh-and-blood man, not merely a paper cutout she had come to play with once or twice a week. She imagined kissing him. The recognition that she might kiss him, that perhaps he wanted to kiss her, flashed across her consciousness like a bright light. How idiotic she had been! How casually hurtful! Suddenly she felt close to fainting; her head became dizzy and her knees wanted to buckle. She realized she had not eaten all day.

"I'm sorry," she said, turning to go.

"You don't look well. Stay a moment. Sit by the window."

"I should go."

"The tea is ready . . . a short, hasty cup and a cookie. Have you eaten recently? Your face suddenly looks white."

"I feel rather strange, I admit . . ."

He came around the counter and led her to the chair in the window. It was where they always sat, a circular fountain table nestled among a forest of green hanging plants. The fragrance of the flowers filled her senses. She felt his hand on her elbow as she lowered herself onto the seat. He held up a finger to say he would be a moment, then he disappeared around the counter once more. Before she could think what had happened, he returned with two cups of tea balanced on a tray, and a small plate of gingersnaps between the cups.

"I promise not to detain you longer than you like," he said, taking his place across from her, "but you appeared faint. Drink a cup of tea and have a cookie or two. They won't hurt you. You'll be the better for it. Then you can go and meet your friend."

"Collie Brennan. The one with the German beau."

"Ah, the one who felt a strong attraction to a German soldier? Yes, I remember. Now sip again."

She tried to imagine George exhibiting such tenderness, but she could not push her mind to it.

"Yes, my friend is coming into town for the wedding," Estelle said, prattling on, she felt, to avoid greater subjects. "She'll be here inside of an hour. It's madness, I know, to be married in December. Somehow Christmas and the wedding have joined together. But it can be entertaining, I suppose."

"Anytime a wedding takes place is the correct time."

"And my friend . . . yes, she still writes about the German soldier. August is his name. She is worried her German soldier will return to see his earlier life and he will disappear."

"That is a legitimate concern, isn't it? The world is in upheaval. You couldn't blame him for wanting to see his homeland."

"No, of course not," Estelle said, sipping the tea again. She felt its warmth spilling into her body. She reached forward and took a gingersnap.

"I forgot to eat today," she said. "It simply didn't occur to me."

"That's not healthy. You must eat in the morning."

"I've been so busy. . . ."

He nodded. She bit into the gingersnap. It tasted wonderfully fresh.

"They're delicious," she said. "Thank you."

"You may always take shelter here," he said, and smiled. "May I ask you a question?"

"Yes, of course."

"Were my flowers . . . did you find fault with my shop?"

"Your flowers?"

"My services, I should say. You had always used me as your florist, so when your engagement was announced, I naturally thought that perhaps I would be of service."

She looked up carefully from the last portion of gingersnap. Could he possibly have taken offense at that? At the failing of a business transaction? Wasn't it clear why she couldn't engage him to handle the floral arrangements? She felt confused and more dazed than ever. She took a last sip of the tea—yes, it had revived her—and carefully answered.

"I've always admired your shop, Mr. Kamal. I hope you understand."

He looked at her carefully. She could not read his expression.

"I should go," Estelle said. "It will be a race to get to the station on time. She has come a long way."

"I've offended you," he said.

"No, not at all. You've been nothing but kind."

"Yes, I talked of business matters when it was something else that brought you here to my door. Forgive me. It was insensitive."

"I'm just so busy these days. . . ."

"I understand. You came because we have had many moments together. Isn't that the case? And leaving one friend for another is always painful. I was a fool to talk about business. What are some flowers, more or less?"

"Your flowers are always lovely, Mr. Kamal."

"You have made the correct choice, Estelle."

His eyes went to hers. She felt herself tremble. Did he mean her choice of a florist or her choice of George? Then she berated herself for being a ninny. She knew very well what he meant. He was saying good-bye as she had said good-bye. It was not about the flowers at all.

"In another world," she said, her eyes directly on his.

"But we live in only one world at a time."

She stood slowly. He stood as well. She smiled a tight smile, then left. The jingle of the doorbell was quickly lost in the traffic sounds.

The house, Collie thought at first glance, resembled a great wedding cake itself. Perhaps it was the snow that covered it in a frosted white— like a rich cream icing—but the house rose up at least three stories tall, blazing and brilliant, as if it could hardly contain its happiness at the approaching wedding. It was six o'clock and already the sky was dark and covered in clouds, but that hardly mattered given the steady lights that pushed rectangular cutouts onto the street from the house.

"The place is a bustle," Estelle said as the cabdriver pulled under the porte cochere. "It isn't usually such a madhouse, but the wedding has taken over everything from morning until night. Father stays at his office until the last possible moment to escape from it. It's quite comical if you give in to it."

"It's beautiful," Collie said, her voice barely able to contain her pleasure at the sight.

"It was built by a railroad baron at the turn of the century," Estelle said. "It's a solid old place, I'll give it that. Mother says the house has been smiling at the prospect of hosting a wedding, and I half believe she's on to something. Now come along. You must be completely worn-out."

Collie noted that the front stairs had been built in the time of horse carriages, because the first step was higher than any she had ever encountered. In former times, one might have stepped directly from the carriage onto the first step, but the cab rode significantly lower than even the smallest carriage. The driver came around to help with the bags, and Collie watched as Estelle discreetly paid him, slipping a folded bill into his hand as he set the bags on the steps. It was one of many observations Collie had already made about her friend's naturalness in her native surroundings. For the first time,

Collie caught a glimpse of the forces that had formed her friend, and she felt the satisfaction of someone receiving an important clue toward solving a difficult puzzle. This was not Smith College, nor a backwater town in New Hampshire. That much was clear already.

A butler or footman—what was the difference, Collie tried to remember—appeared on the top stairs and promised to take over the bags. His name was Charles, and he looked old and tall, as if some of his branches had been knocked away by time, but the center tree had continued to grow. A silly thought, Collie knew. Estelle, meanwhile, grabbed her by the elbows and whispered that it was time to take her medicine. By that she meant meeting her mother, Collie knew, and she let herself be scooted up the steps. Pine swags hung everywhere; an enormous wreath, the biggest Collie had ever seen outside of Macy's or Gimbels, took an entire wall beside the door. It looked like a great green moon, Collie decided, with a Scotch plaid ribbon at its bottom.

"Oh, you've made it!" Mrs. Emhoff said as they came through the door, her hands carrying a folded tablecloth. "We were about to send out the Mounties to look for you. George has been here a half hour at least. He's in the library with your father. Collie, how nice to see you again. It's been years since you were classmates. Estelle told me how you took such good care of her in New Hampshire. How glad we are that you could join us in these happy days."

"Thank you for having me," Collie said.

"Now you really must rescue poor George," Mrs. Emhoff continued. "He's likely climbing the walls by now. They have a fire going, and I've asked for sandwiches. . . . You don't mind if we are less formal, do you? We've got so much to do and the kitchen staff is flat out. Now run upstairs and get Collie settled in the lavender room. Isn't that what we thought? Then come down and join us. I'll just put this away."

She smiled, touched Collie's arm in welcome, then sped off, her voice calling to someone deeper in the house. Collie fell in behind Estelle as they climbed the steps to the second floor. The stairway was large and ornate; carved pinecones served as accents along the balustrades. Estelle called over her shoulder that the stairway had been designed by an architect named Ovid Hobbs, a person of some fame when it came to such things. She said she always hated the banisters because as a child she had wanted to slide down them, but the pinecones made that impossible.

They continued down a long hallway, stopping finally near the end. Collie saw immediately why the room had been called lavender. A pale blue paint, with perhaps a touch of mauve, covered the walls. The bedcover matched, as did the small settee placed near a tiny coal stove. An enormous armoire took up one wall at the south end. It was a solid, capable room, Collie decided, composed of castaways from the rest of the house.

"You'll be comfortable here, I hope," Estelle said, dropping onto the bed. "Please, let's not stand on ceremony. I need you to be my New Hampshire friend, happy and gay. Collie, you are in charge of everything . . . absolutely everything. Whatever you tell me to do, I'll do."

"Your house is beautiful," Collie said. "Did we pass by the library?"

"Downstairs, off where we came in," Estelle said.

"I can't wait to meet George," Collie said, slipping out of her coat. "I feel as though I already know him."

"He's looking forward to meeting you, too. He has a terrible head for names and this wedding, all the fuss . . . it's as if his head were a pitcher and it's nearly filled up. Men really don't enjoy these occasions. I've always heard that was the case, but I never *believed* it until I watched my fiancé go through it. Nevertheless the finish line is in sight. The rest of the wedding party is arriving tomorrow. Then it will have all the inevitability of an avalanche."

Collie caught the last phrase and glanced quickly at Estelle. What was wrong? That deprecatory note, that tone, had been lingering like a ghost in everything she said or wrote concerning the wedding and her marriage to George. Collie had thought that she might have imagined it, but here it was again, rising to light in the first minutes of their visit. She opened her mouth to say something, but then realized it was not the time. Nevertheless, she determined to get to the bottom of it one way or the other. But that would have to wait for later, because Estelle rose to herd her downstairs.

"Into the valley rode the five hundred," she said, "isn't that how it goes? Was it five hundred? I can't recall. Half a league, half league . . . that's all I remember. Now remember, George is the young one! My father is the older man. Lead away. These are my last nights as a maiden, you see. Lead on. Just down past the pinecones here. . . ."

→ *Chapter Eighteen* ←

"A letter for you," Gerhard said, tossing a blue envelope onto August's cot. "I nearly missed it. You should come to mail call, you know? They place these letters into a dead file as undeliverable if they aren't taken."

August sat up, his heart a quick flame. The letter had been sent in a blue service envelope and readdressed by the Red Cross, so that whatever had been written had probably been circulating in a tide of other letters for months at least. How could it have found him? He had returned from Vermont only the day before, and the letter's arrival seemed miraculous. Nevertheless, the sight of the letter made him recoil. His mind hurried ahead and imagined too quickly what news the letter might bring. To live in ignorance was nearly preferable, he realized, than to read the news of his homeland. Letters could be a mixed blessing, as he well knew from watching others gorge, then choke on the information the missives brought, and this letter, trapped in a pale blue envelope, appeared menacing in its deceiving blandness.

He thanked Gerhard, then slipped the letter under his mattress.

"You're not going to read it?" Gerhard asked, obviously surprised.

"Not now."

"I don't know how you can resist. How long has it been?"

"Six months."

"I would tear it open and devour it."

"I need to pick my time. It's been too long. Thank you, though."

Gerhard stared at him, then shrugged and walked away. August lay back on his bunk. He closed his eyes, trying to rest, but throughout the barracks his fellow prisoners talked and kidded one another; it was the best hour of the day, the time before dinner when the guards turned their eyes away and left the prisoners to their own devices. Everyone was cold from a day of work outside, and the guards needed to get inside as well. A cutting north wind had blown all day, raising powdered ghosts in whirlwinds down in the hollows, and the entire camp, August knew, had gone inside to thaw. He rested against his pillow, glad to have steady heat from the box stove pushing warmly into the room. That, at least, was one consolation from working in a logging operation: they never lacked for wood to heat themselves.

The letter, however, would not let him rest. It burned like a coal underneath him. He swung his legs off the bed and went closer to the stove, where a group of prisoners had built a crèche from cigar boxes. It was an ingenious work, and it had become a dollhouse for them all; instead of a scene from Bethlehem, the crèche had taken on a decidedly Germanic appearance. August sat on a turned-over apple box and held his hands out to the stove, his eyes resting on the details of the crèche scene. His skin felt raw and thin, as if the winter had stripped it of its insulation. Two other men sat on boxes in the same semicircle around the stove. They were short-timers, recently arrived, and they retained the jowly freshness of German recruits. August sat and absorbed the heat. His feet tingled as they began to flow with blood again. His fingers came back as if from a land far away. A strange, riotous emotion made him feel dizzy. He wished he had never seen the letter; he wished Gerhard had never retrieved it. He sincerely doubted it could bring him good news, and he did not know if he could stand one more loss, let alone the death of his brother, or the ransacking of his home.

"... sliding days," one of the new men—a blond young boy not more than eighteen—said from his position on the apple box. "My father made a sled and we had a course. . . ."

"We did as well. We came down through the mountains, and the course ran through the pines," the other said—another blond, though this one was darker and thinner, a knife to the other's spoon—and August felt utter contempt for them. The fools didn't comprehend the world they remembered with such fondness was gone. He opened his mouth to say something but then put his head in his hands. He was hungry, he realized, and that made him ill-tempered. Better to work, he understood, no matter how cold. Better to have one's hands and mind busy. Then you would not have letters arriving to drive you mad.

"That world you remember is gone," he said when they failed to shut up about their youthful sliding days back in Germany. He could not help himself. He raised his head and spoke directly to them. "It has vanished. Are you blind to what has happened to you?"

"We understand we're prisoners," the knife said, his voice betraying bewilderment. "That's perfectly clear."

"That world . . . it's been blown apart, you understand?" August said.

"That's dark thinking," the spoon fellow said. "The world is still there, whatever you say."

"Is it?" August asked, and wanted to throttle them. "Do you think the Allies won't bomb us into submission? They won't leave a brick on a brick. And what do you think they will give us to eat? Cows do not prosper when a war rages on. Chickens and pigs, they'll be killed and roasted by the enemy. Where will the food come from? Have you thought of any of this?"

The men shared a quick look. August put his head back in his hands. Why was he chiding them? They were boys. Why shouldn't they remember their pasts fondly? Yes, it would all be destroyed, all of it, but it was evil to ask them to stop hoping. For a moment he pictured Collie. He hated to admit how much he counted on her, on the mere fact of her existence. If she existed, he reasoned, then other good things might exist; she gave him hope.

"Sorry," he said, his voice trembling, and stood. "I'm too wrapped up in my own thoughts just now."

"Understood," the spoon said.

August went back to his bunk and drew the letter out from its place under the mattress. He lay down and turned his back to the room. He held the letter in front of him; it was a woman's handwriting. He slit the Red Cross envelope with his fingernail and felt his breath quicken when he recognized his mother's handwriting on the enclosed envelope inside the first. Hot tears came into his eyes. He held the letter against his lips. The address had been written by his mother. Her hand had been here, on this paper, he comprehended. She had sat somewhere, probably at her darning table, and had written him these words. He closed his eyes and pictured her, his breath slowly turning into a silent sob. He rolled his head into his pillow and tried to get control of himself.

Oh please, he thought. *Oh please, no, no please.*

He could not bear it. He could not bear to hear more bad news. How much was a man supposed to endure? Slowly, so as not to injure it in any way, he slid the inner envelope out of the larger one. Yes, she had sent it to his brigade. A series of postage stamps and directions covered the envelope, each one directing the letter to a different location. A Red Cross member in France had written *prisoner* across the back corner. His entire war history had been re-created, tracing him to this tiny outpost in the White Mountains of New Hampshire. It was incomprehensible. He might have received a note from outside the known universe so remote did the world the letter represented feel to him at that moment.

He began to sob again. This time the tears came so fast they overpowered him. He kept his face in his pillow for a long time. Eventually the others began leaving for dinner. He heard Red or one of his workers ring the meal bell. The glad chimes went on a long time and seemed to carry up into the bright cold of the mountains. His stomach growled. He did not want to miss mess call, but he could no more replace the letter in its hiding place than he could sprout wings and fly across the sea.

My dearest August, my son, the letter began.

He read in gulps; like water once tasted by a dying man, he could not control his intake. *Hard times. Little food. Water pipes broken and the rails blown apart by saboteurs. Internal resistance. Dangerous days.* His lambs still lived, but his dog, his little Kettle—the inheritor of Chowder's place in his heart—had died. She had died of a broken heart, his mother said, from missing him. She was better off, when it came to it. Everyone was well. Frederick had been conscripted and had been sent to France. She did not know where; they did not inform families of the details. She had not heard from him in at least three months.

At this, August turned the envelope over and looked for dates. The date his mother had written at the top of the letter said 7 February 1944. The letter was nine, no, ten months old. That meant Frederick had been sent to the front in November or December of the year before. His brother had spent at least a year fighting if he was still alive or not captured.

August went back and read the rest. Given the news it might have brought, it was reasonably positive. Food and water and the pleasant features of their life had been eradicated, but at least no one had died. Not as of February, August noted. His mother closed with a prayer for his safety and with a mention of his father's blessing. She said again she was sorry about their little dog, Kettle. She asked him to promise to come home safely. They had not given up hope that one day they would all be reunited. That, she said, gave her reason to go on. Write, she pleaded. Send word. He could not tell if she had received any of the letters he had written; the time lag was too great, the distance impossible to cross.

He slipped the letter back into its hiding place, then wiped his eyes and hurried to join the others for dinner. He must eat, he knew. Day by day, that was the only way to approach it. He pulled his collar close around his neck as he ran across the boardwalk toward the dining hall. A guard braced him and asked what he was doing coming late to dinner, and August answered he had needed the latrine, an excuse, he knew, no one ever challenged.

⊰ *Chapter Nineteen* ⊱

Estelle had been correct about one thing, certainly, Collie thought. Christmas and the wedding festivities blended together in delicious ways, forming even the snow—the snow that fell steadily, like confetti to greet a great parade—into celebratory buntings and waves of interesting contours. Everywhere Collie saw pine swags and wreaths, the green pines dappled with white and pale gray ice, so that one looked several times to see the arrangement, the play of pattern and design, before passing on to the next vision. At times like these, riding through the streets in an old-fashioned sledge drawn by a pair of gray Belgians, she felt she had entered a fairy tale. It was all gay, all laughter, and she enjoyed the men, their heavy coats and deep voices, the silly, mad things they shouted to one another. Even George, *Eternal George*, as Estelle called him, seemed lighter and more interesting in the blanketed cockpit of a sledge. The men wore top hats for a laugh, and they had all placed sprigs of pine in their hatbands, and the women had made the drivers stop so that they could demand their own pine sprigs. A crazed scramble followed, with the men dashing about to pull pieces of pine boughs from the selected trees, with the women directing them and sending them back for better specimens. It felt vaguely bacchanalian, and innocent at the same time, and when they arrived at Porters, the enormous steak house reserved for the groom's dinner, one nearly wished to remain outside in the comfort of the carriage, the night flowing like a shaken snow globe all around.

Estelle's father, really, proved to be the ringmaster. He rode in the lead sledge with George's parents, but he kept standing and yelling back to the party, blowing a ridiculous slide whistle, and that, bit by bit, became the theme of the evening. The whistle went from hand to hand until even the promise of its first note became hilarious; Estelle had the opportunity to blow it, and she stood and played her part, her face luminous, her sprig of pine slipping precariously across her forehead. Cheers greeted the whistle, and by the time they poured into Porters—a thick-beamed castle with white stucco walls and cement floors and waiters in red boiled-wool jackets—everyone felt the merry glow of the outdoors enhanced by the fragrance and warmth of the old restaurant.

A magical evening, Collie thought. The waiters scuttled them inside to an enormous table set with a white cloth. The weighty chairs scraped and grinded on the floor, but somehow that fitted the occasion. No one bothered with seating cards or any of the usual stuffiness that Collie associated with wedding parties. The men demanded cocktails immediately, and the waiters, when they delivered drinks, were met by the slide whistle giving their motions a comic sound track. Collie tried to trace the source of the good feelings, but they seemed genuine and without visible origins, so that her glances at Estelle reassured her that her earlier misgivings about George had been mistaken. Estelle glowed. She seemed to be everywhere, nesting among her female friends one moment, then joking with the men in the next, her eyes shiny with laughter. She was getting married!

"Now, now, now," Mr. Emhoff said, holding up his hand once everyone received a glass of sparkling wine. "Now, careful, careful . . . ," he said when he spotted the slide whistle raised to give him the business. "Easy, boys. It's probably not my turn to speak, this is the groom's party after all, but I wanted to say . . ."

Collie smiled and scarcely listened. What a picture they all made in that instant! Everyone wore fine evening clothes and the waiters ducking in and out were picturesque. She imagined a photograph taken at that moment, perhaps from above them all, the frame including the dewy bride and the handsome groom—yes, he was handsome in a subtle, understated way, Collie decided—and the grand fireplace sending out flickers of light that made everything positively medieval. It was life, precious life, and as Mr. Emhoff teetered closer to the end of his remarks, Collie sent her eyes down the table, past the jolly groomsmen, past Mrs. Emhoff and George's mother, until her eyes met Estelle's. And there, suddenly, Collie saw her friend's great sadness. It stole like a phantom across Estelle's eyes; she was clearly not conscious of it; her sight went out in a dull beam.

She must have believed no one watched, because anyone seeing it would have concluded the same thing. Estelle was not happy! The sure knowledge pierced Collie and made her draw back physically, almost as if from a blow, and she looked away out of guilt. But then she leaned forward again to get a better look, and the expression on Estelle's face slowly dissolved, broke apart as she sensed her father's speech drawing to an end. *She is putting on a mask,* Collie thought, and in the wake of that single impression everything else fell into place. Estelle's unhappiness was a restive note, the single element of the night's gaiety that did not fit the communal picture. Collie looked rapidly to see if George had any inkling, but his face looked up in bland amusement at Mr. Emhoff, his thick fingers on a glass ready to raise it for the inevitable toast.

Then the evening resumed; the look on Estelle's face had been like a turtle slipping slowly under the still surface of a lake. It was gone and barely a ripple marked its passing. Someone blew the slide whistle as Mr. Emhoff raised his glass. Everyone stood except George and Estelle. Happiness and prosperity, long days, rich years, then the glasses lifted, the light refracted in the sparkling wine, and George raised both their hands in acknowledgment, Estelle's face locked in a smile, the slide whistle undermining even this small moment.

Collie forced herself to rejoin the hilarity of the table as she resumed her seat. She glanced repeatedly at Estelle, but she did not catch her friend in anything but the merriest guise. No one would know a thing by watching her, Collie realized. A few people began to clink their glasses—encouragement to kiss—and the guests, Collie saw, beamed their pleasure at the awkward predicament. They must kiss; Collie joined in, her smile fixed and immobile, her thoughts passing for an instant to Marie, how she would have loved this evening, how she would have burned the brightest of them all. She watched as George wiggled his eyebrows at the crowd, received the slide whistle in answer, then saw him bend in and kiss Estelle. She curled away slightly, pretending shyness, Collie observed, but what had been a secret at the beginning of the evening bloomed and became obvious at this point. Estelle did not love George. Estelle had been masterful at covering it, and she had fooled nearly everyone in the party, Collie guessed, but now, after their stares had met during Mr. Emhoff's toast, Collie saw the anguish in her friend's eyes.

Estelle kissed George in return, but it was a quick, duckish peck, her lips a bill to keep him at a distance. People laughed. A man at the low end of the table made a rude comment about the wedding night. That brought out a happy roar and George blushed and shrugged his shoulders, and George's father rose and started his own toast. Collie watched him and waited for the beam of her friend's eyes to pass her way again, only Estelle's look had submerged beneath the surface of the social niceties. She played her part, and when George's father concluded and called for raised glasses, Estelle smiled and kissed her fiancé with better feeling, and the slide whistle undercut the seriousness of the moment, and the red-jacketed waiters rushed in like dance partners on a Virginia reel closing together to clear the first course.

Estelle watched George vomit on the side of the road and decided that he was revolting. Not merely for the evening, she realized, but in general. It was an oddly liberating thought to hold so close to one's wedding. It took the pressure off, she decided. She did not have to be perfect; she did not have to make his house overly pleasant, or manage his meals with anything but average competency. To have a revolting husband, she saw now, might have certain advantages. It made her smile to think of it. Meanwhile, he retched again and she smelled the sickening stench of illness and alcohol. The horses shied at his sounds.

"Well, George is off to the races," someone said from the other side of the sledge.

Off to the races was a euphemism, Estelle knew, for becoming sick from alcohol.

"Yes, indeed," someone else said.

They were in the last sledge; the rest of the company had gone on at least an hour before. George had closed the party, toasting with his friends and groomsmen. Even the waiters, Estelle had seen, had become tired of the festivities. At a moment—when exactly, she couldn't say—the party had changed from something lighthearted and happy to something determined and dark. George drank too much. She did not know him intimately enough to know if the problem was chronic or merely a manifestation that came into view at parties, but she suspected the former. She had seen the change in his eyes when he began drinking with a proficiency that surprised her. He was a good drinker until he was not.

"Well, one way or the other, we only rent the booze we drink," George said, mopping his mouth with a white handkerchief when he returned to the side of the sledge.

"Off to the races, Georgie," someone said.

"Not the first time, won't be the last," George said, climbing back into the sledge. "Mighty cold out there, though."

Estelle wished she had gone ahead with Collie and with the rest of the bride's party. She could imagine linked nights like this one, always returning last, always waiting on a final drink. It exhausted her to think of it. George, meantime, slumped against her, cuddling a little for warmth. He flounced the blanket around her.

"You stink of vomit," she whispered to him.

"Sorry."

"Just lean away."

He did as he was told, which was another good feature of George, she decided. Eternal George. The driver cracked a whip and the horses moved on. The earlier snow had stopped now and the stars had come out in bright splendor. George took deep breaths beside her. The driver kept to the back roads so that he could be sure of a coating of snow on the macadam. In minutes they arrived at the back of the house.

"I'll see my own way in," Estelle said, trying her best to lighten her voice, "take care of my fiancé."

"I should come in," George said, but he made no move to rise.

"Good night, good night," the others called.

Estelle waved them off. Their sleigh bells made a merry sound, and she heard them laugh at something. George's laugh boomed loudest of all. Then the slide whistle gave a final rasp and the sledge finally disappeared around the corner of Thurston Street. Estelle stood on the curb and looked up at the sky. She stood looking up for what seemed a long time. The air felt fine on her face. It was a welcome moment of silence. She was marrying the following day. She repeated that to herself twice, before she took one last look at the stars and went inside.

Collie sat at the kitchen table enjoying a cup of cocoa. She had changed into a flannel nightgown. She appeared youthful sitting in the quiet kitchen. Estelle felt a moment of tenderness toward Collie that was particularly sharp. How sweet she was, how pure somehow. Collie would never make the kind of bargain that she herself had made; she would not marry out of convention or for social standing. Those things did not matter to her.

"I'm glad you're still awake," Estelle whispered. "I could use a cup of cocoa."

"I waited up for you, hoping you wouldn't be long," Collie said. "Take your things off and I'll fix you a cup. It's very late."

"Not so late for the city," Estelle said, suddenly feeling happier than she had most of the evening. "You're simply an old country mouse, Collie. But I would love a cup if there's any left. I'll just take off my things."

In two shakes she sat beside her friend with a cup of cocoa steaming before her. She took a deep breath and blew softly on the surface of the chocolate. She wondered, absently, how her life had become so complicated. It could be this simple, she realized, this wonderfully mundane. She had deliberately confused things; she had set her own house on fire and she had no one else to blame. But those were thoughts for later, she decided, not now.

"It was a lovely party," Collie said. "I enjoyed your father especially, Estelle. I had no idea he could liven things up as he did."

"Yes, he likes a good time. That's one of his best traits. And that horrible slide whistle."

"It was just mad," Collie said. "It's going to be a lovely wedding. The caterers have been in. . . . The living room is done. I looked at it with your mother when we came back. It's quite beautiful."

"Oh, it will come off all right, I'm sure. This time tomorrow I'll be a married woman."

"On your *lune de miel*. Where will you stay in Chicago?"

"At the Biltmore. George had been there on business, and he likes it very much. They know him there. They know George everywhere he goes."

"It's very exciting," Collie said.

"Do you think so?" Estelle asked, genuinely curious and bemused. "I suppose it is. Life with George might be very exciting."

Suddenly she felt on the verge of tears. She put her face in her hands. Collie instantly moved to put an arm over her shoulders. Estelle could no longer control her emotions. She broke down into small pieces, sobbing quietly, while Collie held her and whispered reassurances. The weight of the silent house seemed to bear down on them, Estelle realized. Everything waited. Tomorrow the guests arrived, along with great mounds of food, and flowers, and presents, and the house would gain immense gravity until it would sink lower and lower into the ground. They would all move more slowly, bound by the glue of their own expectations, and the thought was horrible, simply horrible, and she cried harder knowing that nothing could prevent the day's arrival.

"I'm pregnant," Estelle whispered into Collie's ear. "Pregnant by George. It was so stupid. So stupid and so utterly damning."

"Shhhhh."

"You must have guessed. I'm beginning to show. Mother has her doubts, but she hasn't said anything. It's the reason we are hurrying along. No one gets married at Christmas! Oh, it's all spoiled, everything is spoiled."

"What is spoiled?" Collie asked, patting her. "Nothing is spoiled. It will be all right. I didn't know. I had no idea. You're not the first. Not even among our friends. . . ."

"I let him . . . ," Estelle said, then fell into a deep series of sobs.

"What is it? Tell me," Collie said.

"I let George . . . he was my vaccination, you see?" Estelle said, recovering her breath at last. "My inoculation against Mr. Kamal. I had too many feelings. . . . I told myself that George was more my sort, safe and knowable, while Mr. Kamal . . ."

"Yes, I see. Of course. It makes sense when you explain it."

"And so I let him. To bind him to me. To bind George and to keep Mr. Kamal at a distance . . ."

"I understand. I do. I see it now."

"No one else knows. I've made a terrible mistake. I've thrown away my life and I knew I was doing it as I did it. Can you imagine what that feels like? It's a form of suicide, you know? It's despicable. I look down at George, I do, but I am the one who is deplorable. He at least is acting on honest feeling. He loves me. I haven't told him that I carry his child, but he wouldn't care. . . . It would make him love me more, you see? I don't even deserve his love."

"It's going to be okay. It will be all right. George will be a good husband. You can see that, surely. And tonight . . . you can have that kind of joy and pleasure . . . that kind of evening. People around you love you. Your parents love you."

"You're being kind," Estelle said, then moved slightly away so that she could clear her head. "And you, Collie . . . I was just thinking that you could never strike the bargain I made. It's not in your character. But mine . . . that's the most painful part. I have had to look at what I truly am, and it is a sad portrait, I assure you. I am a quick purchase. I see that now. The opinion I had of myself . . . that's all plowed under now. That's the most disturbing part. I was deluded before. I believed myself to be a person of character, or principle, and now I see my true nature. . . ."

"You can't think that way. Don't even let such thoughts into your head. I know you, Estelle, and I know what you are capable of. You are not a cheap purchase, as you say. You're not. The war has thrown everything upside down. I see it every day. But maybe you're underestimating yourself . . . and underestimating George. He will be a good father, and he will dote on you. I'm not deaf to what you're saying, but all in the fullness of time . . ."

"You must promise me you won't let yourself forget your feelings for August," Estelle said, feeling suddenly it was the most important thing in the world. "You mustn't tell yourself it isn't real or that it is unimportant. Do you promise? I couldn't stand it if you follow my example."

"I'm not even sure. . . ."

"Promise me. Learn from my mistake. At least then my ridiculous behavior will have some benefit to someone. I have compromised. That's the kindest interpretation you can put on it. Tell me you promise to allow him into your heart if it is inclined that way. Don't put up obstacles. Don't tell yourself it's impossible. You see how impossible things are for me? You don't want that. Promise me."

"I promise."

"I've seen how you look at him," Estelle said with feeling. "It's how I felt about Mr. Kamal. But I was too frightened, too mindful of opinion."

"You may have made the right decision. You can't know everything yet. August is an Austrian soldier, a prisoner. None of us can know what will happen."

"Can't I? I suppose not. What did they say in our introduction to philosophy class? I am presupposing. Oh, I'm just talking through my hat, Collie. It's late and we should get to bed. I'm sorry if I've put too much on you. I had to tell someone. Forgive me. I'm emotional right now."

"You never have to ask my forgiveness. There's nothing to forgive."

"Do you love August? Tell me honestly."

"I don't know him well enough to say. I know I feel light-headed to be near him. I feel that we're meant to be together somehow, but my common sense tells me otherwise."

"Don't give in to that. Not to that. Common sense is precisely the enemy, Collie. You've said you've gone out a few times with Henry, isn't that so? What did you feel? Was it the same feeling you had when you've been in the presence of August?"

"No, but I wanted to talk to you about Henry. He's not as bad as we had first thought."

"I won't soon forget Amos," Estelle said, her voice choking slightly as she said his name. "Oh, I know it can be confusing. How can we know what our hearts want? But if you love August, if you think he's what you need, then find a way. Find a way to be with him, promise me?"

"I will."

Estelle felt herself gathered in a fierce hug. Collie nearly fell from the chair in her determination to comfort her. "Take the long view," Collie whispered. It will be all right in the end. And Estelle, to her astonishment, half believed her friend.

Like candles, Collie thought from her position on the staircase, the guests spread out below her, their faces looking up. Like bright, beautiful candles.

That's how the bride's party appeared to her. The gowns fit exquisitely. And the short veils on their headpieces, a pale cream, seemed the shadow one forms by cupping a hand close to the flame. Estelle's taste, as usual, had been exquisite. The gowns, fitted taffeta with a stiff bodice and a softer skirt, flowed down in superb proportion. Tally's of Chicago had done the gowns, and what had initially seemed an unconscionable extravagance now seemed the wisest sort of expenditure. Even in war one had to dress, Collie realized, and one only married once. She had talked the subject to death with Estelle, but now, seeing them lined up and ready, their bouquets of lilies of the valley trembling in their nervous hands, Collie saw the reason for the cost. You could not fake such dresses.

She heard the low purr of an organ; the organ had been carried in this morning with great huffing and puffing, and Estelle's mother had despaired over the amount of floor space it consumed, but it earned its keep in these final moments. Collie turned to see if Estelle had come up on the landing yet. Estelle's father stood at the top step, his smoking jacket dark and definite among the candles of the bride's party. He smiled benevolently down at everyone.

Then the people on the landing near Estelle's father grew quiet, and suddenly Estelle herself appeared. Collie's eyes moistened at the sight of her friend reaching out to take her father's proffered arm. Someone down below must have reported Estelle's arrival to the crowd, because an expectant stiffness went through the people gathered, and the organ, as if clearing its throat, threw away its earlier musings and began Mendelssohn's stirring "Wedding March." The first notes silenced everyone, and Collie felt the streets outdoors grow quiet, the late-afternoon light become solemn and pale, and then her cue came to advance down the stairs.

She experienced a moment of dislocation: she walked down the stairs comprehending, perhaps for the first time, what it would be like to descend as a bride. Yes, naturally people looked to see Estelle, but Collie came down the stairs carefully, her eyes bright with tears, her free hand sliding on the pinecone banister. She felt her emotions quivering inside her. She imagined herself descending some future staircase toward August. That was a foolish, girlish thought more appropriate to Marie, sweet Marie, than for a young woman Collie's age, but she couldn't help it. She pictured him standing below, his handsome face turned up to see her, his smile broadening as she approached. Was he really the one for her? It was his face she pictured, not Henry's, but had the war thrown them together and made them more attracted than they might have been otherwise? Or did fate simply seal what they could not escape? Their stars aligned, she understood, and in the ten or more steps she took toward the ground floor she promised herself to no longer resist but to give in to her feelings—as Estelle had made her pledge—and to cease combating what sought to bloom with August.

Then the music and the people around her canceled any thoughts except for Estelle. Collie met her groomsman—a man named Neil who had remained indefinite in her mind, a friend of George's, a blustering, vest-popping man who demonstrated his disappointment several times already that he had been matched with this girl from New Hampshire—and took his arm. The music swelled and filled every corner of the room. A number of women held handkerchiefs to their eyes, and just ahead, looking back and smiling, was Estelle's mother. Collie exchanged a smile with her, a small nod, then she had to turn left, separating from Neil, so that they might form a semicircle around the wedding couple, men on the right, women on the left. George stood on the right, his hands folded calmly together at his belt buckle.

Estelle! How lovely she looked, Collie saw with satisfaction as she turned and took her position. Estelle was perfect. Every bride is perfect in her own way, Collie observed, but Estelle had outdone any bride she had ever seen. Her dress, full but not absurdly so, floated down the floor like a fairy broom. Her bare shoulders spread back—Estelle's posture had always been impeccable—but the veil flowed down and covered everything in a gentle modesty. Collie smiled. Here was Estelle, a Smith girl only moments before in cardigans and plaid skirts, in saddle shoes and white socks, who now glimmered like the brightest candle of all. Her confession of the night before . . . what did it matter in the final analysis? Collie knew her friend would try, would be a good wife, and George, Eternal George, might surprise them all. Life was a silly, silly game with impossible rules and unanticipated turns that defied all logic or expectation. Collie understood that now and she vowed to remember it.

Then handing the bride over. A kiss from her father, a warm smile at her mother, and then Estelle's girlhood ended. George stepped forward and held out his arm, and Estelle, not pausing, not faltering, took his arm and smiled at him. Collie nearly wept at the quiet bravery demonstrated by her friend. The minister—an ancient-looking man who resembled a turtle, Estelle had promised, with a pale neck protruding from a black suit, and slow-blinking eyes—raised his voice, and the organ subsided. He lifted his hand

and asked the guests to be seated. The afternoon light from the windows bathed everything in honey.

Collie told herself to listen to the ceremony, but her mind drifted restlessly. She could not concentrate, though she tuned in to hear the classic questions and replies: *Do you accept, forsaking all others, from this day forward, till death do you part?* but the light carried her away. She pictured the late-afternoon light back in New Hampshire, the trees passing it slowly toward the hills, the deer-quiet momentary pause before evening. At this moment, she knew, the birds stopped calling and the light grew faint and only the river remained. Sometimes a late car passed over the covered bridge, giving the tires an echo that raised in pitch and then released once the car gained solid earth again. Mrs. Hammond would be readying dinner and the fire would crackle and snap, and the chairs might scrape as they pulled out for the boarders. At the center of it all August waited, his intelligent hands prepared to play the piano, his lovely smile warm and friendly. *Go to him*, she told herself. And then she raised her hands to clap at the first married kiss of George and Estelle's young lives.

She was married, Estelle realized.

It was not a line one crossed, it was not anything, but as she clung to George's arm, people crowded around them both, she comprehended something had changed. Now and then she caught sight of the gold band George had slipped onto her finger; yes, that had happened, too, and as she accepted congratulations, kissed cheeks, she heard George's booming voice beside her. This was it, then. This was how they would go through life, and she took in details of the moment, the dying sunlight, the music purling and bubbling out of the organ—like a skating party, she could not prevent herself from thinking—and the giddy confusion of the event overwhelmed her.

She felt her mother press near, warmly exchange a kiss, then her father and then aunts and uncles, near-strangers, her father's medical colleagues. Everyone, she imagined, looked relieved, doubtless to have the ceremony finished and drinks being served. A few boisterous laughs rang out from near the stairs, and she saw the outline of several men who had already slipped out to the front porch to smoke cigars. She smelled the cigars and the delicious odor of food from the kitchen, and George discovered a line he liked and repeated: "Well, she nearly got away, but I roped her." The line always brought hearty laughs, and a pat on the shoulder, then they went on, wading through the crowd. Where were they going? She didn't know; in all the frenzied planning, she could not recall a single discussion about what to do after the ceremony. At some point they were to do a portrait, but that could not be now, at this moment, and she looked for her mother to give her guidance.

The three-piece band her mother had engaged began playing. The organ had been replaced and Estelle knew her mother had plans—like a military maneuver, she had envisioned—to cart the organ out through the French doors to make more floor space. She had already recruited the men necessary to do it, and the rental truck waited in the backyard out of sight, and Estelle imagined her mother standing by like General Eisenhower, supervising everything.

Someone handed her a glass of champagne. George, too. He looked at her quickly and raised his glass, smiling, and she did not hate him in that moment. He was not to blame, after all. He was simply George, and she had known what she was doing, and so she lifted her glass and clinked it against his. A few people cheered. She took a good swallow and the champagne hardly bothered her. It felt like water, bright, oxygenated water, and she tossed off the remainder of the glass in a second swallow. Immediately the champagne entered her bloodstream and she remembered she had hardly eaten all day, but that thought passed quickly away. She accepted a second glass of champagne, a lovely tall flute, and she grabbed only a sip before it was taken away and she was turned and the music brightened and George took her in his arms.

They played "A Lovely Way to Spend an Evening" by the Ink Spots. It was their song, Estelle recalled, though where or when it had gained such a valence she couldn't say. George hummed the melody in her ear, keeping time with a measured tap at her waist.

"We're married," she said to him, appraising him frankly. "Does that strike you as strange?"

"Well, it will take a little getting used to, I'm sure."

"We're now a social entity. A wedded couple."

"Say, are you okay?"

"I'm fine. It's just that things happen so quickly sometimes."

"From my end I've been angling for years to win you."

"Have you, George? That may be the kindest thing you've ever said to me."

"I thought you knew it. I was crazy about you all along. Didn't you know?"

"I suppose I never looked at it that way. It always seemed as though we were playing at something . . . and now here we are, married."

"You've got a peculiar turn of mind going on right now, Estelle. No more champagne for you."

"Oh, I want quite a lot of champagne. Gallons of it. I'm pregnant, George. This is a big day for surprises, so there you are. I'm pregnant."

It was a horrible, horrible time to tell him such a thing, and she waited, studying his expression, marveling at her capacity for cruelty. He smiled at someone off to his left, then turned and smiled down at her. This ability to carry on in the face of difficult news would make him a success in business. She saw that clearly. His eyes grew slightly tighter, but then he shrugged and pulled her closer.

"It was going to happen sooner or later," he said, philosophically, she thought. "We want a family."

"Yes, I imagine we do."

"Well then, it doesn't much matter when it happened. It's nobody's business but ours."

"People will calculate the time."

"They can go fry an egg," he said, and spun her. "I'm busting to tell people, but I guess we better not."

"I should say not!"

Was he joking? She leaned back and took another look of appraisal. He had his abilities, it was true. Before she could come to any conclusions, she heard the crowd make a small guffaw, and then her father—he must have mimed a little skit behind George's back, she realized—cut in for a father-daughter dance. George spun off to find his mother.

"Hello, Cupcake," her father said, his breath smelling faintly of bourbon. "You look beautiful today."

"Thank you, Papa."

"Are you happy?"

"Very happy."

"I remember marrying your mother and wondering what in the Sam Hill had happened. But you'll get used to it."

"It feels a little strange right now."

"Of course it does. Why wouldn't it? I'm not stepping on your gown, am I?"

"Not yet."

"Your mother would kill me. She should have been a director. In the theater, I mean. She likes putting on a show."

"Do you like George, Daddy?"

Now it was her father's turn to lean away and appraise her. He pulled her closer after a moment.

"Sure I like George. Who wouldn't? He's a nice young man with a future."

"But do you like him?"

He danced her a few steps around the floor before he answered.

"I know what you're driving at, Cupcake. He's not Cary Grant. I see that. And maybe you always thought you required Cary Grant. We brought you up to think that, I suppose. George isn't Cary Grant, but he will be a good husband, I guess. He'll make his way in the world. And he'll be as kind to you as you are to him, so you're well matched. Not everything is oatmeal and raisins, Cupcake. But you two will do just fine."

"I hope so."

"Of course you do."

Then the music stopped and people clapped and the noise of so many hands highlighted a large laugh out on the porch. Someone nearby said it had begun to snow. Collie swept in and took both of Estelle's hands. Collie smiled her warm, friendly smile, and Estelle felt better about everything.

"Hello, Mrs. Samuels!" Collie said, her voice cutting through the crowd. "What a gorgeous, gorgeous bride you are!"

"Thank you. Yes, the dress worked better than I thought it might. And you all look lovely, too."

"Doesn't George look handsome? He looks rather dashing."

"I told George," Estelle said, bending close and whispering in her friend's ear, "about everything."

"When?"

"Just now. Right on the dance floor."

"Oh, gracious."

"He didn't bat an eye. Not my George. I give him credit for that."

"Why did you tell him now?"

"To hurt him, I suppose. Isn't that the lowest thing you've ever heard? I didn't want him to have a pretty picture in his head that didn't match reality. I wouldn't blame you if you didn't want me for a friend."

"Nonsense," Collie said. "We're going to get you something to eat, and then your mother wants you for pictures. She wants every-one in the library. The photographer may take one out on the porch in the snow. It's begun to snow, you know? That's a good omen. Have you met the photographer? He's a funny man with side whiskers. . . . He looks like photographs of General Lee. . . ."

Estelle let herself be led. Then Collie produced a plate of finger food. Everywhere, at every breath, people swung by to congratulate her, to say how beautiful she looked. Over their shoulders she saw the organ carried away; a blast of cold air from the French doors spilled through the room.

"There goes the organ!" Estelle said and couldn't suppress a laugh.

The efficiency of the operation, the sight of the organ—like a dead hippopotamus surrounded by African porters—scuttling off, struck her funny bone. She was certain it was merely the strain of the day, the nervous energy she could not quite conquer, but she laughed harder and harder at the absurdity of it. What difference did the organ make? They were all inside, they had managed, and now they cast the organ out like an unwelcome guest! She wanted to call it back, apologize, but instead she laughed. Her head felt detached from her body, a fanciful balloon drifting above her shoulders, swayed by the wind and mesmerized by everything around her. How peculiar she felt!

Collie rescued her. And George. George swept by and took her elbow and said into her ear that they were wanted in the library. The whole wedding party. People backed away to let them pass, and Es-telle smiled at everyone as the new Mrs. Samuels, George's wife, an upstanding member of Ashtabula society. George was not Cary Grant, that was established, but he was her husband, and she drifted along beside him, Collie bracing her from the other side, the snow drifting past the window like pieces of a plan she once cherished but no longer needed.

Chapter Twenty

August swung his backside onto the pan of a coal shovel and pushed off from the top of Haymaker Hill. At first he picked up little speed. A boy from Stark, Jeffrey something or other was his name, whizzed past him. The kids skidded like little demons, August saw, but he knew his weight would work to his advantage as he gained speed. A toboggan team went past, too, the front man shouting a warning, but by then August had started to turn and glide like a metal pot with two long legs for handles. He shouted after the toboggan in English, but the faster device had flown into the darkness, the angle of the hill too acute to see their descent.

"Heigh-ho!" August yelled, partially to give himself courage—the hill was steep, and the handle of the shovel jutted next to his privates—but also because they had always shouted *heigh-ho* as boys. A wide grin spread on his face. He saw Gerhard just ahead of him, also twirling slowly. Past Gerhard only the sky remained, the stars blazing as they do in winter. Pinpricks of light in a black felt, August thought.

Then more speed. The shovel made a rasping sound as it skimmed over the icy patches. How long ago, he wondered, had he experienced a sliding night? It had been years, half a war before, and the memory proved elusive. He shucked it away and concentrated on keeping his feet raised. Now the shovel scooted him down the mountain at top speed and he shouted for people to clear away. He saw the children watching, their faces blurred or covered by scarves, and he could not keep himself from laughing. His destination was a bonfire; someone had built the bonfire, and it was that light that had attracted them to begin with. They had seen the light on their march back from a day of cutting, and the children had offered the shovels and August and Gerhard had taken a turn.

More speed. He felt his bottom knocking against the shovel pan as he sped over a tiny jump, then two quick bumps in succession. It was nearly Christmas, he realized. Earlier he had heard the villagers singing "Silent Night," and he had joined them under his breath, pronouncing the lyrics in German, feeling the old holy warmth of the song enter him. It was all madness. Were these the people he had been sent to kill? Were they his enemies? What had it all been about in the final analysis? He closed his eyes and clung to the shovel handle, and he was a boy again, riding his ancient sled down through the Black Forest, and his brother, Frederick, was a mere lad, and his mates shouted and laughed around him. He was no different, he knew, from these boys who ran up and down the hill on this mountain on this night.

The hill leveled out and he skidded to a stop. A boy with a runny nose asked him if he wanted to ride again. August shook his head. The boy wiped a sleeve across his nose and reclaimed the shovel. Then he ran off.

"Over here," Gerhard called from his position in the group of cutters. "We're cold."

Before August could join them a man in a large red mackinaw came closer and invited them to step into the firelight.

"Come on, come on," he said, waving his hand as if to wind them closer, "we won't bite! A hot dog! Have a hot dog. Do you savvy hot dogs?"

August translated the invitation.

"What's all this about?" Liam asked. His color appeared sharp and bright from the sledding.

"They want us to have a hot dog," Gerhard said. "A sausage."

"Do we have a minute?" August asked his two guards.

"Go ahead," said one of the guards, the younger of the two. "But let's move along afterward."

Together the cutting team moved over to the fire. The guards came, too. The heat felt wonderful to August. Ten, maybe fifteen, Americans stood around the fire. The man who invited them busied himself getting hot dogs. A woman on the other end of the fire held them forward, and the man slapped the sausages into rolls.

"My grandfather was pure German," the man said, beginning to hand out the hot dogs as the indistinguishable woman across the fire provided them. "Here, try these. This is an all-American food. Sure, there are plenty of Germans in this country. Why, between the Dutch and Germans, and now the Italians, of course . . . the Germans settled Philadelphia, for instance."

"*Danka*," the men said as they received the hot dogs.

"You could put just about anything on a hot dog," the man said, "but most people use mustard. And pickle relish. You savvy pickle relish?"

August translated and received a hot dog as he did so. He waited for a cue to begin, but the man simply waved his hand in a motion that meant go ahead, so he bit into the hot dog. It was a bland sausage, slightly crispy from being in the flames. August glanced at his team members to see what they thought. He saw they ate mostly out of politeness.

"There you go," the man said, "that's what we eat at baseball games and the like. You savvy baseball?"

August didn't recognize the phrase.

"You know, a lot of people around here were quite concerned when they heard a prisoner-of-war camp was moving in. You can imagine, I'm sure. We're not a very sophisticated community, but you people have been darn white. You have. No one can speak against it. It makes me proud of my German heritage."

August did his best to translate the phrases.

Then, to his amazement, one of his own party began singing "O Tannenbaum auf Deutsch!" It was a boy named Stephen, and he had a lovely voice. August had heard him sing before, in the showers, and during slow periods of work, but now his voice gathered the others, and they repaid the debt of a hot dog with a carol from their own language. August lifted his voice along with Stephen's. Tears suddenly came into his eyes and he had to wipe them with his coat sleeve to keep them from freezing. It might have been an absurd moment, August reflected, but Stephen's voice carried them, and, to his astonishment, a few Americans joined the song. They sang in English, for the most part, but two of the older women in the circle knew the carol in German. A song about a tree, for heaven's sake. Slowly the faces of the Americans became more visible, the light brighter, and August could not help seeing the hard country where the men and women had suffered. They did not look much different from the people of his own village. Here might have been the cobbler, there the blacksmith. . . . The occupations of his boyhood village could have been transferred easily onto these familiar faces.

Then Stephen finished the song. The guards called for them to march. The man in the red mackinaw waved them off and the children continued sliding down the hills like dark sprites. Sparks flew up into the black sky, and away from the fire it was very cold.

Henry Heights watched Amos tiptoe carefully along the first row of river logs and knew it did no good to warn him to turn back. The logs lay bobbing next to a boom pier. They had been abandoned there years before, and they rested like white-backed sheep milling slowly in the river pool. Amos carried a pint bottle of rye whiskey in his hand. He drank from it and then lifted it to the side for balance as he stepped onto another log.

"You're going to go through," Henry said. "You won't like it if you do."

"Come out, you chicken. This is how men logged in Daddy's day."

"It's how men got killed, you foolish jackass."

"Come out."

It was a bitter night. Henry felt the cold in his bones. He pushed his coat collar closer to his throat, but it did no good. He was not dressed for the frigid temperature. Neither of them were dressed to be out on a bobbing cluster of logs a few weeks before the New Year. Henry tasted the chemical burn of alcohol on his tongue and mouth. Despite his best intention to refrain from drinking with Amos, he had given in to it once again. They had passed the night in Ernie's, drinking and shooting pool for a dollar a game against a pair of loggers from Portland, and now this. Henry understood Amos could not be satisfied with the normal course of a night. It was not in his nature to do so. He had to push things; he had nearly talked them into a fight with the Portland loggers, but Henry had negotiated a hasty treaty. Now, not fifty yards from the bar, he had put his life at risk for the holy hell of it.

"I'm tired and cold," Henry said, trying to be offhand, which occasionally worked on Amos. "Let's go home."

"Not until you come out and join me."

"We have no spikes on our shoes, Amos. And we've been drinking. Only an ass would think this is a good idea."

Amos laughed and stepped farther out onto the log raft. At the edge of the pod, Henry knew, the logs would be more active. In the center of the mass they could turn at any moment, but at least the other logs pressing on them lent them a modicum of stability. Near the fringe of the pile, the logs bucked and moved on the icy swirls, surging to spin back to the core. Henry knew Amos would work his way out to them.

"We missed our day," Amos called over the logs and wind. "We missed the era when logging had romance. You didn't mind walking on these when you were a boy."

"Maybe during the summer. You're being maudlin, Amos. Come back out of there before you hurt yourself."

Amos slipped and went down to a knee, but he stood back up quickly, his whiskey bottle passing to his mouth as he rose. He laughed as soon as he had swallowed his drink.

"Men used to ride these like horses," Amos said, deliberately flexing his knees so the log that carried him bobbed slightly. "They walked on water, those jacks."

"What are you trying to prove out there?"

"I'm proving I'm braver than you are, for starters. Proving I don't give a good goddamn for another thing."

"You're drunk, Amos. Come on back."

But he continued working his way out on the logs. Now and then Henry heard the logs hit together and give off a dull thud. Wind carried the sounds away as soon as they were created. The night possessed no moon whatsoever. It was close to the turn of the year, and winter held everything as firmly as it ever would that season.

"She loves that Kraut, you know," Amos said over the wind, his face pointed out to the center of the river. "You're making a fool of yourself over a woman who is in love with a German."

"Says who?"

"It's common knowledge. Everyone knows it except you."

"You don't know what you're talking about."

"Don't I? You think I don't have friends among the guards? It's not hard to see if you have eyes to look. She's playing you for a patsy."

Amos turned slowly around. He had reached the outermost edge of the logs. He made a little bow and smiled. Henry half hoped to see him fall from the logs and be spun between the massive boles like a piece of paper on a typewriter platen. Instead, Amos merely grinned and started back toward shore.

"They trade poetry," Amos said, working his way across the logs, his hands out at his sides, "and he plays the piano for her. She's a traitor giving comfort to the enemy. I'm not the only one who says it. She probably gives him a lot of comfort. She probably spreads her legs for his Heine dick. For his Messerschmitt dick."

"You're vile. Don't talk about Collie like that."

"Like what? You think I'm insane? You're the one lapping after her with your tongue out like a damn dog. She's in love with a German. You know the one. The princely looking one . . . makes me sick to look at him."

Amos slipped again. This time he almost went through the logs, but he caught himself on his belly and worked his way back to his knees. He had spilled a portion of the whiskey, and he tucked the cap back on the top and slid the bottle into his vest pocket. He placed his hand repeatedly on the logs for a third point of balance. Then with great effort, he rose to his feet again. In one motion he rose and took three long steps, jumping two or three logs at a time. With a final surge, he nimbly came back onto shore, but his feet went out from under him and he fell backward, laughing as he went.

Henry stepped forward and jammed his foot on Amos's chest. He pushed him down and kept his weight on him.

"Don't talk about her like that," he said.

"You poor, stupid ass. You like it. You like having the scraps of her, don't you?"

"Don't talk about her that way. That's all I'm saying."

"His German dick."

Henry moved his foot up until it pressed on Amos's neck. He put his weight on his leg and Amos spread out and laughed. Henry kept pressing. The black night saturated him; he felt cold, icy air lifting off the water, and he wondered, absently, if he could crush his brother's windpipe without a second thought. He listened to his brother choke. Amos did not try to fight. He appeared to surrender, to take death, if death was to be the sentence, from his brother.

If Amos had struggled, Henry reflected, he might have killed his brother there and then. It was Amos's acceptance of the death at his brother's hand that made Henry pull his foot away. Amos coughed and took a large gulp of air. Then he lay back and laughed. He dug his pint out of his pocket and sat up enough to drink from it. He emptied it and threw the bottle back at the water, where it crashed on one of the logs and made a small splash as a portion of it went into the black river.

⊰ Chapter Twenty-one ⊱

"He's really quite a remarkable fellow when you get right down to it," Colonel Cook said over the phone. "Been living in New York all this time . . . walked away from the potato farm up in Houlton and managed to make his way to New York. That's where he proved himself cleverer than most. He didn't try to get anywhere special, you see? Just decided to make New York his home, and what with all the Germans and Italians and every other kind of creature roosting in that city . . . he blended right in. Actually had tickets for the opera when they found him."

"How did he make a living?" Major Brennan asked.

He spun in his chair and watched the dull late-afternoon sunlight make its way across the parade ground of the prison. The tale Colonel Cook told was familiar in its outline from general accounts, but this was the first time Major Brennan had heard the story in detail. It was fascinating to hear, but he was also aware of the clock. Collie was due back on the six o'clock train.

"Petty larceny, mostly," Colonel Cook said. "Stole some items. He got a new suit of clothes first thing, and that was the making of him. Blended in . . . looked downright prosperous, they tell me. He spoke English, too, though I guess with a heavy accent. Of course that won't raise an eyebrow in New York. He was a college professor back in Germany. Biology or some sort of science. He had lined up a job at Bellevue, but that's when they caught him."

"Ingenious."

"Anyway, that's the scuttlebutt. I guess the lesson is to be aware of the quiet ones. They're more slippery than the gruff birds. The guy had studied American history in the public libraries so that he would come across as a citizen. Pretty tricky fellow."

"Luckily we haven't had much in the way of escapes up here. Too cold for them."

"Most of them don't have the guts for it. Hell, I wouldn't if I were in their shoes. Where will they get to when it comes down to it? This fellow in New York City was a shrewd customer, but even he got caught in the end."

"Well, it's an interesting story. Thanks for telling me. Now I'm afraid I have to hurry to pick up my daughter. She's coming back this evening from Ohio."

"What was she doing out there?"

"A wedding . . ."

"Well, one more thing before you go, John. Can you give me one more minute? I'm sorry to keep you."

"I'm all ears."

"Well, it's about the postwar world, John. Your name has been coming up these last few months in our discussions. You've done good work up there and we're going to need more of that kind of work in Germany in the next few years. This war's going to end sooner or later and Germany's going to be the right place for you."

"I'm flattered, but in what capacity?"

"Not sure yet," Colonel Cook said in his stiff, workaday voice that was decidedly different from the voice he had used to relate the story of the escapee. "We'll have prisoners. Hell, we have them already. Reconstruction? It will likely come with a significant promotion, John, one you deserve. I guess what I'm asking at this point is whether you would consider reassignment. We could probably get someone else up there to run the camp. Or maybe we'll just call you up when we need you. So take this as an opening salvo, if you would, John. How does it strike you?"

"I'm not entirely sure what you're offering me, Colonel."

"Neither am I, John. I'm simply feeling you out about various options. I'm hoping I can count on you as we go forward. We'll need you, John."

"I'm certainly open to anything, Cecil," John Brennan said, using the Colonel's Christian name. "I've lived overseas before."

"That's one of the reasons you're in the discussions. Okay, that's enough for now. Go grab your daughter. I understand she's been a tremendous help up there."

"Yes, sir."

"Thank her for us, then. We'll be in touch, John. Keep doing the good work we need."

"Yes, sir," John Brennan said, and hung up the phone.

He sat for a moment looking out the window, not stunned, exactly, but nervously pleased. If he could divine what Cecil had been beating around the bush about, it meant a command in Germany. Perhaps a diplomatic appointment. Cecil Cook was prescient; the war would end and Germany would be in desperate need of management. All of Europe would need reshaping, and it was a place for ambitious men to make a mark. He did not know how he fit into that scheme, and neither did Cecil Cook, apparently, but it was thrilling to be considered for inclusion. As he stood and swung into his coat, he felt a pleasant wave of satisfaction that put him in an excellent mood.

In the main office, Lieutenant Peters had slipped a cloth cover over his enormous typewriter and now he tucked it in around the edges. Closing time, Major Brennan realized. Even in prisoner-of-war camps the standard work schedule held sway.

"Running in to meet Collie. You know where to find me if you need me."

"Yes, sir," Lieutenant Peters said. "Shall I call the driver?"

"No, I think I have time to walk. I could use a little exercise. I'm growing stout from all this desk work."

"I understand, sir."

Although Major Brennan wanted the short walk to be alone to think, he regretted his decision to walk almost the moment he stepped off the front porch of the administration building. Really, it was too cold. He tucked his neck down deeper into his overcoat and cursed that he didn't have a hat. It was foolish not to have a hat in such weather, but he never liked wearing one. He walked quickly to the main gate and saluted the guards there. They looked nearly frozen as they kept sentry. Still, that was their job, and it would do no good to let them find a softer way to go about it. He slid through the gate and headed toward the river.

From south of the village he heard the train whistle and he quickened his step as a result. The lights of the village pushed out against the darkness. The pale white covered bridge hung over the river like a swan's wing. When he reached the platform, he found three soldiers waiting. He saluted them all, then watched as an employee from the train company stepped out on the cold platform and checked his watch. It would be a bitter night, Major Brennan realized. The stars glittered with the cold and no wind moved the bare tree branches. It was the type of night that made the mercury drop in the glass. No one in his right mind would try to escape tonight.

Then the train came puddling in, massive and spewing smoke, its bright front light nearly blinding. A conductor swung down as soon as the train slowed sufficiently, and he lifted a folding staircase down to the platform. Two soldiers immediately jumped off, one smoking a cigarette so that the soldier had to squint at the smoke. They looked young, and Major Brennan saluted them quickly. He walked the platform a few steps, hoping to see Collie as she made her way down the train to disembark, but the smoke from the undercarriage obscured everything. Arrivals and departures came in clouds, he reflected.

At last he spotted Collie.

"Oh, Papa, how nice of you to meet me!" Collie said, stepping off the train and into his arms.

"Did you get Estelle married off?" he asked, taking her bag and putting it onto the platform. "Was it a good trip?"

"It was a wonderful trip, thank you. Estelle is married, and I've come to like George," Collie said, her eyes happy and alive. "He's not any girl's dream, exactly, but he's quite dependable."

"Dependability is a great trait in a man," Major Brennan said, feeling the ridiculousness of his remark as it passed his lips. He touched his handkerchief to his mouth and coughed at the cold air, then shifted topics. "You must be weary. And it's horribly cold tonight. The barometer is nearly bursting. Come along."

"It feels haunted when it gets this cold," Collie said, breathing in long pulls. "Ghostly."

"That's exactly right," Major Brennan said, "that's exactly what it is."

Descending in the elevator at the Biltmore in Chicago, Estelle felt the strangest sense of division. Or perhaps that was the wrong word for it. She felt of two minds, of two bodies, as if she had split down the middle and had calved a twin. On one side was the same girl she had always been, the girl she had seen in the mirror for her entire life, the girl with secret thoughts and opinions, a girl who read and spoke a smattering of French, and on the other . . . what was the other? A wife, she supposed. Mrs. Samuels. George's helpmeet. Even the elevator operator, a graying, glimmering old man who wore an organ-grinder's monkey's hat, seemed to regard her differently. Mrs. George Samuels of Suite 372. She felt this wifely demeanor was a costume she could don and use to her benefit, yet it threatened to grow into her skin and become impossible to remove. Somehow a bargain had been struck, but what the terms of the agreement might be, what it meant in the long run, felt as cloudy as a poorly explained insurance policy. One had a sense of it, but scarcely any of the details.

The elevator stopped twice, each time admitting soldiers. Chicago, she had discovered, was overrun with military personnel. One could not go anywhere in the city without seeing uniforms of every description. It was like a parade, really, the men plumed in their wool finery, their obvious satisfaction at being involved in the world's great affairs contained in every movement. Even now, between floors, two young navy ensigns smiled and tipped their hats, their white uniforms glowing in the elevator light. Everything seemed in transit, the men nearly interchangeable, the uniforms the only constant.

When they reached their destination, the military men stepped aside to let her pass into the lobby. George had already gone down to breakfast. She had argued to have breakfast in the room, but he had made an appointment to meet with someone from Midland Bank, a mortgage specialist whose business, she must understand, was invaluable. It was the only opportunity to see the man while in Chicago, and so they had a date for breakfast, where surely she would be a third wheel. That was another confusing feature of being married; one was not always sure if one was wanted. Nevertheless, she found the dining room easily enough and stood for a moment at the maître d's station while she scanned the various tables and chairs. She spotted George and the other man—a sleek, seallike man of about forty with white-blond hair and a slightly arched back—seated in a banquet looking out on the street. They appeared rapt in conversation, but as she approached the table they looked up and stood, the business associate's napkin falling off his lap onto the floor.

"Estelle . . . may I present . . . ," George started, but then stopped when he saw the comedy of proceeding while the man bent over to get his napkin.

"Sorry," the man said when he retrieved the napkin. "Harry Palconowski."

He held out his hand. Estelle shook it. It was a dry, light hand.

"I ordered you coffee," George said, stepping out and making
room for her to slide in between them. "We were just saying, the
breakfast is quite smashing for wartime."

"Smashing?" Estelle asked, unable to help herself.

"Good, then," George amended. "Harry here was saying we must
see the Field Museum. They have a *Tyrannosaurus rex* on exhibit. Best
in the world."

"If you like that sort of thing," Harry hurried to assure her. "I
happen to take an interest. When I was younger, I thought I'd like to
be a dinosaur hunter."

"And then what happened?" Estelle asked, trying to conceive of
this man—yes, he reminded her of a seal, with a sharp nose and soft
eyes and heavy lashes—living and working anywhere except in a
five-block radius from where they sat.

"The usual hubbub of life. Isn't that always the case? One makes
plans, then the world intrudes. I can't kick, though. Midland has
been fine to me."

"Harry is the vice president in charge of the entire Midwest,"
George said, looking up to catch the eye of the waiter now that
everyone was at table. "At his age, that's practically unheard of."

"What compounded the difficulty of escaping," Harry said to Estelle, "was that I happened to be good at this sort of thing. This
banking . . . not everyone is. And when you are good at it, they
throw enough money at you to make you forget your former ideals.
In an odd way, if I had been a disaster at this position I might be a
dinosaur hunter today. So a success is always a failing on its flip
side."

"I never thought of it like that," Estelle replied, seeing this Harry
Palconowski in a more charitable light.

"But of course here I am interrupting your honeymoon. Your *lune de miel*," Harry said, his gaze resting on Estelle's. "I hope you'll forgive me. I tried to tell George we could meet another time, but he insisted that you wouldn't mind. He said that was the remarkable thing about you."

"I don't know how remarkable that is. I hardly had a choice in the matter. Did I, George? But you know, that's the second time someone has referred to my *lune de miel*."

"It's meant more broadly by the French than we understand it in the United States. We use it to talk about the brief vacation after a wedding, but to the French it connotes the entire month . . . that the first month of marriage is a month of honey. One moon-full, as it were."

Estelle gave the man credit and took a third look at him. He was not entirely pleasant to look at, but she could see why he was successful in business. He had a sharp, magpie mind that picked up glittering pieces of glass and held them up to see if they contained value. At least, she mused, that was the initial impression he gave. She was pleased to be interrupted in her train of thought by the waiter, who took their orders in an efficient manner without writing them down.

Then for a short while the men discussed business. She realized almost immediately that she could follow the issues, though she found them tiresome. She wondered why anyone would devote his life to such a practice. It was illuminating, however, to watch George in action against a worthy adversary. Mr. Palconowski would not be intimidated by George's usual brusqueness. George himself, in deference to Mr. Palconowski's lofty position as vice president of the Midwest—whatever that meant precisely—did not drive as she was used to seeing him drive. This was her husband, she reflected, and here was the start of their future together.

She was still watching when Mr. Kamal walked into the dining room.

Her heart stopped. To have something to do, she reached for her coffee, and it was only by looking away and then returning her eyes to Mr. Kamal's retreating figure that she realized she had been mistaken. It was not Mr. Kamal after all, only another Indian man, probably a Sikh from his appearance, and she had supplied the necessary details to bring him to life as Mr. Kamal. Her hand shook as she brought the coffee cup to her lips.

"You look as though you've seen a ghost," Mr. Palconowski suddenly said in a momentary pause from his fencing with George. "Are you feeling all right?"

"I'm fine," she managed to say, "I choked a little on something."

"Crust of bread always works for me," Mr. Palconowski said. "All things advance before a crust of bread."

She did as he suggested. The men returned to discussing business, though Mr. Palconowski—Harry, she told herself—promised it would take only a moment longer. *Dull stuff,* he'd said. She ate two bites of the crusty French bread on the table and only when she was certain she could contain herself did she turn and pretend to take in the dining room. There was the Mr. Kamal look-alike, sitting with a woman Estelle imagined to be his wife, two small children wedged between them. She felt her heart regain its rhythm and her breathing came back under control. She tried her best to keep her attention fixed on the two men at her table, but her mind roamed back to the flower shop and to the scent of spiced tea and lilies, the charming fountain table bathed by early sunlight.

"I am going to kiss you," August said, and he did.

As simple as that, Collie thought. At the same time she kept a hand up against his chest, his heavy coat making a flapping sound in the wind, and she tried ineffectually to prevent him from claiming too much by the kiss. His cheek scratched hers; his lips tasted of coffee and powdered milk and something else she could not identify.

"August, stop," she whispered after a moment. "Please. That's too much."

"I've dreamed about kissing you," he said, his voice tight, his arms pulling her into him.

"Yes, yes," she said. "Yes, I know. I have feelings, too. . . . But this isn't the time or place. . . ."

He released her slowly. A part of her wished he would never unclasp his hands. He finally took a step back and kissed her hand. A mitten covered it, but he kissed it anyway. He kept his eyes averted.

"Forgive me," he said.

"There's nothing to forgive."

She smiled. He was devastatingly handsome, she saw once again, but now it was a more mature beauty. His kiss continued to vibrate through her body. She could hardly believe what it felt like to be kissed by him. She reached out and put a hand on the horse nearest to where they stood in order to steady herself. The horse took a half step sideways and nickered a little in its throat. She had come out to the horses on her lunch break, to her usual spot, and here was August harnessing one of the animals. He had not delayed or equivocated; he had stepped toward her as soon as he had seen her and kissed her. It was the first she had seen him since their last moment together as he departed.

"You surprised me," she said, still trying to regain her balance. "I didn't expect to see you here."

"I'm sorry. I have thought of you over and over . . . and then suddenly you were here as if I had conjured you. And I thought perhaps you wanted to kiss me, too."

"Yes, I did. . . . I mean, yes, I'm not angry. It's just . . . ," she said, having difficulty forming her words.

"There is a great gulf between us, I understand," he said. "A world apart. Our countries are at war."

"Something . . . yes, I suppose. But we are suited in other ways, I think. I don't know what I'm saying. You confuse me. Our situation . . . but I am glad you kissed me. Very glad."

"Yes, I understand."

He smiled. She reached out a hand and squeezed his. She wanted to reassure him. He had lost weight, she realized, during his time in Vermont. He did not look entirely healthy. Rations, she knew, had been difficult to procure, yet the logging work continued. Her father felt himself in a bind; it was always a bind, and he spent hours on the telephone haggling with supply officers for more food. She could see the effect the limited rations had on August. His skin had become somewhat sallow and his hair, always luxuriant, had taken a dull sheen. His teeth appeared slightly too prominent.

He met her eyes, then stepped back and finished harnessing the horse. After the night of bitter cold, it felt glorious in the sunlight. The horses stood in the makeshift pole barn, their bodies warm and comfortable, only their shadows cooling the air when one passed through them. August ducked under the large Percheron to buckle a belly cinch. He straightened the halter straps along the horse's cheeks, then spent a moment making sure the horse's right ear was not pinched. Collie watched everything he did.

"How was your trip?" August asked when he had the horse ready.

His voice had changed a little, reverting to a more formal tone.

"It was a lovely wedding."

"I'm glad. That was your friend Estelle, wasn't it?"

She nodded.

"That's a good thing to think about," he said. "You traveling and happy. I search for happy things to occupy me. I have a storehouse of memories that I pick up like stones and examine them."

"And how have you been?" she asked, conscious of the absurdity of such a question to a prisoner of war. "You've been gone a long time it feels like."

He shrugged and put his hand on the horse's forehead to pet it.

"A letter from home arrived," he said, "but it was out of date."

"From whom?"

"My mother. She wrote with news, but the letter is too old to say much. It was good to see her handwriting, though. She reports that it is bad in Germany and Austria. The Russians are advancing from the east. The Russians are animals, you know. They will kill everything in their path. They will not leave a stone on a stone."

He said all of this in careful English, his words pieced together slowly.

"Do you fear them?" she asked.

He nodded and continued.

"If they reach the Rhine, then all is lost."

"I can't say I'm sorry. I am sorry for you but not for your country."

"I understand. Do you see why it is difficult for you and me? We are dreamers. The world doesn't cooperate. Is that the word? *Cooperate?*"

"Yes, I take your meaning."

"The Allies will try to attack the Ruhr Valley. That is our manufacturing center. The Rhine is the last line of defense. Hitler is calling on the young and old to defend the Fatherland. Boys are now fighting. Young boys without whiskers. The old men have left their firesides, and they are fighting for their lives."

"I'm sorry."

He bent back and rubbed the horse's neck. He appeared exhausted and haggard now that he was fully in the sun. She wondered if her father saw the prisoners' conditions clearly. It was easy to overlook such things in their gradualness.

"We brought it on ourselves," August said simply, petting the horse's neck. "You cannot forget that. We would like to forget that fact, but we can't. The Russians have a tank . . . it's known by a letter and a number . . . a T something . . . and it cannot be stopped. It can shoot our tanks from a mile away and decimate us. That's what we hear. We send out old men to fight with grenades strapped to sticks. We cannot hold out."

Collie studied him. How had she never quite understood this before? One country's victory meant the obliteration of another. A country was an abstraction; war meant the death and annihilation of hundreds of thousands of human beings. It meant the eradication of entire families, of sons and daughters and loved ones, irrevocable loss that could not adequately be represented by a newspaper account or a radio report. The war was progressing; even in the Pacific the Allied forces had gained ground. Reports of troops advancing on Berlin came every day now. The German and Austrian people would suffer. That was the price they paid, but that did not make it any more conscionable.

"Maybe if hostilities cease," August said, his eyes on hers again, "we can sit and talk like any young man and woman. That is my hope. They will send us home eventually, but what will we find? It will all be gone. We are fighting for a dream of what we were."

"I'm sorry."

"May I kiss you again?"

She nodded.

He kissed her. This time the kiss expressed longing and sadness. He did not put his arms around her as he had done before. He kept his hand on the horse's halter. His lips lingered lightly on hers. The kiss still vibrated through her body.

"Does this horse have a name?" she asked when he lifted his lips from hers.

"He is known as Crackerjack. What is Crackerjack? The guards could not explain it to me."

"A caramel popcorn. Sometimes with peanuts."

She thought of the phrase in German. She pronounced it to the best of her ability.

"Yes, I see. We have such a thing. It's a funny name for a horse.

Now I must go. They will want the horse for the dragging. Cracker-jack. We are bringing out logs nearby today. So many trees!"

She could not help herself. She stood on her toes and kissed him. She was uncertain what she meant the kiss to convey, but she could not imagine letting him walk away without once more feeling his lips on hers. He put his hand against her cheek when she drew back. His hand, she noted, had been roughened by the labor of the last half year. He was no longer the lithe young boy who must have sat at a piano and practiced scales in his Austrian homeland.

"You are the only good thing to come out of the war," he said. "My only hope."

"And you are mine."

"And my friend Crackerjack," he said, petting the horse a last time and starting away. But she called him back. He walked Crackerjack in a circle and came to a stop in front of her.

"I nearly forgot," she said, and she dug in her purse and produced the clover necklace she had weaved. She handed it to him.

"I ran out of flowers on mine. But this is to make you think of me each day," she said. "It's a forget-me-not."

"I don't need it, but I will treasure it. You are in my thoughts always, Collie," he said, his eyes directly on hers. "I wake to you and I go to sleep to you. It may be unfair to say that I love you, but I do. I don't know if the world will let us be together, but it can't change my feelings for you."

Crackerjack made a push to get his mouth on the flowers, and August pushed him away just in time. He laughed and petted the horse, then tucked the flowers in the breast of his jacket. He made a clicking sound with his tongue and led the horse in a second loop to get him moving. Sunlight caught the buckles of the harness and reflected back like bright sparks. Collie held her hand up to her eyes to shade them, her back cold from the shade of the pole barn.

PART FOUR

Chapter Twenty-two

Estelle felt a tide of nausea rise and she wondered if she would vomit. She could not predict it any better than if she had been an onlooker. The baby rode inside her like a fish, swimming and doing as it liked, every now and then sending up a disagreeable sensation of nausea and light-headedness, and she despised its willfulness and its sense of timing. Even now, with the painters and paperhangers standing about waiting for instructions, she was not sure she wouldn't vomit on their shoes. They stared at her, obviously ready to receive instructions, but she was afraid to open her mouth for fear of what chain reaction it might begin.

She held up a finger to give her a moment, disguising it as though she required a moment of thought when it was merely a noxious swelling in her intestines. Fortunately her mother-in-law came to her rescue and told the men to take a ten-minute break. The men appeared unconvinced, but they backed slowly out of the dining room and Estelle heard them speaking together as they went into the backyard. They spoke Italian.

"You're nearly green," her mother-in-law, Gladys, said. "Come and sit down immediately. I don't know why these men can't clean up after themselves. . . . They let everything go so that they can have the satisfaction of uncovering it all at once. . . . It's a trick to make their work look better than it is."

"I'll be all right," Estelle said, swallowing her gorge and feeling minutely better.

"These paint fumes are enough to make anyone feel ill," Gladys said. "I have the beginning of a headache myself."

"I'm okay now. It's passed."

"Are you certain? In your condition . . . I tried to tell George it was too much to take on for an expectant mother. A new house and a baby . . . it's really too much."

"I'll be fine in a moment," Estelle said, taking a seat on one of the straight-backed chairs perched around the open living room. She lowered her weight carefully, and the young fish swirled in happiness. She reached into her sleeve and took out a lace handkerchief. She would not admit to anyone what the handkerchief meant to her for fear they would think her strange. But she had come across an antidote for nausea: the scent of hay. For reasons she hardly cared to examine, the smell of hay calmed her and settled her stomach. As a result, she kept a tiny bundle of hay in her handkerchief because no one would think it odd for a pregnant woman to touch her nostrils with a cloth. Now, with the fumes everywhere, and her mother-in-law's anxious face studying her, Estelle took deep breaths of the hay and thought of barns.

A second part of her consciousness looked about the house. Yes, it probably was too much, but she had been so eager to leave her in-laws' home she would have moved into a circus tent if George proposed it. The getting of the house, the bank payments, the risk assessment, the sense George had that this would one day be a "very good neighborhood indeed" had made the acquisition painful and overly long. While other men might simply have decided on a house and purchased it, George, she knew, measured his business acumen by it. It was also an advertisement for him, and so when he had gathered together this band of Italian craftsmen and put them to work finishing the house, she had gone along with it. They had the Duck Pond club, anyway, for meals and entertainment, he said, and so what if they had to bunk out a while with his parents? A penny earned, and all that.

He had underestimated the baby, however, and she had tried to make him understand what a pregnancy entailed, but he was not attentive in that way. Faced with an economic uncertainty, or a ques-

tion of finance, he was unmistakably the man for the job. He drew a
line between the world of men and the world of women, she reflected,
and was not fully aware of their intersection. Gladys, Estelle knew,
saw this feature of her son, and, to her credit, did what she could to
make him pay attention. Gladys, too, was in a tricky position, Estelle
realized. She did not want to be the meddlesome mother-in-law, but
at the same time she had somehow become responsible for her
daughter-in-law's health and welfare. It was all quite exhausting.

"I think the blue, with carriages . . . the one they showed us in
the store. We have several rolls of it here somewhere," Estelle said,
aware her eyes were looking far away while her mind percolated
with the details of decorations. "For the dining room . . . how do
you think that would look?"

"Oh, very nice. You know best."

"And a cream for the living room. Maybe the wainscoting in the
dining room should be cream as well to draw the colors together.
That would match and lead the eye. . . ."

"Oh, yes, yes, I see just what you mean."

Poor Gladys, Estelle mused. If George was *Eternal George*, then
Gladys was his opposite, a sort of hummingbird-of-a-woman who
lived on lettuce and air. Her slimness made her easy to bully, a horrible propensity that Estelle had discovered in herself. As she grew
denser with the child, she felt she could command anything from
Gladys, and that, she knew, was unconscionable. She had written to
Collie about it and confessed everything, but Collie, as usual, dismissed her friend's capacity for cruelty. Collie, in certain ways, was
too innocent for her own good, Estelle had concluded.

"Yes, I think that should be all right. If you wouldn't mind calling
them . . . ," Estelle said. "I'm feeling back on my game now."

"Yes, of course," Gladys said, and hurried off to call the men.

Estelle heard her pigeon voice, and then the men returned. The
foreman, a heavily mustachioed man named Anthony, came for-

ward to take the instructions. Estelle knew the man did not think much of her. She had picked up a few words from his quick Italian— as much the tone as anything—that had disparaged her choices. She had inquired several times of George about who these men were, why were they not fighting the war, where had he found them? He had brushed aside all of her questions, insisting they should use them while they were available, and it was this sense of an under-the-table deal that colored all of her exchanges with Anthony.

"I think the carriage wallpaper for the dining room," she said, watching his eyes. "With a cream wainscoting. Then, if you please, we'll have the cream duplicated on the living room walls. . . ."

"*Si, signora.*"

"Will that look all right?" she asked, testing him.

"Yes, very nice. No . . . ," he said, but apparently could not think what else he wanted to say.

"Yes?"

He lacked the word for *trim*, she realized, because he walked over and pointed to the doorframe.

"*Uno* color?" he asked.

"He thinks there should be a trim color," Gladys said, staring at him as though he were a bear on a bicycle.

"He may be right. We can decide that later," she said directly to Anthony, "once we see the paper on. We don't want it to look like a bordello in here."

She used the word *bordello* to get a rise from Gladys, and it worked. The tiny woman blushed.

Estelle waited while Anthony issued instructions to the men. They deliberately showed no expression. She finally decided not to care one way or the other. She stood and went with Gladys to make a quick inspection of the work so far. That was part of the established routine. She would go through the house, trailed by Gladys, making mental notes of what remained to be accomplished. Under different circumstances, without a fish exercising in the natatorium of her stomach, she might have taken more pleasure in the details. Once she had the notes, she did her best to explain them to Anthony or whatever tradesman happened to be responsible for the construction.

Today, however, she performed a cursory inspection. As soon as she had made a lap around the downstairs—she did not bother with the upstairs, which felt, at times, like yet another country to conquer—she pronounced the progress *bene* to Anthony. He nodded and asked a question about the color for the kitchen cabinets. They had been over it before several times, and she realized he did it simply to annoy her.

"It will all be fine," she said, gathering her coat and Gladys. "It's all looking very good."

"I don't know where George gets these people," Gladys said once they had stepped outside. "I really don't. I think he enjoys the underworld feeling about them."

"Maybe George is a gangster," Estelle said, watching the shock spread on Gladys's face. "You never know. I read an account in *McCall's* about a woman who was married to a man who had killed three women in their own basement. Anything is possible, Gladys."

"In their own basement?"

"Yes. A bloodthirsty man, apparently. After she had gone to bed, he had roamed around in the darkness like a modern-day Jack the Ripper. Very gruesome. You don't think George could be involved in something like that, do you?"

"Oh, Estelle, of course not!"

Estelle took her mother-in-law's arm as they went down the porch steps. The porch was the element of the house she liked best. It was wide and wrapped all the way around the house in a Victorian style, she supposed, but it always struck Estelle as a skirt held out in a curtsy. It required no effort of imagination to envision summer evenings on the porch, lemonade and fireflies, perhaps neighbors out for walks casually dropping by. George had promised her a porch, and he had made good on the promise. She gave him that much.

At the street curb she turned around and studied the house. She tried to see it apart from its surroundings. George had plans to build half a dozen houses along the street with his partners. It was an odd thing to see this kind of construction given the choked supplies most citizens experienced. But George had his ways; trucks came and went, and she could not believe it was all quite on the square, but she didn't question it too sharply. She imagined George stood to make a tidy fortune at the war's end. As he said, people would return and begin making families, and it was not war speculating at all. It was merely being ahead of the curve, he said, and so the muddy yards and the cement foundations up and down the street—he gave her permission to name the street as long as it was something American-sounding and she had called it Persimmon Drive—suggested progress and forward-thinking. They would be rich, she knew. Not rich as her father was rich, but rich in a way that would satisfy George, in a way that would make money almost beside the point, and she was not sure what she felt about that.

"The March weather makes it all look rather tentative," Gladys said, sharing Estelle's view beside the car. "But we shouldn't judge anything until the landscaping is finished. George says he has a very good man for the job . . . a man who worked on some of the most prominent parks in Europe."

"Of course George does."

"I don't know how he learned to do all this, but he certainly keeps himself busy."

"He certainly does."

"Building houses for people . . . In the end, that's rather noble, isn't it?"

"As long as he's not burying corpses in the foundations," Estelle said, sliding in behind the driver's wheel and reaching across to spring the passenger door for her mother-in-law. "As long as he's not doing that."

"The Russians are cutting the arms and legs off the German dead and feeding them to the livestock," Gerhard said at lunch break, a slender stalk of grass bobbing in his mouth as he spoke. "That's the report. It's done for now. Everything is lost. We're better off here. It's going to be a horrible business before it's all finished."

"Hitler should surrender," Patrick said, spitting the words. "He's become a laughingstock."

Patrick was the young boy now in charge of the twitch horses. The other two members of the cutting team, Emmet and Liam, had gone with the guards back to camp for a hot lunch. August preferred to stay in the woods; the sun was warm and pleasant, though it had turned everything underfoot to mud. Now it was late March and spring sunshine crept over the mountains each morning and the river smoked in the increasing warmth like a train waiting to leave.

"He'll never surrender," August said. "It's not in his character. He has promised to shoot anyone who speaks of surrender."

"That's what the American news reports say," Gerhard said. "We can't believe everything that we hear."

"Do you doubt the Germans are on the run? The Allies have crossed the Rhine now. It's a matter of days or weeks."

"The Russians will retaliate," Patrick said. "My grandfather said they have tails, some of them, like wolves."

"Your grandfather has read too many fairy tales," August said. "But they *are* wolves, true enough. They'll rape anyone they can."

"The German girls cover their faces with grime and coal dust to make themselves look older," Gerhard said. "The Russian authorities will do nothing to prevent the rapes. It's always been that way between us."

"Between the Germans and Russians?" Patrick asked.

Gerhard nodded.

August ate a piece of sausage wrapped in a mouthful of stale bread. He had not remained in the woods through lunch hour to hear yet another account of atrocities. In the beginning there had been a dreadful fascination to the subject, but now it seemed ghoulish to speculate about the circumstances in Germany. The conditions were dire, certainly. No one disputed that any longer. The last residue of Nazism had disappeared from the barracks. No one performed the *Deutsche Gruß*, the Nazi salute, with anything less than irony. It was humiliating to see it, to think that it ever held significance.

It was a fine noon, August made himself note. That was something for which to be grateful. He was always on the lookout now for something to count on the positive side of the ledger. Many of the men agreed that New Hampshire was a place they had come to love. Perhaps *love* was too large a word to apply, August reflected, but he admired the land, the green woods, the mountains that stretched off to the east. As a sort of parlor game, the men had often asked one another: if the authorities permitted it, would they remain in the United States rather than return to Germany or Europe? August had always answered in the affirmative, although only under the proviso that he could travel home to see his mother and father and his brother first. That would be his primary mission once the war ended.

"We should go to Canada," Gerhard said absently, tapping a stick on one of the logs they had cut that morning. "We've talked about it. We've talked it to death. We should go. Others have made it."

"And others have been shot dead in escaping."

"Who has gone to Canada?" Patrick asked.

August eyed Gerhard. It was a plan they had talked about repeatedly, and he wasn't sure whether they should take Patrick into their confidence. August doubted the boy would tell, but you never knew.

War had taught him to shut his mouth. Nevertheless, the cat was out of the bag, and it was not exactly a secret that the men had talked of Canada as if it possessed the answers to everything, a Shangri-la where life could regain its flavor. August shrugged. Gerhard explained it to the boy.

"Some of our countrymen have worked their way north to Canada. At least that's the word leaking around camp. The Canadian government is more forgiving than the Americans'. We are not far from the border," Gerhard said, raising the stick and pointing to the northwest. "It's not a mere dream. It's tangible."

"A couple days' walk," August added.

"There's talk they will send us to England when we leave here. For more labor," Gerhard said bitterly. "More forced labor. In Canada you can ask for political asylum and it will be granted."

"Do you know that for a fact?" Patrick asked.

"No," August said, "and that is part of the problem. We can't know for certain. Too many questions will raise too many suspicions. Much of what we are telling you is rumor. It may all be a story we use to give ourselves hope. Some men have been shot on the way."

"I'd go with you," Patrick said. "Anything is better than staying in prison."

"Canada could be a prison, too," August said. "We can't know."

August heard the guards and the other men returning from lunch. He lay back on a comparatively dry spot of soil and watched the sun move through the treetops. As always, he thought of Collie. He had kissed her twice in the last week, both times briefly and with great nervousness that they might be discovered, but he could call the moments to mind with infinite detail. Once, it had been outside the kitchen in the early evening when everyone else had gone off to wash before dinner; another time it had been close to the river in the morning's first hour. The risk was all hers. She would be vilified if their meetings came to light; her father would feel betrayed.

Gradually sleep overcame him. The sun felt wonderful on his skin. He caught the scent of horses now and then, and underneath it the unmistakable breath of mud and water mixed. Spring, he thought. Then he felt himself slowly spinning down, his body letting go, and he jerked twice as his muscles relaxed. Canada, he thought with his last bit of consciousness. That was the solution. Two days of hard hiking. Maybe three. They could keep to the back roads, keep to the woodland game paths they knew from their work on the cutting teams. It was a dream, but it had begun to pull at him. As he fell asleep, he felt himself circling down, falling, and it was always toward Canada and the image of Collie waiting for him there, her hair lifted in the wind, the sound of war washed away and left behind forever.

Collie knelt for a moment and placed a fan of irises on Marie's grave. The grass over the grave had grown in and joined with the surrounding plots so that, except for the newer headstone, one would not have known how recently Marie had joined them. Still, it was a pretty place; wildflowers, small bluebonnets, had already speckled the ground. A section of the cemetery held the brown headstones of the town settlers. Down a slope, overlooking the mountains, a newer section had been carved free of the pressing woodlands. Marie had been buried in the third row, her dates deeply chiseled into the gray granite. Here she had lived, and here she had died, Collie realized. What a vigorous, beautiful life Marie had led. Collie smiled and felt a mist of tears cover her eyes for a moment. The sweet, sweet girl. How she missed her.

She stood for a moment and didn't do much of anything. It was a fine day. She glanced at the other gravestones, most of them familiar at least by name. She took deep, even breaths and let her eyes roam up the mountainsides. Marie could rest here, she thought. If one had to die, one had to leave life, then this was as good a place as any to rejoin the soil. Small consolation, she reflected, but true nonetheless.

She took a seat on the stone bench located inside a scatter of Patch family gravestones. The Patches, she knew, were a prominent family in the area, and they multiplied and spread their interests everywhere, and it did not surprise her to discover the bench positioned among them. She sat and drew out the letter she had collected from the secret hiding place near the twitch horses' pole barn. It served as the drop box for August; once each day she swung by on the pretense of seeing the horses and made a quick exchange: her letters for his. He had never disappointed her.

She smiled when she opened his letter and saw his declaration of love. Marie, she thought, would have adored the secrecy of the situation. For Collie, however, each exchange of letters made her revisit her guilt over betraying her father. It was impossible to stay away from the letters, naturally, but she wished fervently that they could communicate open and honestly. She would have given anything to stand before the community as two lives joined, but that was out of the question.

His letter touched on the usual themes: food, the work, the scent of pine in the morning, something amusing someone said. His English had improved as had her German, and sometimes he gave her small assignments to translate, usually a phrase that contained a delightful surprise for her. His last paragraph he spent in telling her why he loved her. She read the sentences slowly, one at a time, letting each one ring like a finely cast bell before its tone faded away. When she finished she held the letter against her chest and wondered how she had not known love could feel this way. With all the heated talk, the songs, the movies, the sentimental poetry she had consumed, she had not realized love could be the common back-and-forth between a man and woman, "every day's most quiet need, by sun and candlelight," as Elizabeth Barrett Browning had promised.

That was what she felt. His love and attention did not surprise her so much as give structure to her day, to her thought, to her hope.

She stayed a while longer, then made the mile walk back to the boardinghouse. She found a good twig to serve as a walking stick and carried it at her side, slapping at bushes and branches that sometimes intruded on the path. Her father waited on the porch. He smoked a cigarette and had a newspaper open on his lap. It was against the rules to drink in the boardinghouse, but Collie smelled whiskey laced in with her father's coffee. She imagined Mrs. Hammond turned a blind eye on the minor transgression.

"There you are," her father said. "I wondered where you got to."

"I went to the cemetery."

"Well, good," he said, and patted the chair beside him. "Have a seat."

"Some coffee you have there," she whispered.

"Don't spoil it. Mrs. Hammond and I have come to a truce. I drink only out here on the porch. That way she can preserve the dignity of her establishment and claim with honesty that there is no drinking inside the boardinghouse. See? The root of all diplomacy is equal parts hypocrisy and deliberate ignorance."

"Well, I intend to hold it over your head if I ever need to get on Mrs. Hammond's good side."

"Oh, she likes the evilness of it. It gives her something to fret about. Listen, dinner should be ready shortly. Henry Heights stopped by a few minutes ago. I invited him to join us, but he said he couldn't spare the time. He's on his way up north to get his brother."

She nodded. She watched her father take a sip of his coffee. He held the liquid in his mouth for a moment before swallowing it.

"What do you think of him anyway?" he asked, trying his best to be casual about it.

She looked at him carefully.

"Why do you ask?"

"Just curious. Just a father's curiosity, that's all. He's always been very . . . very polite in our dealings. He does seem set on you, Collie. You know that, don't you?"

"That's nonsense."

"You know very well it's not. What don't you like about him? I've tried to put my finger on it, but I haven't been able to do it."

"I don't dislike him," she said, feeling uncomfortable, profoundly so, with the letter from August fresh in her mind. "He's a perfectly nice young man."

"Oh, I guess it's none of my business."

"No, it isn't."

He looked at her, appeared worried for a moment, then laughed.

"Okay, okay, okay," he said. "Enough of that. I know when to retreat."

"I'm going to run in and wash before dinner."

"Yes, and I'll finish my coffee. Beautiful evening."

"How about you, Papa? When are you going to find a woman to your liking?"

"Oh, please. I deserved that, but let's agree to a truce."

"You seem to need to strike truces with the women in your life."

"Surrender is more like it."

"I was being charitable," she said, and rose to go inside.

Mrs. Hammond met her at the door.

"Dinner in five minutes," Mrs. Hammond said.

"Dinner in five minutes," Collie repeated for the benefit of her father. "Hope that coffee left you with an appetite."

Collie smiled at Mrs. Hammond, then hurried up the stairs. She had ascended half the staircase before she remembered she still had the walking stick in her hand.

Estelle felt she had come to rely on cocktails. It amused her to discover her taste for booze. Of course, she mused as she set out the bar things for the evening get-together, she would never call it *booze*, or *hooch*, or any of the words George liked to hide like small explosives inside his genial conversation. He had changed that much, at least; gone were the British phrases he had employed to distraction in the beginning of their courtship, replaced, she noted, by a sort of film noir talk. He spoke from the side of his mouth now, aping actors in those dark, venetian-blind dramas popular among a certain segment of the population, though he just as often spilled out into general American boosterism. He was Babbitt, really, the character made famous by the Sinclair Lewis novel of the same name, a backslapping, joke-telling, inveterate joiner. A Lion, an Elk, an Odd Fellow, a Mason, a Knight Templar, for all she knew . . . she could not keep track of his associations. She did not ask what that made her, naturally, and so she had come to rely on cocktails, an evening medicine that made the days tolerable.

It was nearly five thirty. Cocktails to six fifteen, then the short drive to the Duck Pond, then more drinks, dinner at seven or seven thirty, a dance or two—or a lap around the track, as George would likely call it—and then back home. It was much the same every Friday night. She looked at the bar things one more time, checked the ice in the bucket, then went and lighted a fire in the brick hearth. The logs were laid and the flames came right up. The fire was supplemented by construction pine, bits of two-by-fours and trim that George cut up on Saturdays. Everything to a purpose, he liked to say, and perhaps he was right about that.

Car doors sounded in the driveway, almost, she thought, as if conjured by the flames of the fire. She went to the window and peeked out. Two couples, three vehicles. She recognized the first couple: Polly and Missy Kent. They were two old shoes, but the second couple, bright and blond and obviously looking around at George's domain—customers, Estelle knew—stood on Persimmon Drive and ran their eyes over the various houses that had been built and inhabited in the last few months. Prospects, George would say. Everyone, he liked to claim, sold something. Everyone was buying or selling, sometimes both, and this latest couple, unannounced before arriving, surely came to look.

She heard George's voice, doubtless singing the praises of the most recent improvements. Streetlights turned on, sewer in place, speed limits set, local school with a promise to put a new wing on the east side of the building . . . she could do the spiel as well as he could. He had sold five houses; five waited. He was now putting in feelers over at an industrial park he and an investment group had turned up, a potential golf course he was calling Shady Ridge. Houses sitting on adjoining golf courses, he prophesized, would end up being the coming thing.

Polly came in before the others.

"There's my girl!" he said, opening his hands along the lines of his pants like a singer finishing a ballad. "I told them you would have a witches' brew waiting. . . . How are you, darling?"

He came and kissed her cheek. She handed him a Scotch glass.

"Do the honors, would you, Polly? I need to check on the baby. Who are the new candidates?"

"The Blonds? That's what George calls them behind their backs. Mr. and Mrs. Blond. He's just been transferred in . . . from California, sat out the war with a herniated disk or broken hip or something. She's a Miss something or other. A beauty queen."

"Are they interested?"

Polly began shuffling glasses and nodded.

"George thinks tonight will put them over. He's counting on you."

"Of course he is."

"Sell the woman and the man will follow. Isn't that the motto?"

"Fix the drinks, Polly, and let me run upstairs."

Louisa, a heavy black woman with one eye pushed down so that it was nearly closed, met her on the upstairs landing. She carried a dirty diaper in a gray pail. She walked softly and put one of her fingers to her lips to signal *shhhhh*. Hazel, baby Hazel, was asleep.

"She went down?" Estelle asked, hiding her irritation at the baby going so early to sleep. Sleep made the sitting job easy for Louisa and the following morning difficult for Estelle.

"Just like a little lamb," Louisa said. "Hardly stayed awake while I changed her britches."

"That's precious."

"She's a *good* baby, ma'am," Louisa said, emphasizing the good in a way, Estelle reflected, no mother could resist.

"I'm glad you think so, Louisa."

"No thinking about it. She just is, that's all. Sleep like that, that means she was born with a clear conscience."

"Really?" Estelle asked, intrigued with this little sample of folk wisdom despite the sound of the guests coming in downstairs.

"Oh, yes, that means she is not guilty over Cain's original sin. Not at all."

"Wasn't it Adam and Eve's disobedience that was the original sin?"

"Oh, I always believed that they didn't like it in that nasty old garden. Going around with hardly a stitch of clothes . . . why, you tell me if you would like that! No woman would. One way or the other, your little Hazel is as empty as a cup when it comes to guilt, I'm saying. She be a good sleeper all her life."

"That's a blessing."

"Sure it is. Now let me take care of this here, and I'll come back in and sit with her."

Estelle nodded. She tiptoed in and hovered over Hazel's crib for a moment. She really was a darling child, with red highlights in her downy hair and blue eyes that contained half of the world's wisdom at least. Wise eyes, everyone said, and it was true. Hazel lay on her belly, her tiny fists curled in fierce blocks at her side. Estelle bent down and kissed her. *A baby*, she thought. *A tiny infant lives in my house and belongs to me and I am responsible for her welfare.* It was absolutely extraordinary to consider. She touched Hazel's fingers and counted them. The baby's breath came out in little pants, like a small creature, a puppy, perhaps, and Estelle leaned farther into the crib to feel the child's breath against her cheek. How strange life could be. She did not much care one way or the other about George—oh, she did, she did, she reminded herself, except he felt like a family servant, a clever gardener who came in at times to check the plants and then disappeared—but she was mad about her child. It terrified her to think how much she loved Hazel. Her teeth sometimes gritted when she held her, so passionate was her feeling for the lovely little infant. She kissed the crown of Hazel's head and backed slowly out of the room. She wondered, as she went, if all mothers felt such love for their children.

Then she hurried down to join the guests.

"Here she is!" Missy Kent said as Estelle came down the stairs. "The Queen of Persimmon Drive!"

"Hardly a queen!" George said, his hand on a brown drink and his color high. "More like the Empress of Japan. Someone imperial and faultless . . . this is my better half, as you probably surmised. In all her glory."

He said this to the Blonds. Estelle was forced to introduce herself, an event that happened sometimes when George was selling hard and forgot names.

"I'm Estelle . . . and you're?"

"The Emersons. Pat and Patty," the male Blond said.

"Not really?" Estelle asked, genuinely incredulous. "You're having me on."

"We confess," the woman said. *Patty*, Estelle reminded herself. "It's really quite ludicrous. We're aware of it, but those are our names."

"How cute!" Estelle said, accepting a drink from Polly. It was

Scotch over rocks, and she swirled it for a moment to bleed the ice. "Well, here's how, Pat and Patty. Welcome aboard."

"They were looking for property," George said, "and Kiley French put them in touch with me. How about that? They may be settlers out here with us on the great frontier."

"Everyone's moving into George's orbit," Missy Kent said, drinking something faintly orange. "We might as well turn in all our house keys and surrender."

"It seems like a lovely location," Patty said.

"Not yet it isn't," George piped up. "It's a promise of what it will be. That's how I like to phrase it. But you give it five years and the house prices will double. The war's ending and people are going to be spilling out of the cities, you mark my word. Now, you may be transferred away in a year or two, but this house . . . I'm telling you, buying on this end, buying cheap and selling dear, that's the way the two-step goes."

Estelle took another drink. She admitted a dread fascination in watching George rope in customers. The Emersons, for instance, looked like perfectly nice people. They smiled and took a second round from Polly, and she imagined they had a solid life together. They reminded her of draft horses, or a matched pair of andirons, anything put together side by side to manage a job. George was right about their blondness; it was a disarming glimmer, a shiny gleam as if they had come out of the packing material much more recently than anyone else she had met. As she studied them, she guessed they were not sure what to make of George. He enthused an infectious combination of bonhomie and shark salesman, and one had to smile as he chewed on one's leg.

"Won't you move over to the fire?" Estelle asked, feeling the lovely swell of alcohol pushing the day away.

"We should go soon," Missy Kent said, though she led the group to the hearth. "They're doing a roast beef and they always run out."

"It's damnable the way they do that," Polly said, "as if they wanted to tempt us by what we can't have."

"Still, it's a good club," George told the Emersons. "You can't find a better brand of people. All the right sorts, honestly. The Duck has been an institution around here for, geez, I hardly know. I can't remember when we didn't have the Duck."

"'Going to the Duck' is the euphemism for getting drunk," Polly said, his eyes bright and watery with his first drinks. "At least usually it is."

"We're making it sound scandalous, but really it's quite a welcoming place. The kids have birthday parties there . . . and the pool in the summer," Missy said, "is really heavenly. A lot of the moms live on those lounge chairs all summer long."

"And the kids play together," Polly said. "It's all one lovely conspiracy."

It was interesting, Estelle realized, to hear their lives explained to newcomers. What wasn't mentioned, of course, was the difficulty of getting into the Duck in the first place. One had to be sponsored, then vetted, then interviewed, and so on. A financial checkup, too, she imagined, although she had been a member through her family so long that she could not really recall those specific details. But one did not simply walk through the door and pull up a barstool at the men's grill. Not at all. The golf course was in demand and the greens' fees stiff, and George, she knew, would flash everything in front of the Emersons as if they merely had to acquire a house on Persimmon Drive to make it all happen. That was his special selling technique.

Then it was time to go. Polly drained off his glass after calling bottoms up. The others followed suit. George lifted a fire screen in front of the spitting pine scraps while Estelle called up the stairs softly to Louisa that they were going now. Louisa appeared at the top of the stairs and nodded and whispered down that Hazel was still asleep like an angel. Estelle promised they wouldn't be too late.

In the car on the way to the Duck, George said he thought the Blonds were ready to bite.

"Another triumph," Estelle said, trying unsuccessfully to keep the sarcasm out of her voice.

"Dinner should close them. I hope they have enough of that damn roast beef tonight. I need to talk to the manager, what's his name?"

"Steve," Estelle said.

"Right . . . I can never remember his name. I wonder why not. I must block it. Anyway, I'll say, Steve old boy, let's stop being chintzy with the roast beef. If there's one thing you can't go cheap on at a club like the Duck . . ."

"That would be roast beef," Estelle couldn't help herself from saying.

"One of those kinds of evenings, is that right?" George asked, looking over as he navigated up the long, treelined driveway to the Duck.

"We always have one of those evenings, George. It's our fate."

"Be better if you worked with me instead of against me."

"I always work with you, George. I just don't always like that I work with you."

"You're too clever for me by half," George said, and yanked the car into a slot under a chestnut tree. "Anyway, see if you can keep that Patty interested. She's the one who will make the decision. She wants to start a family."

"Do I get a commission?"

He leaned over quickly and kissed her cheek. Then he popped out of the door and came around the car—the Queen of Persimmon Drive, the Duke of the Duck Pond.

~ *Chapter Twenty-three* ~

As the German prisoners found their way to seats in the temporary theater, Major Brennan nodded to Lieutenant Peters. Every guard had been alerted; all hands had been summoned. Lieutenant Peters had seen to that, issuing the order. It was the same order, as it happened, that they had employed to announce Hitler's suicide in the last days of April 1945. They had reported his death and the subsequent immolation of his body factually and without passion. There was a trick to handling such things, and Major Brennan believed in frankness. *Lance the wound,* he had told Lieutenant Peters and others after receiving news about Hitler's death only weeks before. It served no purpose to deny or underplay these events. The worry over how the German men would react to the death of the Führer had been misplaced. If anything, the men appeared relieved, glad to have the end of the war so clearly marked. Hitler's abiding fascination had been dispelled in a single five-minute span as Major Brennan had read calmly an account of his last hours, including Hitler's marriage and breakfast reception with Eva Braun. The men had filed out after a few questions. Surely the conversations had continued in the barracks late into the night, but there had been no obvious repercussion, no attendant protest.

Tonight, however, might prove to be different. When Major Brennan stepped onto the front porch of the mess hall, the German men came promptly to their feet. The Germans, Major Brennan marveled, never failed in that regard: while an American assembly might begin in a lazy, distracted manner, with men climbing to their feet in ragged order, the Germans, as always, stood rigidly alert, obviously prepared to grant a senior officer their full attention. Under other circumstances, it might almost have been humorous, but tonight Major Brennan merely made a motion with his hand and asked that the men be seated.

The men sat. A wind pushed the makeshift movie screen that had been suspended from the front porch of the mess hall. Major Brennan heard it flap behind him. He waited a moment to make sure the men had settled. Then he turned to Collie and asked if she was ready.

"Yes, Papa," she answered.

He started once, opening his mouth to begin, but then stopped. How did one start on such a topic? He braced his shoulders back and took a deep breath.

"In the past few months," he said in a loud voice, "we have heard reports about prisoner-of-war camps in Germany and Poland."

He waited while Collie translated.

"Many of these stories have been met with skepticism, because, I think, we did not wish to believe the truth of what had transpired. Gradually, however, the nature of these camps has begun to astonish the civilized world. Our eyes see, but our minds cannot accept the evidence of our sight."

He waited again for Collie to translate.

"Tonight, we have a film record of what these camps have kept hidden for several years. The film has been provided by the State Department of the United States. Copies of the film have been made and distributed throughout the United States and across all corners of Europe."

Collie translated. Her voice, he marveled, was steady and strong. He saw the German prisoners nod at her words.

"You may ask yourself, why am I being shown such a film? The war is coming to a close. It is time to shut the door to such memories. But it is the position of the State Department, and of the United

States of America, that German prisoners should be shown evidence of the horrors the Fatherland visited on the peoples of Europe. We do this not to shame you but to bring to light the full depravity sanctioned by the leaders of your nation. This is of the darkest character. This is the ultimate expression of human cruelty."

When Collie finished translating, Major Brennan raised his hand to indicate to the projectionists to run the film. Major Brennan quickly stepped out of the beam of light that flashed from the roof of the closest barracks. For a moment nothing became visible on the screen except numbers. Then gradually images began moving on the screen. A pile of skeletal bodies lay in a discarded heap, with a bulldozer slowly pushing the bodies toward a mass grave. The pictures moved without narration. Major Brennan watched the diesel smoke coming out of the exhaust vent on top of the bulldozer; it was incomprehensible that such a machine could be employed to maneuver human corpses. The bodies rolled in stiff, reluctant waves, like flaccid bolts of material pushed along an earthen floor. Major Brennan lighted a cigarette and felt his hands trembling.

The rest was a variation on the same theme: ghostly men and women with enormous eyes, malnourished, gasping, their expressions pleading. More bodies, more corpses. The camera occasionally went inside a barracks, the bright lights illuminating crowded bunks of starving people languishing in a boned silence, heads hardly able to turn at the light. *Hibernacula*, Major Brennan thought, watching them. Winter caves for bats.

Major Brennan moved his eyes from the images on the screen to the men watching the film. No one made a sound. The film went on a long time. The wind occasionally pushed the screen back and forth and made the images hard to see. Then the cloth settled again and the horror returned.

"We told you this was happening!" one man finally said, but who it was, or even what portion of the crowd had given voice, Major

Brennan couldn't say. Then another said, "No one listened! We told the officers, but no one listened!" Those voices freed the crowd of men to a degree and let them move slightly in their seats. The usual human sounds returned: a scuffed shoe, a cough, a sneeze, a match-strike.

When the film finished, the light flicked off. Major Brennan returned to the small porch. He stood for a moment and then slowly began the words to "Our Father." The Germans joined him, speaking their own language. "Forgive us our trespasses," he said, his voice wavering, and "for those who trespass against us." When he finished the prayer, he nodded to Lieutenant Peters to dismiss the men. They filed out in silence.

Later that same night, Collie heard August playing the piano. She knew his style immediately. Other people played the piano, some even with greater fluency than he, but none played with his quiet, elegant style. The notes came to her as she locked the office. Her father had gone off after the movie, taking two of the younger officers into Berlin for dinner. The men were being transferred back to Boston the next day. It was a good-bye dinner, strangely juxtaposed with the horrors they had witnessed during the film from the extermination camps. But that was the way with war, Collie reflected. A thousand things happened in a single day.

She did not pretend to go anywhere but the refectory. She found August sitting at the piano in the dimness. It might have been a bit a cliché: the troubled young soldier losing himself on the piano keyboard after observing his countrymen's depravity. But it did not feel that way. He played to find something in the music, not to lose himself, and she stood for a moment in the doorway watching him.

She loved him. That was clear now. It was like loving her hand or face or breath. Inside of her head, she was no longer alone. She did not think only for herself but for them both, for what he might think or need or desire. She imagined she held the same place in his thoughts. When he looked up to see her, she crossed the room quickly and went into his arms. He kissed her. Then the kiss grew and built and she felt his hands on her, everywhere, and she kissed him deeper, deeper, slowly stretching across his lap. She could not resist. What was the point of resisting? She felt his strength and his urgency, and she did not try to stop him but added her own urgency to his. They might have been a fuse burning, she felt, and it was insanity to do this here, to enter this level of wantonness where so many people might surprise them, but it broke on her with quick, sudden snaps.

She nearly drowned. She nearly lost herself entirely, but finally pushed herself away. She took two steps toward the door, then fell back into his arms, kissed him, pushed away again. She did not speak and neither did he. The room was dark except for the outside lights and the only noises she heard were sounds their bodies met sparking together.

She shook her head no when it had all gone too far, then she crawled off him, an animal, a lost, ravaging creature, and his hands trailed after her. She felt his arousal, his determination, but she kissed him again and again, slowly pulling away, slowly easing out of his orbit. She kissed him a hundred times on his neck, his forehead, his hands. Then she turned and nearly ran, her head detached from her body, her blood slinking in warm, flushing currents through her lips, her legs, her groin. She pushed through the door and walked out, relieved, almost, to see a group of prisoners stepping along the boardwalks, the moon, half empty, swinging like a garden gate on the ridge of the Devil's Slide.

❧ Chapter Twenty-four ❧

Albee Spencer's office smelled of cigars and bay rum, but mostly of cigars. It was a dark, dingy office, with an overhead fan twirling as if trying to screw itself out of the ceiling. Estelle could not find a comfortable place to sit, which was not to say that the chairs were uncomfortable but merely poorly placed. One straight-backed chair sat in the corner, and a vast, blue-gray couch took up the northern wall. The standard desk chair that had been put into service in front of the gunmetal desk sat on wheels and looked unsteady. Given the various options, she was not sure where she wanted to sit.

A moment later Albee Spencer came in. He was a dense, bald man of about fifty, with extraordinarily full eyebrows and a pair of bright red braces straining to hold his pants up against a large belly. He resembled a rolling pin, Estelle thought, or a novelty bottle with maple syrup inside. She had seen those kinds of bottles at the state fair, and she had never imagined they might be modeled after someone. For all of that, however, he moved like an anxious bear, stopping midway into the doorway to shout something back at the larger office behind him. The sound of typewriters propelled him into the room. He crossed quickly to his desk and sat down. He did not shake hands or give her any better indication of why she had been asked to visit him.

"You wrote the article on the Red Cross?" he asked, his eyes down at the papers on his desk.

"Yes. . . ."

"Are you going to sit or run out the door? Am I so terrifying?"

He looked up. He had soft eyes, at least, Estelle thought. She sat on the front edge of the desk chair. It rocked a little forward and she had to balance herself.

"Your name is . . . ?"

"Estelle Samuels. I was Estelle Emhoff."

"Dr. Emhoff's daughter?"

Estelle nodded.

"That explains it," Albee Spencer said. "You write passably. We need a number of things covered. Are you interested?"

"Covered?"

"Yes, yes, as a reporter," Spencer said, his temper just bubbling underneath. "Yes, covered . . . local events, school board meetings. Nothing too exciting. You're not going to be Nellie Bly."

"A reporter?" Estelle asked, still trying to make sense of the request.

"Yes, a local events reporter. This piece you did on the Red Cross . . . it's the kind of thing I'm looking for. Right now we're shorthanded. The war has taken away most of my reporters and the young kids . . . they think they're going to come in here and break the story of the century. And they can't write. I need someone steady to go around and write up the stories we need covered at the *Bugle*. Does that interest you?"

"I've got a baby."

"Did I say that you didn't? I'm not thrilled about hiring a woman, believe me, but I'm shorthanded, as I say. You seem to have the knack, and what you don't know we can teach you. If you don't think it's a respectable occupation for a woman, then don't waste either of our time. I've got a thousand things to do today."

"How much would you pay me?" Estelle asked, more to have something to say than to negotiate terms. She felt dizzy and out to sea. What was he proposing exactly? This curious little man.

"We'll pay you by the story. You don't have to come into the office unless you're submitting a story. You'll be a freelancer ... ever heard of that? A stringer, we could say."

"I've heard of it."

He suddenly pushed back in his chair and reached for a cigar left on the edge of an enormous ashtray. The cigar had gone out. He started it again.

"Look ... it's a pretty simple proposition. I need some things covered. You're local and you write well enough and you're probably in the area for the duration. I'm not expecting more than you can handle, believe me. Most of the events can be covered in an hour or two. Do you have a typewriter?"

She nodded.

"Okay, so you go take notes, you write it up, then you hand it in to the copy boy. Make sure you write a lede and leave something to cut at the bottom. It's not *Gone with the Wind*. It's just local reporting. We'll send a photographer out with you when you need him. I've got a school board meeting tomorrow night and a PTA meeting over in Lawrence Thursday. What do you say we start with that and see where it goes? If you can write more personal stuff ... flower shows, family reunions, that's all to the good. You can check with me."

"You're offering me a job?" Estelle asked, still not comprehending. Or rather, she comprehended, but she wanted to hear him say it.

"Yes. A job."

"I'd have to talk to my husband."

"You do that and get back to me. Don't sit on this, though. I've got to have someone."

"Well, thank you," she said, rising.

The smell of the cigar was really quite something, she reflected. She wasn't sure how to make her exit, so she held out her hand and Mr. Spencer shook it. Then she went back outside into the general office and the swarm of typewriters.

She could not have been more astonished, she realized as she pushed onto Carolina Avenue. The noise of the street seemed to surround her, and she stepped for a moment to the protection of the line of buildings that rose on both sides of the street. She placed her hand against the granite foundation and tried to catch her breath. A job. It was the last thing in the world she had expected to blossom from her article on the Red Cross activities in the Ashtabula area. She had written it at the request of Shirley Grant, a volunteer at the Red Cross in the next town over, and she *had* taken her time with it. It was to run with her name attached, after all, and one didn't want to appear a proper idiot in the newspaper. But now, suddenly, Albee Spencer—George knew him and liked him, and her father had mentioned him many times over the years—had offered her a position. Not a position, she corrected herself, but an arrangement, an assignment. . . . What was the word she was searching for? She didn't know. She pushed herself away from the building and felt a nervous thrill burning in her stomach. But what about Hazel? She could not simply abandon her child to traipse around the county writing up stories about local budget issues. George would be furious; so would her parents. On the second consideration, it made very little sense, even if it was flattering to be asked.

She steadied herself. Louisa had come in to watch Hazel for the morning. There had been some talk about joining George for lunch at Collin's Grill, but he had canceled last minute. Estelle had not informed George of her meeting with Albee Spencer; she had never thought about it, honestly, except that there might be something about the Red Cross article that had come to his attention. She had rolled the appointment into a round of errands to run and as she slowly gained a sense of herself once more, she pulled a to-do list from her purse.

It was difficult to concentrate. A reporter! Women were performing all sorts of jobs they hadn't considered prior to the war, but a reporter! She walked slowly down Carolina, then crossed at the corner of Ellis and Montgomery. Her mind played with the idea. She could manage it, she thought. She could have Louisa in when she was needed, and for the evening events. . . . Hazel would be asleep, so there was no difficulty there. If she were being honest, she had always prided herself on her writing. Even at Smith her papers had received fulsome attention from the professors. Now Albee Spencer had singled her out as a potential journalist. It was gratifying, she admitted, even if it seemed to lead nowhere. It would be dull work, she imagined. School board meetings, and town budget hearings . . . George met often with zoning boards and the like, and he always came back incensed at the bureaucratic sludge he encountered. To cover those proceedings, Estelle reflected, would be tedious in the extreme. But it would be work, honest work, and for the first time in months she felt that her life had not ended upon giving birth. She *loved* Hazel, that was indisputable, but were the rest of her days meant to be spent supporting George in his endeavors and drinking at the Duck Pond and tending to Hazel? It was wonderful to be a mother, the highest station a woman could set for herself, but if it meant so much, why did she feel such a thrill at being asked to report for the *Bugle*?

She had been paying little attention to where she was walking, and when she looked up she found herself nearly in front of Mr. Kamal's flower shop. The front had been redone, but its style was unmistakably Mr. Kamal's. If she had paused to think, she would have turned away, but she felt so much under the influence of her recent conversation with Albee Spencer that she simply opened the door to Mr. Kamal's shop and stepped inside. The scent of flowers assailed her; she smelled roses and something deep and green. The shop looked prosperous. A young woman stood behind the counter; someone had added a bright parrot to the interior. The bird was in the process of climbing up a branch in the center of its cage, and Estelle marveled at the ingenious way it used its beak to steady itself.

It made a short ratchet sound, and the young woman—she was an Indian woman, quite beautiful, with a tiny dot in the center of her forehead—shushed it and came around the counter.

"May I help you?" the woman asked.

She possessed the same unusual intonations used by Mr. Kamal.

"I was just passing by and I realized I hadn't seen Mr. Kamal in such a long time. . . ."

"He is in the back resting. I'll call him."

"Oh, please don't. It's nothing important. He's not ill, is he?"

"No, just lazy!" the woman said, and smiled. "He was up late last night with a sick child. Our apologies."

"The store looks wonderful. You've made changes."

"What is your name?" the woman asked. "I'll tell him you stopped by."

"Estelle Samuels."

"Very good, Mrs. Samuels. I'll be sure to tell him. Are you positive I can't be of service?"

"No, thank you. I was just running errands."

"Feel free to look around."

The parrot emitted another squawk. Estelle smiled and thanked the woman again, then she hurried out the door. She must get hold of herself, she thought. She turned right and walked toward Anderson's Bakery. She needed to sit and collect herself. Who was that woman, she wondered, and what was she doing in the flower shop? And a child? Could that have been their child? No other explanation quite fit the facts, at least not initially, but Estelle felt too muddyheaded to make sense of anything. She needed to stop acting impulsively. She would have coffee and perhaps write a letter to Collie. There was so much to tell, so much to relate. The world was a very funny place.

Chapter Twenty-five

Estelle held Hazel in her arms while the operator tried to put her through to New Hampshire. Stark, New Hampshire. The operator had made her repeat the name twice, unable to locate it, and she had finally been forced to go to a supervisor who took it as a challenge. Now Estelle waited. It was only a little past seven in the morning and the nursery was quiet and soft, the way she most loved it, and her baby nuzzled her and cooed. Hazel had taken her bottle and now occasionally rubbed her eyes in sleepiness. Estelle kissed the top of Hazel's head and smiled at the gentle softness returned to her by the infant.

Then the phone clicked several times and finally the operator—the supervisor, Estelle realized—came on and said, "Go ahead. Your party is there," and Collie came on from the New Hampshire side.

"Estelle? Estelle? Is that you?"

"Collie? Sweetheart, I received your letter yesterday. I would have called last night, but it was too late and I feared I'd wake the whole boardinghouse," Estelle said. "You have me scared, Collie. What's going on there?"

"I'm going to marry him. I'm going to be with him. I don't care anymore."

"But how? How could you possibly? I know you have strong feelings for him, but how will you manage it?"

Collie's voice grew very quiet. She whispered.

"He's going to Canada. We'll live there. It's the only way. We've worked it out. We leave letters for each other near a post where the horses are kept. We've made plans. We've promised each other."

"When will you go?" she asked, trying to take it all in.

"I can't tell you that. But soon. Very soon."

"It's dangerous, though, Collie. It's very dangerous, isn't it? It must be."

"Yes, it is," Collie answered, her phone hitting against something. "Dreadfully so. By law, they can hang an escaped prisoner in a time of war. It's treasonous to help him."

"Can't you wait? Can't he return to Austria and then work his way back to you? Your letter wasn't clear. . . ."

"They're not going back to Germany or Austria. They're going to forced labor camps in Britain. My father hasn't entirely confirmed it, but he won't deny it, either. There's massive work to be done in London . . . all over the United Kingdom, really. The bombing left the country decimated."

"Collie, I'm worried for you."

"Do you think I'm making a mistake? Tell me honestly. I have no one to confide in about this. It's so enormous I can't get my head around it."

Estelle felt every word she had ever spoken freeze in her throat. What did she know? What did she know about anything? She had married for convenience, for reliability, for social standing. How could she possibly render an opinion on Collie's reckless plan? Of course it was wild and perhaps even doomed, but how did that compare to her own stolid life with George? Could she advise her dear friend to ignore every impulse, every warm current of her body, so that she could someday marry a man like George?

She shook her head and kissed the top of her baby's skull.

"You are not making a mistake, darling," she whispered. "You are not. I can't speak to the safety of your plan, but cling to him. Stay with him."

"I will. I promise."

Then Collie stopped. Estelle heard her crying.

"My heart feels like it might burst," Collie whispered between deep breaths. "I love him so."

"I know you do. You have loved him from the start."

"I don't know what will happen, but plenty of brides have lost their men to the war. I'm not alone, heaven knows . . . not in that. So really I've decided to love him as much as I can for as long as I can. Do you think I've made the wrong choice?"

"No," Estelle said, kissing the baby again, her heart splintered and jagged. "You have made the perfect choice. You have made the only choice. I admire you so much for your choice, Collie. I want you to know that."

"I don't feel it was a choice. Not really."

Estelle walked the baby and switched arms. She pinched the phone between her ear and shoulder.

"What about Henry? Is he in the picture at all?"

"I've gone out with him twice more. Really, it's to keep people from spying too much into my business. Henry's a good man, but he's not for me. He knows it deep down, but he doesn't like to examine it too closely."

"Stay away from Amos. Don't let him get wind of your plans."

"No, I won't," Collie said, then her voice changed into a reedy whisper, lighter even than what it had been previously. "Estelle, August is leaving any day. He hasn't told me when, but I know it must be soon. He has his plan made. He says he's simply going to walk away from the war."

"Do you think he can pull it off? Oh, Collie, he's risking his life to be with you."

"I don't know. He can get away, certainly, but I don't know if he can make it to Canada. There are so many eyes watching."

"What about your father? What will he say?"

"He will be disappointed. He will know I had an idea about the escape. But Estelle, we have a right to some happiness, don't we?

Doesn't everyone have that right? The war is over, or nearly so. In some ways, this has nothing to do with my father. This is August's life. He has to do what he thinks he should do, and so do I. We only want each other."

"That's not much to ask of the world, is it?"

"I hope it's not too much."

Hazel squirmed in Estelle's arms and emitted a small cry.

"Is Hazel right there with you?" Collie asked. "How are you, Estelle? Tell me how you are. I've been so involved in my own dilemma that I haven't even asked."

"Hazel is right here saying hello. I'm doing fine. I'm doing those silly articles for the newspaper job I mentioned. Hazel is just wonderful. Nothing momentous is going on, I promise. George is nearly done selling his properties out here. He's done very well for himself."

"Good old George."

"Yes, good old George. He should be coming downstairs any minute, so I should hop off. Okay now, darling, I'm sending you all my love. I wish I were as brave as you. You are very, very brave."

"Good-bye, Estelle. Let's see each other soon."

Then for a moment neither of them said a word. Estelle felt her eyes fill with water again.

"It will be all right," Estelle whispered. "You were meant to be with him."

"I hope so," Collie said, and then whispered good-bye.

Estelle carried Hazel to the window and looked out at the street traffic slowly coming awake.

Collie took the train to Berlin. She needed to get away from camp and she also needed to withdraw her savings. It wasn't much—a little over one hundred dollars—but it was the best she could do. She would give it to August. Whether she went with him or not, whether he could escape on his own or go with Gerhard, he would need money. She could do that much, though even that set her against her father. She hated her position. She hated deceiving, or working in any way against her father's role at the camp. But she felt, at least as the train moved gently through the springtime forests, that she served a higher cause than her loyalty to her father.

As soon as she arrived in Berlin she made her way to the Narragansett Savings Bank. It was the bank everyone used, and she was relieved when she approached a teller without seeing anyone she knew. She asked him for a withdrawal slip and filled it out, requesting the entire amount save five dollars to keep the account open. The teller, a short, bald man with thick glasses, made no comment nor displayed any interest in her transaction beyond the routine of digging out the money from his cash drawer. He counted it out on the counter between them, then nodded at her.

"Anything else?" he asked when she did not immediately pick up the money.

"No, no thank you," she said, flummoxed by the ease with which she could begin her duplicity.

"Is it looking like rain after all?" the teller asked. "I heard a report that says we're due for it."

"Just a little overcast, I think," she said. "It may rain later."

She gathered the money and put the bills inside a small wallet, then dropped it into her purse. Her heart and pulse hammered with ridiculous weight. She was not cut out to be a spy, or an undercover operator, clearly. She tucked the purse onto her arm and began to turn away when she spotted Henry making his way toward her.

"Now this is a pleasant surprise," he said. "But why didn't you let me know you were coming to Berlin today? I would have met you at the train."

"I wasn't sure of my plans. And when I did . . ."

"Well, no matter," he said. "I'm headed to lunch. Would you join me? It's close enough to noon, I think."

She tried to invent a way to put him off, but her mind felt empty. Truly she was not very good at subterfuge. She smiled and tucked her elbow closer over her purse. She found herself nodding before she had made up her mind consciously.

"If it's short," she said. "You're very kind to offer, but I have a dozen errands to run."

"Just a quick bite. Let me do a little banking here, and then we can stop in at Wentworth's. Have you been before? It's a workingman's saloon, really, but they make the best stew in the area. I insist you try a bowl."

As he talked, he handed papers and checks to the teller. The teller did not even ask what to do, apparently accustomed to Henry's transactions. He stamped a number of the documents, made out slips, and in good order handed back a small bundle to Henry, which he slipped into the breast pocket of his overcoat.

"There you are, sir," the teller said. "Have a lovely afternoon."

"I plan to," Henry said, then put his hand out to escort Collie forward.

Although it had felt like bad luck at first to run into Henry, Collie realized it served a purpose. If her visit to Berlin aroused any curiosity, she could say she had lunched with Henry. Besides, it gave her a moment to think. She kept her elbow on her purse as she walked beside him to Wentworth's. She jumped slightly when the bell on the door jingled as she pushed through. The restaurant was exactly as Henry had described it: it was a saloon, complete with red-and-white-checked tablecloths and an enormous bar with beer taps rising like masts from its center deck. It was crowded, too, with loggers and workmen. A coal stove burned in the fireplace. Its heat was welcome.

"We'll be with you in a second," a waitress said to them. "Grab a seat if one opens."

"That's Hermione," Henry whispered over the crowd noise, "she's quite famous. She killed her husband with a pickax one winter night. The court decided he deserved it and only sentenced her to three years."

"I'll be certain not to offend her, then."

"That's the plan . . . ," he said, and then touched the small of her back when a table opened just past the front window. Two loggers had occupied the table, and they left it with a nod.

"There you are, governor," one the men said. "For you and your bird."

"Thank you," Henry said.

They sat and waited while Hermione came over and cleared the logger's dishes. She worked efficiently and piled everything onto a tray before lifting it up to her shoulder. Collie found her fascinating. She had thick arms and rusty-colored hair, but she moved with great assurance and unquestionably ruled the dining room. Collie would have liked to ask her a few questions about what it meant for a woman to overturn convention, but that was impossible.

"Will you have the stew?" Henry asked. "I don't mean to push it on you, but it's famous. They make it fresh every day."

"I'd love a bowl."

"And what to drink? Is it too early in the day for a cocktail?"

"I think just coffee for me, thanks."

"I guess that's a better idea. Coffee, then," he said, catching Hermione in passing. "And two bowls of stew, please."

"Simple enough," Hermione said in a voice that had a slightly foreign lilt to it. "Bread with that?"

"Yes, sure."

Off she went. Collie felt herself sag in the chair. It felt good to be out of the chilly spring air, good to have a place to sit. She hadn't known she had been chilled. She took off her gloves and used the moment to look around. She liked Wentworth's a good deal. It felt to be an authentic place, trying to be no more or less than what it was.

"A good place, isn't it?" Henry asked, reading her.

"I was just thinking that."

"Funny that we ran into each other. The New York Opera is coming to Portland, and I wondered if we could go see it together. I was going to call you this afternoon to invite you."

"That sounds lovely," she said.

"It won't be for another month, but if you're interested I'll be sure to get tickets. Mother might want to go, too. We're not a big opera family, so I don't mean to give you that impression. But we try to support the arts when they journey north. Mother insists on it."

Before Collie could say anything to that, Hermione returned with four bowls of stew loaded on her arms. She set one in front of each of them and continued on her way. "Coffee," she said, reminding herself and them that she needed to bring them something else. She hurried around the dining room and it was impossible to ignore her.

"Good?" he asked when she had taken a sip of the stew broth.

"Very good. Very fresh, as you say."

"Sometimes they use moose meat, but I can't tell the difference. The loggers swear moose makes a better stew. Amos will go out of his way to find a moose stew."

"How is Amos?"

Henry smiled a rueful smile. Amos, she knew, would always remain a project. Henry's smile contained that knowledge. Amos would keep going, keep churning, until one day he ran into an obstacle, or another person more deadly and unpredictable than he was. Then he would die, or end up with his health ruined, his body broken, and he would haunt Berlin in a haze of alcohol. His epitaph was already written and waiting for him to fulfill it. She did not know how she understood that suddenly, but she did.

"He's up north with a survey team," Henry said, spooning more stew into his mouth. At the same time Hermione returned with coffee and a bowl of brown bread. She put a plate holding a yellow thumb of butter onto the table beside it. She didn't ask if they were satisfied or required anything else. She had work to do and left as soon as she deposited the bread and coffee.

"Looking at land?"

"From a barstool, probably. Yes, that's the idea. He does better away from the office. His colorful nature needs a lot of air."

She nodded.

"And you? What have you been doing?" he asked.

"The stew is very good," she said, and meant it.

"I told you. We'll turn you into a logger yet."

"I'm not doing much," she said, returning to his question, "except requisitioning trucks and sending off gear. Things are coming to an end. My father thinks the camp will run through the summer, but it's hard to say. We're emptying things around the edges."

"Will you be glad to have it over?"

"I suppose so. But it's been exciting, too. Lieutenant Peters says we will all miss the war when finally it is over, and I suspect he has a point."

"And what will you do next if you don't marry me?"

He smiled. It annoyed her to have him throw that into the conversation, especially today. But she dared not rise to the bait, so she shrugged her shoulders. She wondered what he would say, what any of them would say, if they knew she contemplated running off with a German soldier to a place she had never visited with no assurance that they would not be shot for their troubles. It made her wonder if everyone, every last person in the saloon, didn't have a secret agenda that they kept close to their hearts. Even Henry, for all she knew, might be revealing only a small portion of his character to her. It made her feel peculiar to think it.

"You need to find a north-country girl," she said. "I don't fit the job description."

"You do, actually," he said. "But I didn't mean to be glib about marriage. You make me nervous, Collie, and I'm not always at my best around you. I try to be. I want to be, but I suspect I try too hard. It's funny, too, because I am not like that with other women."

"You've been very kind to me, Henry. I've counted on you while we've been here."

"But you don't love me, do you?"

He smiled. He might have been asking about the weather from his expression. He knew the answer already, she realized, but he required himself to ask just in case. She looked at him carefully. She didn't want to hurt him, but she could no longer maintain the exercise of being with him.

"No, I don't love you, Henry," she said as softly as she could.

"Do you think you could grow to love me? Isn't that what they ask in all the stories?"

"I don't dislike you, Henry. I'm fond of you. I don't have anything against you. Even that business with Amos . . . that's all forgotten. Let's not make this more uncomfortable than it needs to be. You may not believe it, but I tried to love you, Henry, but my heart isn't easily persuaded. My friend Estelle claims we all have a sun that we grow toward. She loves plants, so she thinks in those terms, but it's true."

"And I'm not your sun?"

She didn't say anything.

"And the German soldier . . . he is your sun?"

She didn't say anything to that, either. Henry wiped his mouth with his napkin. He smiled and it was the same rueful smile he had possessed when he spoke about Amos.

"Well, the poor bastard, I feel sorry for him anyway. After this is finished, they're being sent off to London. It will be two years or more before they make it home. My father just gave me the report."

She kept her eyes steady, although the news, delivered so off-handedly, shocked her. If August heard it he would be off to Canada the next day. He would not surrender to another two years of imprisonment and labor. Many of the men wouldn't.

"I knew that was a possibility," she managed to say after another long moment. She put her spoon into her stew to cover herself.

"If you change your mind," he said, "don't be shy about it."

"Thank you, Henry."

"Amos was right after all," he said. "He always contended you had feelings for the German boy. I thought he was just saying it to be cruel."

"I never meant to be cruel."

He didn't say anything else, and when Hermione passed by again he asked her for the check.

❧ *Chapter Twenty-six* ❧

"It has been confirmed," her father said beside the fireplace in Mrs. Hammond's boardinghouse. "I don't deny it, but Henry overstepped by saying anything. I needed the Brown Paper Company people to understand the men's position, and I probably said more than I should. But, yes, the prisoners will be transported to London aboard two ships. They won't be told until they are halfway across."

"They will assume they are going home?" Collie asked, trying desperately to keep her voice level.

"They'll assume what they assume."

"That's very cold of you to say it like that."

Her father regarded her. He appeared tired, she realized. But a weight had also been lifted from his shoulders. They all saw the end of Camp Stark. It might be days, it might be weeks, but the ending advanced on them each hour just as the Allied forces broke off pieces of Germany and claimed them. There was a sense, almost, of school ending, a broad summer extending outward in its deliciousness. That weight had been lifted, but she understood she had brought him an additional burden.

"We're at war, Collie," he said sternly. "These are men who fought against us. We have treated them humanely, which is more than I can say for their treatment of the Jews. They are being sent to clean up the devastation they wrought on a nation that is our ally. I have sympathy for these men, but only to a point. I know where my loyalty rests."

Collie nodded. She could not press. He would intuit why she asked. He understood, furthermore, that it was a death sentence for many of the prisoners. It did no good to point that out to him. Who would know better the men's condition, their frailty? Weak and infirmed, they could not survive another two years of forced labor. The blow to their morale alone would be enough to kill many of them. All of that rested inside his orders. It was the weight of command.

The fire snapped once and a small puff of smoke escaped the draft. The fire was not needed. The afternoon had turned fine and warm, and now the fireplace lazily burned the last of a log end. In an hour the fire might be needed again, but for now it laid glimmering in the softening afternoon light.

Her father leaned forward in his easy chair. He had been reading the newspaper and it slipped from his lap. He caught it before it slid entirely off and repositioned it on his legs.

"Collie, I understand your concern. I do. But you were not supposed to have this information. Henry should not have told you that. The order might be overturned down the road. Didn't your mother always tell you not to climb a mountain until you come to it? It's like a great billiard game right now, with the balls rocketing every which way, slamming into each other. Sorry, that's a poor metaphor, but you get the idea. Nothing is certain for the time being."

"But the order came in?"

"Yes," he said, softening his voice so it would not pass to the sharp, owlish ears belonging to Mrs. Hammond, "but only as a point of information. It's not for public consumption, and the press knows nothing about it."

"Can you imagine what it would feel like to believe you are on your way home and then suddenly to be told you are not going home after all but to a foreign country where you will again be regarded with suspicion and again be asked to work for slave wages?"

"Yes, it's regrettable. Staff is concerned the men will revolt."

"Could you blame them if they did?"

He raised his handkerchief to his lips. He was a kind, decent man, she knew, but she could not help cornering him on these essential points. Still, it was wrong of her to do so; he could not countermand what came from above him. She must get hold of herself, she realized. Her mind passed to August. If he caught wind of these orders, he would leave. It was as simple as that. In his position, she would do the same thing. All of the men would.

"Listen, sweetheart, I'm sorry," her father said. "I am. I know we've come to care about these men. I know you have feelings for the German boy. But these times are not like other times. You cannot judge things the same way. Besides, I have good news."

"What news, Papa?"

"I have been transferred to Germany. It's nearly certain. As soon as the camp closes here, I'll be sent over. It looks like I will supervise a prisoner-of-war camp there, but for officers. It's all being worked out, but that's my next post."

"Congratulations, Papa."

"If you want to come with me . . . ," he said, and said nothing else.

If you want to come with me, she knew he wanted to say, *you might be able to see your German love in Europe.* That was his offer. In some way that wasn't quite clear, it was the balance he hoped to strike with her. She understood that. She looked at him carefully. She loved her father. His kindness, his soft, gentle demeanor, never meant more to her than it did in that moment. August had said the men respected him as commandant. Yes, he was a good, kind man working for the best interests of all concerned. It was not easy, but he did it as well as any man could do it.

She stood and went to him. She kissed his cheek.

"Thank you, Papa," she said.

"Time makes everything right in the end."

"I know, Papa."

"It's a hard turn for the men, but they lost a war."

"I understand."

"Don't hate me for it."

"I could never hate you, Papa. I hope you'll never hate me."

She pushed away and went upstairs. She heard him turning the pages of the newspaper as she climbed the steps. She glanced once more at him and tried to commit the image to her memory, because, she feared, it would be a long time before she saw him again.

Estelle typed in the living room, close to the fireplace, so that the sound of the machine would not wake Hazel. She liked typing on the small table tucked close to the window where she could see the comings and goings outside, while still having the heat from the fireplace. She also enjoyed having the fireplace for a wastebasket; one mistake on the typescript and she simply pulled the paper from the platen, crushed it into a ball, then tossed it into the flames. She liked the finality of that. She wished all mistakes could be committed to a fire as simply as paper.

She glanced down at her notes and listened for Hazel. The child was an excellent sleeper, which was a mercy. She listened, too, for George; he would be home soon, banging and clanging, his step made stupid by drink, his keys a hum of metallic noise as he came through the door. She hoped he would not be too jolly. She had a deadline for early the next morning: the Ashtabula Board of Education had met on a bond proposal. The proposal had been floated as a remedy for a lack of space due to an increasing student population, but several of the board members had pointed out that with war expenses compounded by an unknown future, it was not the time for the town to borrow money. Estelle had several winning quotes and she looked for ways to fit them into the prose. It was like working at masonry, she felt, fitting things together, placing them just so before the mortar dried completely. Certainly it resembled masonry more than actual composition, she thought. Nevertheless, she found it rewarding work.

She was halfway through the article when George arrived, heralded by the slam of a car door and the small chimes of his keys. He was a great believer in locks, she reflected. He was never happier than when he was opening or closing something, securing it or breaking it free. A lesson about his personality rested in that understanding, but she wasn't sure she could name it satisfactorily. She forced herself to concentrate so that her fingers could be working the keys as he came through the door. She had learned that as a trick to keep him heading upstairs toward the bedroom.

But tonight it didn't work. He loomed in the doorway, a silly grin on his face, his right pocket pulled out like a rabbit ear extending from his hip. His scent came to her even from across the room: liquor and cigarettes, maybe perfume, maybe the heavy odor of laundry in need of change.

"Hey," he said.

She looked up and smiled.

"It's Saturday night," he said.

"So?"

"That's a night for . . . you know," he said, coming slowly across the room to take a position with his back to the fire. "Saturday night . . ."

"You sweep a girl off her feet, George."

He raised his eyebrows and smiled. She guessed he had been at the Duck.

"The deal's going through," he said after a moment. "Put that in your paper. Put that in your *Bugle*," he said, attempting a joke. "How do you like them potatoes?"

"Isn't the phrase 'apples'?"

"I like 'potatoes' better."

"When you say 'the deal,'" she said, trying to make herself speak rationally to him, "I assume you mean the golf course deal on the industrial property—"

"S'right," he said, cutting her off.

"You should go to bed, George."

"You can have anything in the world you want," he said, marveling at the concept even as it crossed his lips. "Not yet, but soon. Anything."

"I'm very grateful, George. You're a wonderful breadwinner."

"Aren't I?" he said, rocking a little on his heels. "This road? Persimmon Drive? Ten houses. Around the golf course . . . thirty maybe. You do the math."

"That's impressive," she said.

He nodded. Then he changed subjects.

"How's the brat?"

"I wish you wouldn't call her that."

"She is a brat. But she's our brat."

"Still, it's not a good habit to get into. . . ."

"One more check of disapproval. I know a game we can play. It's Saturday night, so we can play games, can't we?"

"I have some work to do, George."

"Of course you do . . . let's have one drink."

"Maybe you've had enough."

"You swill your share easy enough."

"That's a fair point, George."

He looked at her, apparently trying to focus. He was in rough shape. She worried that he might fall back on the fire.

"I'll get you a drink if you promise to sit down."

"You have one, too."

"Sure, I'll fix us both one. But you have to sit."

"You never said how the brat was."

"Hazel's fine," Estelle said, standing and going to the portable bar they kept near the French doors leading out to a patio. "She's very sweet."

"S'course she is."

"You promised you'd sit if I fixed us cocktails."

He nodded, then moved slowly to an easy chair. He collapsed a little as he sat down into it. He put his toes on the heels of his shoes and shot the shoes off toward the fire. They made a loud clumping sound. Estelle mixed two light drinks. She added extra soda in George's whiskey. She brought him the drink, half expecting him to be drowsy, but his eyes were open and his grin had returned.

"So we should play this game," he said, "the one I proposed."

"Okay, we'll play a game," Estelle said, going back to her seat beside the typewriter. "How do you play?"

"It's easy. It's easy as Parcheesi," he said, dumbly rhyming. "The whole thing is we try to go through an hour without you disapproving of me. How's that?"

"I don't disapprove of you, George."

"Sure you do," he said, and raised his glass. "That's no secret. You can't hide a thing like that. You married below yourself, Estelle."

"George, this is ridiculous."

"*Bshshhhh*," he made a dismissive buzz with his lips. "The funny thing is, I'm going to make you rich, but you won't care a hang for it, will you? Money isn't the object, but I sure as hell don't know what the object is if it isn't money."

"Maybe it's happiness."

"Money will help make you happy, believe me. It's going to make Hazel happy, too."

"That remains to be seen, George."

"Do you love me, Estelle?" he asked, his head suddenly jerking a little from booze as he turned to look at her directly.

But he also appeared alert. One should never underestimate George, she reminded herself.

"I married you, didn't I? Had your baby?"

"But I don't think you love me. Isn't that funny? We're just a little dollhouse here, with Mommy and Daddy and Baby, paper cutouts. . . . Why did you take that job?"

"My reporting?"

He nodded.

"I guess you could say for fulfillment. I know that sounds grand and phony, but that's the honest answer."

"The guys in the office give me hell about it."

"Why?"

"They figure I have you working as a spy to get information about town doings. That sort of thing."

"Are you serious?"

He nodded again and took a larger drink. He rattled the ice cubes at her.

"They think you go to these selectmen meetings and report back to me. They figure you give me the real dope and report the rest for the regular slobs."

"That's one of the craziest things I've ever heard."

He shrugged. It was a boozy shrug. For a moment she saw the little boy in him. Eternal George, she thought. Eternally a boy.

"I spoke to Collie today," she said, attempting to change the subject. "This morning, actually. She sends her love."

"Bet she's having a Saturday night," he said, and winked.

"Drop it, George."

"What she say?"

"She was very happy, that's all. The camp is getting ready to close."

"She still in love with that Kraut?"

"She didn't say."

George hoisted himself out of his chair and went to the bar. He poured himself another drink, this one much darker than the one she had given him.

"You make that call without spending any money?" he asked her.

"How could I?"

"I'm simply saying money made you happy today, didn't it? Helps to have a little jingle in your pocket."

"I never said it didn't."

"You don't have to say things to mean them, you know."

She sipped her drink. Then she stood and put a log on the fire. Two logs. She sat back in her chair. She felt a mild headache beginning along her forehead.

"Why are you being quarrelsome, George? Did something happen today?"

"I'm not quarrelsome."

"Okay."

"That's a trick, right? If I say I'm not quarrelsome, then I'm quarrelsome. That's pretty good, Estelle. You learn that at Smith with all the other Smith girls?"

"Now you're being offensive."

"Am I? Pardon-ay moi."

She stood and lifted the fire screen in front of the fireplace. Then she carried her drink out to the kitchen and put it in the sink. She didn't know what she would do about the article. The only solution was to rise especially early before Hazel woke and finish it then. She went back to her desk and tidied the papers on it. George stared straight ahead at the fire.

"You're still in love with that nigger, aren't you? The one in the flower shop?"

"Good night, George."

"That's the truth," he said. "An Indian man. A swami. I'm not good enough for you, but that nigger bastard is just fine."

She didn't say anything else. She went upstairs quickly and went into the nursery. She locked the door. They kept a small bed beside the crib for Louisa when she stayed over. Now Estelle sat on the edge and put her face in her hands. It was the liquor speaking, she knew, but it was also his personality coming out. One couldn't disguise true feelings forever; eventually the mask fell away. She folded over onto her side and cried into the pillow. She kept her sobs quiet so that she didn't wake Hazel.

❧ *Chapter Twenty-seven* ❧

"We could be killed," August said against her hair, his lips moving over her forehead, to her neck. "You understand that, don't you?"

She nodded. She could not move or think or say anything. She stood in his arms and tried to understand what they had just promised each other. Did the words truly mean what she thought they did? Did they just promise to go together to Canada, to risk everything, to leave everything, and simply walk away from the war? It seemed impossible. It reminded her of a childish game where one or the other person would pull back from a dare and say she or he meant it as a joke. But this was no joke. She had told him about the forced labor waiting for him in Britain; she had watched the information strike him as if with a blow. He shook his head in disbelief. He vowed immediately to escape; he refused to entertain the idea of more time in prison.

She put her cheek flat against his chest. He kissed her over and over, and she felt her body losing its outer skin and sinking into his. That was impossible, of course, but she felt the evening air around them, the dampness of spring, and his warmth held her and covered her. Yes, she told herself. She had meant exactly what she had declared a moment before. She would go with him.

"I don't care," she said, her head buried against him. "I'm willing to risk it."

"It's not far, but it's dangerous. Gerhard will come with us, and he is skilled at this type of thing. We must travel quickly, you understand? The longer we take, the more risk we endure."

She nodded. Her blood made a racket in her body. She still had difficulty believing they had struck such a dangerous, fateful bargain.

"Are you sure you can do this?" he asked.

"Yes, as sure as I can be. As sure as I know that I love you."

"We will marry. We will make a home. When this is all over, we can decide what we will do about everything. But the war is like a big threshing machine. Do you know that machine? It cuts the grass and sweeps everything up with it. We live between the blades of a thresher. That's the phrase we say in my home country."

"Yes, I understand."

He kissed her again. They were safe, she knew, standing in their meeting place beside the draft horses. The rest of the men were at dinner. The guards no longer kept a sharp vigil. For all intents and purposes, the war had ended. She saw no point in forfeiting a pair of lives to a war that had devoured so much already, had glutted on blood and bones across the seas and lands for years. Surely to leave it now was a fair compromise. If not for her father, and the pain it would bring to him, she would not have hesitated more than a moment. The war was not a thing. It was merely a word, a horrible, vicious word, and its power, she felt, had begun to slip away.

"We will go tomorrow night," he said. "Gerhard said the weather is improving. We will leave immediately after last roll call. We can leave from here. We can simply step into the forest, and that is all. If anyone objects to us, we can say we needed to check on the horses. But no one will stop us. We can travel all night."

She nodded. It was the plan they had talked about before. It was treason to discuss it, but *treason* was also another mere word. She felt tired of words. She felt tired of every word that tried to separate her from him. She felt tired of *war* and *German* and *guard* and *tower* and *prison* and *bullet* and *bars* and *rifle* and *Reich* and *Hitler* and *Japan* and *shortage* and *drive* and *victory* and *loss* and *wounds* and *nurses* and *doctors* and *Blue Stars*. The words oppressed her, and she felt them pushing her deeper into his coat, into his arms, while he kissed her cheek and whispered that he loved her.

"We should go," she said after a little longer. "You'll be missed."

"I pledge myself to you," he said. "Do you see?"

"Yes, and I to you."

"You could travel to Canada by yourself and wait for me. It's not too late to do that. It would be safer."

"We talked about this already. I can walk perfectly fine, and I may be able to protect you in some circumstances. There's a case to be made on either side. If it goes correctly, we will be in Canada in two days. Not more."

He pushed her away slightly and regarded her.

"You should go and meet me there," he insisted. "Gerhard and I will make it. We can find each other when we cross the border."

"We can't know that. We could be lost to each other and that would kill me. No, I want to travel with you. I want to risk whatever you risk. I couldn't stand to be separated from you again."

"It's not fair to ask it of you."

"You didn't ask. You never asked. It's what I want. It's the only thing I am living for now."

He kissed her again. Then he looked quickly around, testing the sight lines to ensure he had not been spotted by the guard towers.

"If anything changes, I'll leave a message here," he said, nodding toward the chink in the wall that they used as a mail drop. "Check it at dinner. I won't come to see you then. I'll stay away from you until we are leaving. "

She nodded. Then she kissed him. She kissed him with all her passion, with everything she had inside her. He would be her husband. He would be her life.

"Tomorrow," she whispered when they broke apart. "Eight o'clock."

He kissed her hands. Then he turned and dashed off, his form the shape of her beloved.

"Is this seat taken?"

Estelle looked up to find Mr. Kamal standing in front of her, his dress somewhat formal, his expression amused. Her heart made a strange leap, but whether for good or ill she could not quite say. She had a notebook open on her lap and was busy transposing quotes into a story she was writing about the Barnum & Bailey circus arriving at the end of the month. Hazel slept in the pram beside her, her tiny face shaded by the hood.

"Mr. Kamal!" she said, trying to gather herself.

"But you're working! I'm sorry. I should have known."

"No, absolutely not. No, please, sit and join me. Just please keep your voice low, because I don't want to wake the baby."

He bent over the pram and examined Hazel. He smiled as he straightened.

"She's very beautiful," he whispered.

"She's a good baby."

"I will join you for a moment, if you don't mind. I've been on my feet all morning. And it's so unseasonably warm."

"Yes, it's quite warm," she said, and slid her notebook into the pocket at the pram rear. "They're calling for rain tomorrow."

"The farmers need it, certainly."

He sat on the other side, away from Hazel. It was strange to see him in formal Western wear—a suit with a white shirt and an emerald checked tie. He looked quite handsome in it, though not entirely comfortable. He pinched the crease of his trousers as he crossed his legs. She smiled to see this small tic she remembered from her days visiting him. It was an endearing unconscious habit.

"What are you working on?" he asked. "I stood for a moment

before you realized I was nearby. You were very involved with what you are writing."

"An article for the paper. On the circus coming to town, of all things. Not earthshaking, I'm afraid."

"Who is to say what is earthshaking? To a small boy or girl, the circus coming is big news indeed."

"That's true, I suppose."

"Your writing is very clear, you know? I look forward to reading your articles because I can always hear your voice inside the words. I could pick out an article written by you from a hundred different articles."

"Thank you."

"I'm sure I'm not the only one to tell you that."

"You'd be surprised. Reporters hear little about their work unless there's a problem with something. My editors say we're society's wallpaper. Newspapers, I mean."

"Your articles are mentioned frequently in my shop. People notice."

"I don't know if that will paralyze me next time I go to write something."

"It shouldn't. It should encourage you."

Estelle heard Hazel move slightly in the pram and she leaned forward to check on her. At the same time, her mind felt filled with thoughts of Mr. Kamal. How natural it felt to sit with him! She had missed his calm solicitousness, his kind regard for others. It provided a stark contrast from fools like the men she sometimes interviewed or even George. George would be like a tin drum beside him.

"She's restless," Estelle said of Hazel, her eyes returning to Mr. Kamal's. "She hasn't been feeling well lately."

"Nothing serious, I hope."

"No, just the hurdles of infancy."

"You are enjoying motherhood?"

"Yes, to my surprise I am."

He crossed his legs in the other direction. He tilted his head back slightly to take the sun. It was lovely in the park, Estelle reflected. The oaks had come into full leaf now and the fountain—an arching fish with a spout of water flowing from its mouth—bubbled and kept the air fresh.

"I also have had a busy morning," he said, his face still up in the sunlight. "I am a full citizen now. I participated in the ceremony this morning."

"That's wonderful news, Neem."

"The ceremony was brief, but many of us cried."

"Did you cry?"

"No, I felt a longing, however. A curious mix of emotions. They served us punch afterward. I don't know why, but that detail has stayed with me. Punch. It was the first thing we consumed as new citizens."

"You should be very proud."

"I am. And I am going forward with the adjoining store . . . as we talked about. It will be a bookstore, my other passion. Flowers and books. My sleepy little shop will lose some of its character, but it's all for the good."

"I'm so glad. Things worked out as you had hoped."

"Not everything," he said, and lowered his gaze to regard her.

Were they going to have this discussion at last? she wondered. She felt blood come into her face. She lowered her eyes. Her hand trembled slightly as she reached out to tuck the netting tighter around Hazel's pram. She marveled that he could still stir her so deeply. Part of her yearned to cut the conversation short, to stand and claim an excuse, anything, to conclude their meeting. But the greater part of her spirit longed to stay, to hear everything at last. She felt a small war taking place deep in her soul, a confusing jumble of emotions. What was the point of visiting that land again? The pain of it all, the useless loss, overwhelmed her and she decided to speak frankly once and for all.

"Did you have feelings for me, Neem? When we visited often . . . what were you thinking? I never knew, you see. Not entirely."

He looked at her levelly. Her eyes traveled into his.

"I loved you," he said simply.

"Why did you never declare yourself?"

"I did in every way I could. I thought you knew that."

"But you didn't express your true feelings. Never. It was all a puzzle that I had to put together and I never could. I lacked the important pieces."

"I did my best."

"Did you think because our backgrounds . . . the differences between us . . . did you think that was insurmountable?"

He nodded.

"Weren't they?" he asked.

"I don't know," she said honestly. "At times I thought they were, but now, looking back, they don't seem so formidable. It pains me that we failed to try as hard as we might have."

"I waited every day for you, hoping you would arrive."

"And for me . . . coming to your shop . . ."

She put her face in her hands. What a horrible misunderstanding! What a lack of courage on both of their parts. But that, she reminded herself, was not entirely true. She had known what she was doing; she had accepted the bargain, the familiar bargain, she amended, of George and all he stood for. That was the most painful element of all. *She* had been a coward, seeking comfort over love, familiarity over her heart's desire. Was familiarity, then, her true desire? The house, the money filling the bank like a water leak seeping into an old basement, the presentable Eternal George. Was that her true heart's desire? It must have been, she realized. She was a shallow, horrible woman, every bit as despicable as George himself, an assistant who held his dreadful tools out for him on a tray while she looked away and pretended not to be a participant. She could be bought, she had been bought, and to pretend otherwise was pointless.

"I'm ashamed of myself," she said, looking up finally.

"No, don't be ashamed."

He took her hand.

"I am," she said, and knew it to be true. "And the irony is that I have inflicted my own wound. You were nothing but kind, just as you say."

"Yes, but I see now I did not carry through. I left too much unsaid."

"Maybe the differences would have been too much," she said. "But we might have tried."

"Yes," he said.

She drew back her hand. It was too late now. The world had kept spinning and the days had passed and swallowed them both. She wanted to ask about the woman she had met in his shop, but that was not fair. It didn't matter anyway. She was married to George, was a mother to Hazel, and those were the borders of her life. It was too late to change any of that.

"I will always wonder if you were my great love," she said.

She leaned across the bench and kissed him. Then she stood and pushed the pram down the sidewalk toward the street. She bent over the opening to see if Hazel had come awake at the motion. But she slept soundly. Estelle pushed the pram slowly through the park, forcing herself to feel the shade of the trees and the brilliant light of the morning.

The clock refused to move. Collie had watched it all day, reacting to each minute that ticked off against the wall, to each phone ring, to each clatter of the typewriter, to each shuck of paper as Lieutenant Peters pulled it free from the typewriter platen. Her nerves felt impossibly alive. Tonight, within hours, she would leave with August. She would meet by the twitch horses and step into the forest and they would be fugitives. Yes, fugitives, escaped prisoners. In some ways, her status would be more dire even than his. It was their duty to escape, but her part in it, her complicity, would be a betrayal of everything she knew, everything her father stood for. She would receive no sympathy, no quarter at all. She understood that. Nevertheless, she felt as though she had been cast to live out this part, that it was inevitable as nothing else she had ever known could be. From the moment she had first set eyes on August she had been traveling toward this day. Her heart had brought her to it. Now she simply followed as she would follow air.

At four her father stepped out of his office and said he was finished for the day. He held his handkerchief to his lips. She knew, by a glance, that he did not feel well. Occasionally the residue of the gas rose in him and restricted his breathing. He usually blamed it on the weather, but today he simply appeared exhausted. She stood from her desk and went to take his arm.

"You don't feel well," she said. "I can see it. Let's get you to rest before dinner."

"I'm all right. Just need to take the weight off my feet for a few minutes."

He panted slightly as he said this. He held the handkerchief to his mouth.

"Why don't I call a car for both of you?" Lieutenant Peters said, looking up from his desk. "We're done here today, aren't we?"

"Did you get the transport finalized?" her father asked, resting his hand on Collie's desk for balance. She stayed beside him in case he felt light-headed.

"Yes, sir. It's all arranged."

"Yes, well then, maybe so . . . a car."

Collie hurried to gather her things. A part of her mind marveled at the details. *Now I am putting the typewriter cover on for the last time,* she thought. *Now I am clearing the desk and placing the extra pens and papers in the drawers.* It felt extraordinary to be doing the ordinary with so much waiting at the end of the day. Her stomach grew tight and uneasy. She slipped on her jacket and then went and took her father's arm again. He looked at her. Then he nodded, his lungs, she understood, giving him difficulties.

"Thank you, Lieutenant Peters," she said, realizing, as she did so, that she would not likely see him again. He was a good, honest worker, a kind man, and she wished she could tell him what he had meant to her in this final minute. But after making the call for the driver, he had already returned to his typewriter and his fingers blasted across the keyboard, creating a sound like wooden rain striking the roof. She smiled at him as she went out. He did not look up.

"Feeling a little rocky," her father said as he settled into the backseat of the Ford. "Not sure why. It came on all at once."

"To the boardinghouse, sir?" the driver asked, looking in the rearview mirror.

"Yes, to the boardinghouse," Collie answered. "Right away, please."

In no time they arrived back at Mrs. Hammond's place. Collie climbed out first and helped her father gain his feet. The chlorine gas, she knew, occasionally sapped all his strength. She thanked the driver and almost called him to help her with her father, but at that moment the major squeezed her arm with his elbow. He did not like to show weakness in front of the men. She stiffened herself and gave him more to lean on; he climbed up the steps and then swung around to sit on the glider.

"You should lay down, Father," she said. "Let's take you upstairs."

"I'll need a rest before I try the stairs, I'm afraid," he said, then had difficulty saying the last two words. "Fresh air."

"Yes, for a moment, and then to bed with you."

She sat beside him. Already the light had begun to soften. It was afternoon, not evening, but shadows covered the porch. It was chilly away from the light. She held her father's hand as he tried to regulate his breathing. Twice he coughed violently into his handkerchief. The sound of his coughing made her wince. How could she leave him? How could she wound him as she planned to do? She felt heartless and vile. Naturally she did not intend her actions to be an assault to him, but he might perceive it that way in any case. She would have given anything to confess to him, to have told him about the anguish she experienced, about her love for August, but that was impossible. Maybe in time he would forgive her. She squeezed his hand as she thought that, and he returned the pressure.

"I'm ready for this to be over," he said, his eyes scanning the river. "I don't like holding men in prison. It's not natural, no matter what they've done. I understand it in my head but not in my heart."

"You've been fair to them, Papa."

"Have I?" he asked. "I hope so. I've tried to be fair, but you never know. I counted on you, that's certain."

"I was happy to help, Papa."

He didn't say anything but kept his eyes on the river. She could not let her mind fill with too many thoughts of him. For a moment she felt like a little girl sitting beside her father. Then he rocked forward and slowly climbed to his feet.

"Maybe I better try the stairs," he said. "I think I need to lie down."

"I should have asked the driver to help."

"We can manage."

But they barely did. At last, after a great deal of trembling and awkward climbing while the banister rattled with the force of her father's weight, she propped him on his side on the bed. He preferred to be on his side when he suffered these attacks, she knew. She

brought him a towel and left a waste can by the bed in case he
needed to vomit. Then she sat on the edge of the bed and tucked an
afghan over his shoulders. His breathing began to ease slowly despite the exertion of climbing the stairs.

"I'll let you sleep," she whispered. "Sleep as long as you like. I'll
wake you for dinner."

"Tired . . . ," he said, already drowsy.

"I love you, Papa. I love you very much."

He nodded. She stood and tiptoed to the door. She kept her eyes
on him as she swung the door shut. *Good-bye,* she thought. *Don't hate
me. Please don't hate me.*

The madness of small moments. That's what Collie thought as she
took a single step away from the mowed area where the twitch horses
were tethered. With one short step she entered the woods. One step
changed everything, she reflected. A moment before she had been the
major's daughter, a translator, a valued member of the community,
and now, suddenly, she had entered the war. The war had come to her
at last, ironically in its last throes, and she reminded herself that she
must make that change in her thinking as well. If she were caught, she
might be hanged as a traitor.

It was a soft night. It was still early. The guards had become lax,
she knew. Why would the prisoners wish to escape when the camp
was about to close? That was their thinking, she imagined, but they
did not know about England. England changed everything. By informing August she had acted in a treasonous way. She didn't care.
Not really. She felt finished with rules and regulations, compromises
and imprisonment.

A few minutes later they appeared. August and Gerhard. The
sight of them chilled her. They were German prisoners, soldiers, and
she had thrown in her lot with them. Even the prospect of being

near August, holding him, marrying him, felt secondary. She had not been prepared for that.

But he kissed her. He held her. And she felt better for it.

"We start," Gerhard said in German.

She nodded. Her heart beat rapidly in her chest. Two more steps, a mile, and she could no longer turn back. She knew that. The guard towers flashed their lights round and round, but she understood no one took them seriously any longer. The guards with dogs made circuits only occasionally. The war had ended for everyone but her.

She followed them through two long connecting paths, the woods pressed close in against her. They had no rucksacks, nothing. Neither did she. She had money in her pocket, a small purse of personal items, and that was all. She had matches in the other pocket and paper and candles. August had given her a quick list. They had no food. They planned to drink from streams, she knew. The less they took, the less suspicion, Gerhard had said. It was just three days of walking, perhaps only two. They could make it with nothing but what was in their bellies already, he insisted.

Walking, following their backs, she wondered if she wasn't making a horrible, horrible mistake. Besides the peril she put herself in, and besides the anguish her departure would bring to her father, did she even know this man she followed? She said she loved him, but what did that mean? Did it mean she should go with him through the woods, hike to Canada, collaborate in his escape from an American prison? It felt insane and wildly irresponsible, and twice, three times, a thousand times, she had to bite her tongue to not call out and confess it had all been a colossal mistake. The reality of what she had dreamed about suddenly confronted her. What a fool she had been. What a romantic, dazed idiot.

Fortunately they moved too rapidly for discussion. Gerhard seemed to know exactly the way to go. He was a farm boy, August had said. August trusted him. Gerhard possessed woodcraft, August promised. Collie followed and tried to still her mind.

Near midnight they stopped. A small stream ran through the understory. Gerhard fell on his belly and drank from his cupped hand. August turned to see if she was all right, but Collie fell on her stomach beside Gerhard and drank as well. Mosquitoes had collected near the water and buzzed in her ears. The water tasted of mint and metal.

"We should travel at sunset and sundown. At night if we can see," Gerhard said when they finished drinking. "Traveling in the daylight is too risky."

"We will sleep in the daylight hours," August agreed.

"How do you feel?" Gerhard asked.

But to whom he directed the question was impossible to say. Collie bent and retied her shoes. Her feet hurt. Not horribly, but they hurt. She wore the same clothes she had worn to hike with Marie. She had not spent a moment talking to August. That felt curious. Was it shyness she felt? she wondered. If so, he suffered from it also. He directed his attention to Gerhard. Only Gerhard seemed natural.

"We'll walk to sunrise," Gerhard said. "Do not speak. Make as little sound as possible."

Collie nodded. August nodded to her right.

"I doubt they will come after us until the morning. With you, Fräulein, there may be more eagerness to find us. More incentive, perhaps."

"I'm sorry," she said.

Gerhard shrugged. August did nothing.

"Let's go," Gerhard said, and got to his feet.

They moved better this time, she realized. Maybe her eyes had adjusted to the darkness, but they followed the path with little difficulty. Twice they passed over streams and they waded across. Once, they started a deer—Gerhard whispered that it was a stag—and it lifted through the woods and disappeared in no time. Still, the noise it made in passing sounded loud in the surrounding silence. They did not move while the deer ran.

When the sun began to lighten the sky, they started looking for a place to sleep. To Collie's eye, the forest looked the same. But Gerhard whispered that he wanted someplace with height. "Lazy men do not climb hills," he said, meaning that they reduced their risk of being surprised by hunters if they gained height. He led them up onto a small knoll covered by beech and birch stands. He searched the top until he found a depression.

"Here," he said. "We will cover you."

It took her a moment to understand. They were going to ground, she realized. Like animals they were going to bury themselves through the daylight hours and reemerge with the sunset. She guessed this must be part of the plan they devised. She laid down in the depression and let them cover her with branches and leaves. It felt like being buried, but she did not let herself think of it.

She listened to them as they found their own resting spots. Gerhard was the last to cover himself. By the time he was silent, the birds had begun to call. She listened to the birds. They sang in their spring voices, insistent and crazed with the desire to find nesting sites. Black flies and mosquitoes buzzed at her ears, but she did her best to let them be. If she began slapping them, she knew, she would be unable to stop.

She slept and woke. Slept again. When next she woke Gerhard was out of his sleeping den. He stretched and tried to get his muscles loose. She crawled out of her hollow. The skin around her eyes felt swollen from insect bites. Thirst pulled at her belly and veins. She didn't know, honestly, if she could go on. It felt too mechanical, as if they were toys someone had wound tightly and abandoned to spin on a dining room table. When August came out of his chamber, he conferred only with Gerhard. He seemed uncomfortable with her, and that was by far the most extraordinary thing of all.

"We walk," Gerhard said in German. "Single file, silence."

Now the going was harder, Collie discovered. The path brought them to a swampy mess, and though they searched for trails around it, they failed to find one. They had to wade in up to their waists, and beneath the surface of the water her feet found snags and horrible roots that tried to trip her. The insects relished their proximity to the water. They roared in her ears, and when she slapped at them her hand came away bloody.

They stopped near midnight again. The sky emitted no light. Whatever the stage of the moon, it provided nothing. It made their passing more secretive, she understood, but it also made it difficult to walk without tripping and falling. She grew increasingly conscious of August's indifference to her; he did not turn and help her, nor did he seem to care that she had joined them. If anything, Gerhard was more solicitous than August. Collie felt hatred for August building in her. Had she left everything, everything behind to be treated like a minor third party? She did not need to escape to Canada, after all. She could have traveled by train and waited for them there, exactly as they had discussed. It was only out of concern for him and for the possibility that they would become separated that she had struck out with them on the escape.

Near daybreak they began looking for another hill. Gerhard found one slightly to the east, not exactly the direction they wanted to go, but it didn't matter. The air was better on top of the hill. Collie felt exhausted and welcomed the chance to stop. Her feet hurt and her clothing hung in wet, heavy cords against her skin. Her hair, her skin, everything about her seemed primitive and unraveled. Whatever dreams she had possessed, whatever thoughts she had toward August, seemed even more foolhardy as she climbed into the depression and waited for Gerhard to cover her. She was shocked when August suddenly fell into the hole beside her and waited while Gerhard covered them both.

"I'll come for you," Gerhard said. "Stay where you are. Don't startle at anything. Today they may be nearer. They could come with dogs, but don't flee or respond. Stay where you are. The wind should cover us."

Collie had no idea whether his plan made sense. Frankly she was too intent on August stretched beside her to give anything else a thought. He lay with his face toward her. She looked at him, and, little by little, the light brought his features to her.

Then he pulled her to him and he held her.

Major Brennan woke to the sound of the siren. It came as a rude shock; he had slept too long, had slept, in fact, through the night. He felt slightly annoyed at the sound of the siren. Why were they running it with its horrible voice? No answer came to mind. He doubted that anyone would try to escape. The men were due to be shipped out at the end of the month, three weeks away. In two weeks' time they would be back in Fort Devens awaiting transport.

Then it came to him, half mixed in sleep, half in a painful consciousness.

His daughter had left. Or if not left, she had facilitated the escape of her young German. He could not know it for certain, obviously, but the fear of it, the shame of it, entered him and made him wish to remain in bed rather than answer the demand of the siren.

A few minutes later, as he pulled on his trousers, someone knocked on the door.

"A minute," he said, but his voice had not warmed enough to speak, and his words came out choked and incomprehensible. He repeated them. He heard the driver stand away from the door. Major Brennan finished dressing hastily, then went out into the hallway.

"Meet me at the car, Private," he said. "I'll be just a moment."

The private nodded and turned smartly around. Major Brennan went to use the water closet. Afterward he splashed water on his face. He flicked the water free from his skin, then went down the hallway and followed the stairs to the second landing. He stopped at Collie's door and knocked. He waited a moment, then knocked again. When she did not wake to let him inside, he pushed open the door. The bedcover had not been pulled down. A pale light floated into the room. He stood for a moment, his mind not caught up to his physical presence in the doorway. What did it mean? He had difficulty grasping the import of the empty bed. Had she gone?

At the same time, he grew aware of the sense of familiarity of this moment. How many times had he checked on his daughter at night, making sure she was safe and warm, the covers up, the sweet, soft sound of her breathing the only noise for blocks. For years she had slept with Puzzle, her striped, six-toed tabby, a valiant, trusting cat that had traveled with them through their postings. Yes, he remembered Puzzle. He remembered the sense of communion he had felt with the cat, both of them protecting her, the light catching the cat's eyes and reflecting it. How long ago had that been? he wondered now. And where had she gone?

But he knew the answer. Not the precise answer, naturally, but the general outline of what she attempted. He wanted to kill young Henry Heights for telling her about the men being shipped to England. She would not accept such a turn of events quietly. It played against her sense of justice. Added to that was the love she felt for the German boy, August. It made for an irresistible combination of emotions.

Halfway down the stairs he heard Mrs. Hammond in the kitchen, starting breakfast. That good woman, he thought. He wanted to go in and ask if she knew anything about Collie, but by doing so he might as well take out a billboard and broadcast the news across the hamlet. No, he made his step lighter and hurried toward the door. He stepped out on the porch and closed the door softly behind him.

"How many?" he asked the private as he climbed into the jeep.

"Two, sir."

"Morning roll?"

"Yes, sir."

The private would not know about Collie.

"Pretty late in the game for this," Major Brennan said.

"Yes, sir."

The private started the jeep and put it into gear. Major Brennan watched the light on the river as they drove toward the camp. A few fish poked rings in the still surface. He watched a kingfisher glide down and scrape at something in the water, its claws coming up with a bracelet of wiggling fish. He wondered, absently, who would be the first to call. Colonel Cook, he imagined. Cook would call and get to the bottom of things, as he liked to say. *Funny business,* Cook would say. *Your own daughter, eh?*

⊸ᕯ *Chapter Twenty-eight* ᕤ⊸

C ollie woke in his arms.

Even now, even with her own filthiness, with the incessant whine of insects, the fear that any moment, any sound might be the beginning of their capture, she could not wish herself to be anywhere else. His body fit hers; she fit her body to him, and now, in the first strings of evening air, she knew that she had made the right choice. He had whispered that he had been nervous around her at first; he had said the enormity of what they had undertaken, what he had asked of her, had struck him nearly dumb. He wondered several times aloud if he had had the right to ask her, to encourage her, because look where they were, in a dirty hole covered by branches. That had been the source of his distance. He had felt guilty and ashamed, unsure that he had the right to have her beside him. But their long day in the tiny bunker had changed all that. When Gerhard came to retrieve them, she felt they had become a gnarled root, forever grown together and divisible only by fire.

"We should go now," Gerhard said.

His face looked swollen from insects. He looked thin, too, and disgustingly dirty. But he also looked—as August did—freer. That was an abstract notion, she knew, but it fit nonetheless. Despite their fatigue and hunger, they moved with greater certitude. They had a goal at last and it was a simple one: *walk to Canada*. Nothing else mattered for the time being.

"Are you starving?" August whispered to her as they began.

"I'm hungry," she answered, "but I'll be all right."

"If they are coming for us, they can catch up to us today," Gerhard said. "We should be particularly careful."

"They will be watching the border," Collie said. "You can count on that."

Gerhard nodded. She took the middle position. They walked into the darkness. Her body had difficulty moving after being constricted in the foxhole for so long. In time it loosened, however, and gave way to the grinding hunger she felt in her belly. She had never known hunger like this. It did not hurt, or call attention to itself; it grew and spread, taking more of her body as the hours passed, reminding her that she was merely an animal in the end.

After an hour or two they came to a small collection of houses. It was difficult, from a rise above it, to determine how many dwellings it contained. A few dogs barked, but whether the dogs had picked up their scent, or barked at other animals moving through the woods, proved impossible to tell. Collie stared down at the few lights that marked civilization. Now she keenly felt the foreignness of her existence. She was no longer welcome below. She was a traitor, an escaped prisoner every bit as much as the two Germans, and she felt uncomfortable at that knowledge. But it was a simple fact and she accepted it.

"How do we know where we are?" she whispered.

"We hope," Gerhard said. "We hope we have followed the correct course."

"There is a river below," August said. "Is it the river we need?"

"I don't know," Gerhard said. "It might be. We can't very well go in and ask for directions.

"If we keep going north it has to be right," Gerhard continued. "We can count on that."

"That makes sense," Collie said.

"But we want to get to the border as soon as possible. The sooner we cross, the better."

Collie felt August take her hand. The closeness she had felt for him through the long day in the trench remained with her. She kissed him.

"North," she whispered.

In the small hours they came to a cabin. Collie smelled smoke long before they struck the cabin. She smelled water, too, and in time realized they walked close to a large lake. The cabin sat on the western shore of the lake. The cabin was dark, but the smoke suggested someone inhabited it. For a long time they stayed in the woods and watched. It was possible whoever had used the cabin had departed, leaving the fire to burn itself out. They could not see a vehicle. It was likely the visitors had come by boat. From what they could see, which was not much, the cabin sat amid a well-forested bank. No one had cleared out behind the building. Although it was too dark to say for certain, they could not see any power lines. It was a primitive cabin, a fishing cabin away from everything.

"We'll stay here until morning," Gerhard said. "We might learn something. It won't be long."

Collie knew without discussion what they intended. They intended to capture the people inside the cabin. If the cabin proved unoccupied, they would raid it for food. The isolation of the cabin made it an ideal target. Once captured, the inhabitants could do nothing to alert the authorities. They had never planned to walk all the way to Canada without food. This had been their plan. They meant to find opportunities and exploit them.

It made her feel uncomfortable, but she understood the tactical necessity. They needed supplies and they needed information. The cabin potentially held both things.

When light began growing in the east, Gerhard spoke rapidly to August. She understood a few words, but not all. Then Gerhard circled away. He meant to come at the cabin from the other side. It chilled her to observe them behaving as soldiers, but she could not blame them. It was a question of survival.

"There," August whispered, nodding toward the cabin. "A light."

"Someone is making coffee."

"Yes, and more smoke. They're bringing the fire up."

Someone opened the door and stepped out. It was a man, she could see. An old man with gray hair. He walked to what appeared to be an outhouse and entered. He came out a few moments later. He walked down to the lake and squatted beside it while he washed his face. She heard the water trickling between his fingers and splashing back into the lake. It gave her an odd feeling to spy on a person. It was interesting as much as it was repellent.

"He has a canoe," August said. "See?"

It was like a puzzle of some sort that came to life as the light grew. Yes, she saw the canoe. It was dragged high on the bank and tilted over onto a rock to keep the rain out.

"Now we wait to see if he is alone," August said, his eyes fixed on the cabin. "But it looks like someone is still moving in the cabin, so I doubt he is by himself. Maybe his friend, maybe his wife."

"What will Gerhard do?"

"He will approach from the north."

"How will you know when to start?"

"When we are certain about how many are down there. We'll wait until they are out of the cabin so that they can't get to any weapons. Then we will advance."

"Were you a good soldier, August?"

He nodded.

"Yes," he said, "very good. I am patient. Patience is a soldier's best weapon."

"And Gerhard?"

"Excellent."

She didn't ask anything else. She wasn't certain she wanted to know anything else. Soon, she hoped, that part of their lives would be behind them. The war would be behind them.

A woman exited the cabin next. The man's wife, Collie imagined. The woman also had gray hair. She went to the lake and washed. Then she sat on the overturned canoe and watched the water. She took out a cigarette and lighted it. The man, her husband, came out of the door carrying two cups of coffee. Each motion—the door closing, the whine of the screen door—made a distinct sound that carried out onto the lake. The morning was very still.

August began moving before Collie could do anything. Immediately she spotted Gerhard approaching from the other direction. They closed down on the cabin and she hurried behind. They would terrify the couple, she understood. She watched as Gerhard and August angled toward the cabin, cutting off the couple's retreat. It was not difficult. The couple sat and drank their coffee, unaware of the soldiers closing on them.

Gerhard arrived first. She saw the couple rise, wave, though their body posture demonstrated hesitancy an instant later. Who was this man? they seemed to ask. Then August reached his position and the couple became more animated. The man began walking briskly back toward the cabin, but Gerhard cut him off and held up his hand. August joined him. By the time Collie reached them the couple had begun to piece things together. She saw it in their faces.

"Don't worry," she said to them, "I'm an American. We don't mean you any harm."

"Go back and finish your coffee," August said to them. "Is there food inside?"

"Yes," the woman answered.

"Is there anyone else here? Are you expecting anyone?"

"Our son and his wife later today," the man said.

"We'll be gone by then, don't worry," August said.

Then he translated the couple's answers for Gerhard.

"Collie, sit with them," Gerhard said in German. "Find out where we are. Find out how we get to Canada. Explain that they will not be hurt if they cooperate."

"Is there a weapon in the house?" August asked.

"A shotgun," the man said.

"Is that all?"

The man nodded.

"Is there a road or did you come by boat?" August asked.

"By boat."

"Any other means to get here?"

The man shook his head.

"We won't hurt you," Collie said, "come back and finish your coffee."

The man took his wife's arm and led her back toward the lake. Collie followed them. The sun had risen above the horizon and began to skid light across the water.

Chapter Twenty-nine

Mr. and Mrs. Lepage. That was the couple's name. French Canadian originally, Collie guessed, but now proud Americans. The man wore a plaid shirt tucked into corduroy trousers and was older than Collie had first observed. Seventy at least, she thought. His face was sharp and edged along each cheekbone. He had undergone surgery, she saw, on his neck. A series of stitches ran back and forth down toward his clavicle. Collie wondered what it could have been to demand a second and third visit from the surgeon. She thought to ask, then silenced herself. It was none of her business.

The woman was slightly younger, Collie guessed, but in less robust health. Her back was slightly humped in the way old women's backs sometimes became humped. Her arms were thin, too, and she smoked without any pleasure. Her hands shook when she brought the cigarette to her mouth.

"You're Germans?" the man asked.

He couldn't quite figure out what they were doing there, Collie saw. She could not put herself in their place. How did Germans arrive at their doorstep in this lonely cabin? It was an impossible puzzle for them to solve.

"Not Germans. Not really," Collie said, though that was nonsense. "How far are we from Canada?"

"Five miles," the man said, and pointed down the lake.

"What's the border crossing like?"

The man shrugged. The woman answered for him.

"It's a road with a drop-down gate," she said. "A red and white gate. Is that what you mean?"

"How close can we get by boat?"

"Within a couple miles," the man said. "It's just a hop over."

The man kept his arm on his wife's shoulder. They did not look frightened, Collie decided. They looked perplexed and somewhat annoyed. The woman chain-smoked. The man drank his coffee. Light continued to grow on the water. Collie fought the desire to explain herself to these people. She would have to learn such explanations were pointless. It would take too long, involve too much, to make it worthwhile. Better to remain silent, she told herself.

A few minutes later Gerhard and August returned. They carried the shotgun with them. They also brought food tied up in olive cloth. They spread the cloth out on the boat. Collie told them what the Lepages had said about the lake, the guard station at the border, the overall distance. Gerhard made her ask them again. This time they answered with less nervousness. They seemed to want to be helpful. August ate. Collie helped herself to a heel of bread and a sausage. She drank coffee from a tin cup. It tasted delicious.

"Has anyone been through here?" August asked, translating for Gerhard. "Any search teams?"

"You're from Camp Stark," the woman finally realized.

"Yes," August said. "We are going to Canada. We wish to hurt no one. We'll be on our way in a moment, so you don't need to worry."

"Nobody's been through. This is out of the way, this cabin," the man said. "We fish, that's all."

"And bird-watch," the woman added.

Collie ate a MoonPie. The MoonPie tasted better than any food she could ever recall eating. The chocolate frosting burned the roof of her mouth with pleasure. Gerhard turned away from the couple and ate rapidly. Watching him, Collie had a glimpse of how they must appear to the couple. Like traveling dogs, she thought. Like a pack descended on them.

After he ate, Gerhard directed a hundred questions to the couple about the border crossing, the end of the lake, what they might expect to find at each interval. Five miles, that was all. Collie heard it with her own ears. By nightfall, if things went well, they would be in Canada. The man explained it was only one small station in miles and miles of forest. He had never bothered to think much about it, but the border was porous, he said. It wouldn't take much to make it to Canada if one were determined to get there.

"But I would stay to the backcountry," the woman added. "I wouldn't cross at the border. I doubt you would, but farther north you'll find the border empty. Your biggest problem would be to know when you're in Canada."

"Just keeping traveling north," August said, and the man and woman nodded.

Collie went to use the outhouse, and when she returned she found August and Gerhard in a debate about the best course of action. The dispute seemed to be whether it was smarter to travel by boat or to stay on foot. She went to the lake and spent a long time bathing herself. She combed her hair with her fingers. The woman, Mrs. Lepage, came over and stood beside her.

"You're American," Mrs. Lepage said. "I thought you were pretending when you first said it."

"No, ma'am, I'm American."

"Why are you with these men?"

"That man and I are going to be married," Collie said. "The blond one. The other one is a friend."

The woman nodded. It seemed absurd when you spoke it aloud, Collie realized. She tried to read the woman's expression, but the woman hid her feelings well.

Collie stood and found the sunlight. She turned her face up to it. She felt better. Her stomach felt calmer and her skin felt cleaner. She wondered, as she let the sun warm her, what she had imagined the journey would be like. Had she ever conceived of it? she asked herself. She had been too in love with August, too trapped in her own head to contemplate what the step-by-step journey would entail. Her ignorance fascinated her. She had more in common with Marie than she might ever have imagined.

"Take what you need. We won't stop you. We have no one to report things to, so you will be in Canada before we can say anything to anyone. We'll need to go out in our son's boat, but he won't arrive until evening and we won't cross the water at night. You have until tomorrow. I give you my word on that."

"Thank you," Collie said.

"You're tired of the war," the woman said. "I understand."

"Yes."

In the end, they decided on the boat. The man told them they should keep to this shoreline, the western shoreline, and follow it north. The lake went three and a half miles in that direction. He doubted anyone would bother them or even see them. Near the border, he said, pull over and tie up the boat and do the rest of the trip on foot. When they crossed a stream they would be in Canada. The stream was called the Kangatooweet, not that it mattered.

"It's a broad stream this time of year," the man added. "Spring runoff. You can wade it but it's fairly wide. Later in the summer it's nothing at all. You can step across it."

Collie watched the couple for signs of treachery, but she couldn't detect any. What did they care anyway? They were at the other end of their lives and the war; up here, next to a lake in northern New Hampshire, must seem worlds away.

"We're sorry," August said as they packed up and prepared to leave, "to have interrupted your morning."

"It's the most excitement we've had in years," the woman said. "Keep north."

"You can't miss it," the man said, which was meant to be a joke, Collie realized too late to laugh.

"We'll leave your canoe tied up and we'll leave the shotgun in it," August said. "Thank you for the food."

When they were ready, the man pushed them off in the canoe. Gerhard sat in back, August in the bow. Collie sat in the middle. The cabin disappeared in no time. The men paddled well. It was pleasant, Collie mused, to be paddled across a northern lake by two stout young men. She felt herself dozing. The sun grew stronger. It was not until they were halfway down the shoreline, halfway to where they planned to leave the boat, that they heard the insect whine of an outboard motor cutting across the lake on an angle to intercept them.

ollie watched the motorboat cross the lake toward them, its wake spread out behind it. She was able to make out the figure of a man standing at the steering console. He aimed directly at them, which was unsettling. She squinted to see if the man wore a uniform, but it was impossible to tell at such a distance.

"How do we play it?" August asked in German.

"We are visitors who have borrowed a canoe, that's all," August said. "Say no more than necessary."

"Let me speak," Collie said, watching the motorboat begin to come into focus. This was why she had accompanied them, she realized. Exactly for this moment.

"Damn him," Gerhard said. "Damn our luck."

Collie felt better when she made out that the man did not wear a uniform. He was gray-haired and dressed for the outdoors, his head sporting a large, floppy hat with fishing flies tucked in the brim. He cut the engine when he was a little ways off and let the boat glide closer. He was heavyset and smiled broadly. He had nothing to do, Collie realized, and had simply brought the boat out to say hello.

"Sorry, thought you were the Lepages," the man called in the new silence created by the disappearance of the motor. The wake caught up to the boat and to the canoe and lifted them both several times.

"Good morning," Collie called back. "We borrowed their canoe. We thought we'd do a little bird-watching."

"They back at the cabin?"

"Yes," Collie said. "Having breakfast."

"Johnny Delacrois had a heck of a night fishing up around Cutter's Point. I was going to tell them. He was trolling but he had five or six good-size togue."

"We're just out for a paddle," Collie said, trying to fit her words and tone to his. "No fishing this morning."

"You visiting?"

Collie wasn't sure how to answer that one. She nodded. Let him think whatever he liked, she decided. The man studied them for a long moment. He was proud of his boat, she realized. That was a large part of it. He liked having a boat that could speed across a wide expanse and catch them. His face looked juvenile and at the same time canny and suspicious. She found herself detesting the man and his idle curiosity.

"All right then," the man said, "maybe I'll swing down and have a cup of coffee with the Lepages. I may see you back there. Sorry to come up on you this way."

"We won't be long."

The man started the engine. It was obscenely loud on the quiet lake. He puttered around in a half circle, then gradually opened the throttle as he headed toward the Lepage cabin.

"What do we do now?" August asked.

"Keep paddling," Gerhard said. "He can report us as soon as he gets back across the lake."

"He'll contact the border patrol and tell them our plan," Collie said.

"We need to hurry," August said.

They paddled with more determination. Collie felt her stomach knotting into a ball. She listened for the sound of the outboard, but it didn't come for a long time. That surprised her. She imagined the Lepages would tell the man in the motorboat what had happened and the man would skim across the lake immediately. But that didn't occur. She waited for the sound and felt grateful for every second that passed in silence.

Not far from the end of the lake they beached the canoe and pulled it up beyond the tree line. Clouds had filled the sky behind them and a light rain began to sprinkle and turn the white lake rocks dull gray. Gerhard told them to wait while he made a short scouting foray. He wanted to gain height and look around. He disappeared into the woods, moving west. Collie watched him go. August came to her and took her in his arms.

"It will be all right," he said. "We are almost there."

"It feels like too much right now."

"A few more miles and then it will be over. We'll be free. Are you sorry you came?"

She shook her head. It did no good to think what one should or shouldn't do. One acted, fumbled blindly, and then accepted the consequences. One could only pretend to have a plan, a purpose, a design. Life was far more random and chaotic than she had given it credit for being before. She understood that now. She leaned closer to him. She loved him. She loved him down in her core and she realized she had always been traveling toward this moment. Toward this instant.

She opened her mouth to tell him, to say what was in her heart, when Gerhard reappeared through the forest. He came quickly, jumping down the hill in places, his voice tight when he reported what he saw.

"He's hunting us," Gerhard said.

"Which one?" August asked.

"The man in the motorboat."

"Did you see him?" Collie asked. "I don't understand."

"No, but that's why he hasn't gone across the lake again. He must have had a rifle in the boat with him."

"But you don't know for certain," August said.

"No, but we can't wait. There is a road up ahead. When we cross it we will be near the stream."

It felt, Collie realized, like a childhood game. Like hide-and-seek, only now the stakes were life-and-death. Maybe Gerhard was wrong, maybe the man simply had trouble starting his motorboat, but she did not believe that. She thought back to the man's ugly face, his floppy hat. He would see their escape as a chance for bravery, as a chance to become a hero of some sort. If he had a rifle, yes, he would come after them. She knew that. It fit too many parts to be incorrect.

They kept to the shoreline and hurried forward. Gerhard led them. The undergrowth along the shoreline was formidable. Twice they had to stop and wade into the water, then out again in order to continue. It felt like walking beside a jungle, and the rain falling did nothing to make the going easier. The rain came more stiffly now, filling everything with a soft patter. It turned the ground to mud and made the footing treacherous.

Collie did her best to keep up, but she felt she slowed them down. She thought about telling them to go ahead. They could move faster without her. But then, even as she thought it, they came to the small, two-lane road at the head of the lake. It was not paved. It passed over a culvert that permitted the stream water to flow into the lake. Beyond the road, beyond the stream, lay Canada.

Gerhard would not let them move forward. He held out his hand and then pushed it earthward, telling them to get down. A car passed. A second one followed. Collie could not see the vehicles for fear of showing her face when she looked for them. The cars did not slow or give any indication that they had been discovered. The cars continued forward, and then no sound reached them at all except the steady drone of rain on the new green growth.

She put her head on August's shoulder and turned and looked up at the sky.

"I love you," she said. "I've loved you from our first moment."

"And I you."

"*Ich auch*," he said in German. *I also.*

Before she could speak again, Gerhard hissed them to their feet. She scrambled up and ran and in an instant she crossed the road. Her eyes, she thought, rested now on Canada. August took her hand when they came to the stream and she half fell, half staggered into the water. Then the water pressed against her and she felt the strain of it trying to drag her downstream, back toward the lake. She heard a third car, this one more urgent, suddenly come across the culvert. They were exposed, she knew, now that they were in the water. It was all confusing, all a mad dash, and she wondered, with surprising clarity, if they had made it to Canada after all. She wondered if crossing the streambed by half made them free, and she turned to August, and she smiled, and he smiled back, and then she heard the sound of the car doors snap open and the rain knitted them to the surface of the stream and she smelled lush green growth and the sky that had broken and fallen on them all.

❧ *Epilogue* ❧

This, then, was Collie's war.

It was not much of a war when weighed against the death of millions, but years later, recalling her time in New Hampshire, this was the moment she spoke about. It was rare that she let the full recollection come to her, though she lived with it as a shadow every day for the remainder of her life. *August,* she sometimes thought at the oddest moments, kneeling in the garden, or bending to pick up a basket of laundry. Then for just an instant he would be there, her boy love, her first heart, her soldier true.

He was an Austrian and he had run north for his life, and she had traveled with him. That was the story she told to her children, to her grandchildren, but only at some late hour or in some setting that forced the memory on her. Her recollection rested on a single day spent beneath hastily cut branches, buried in a small hole on a hillside in New Hampshire, and she did not like to cheapen it by recounting it. That was Collie's war. And the first sight of him—yes, she could remember that, but in time, in the many years of her life, that memory mixed with others so that she could no longer count on its veracity. He was a shining boy, a handsome man, and she could still recite the poem. *The world becomes more beautiful with each day.* The paper transcription, his offering, lived in a small corner of her jewelry box, kept secret even from her husband of thirty-seven years, discovered, finally, by her two oldest daughters when they moved her into the nursing home.

There were times, many times as she grew old and brittle and sat in front of a gritty television garbled with static, that the memory reformed and changed. Mercifully, she could not always remember what had happened in those last moments against the Canadian border. She could no longer envision Gerhard's head breaking open like a fresh melon, his blood bleeding out into the water, his steps becoming ponderous in their final heaviness for a moment. She screamed then, but she no longer remembered even that with any clarity. Gerhard fell forward and the water reached up to receive him and his blood became a red flag opening in a wind close to the earth. It spread over her legs, and then the second bullet, or maybe the fifth, or tenth—how could she know?—came for August. She heard it in the chamber of the rifle, in the explosion of gunpowder, in the air, whistling and sharp, as it spread and entered him in the neck and ended his life. She held his hand when he fell forward and for many moments she stood in the water, his body slowly rolling downstream, its weight forcing her to follow him, one step at a time as his weight tumbled and pulled her. She yearned for her own bullet, but it never came. Then men splashed into the water and she felt herself pulled back and she refused to let go of August's hand. They broke her grip finally and she had screamed to let her go. She intended to follow his body into the water, back to the lake, but they would not permit it. The water rushed over his beautiful face and pushed his hair into a wedge behind his skull.

That's what she remembered. That was her war.

Afterward, of course, profound embarrassment. A long trip to her father's sister in Philadelphia. A convalescent visit to Estelle's home. Many hushed voices around her. It had been a rash, childish stunt, people said. It had been the result of immaturity and the loss of her mother. Young girls, they said, let their hearts get in the way. And for many years—in her productive decades filled with children and work, the endless cleaning, the meal making, the sick infant, the unmade beds, the open hampers—she had agreed with them. It was a folly of youth, is how she put it. It had been a foolish fling, one, looking back, that she must surely regret.

But she always understood that was not the whole truth. August had not been a folly. To believe that would be to believe her own life had been a foolish, meaningless passage of days. If she knew love now, then she must have known love then.

In her last years, after her husband died and when her children had gone off to pursue their own lives, and while she sat in the padded chair of the nursing home that harbored her for the final days of her life, sometimes in the late afternoon August returned to her. He was not the corpse rolling in the water then, not the slack hand in hers, but the young, gallant August, the sweet boy she had loved with all her heart. It was not wrong to remember that, she didn't think. Dozing, half surrendered to her afternoon nap, he sometimes appeared to her. He was a boy, just a boy, and he held out his hand— the same hand that she had clutched so desperately in those final moments—and smiled at her. Sometimes, in the deepest dreams, she went with him. They crossed the stream and they climbed the bank on the other side, and she turned to him and kissed him. And that was a different life, one equally beautiful in its way, and he led her northward into the new land, and she went with him, always with him.

I, also, he said. *Ich auch.*

Author's Note

This is a work of fiction set in a historical setting, and as a result I have felt free to invent elements as needed for the narrative. I have also rounded off certain square ends, made the timeline tidier or more convenient in places, and created events only touched on or suggested in historical accounts, all in service to the story of a young woman and man falling in love in that troubled and difficult period. I have softened much of the prison experience, or kept it from intruding too far into the narrative, because my focus rested primarily on the fate of the story's couple. Prison life, even under the best circumstances possible, was dire. Food was short; war reports came frequently, often carrying news hard to hear.

One small footnote. Near the end of the story, August and Gerhard attempt to escape to Canada. While we never learn the fate of the other Camp Stark survivors in this story, it should be noted that many German prisoners were indeed sentenced to forced labor in England. They found out about this final sentence only when they were already on board ship. To add to the cruelty, they thought they were going home when the ships were diverted to Britain. For many, this proved the final straw. Many German POWs took their lives by stepping off the ships at night. Even the prospect of drowning in the wild northern seas was preferable to the thought of more forced labor in a foreign land.

The fabric of this story was shaped and formed by my reading of *Stark Decency* by Allen V. Koop and Hartmut Lang. For any reader looking for a comprehensive account of Camp Stark, I cannot send you to a better source. For many years as a professor in the University of New Hampshire system, I had heard vague rumors about a camp, some sort of prison camp holding German soldiers, that existed during World War II in New Hampshire. The idea seemed preposterous to me, but gradually I learned of this singular chapter in the state's history. Reading *Stark Decency* gave me the first inkling that there might be a story worth telling not far from my own front door. In time, the scope of the German prisoner-of-war camps became clear to me, and I remained astonished that I had never encountered such histories in my years of schooling. My guess is that most Americans, if they think of prisoner-of-war camps based in the United States during WWII, usually recall the Japanese internment camps. In the years I have been working on this novel, I have come across many people who could not quite believe it when I told them German soldiers were incarcerated in a tiny village in New Hampshire a year prior to Hitler's final days.

Any errors in this historical account are entirely mine. The characters herein are fictional. Although I was impressed in many instances by the good nature and competency of some of the historical figures involved, I did not "base" my characters on any particular individual. I may say, however, that I was enormously pleased to find that the people of my home state—New Hampshire—acquitted themselves with great courage and decency during that era. I have always found the people of New Hampshire to be kind and level-headed, and so it did not surprise me to read that they had been fair and evenhanded in their treatment of German soldiers. I am proud to say I would have predicted it.

In 1986 the people of Stark held a reunion with the former German captives. It was held in the town hall, a classic New England white building with trim lines and a woodstove as a source of heat. By a strange twist, the cowboy song "Don't Fence Me In" became a sort of anthem for the Germans and guards in the 1940s. At the reunion the former prisoners and their keepers rose and sang it together, most of them crying. Afterward many of the Germans and American guards confessed that their time in Camp Stark had been a highlight of their life. It was a decent place, where captives were treated humanely, and where two cultures, engaged in a horrible war, came together in unity. That was the spirit I attempted to capture in this story and to embody in the love between Collie and August.